FROM GALE-SWEPT CHICAGO
where the corpses of black GIs were found gunned down by unknown hands, and a beautiful woman reporter became an unlikely ally in hunting the truth . . .

TO THE HALLS OF POWER IN WASHINGTON, D.C.
where a bureaucratic maze hid a cancer of corruption eating away at the heart of the military . . .

TO A HIGH-SECURITY U.S. ARMY BASE IN GERMANY
where a beribboned master sergeant and a desperate GI deserter represented the final pieces of a puzzle of nightmare evil . . .

Tarbert Weir had a new kind of war to fight, a new kind of enemy to beat, and the old-fashioned kind of guts to do it with . . .

## A MATTER OF HONOR

"Fast paced and gripping."
—*Worcester Telegram*

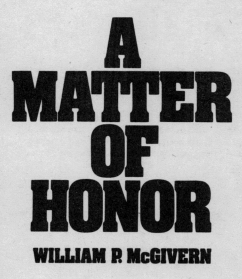

# A MATTER OF HONOR

## WILLIAM P. McGIVERN

BERKLEY BOOKS, NEW YORK

This Berkley book contains the complete
text of the original hardcover edition.
It has been completely reset in a typeface
designed for easy reading, and was printed
from new film.

A MATTER OF HONOR

A Berkley Book / published by arrangement with
Arbor House Publishing Co., Inc.

PRINTING HISTORY
Arbor House edition / February 1984
Berkley edition / July 1985

ISBN: 0-425-08091-9

A BERKLEY BOOK® TM 757,375
Berkley Books are published by The Berkley Publishing Group,
200 Madison Avenue, New York, New York 10016.
The name "BERKLEY" and the stylized "B" with design are
trademarks belonging to Berkley Publishing Corporation.
PRINTED IN THE UNITED STATES OF AMERICA

# Acknowledgments

Special thanks to the stalwarts who contributed thoughts and information for this book: Maggie Daly ("Mother Chicago") and Patricia Leeds, both of the *Chicago Tribune;* Helen McGill Tubbs of Rome and New York; officers Nick Kitowski and Sergio Rajkovich of the 18th Chicago Police District, for sharing insights into their city, and especially Cabrini Green and Dr. Kenneth Lambert of St. John's Hospital in Jackson, Wyoming, for befriending Duro Lasari and giving him hope when he needed it most.

# A MATTER OF HONOR

# Chapter One

THE YOUNG SOLDIER was shot three times in the back from a passing car as he swayed and urinated into a vacant lot on Chicago's south side. Ballistics determined later that Private Randolph Lewis, identified by fingerprints, was killed instantly by two .45 bullets which smashed into his neck and shoulders. Lab reports disclosed a high mix of alcohol and narcotics in the black soldier's bloodstream.

An old wino heard the shots, watched a car turn out of sight a half block beyond a row of darkened buildings and a pair of bright ribs-and-beer bars. Slumped in the doorway of a burnt-out hand laundry, the drunken man listened with a vacant smile as echoes of shots exploded like firecrackers in his head. A pair of hookers in skinny boots and short leather skirts saw the soldier pitch forward into the weeds just down the street from a bar called The Studsville. The winking neon sign glazed their impassive brown faces with glittering reflections.

When the gray sedan flashed past them, the women exchanged glances and closed their striped umbrellas. Down the cold, rain-slick street a pimp signaled urgently, then disappeared into one of the ribs bars, windows streaked with whitewash signs for red bean soup and broiled ribs. The women shook the drops from their umbrellas and drifted toward The Studsville. A blast of hard rock music swept out as they opened the heavy glass doors. The old drunk in the charred doorway heard the sharp musical beat and thought someone was firing again. He coughed in alarm and almost

1

choked on a mouthful of sweet muscatel.

The soldier lay on his back with rain falling into his open eyes. Drops of blood-spattered beer cans and broken bottles around him. A few seconds after the shooting, two teenaged blacks ran from alley shadows toward the body. With rapid, practiced movements, they turned out the dead soldier's pockets and stripped off his belt, wristwatch and boots.

A wide-bodied jet with wing lights flashing roared above the city on its base leg into O'Hare International Airport. The 747 flew the length of the misted skyline, sounds of its jets muffling the rising whine of a police siren approaching the murder scene. The teenagers scrambled from the fetid lot and ran for the alley. A Chicago police squad roared past The Studsville, its dome light sending crimson strokes across the storefronts and wet sidewalks and finally stopping over the soldier's sprawled body.

There were no witnesses to the murder. No one had heard the shots except the wino, who was volatile but incoherent. In his excitement he had vomited down his long brown coat and the uniformed officer turned away quickly from the sour-sick smell of fermented raisins. The soldier had been drinking in The Studsville till around midnight. He had talked to no one but the bartender, telling the man he was waiting for a friend, had ordered bourbon with beer chasers until the bartender told him he'd had enough. It seemed clear the soldier must have stopped to relieve himself in the empty lot; his Army trousers were unzipped, his genitals exposed. There were fresh skid marks in the debris near the gutter. Somebody in a car had blown him away. Naturally, a cop commented, no one had seen a fucking thing, couldn't give them a make on the heap or the plates. The wino shouted it was like a Fourth of July celebration or champagne corks going off or some damned thing.

A police ambulance arrived and the two attendants waited in the cab while a coroner's official turned up his coat collar and bent to examine the soldier lying in the sleeting rain.

The winds off the dark, choppy lake were intensely cold. Traveling high over the shoreline, they battered against the gleaming buildings along Michigan Boulevard and created blowing heaps of litter along the broad sidewalks and wet gutters.

Gale Force alerts had been reported by the Coast Guard monitors at Navy Pier. Small-craft storm warnings were flying at all ports and marinas. Late TV news shows flashed shots of pedestrians with inside-out umbrellas, teetering precariously as they rounded corners in the business district during rush hour, almost immobilized by the blasting winds.

At an intersection north of Diversey and Clark, a young man named Duro Lasari stood watching the ground floor lights in an old-fashioned brick building. It was after one o'clock, the streets and sidewalks were empty. Only an occasional police or fire siren rose somewhere above the wind. In the next block an all-night luncheonette was still open, its front window a square block of light on the wet pavement.

Duro Lasari blew on his hands and pounded them against his arms. He wore solid work boots, jeans and a wool-lined canvas jacket, but the wind cut through his clothes like razors. His eyes were watering, tears freezing on his cheekbones.

Lasari watched the people working under the overhead lights in the storefront office. A pair of desks faced a large window streaked with dirt, the outside sill crusted with old snow. Behind the window four figures moved from desks to shelves to files. A trim, mature lady in a plaid pantsuit sat at the biggest desk. She seemed to be in charge, frowning over files, signing papers and talking on the phone. Two young males were sorting papers and typing records. And there was a red-haired girl who came in at odd hours. The first night she'd come in at eleven, the next a quarter after ten, and tonight it was almost midnight before she had pulled up in a cab and gone inside to a desk. Through the cold sting of wind in his eyes, the office staff looked almost unreal to Lasari, like figures moving under water. He squinted his eyes to read the painted sign on the office window:

VETERANS' ASSISTANCE SERVICE
PLEASE COME IN

Duro Lasari had been standing at this intersection for three nights in a row, trying to make up his mind to cross the street, to enter that office, and talk to someone about his problems.

He pounded his arms and decided to circle the block one more time at a rapid walk to get his blood circulating and then he'd do it, he'd go into that office as Carlos convinced him he had to and explain his side of what had happened.

His full name was Durham Francis Lasari, but he'd always been called Duro, in school, down in Florida, the Army, everywhere he'd worked, never Durham or Francis. Nobody in his platoon, none of the doctors at Fitzsimons knew him by any name but Duro Lasari. He remembered only two times when his mother had called him Durham. Once had been the Christmas in North Carolina when he was seven and had given her earrings like gold bells and the other he couldn't remember.

Walking south from Diversey, Lasari pushed his hands deep into the slant pockets of his canvas jacket. In an alley, two old men argued over a bottle of wine, each struggling to pull it away from the other, their querulous voices low-pitched, almost intimate. In the next street, just beyond the frame of light from the luncheonette, three Latino boys in Navy pea jackets and Chicago Cubs baseball caps stood watching Lasari expectantly. Smoking brown cigarettes, they shadowboxed about in shuffling circles, commanding the whole width of the sidewalk, the heels of their ankle-high boots tapping out a noisy staccato.

Lasari crossed the avenue to avoid the trio and continued south on the shadowed street. His maneuver was strategic, not tactical; the rule now was to keep out of trouble, any trouble. A brawl, a mugging, a physical confrontation, even a minor traffic violation, could lead to a police station or a hospital where there were always clerks with questions and forms and typewriters and demands for ID. Duro could handle himself, that wasn't the problem. It was what could come later, the red tape everybody was so eager to wrap and trap you in.

With average height and a quick, slender body, Lasari had broad, strong hands and knew how to use them. It was the baseball caps the three boys were wearing that had triggered the anger, then the caution. Punks, Duro thought, show-off, no-talent punks. The caps reminded him of the two spring seasons in high school and the time in Florida when he had believed that baseball would be his ticket to somewhere. He'd had a strong, accurate throwing arm when he'd played baseball in high school in Durham, North Carolina, and the one year in the semi-pros, and great range because of his speed and hands.

A scout from Triple-A, a graying man who'd pitched for the

Dodgers when they were still in Brooklyn, told Duro his fielding and base running weren't the problem, it was hitting. *"You* can hit a waist-high fastball, kid," the scout had said, "but so can *everybody else.* A big league curve, you got to be able to go into the locker with it and make contact. Otherwise, you empty that damned locker and say goodbye."

But the training, the coaching, the sweating and straining in the humid and fruit-scented air of ballparks in Lakeland, Florida, hadn't worked for Duro Lasari. The team had dropped his option at the end of one year.

Lasari pulled the collar of his jacket tighter about his neck and leaned into the wind. His hair was thick and dark, his face hard and intense. His normal expression, the one he showed the world, was one of careful, cool appraisal, a look of dignity and reserve that was also challenging, a defiant and racial fineness defined at its purest in the centuries-old portraits one could see in the museums of Florence. Duro had seen such paintings in books, amused at the shadow of himself that showed out of fading oils and in the sharp, dark eyes of courtiers, shaded by plumes and soft hats.

A police car turned into the block ahead of him. It was cruising, not on call, and its dome light was dark. Yet anyone on the streets in this crumbling neighborhood at this hour could be routinely stopped for questioning. Without hurrying or changing his pace, Lasari turned and walked back to the luncheonette and ordered black coffee with rye toast.

His car was parked across the street, a black Pontiac GTO, a dozen years old but in show condition. The waitress saw him looking out at it as she put his coffee down on the counter.

"It's like yesterday," the waitress said. She stared at the old Pontiac, gleaming in the rain. She was about nineteen, plump and soft, with curly blonde hair. "Like *I* remember yesterday, anyway," she said. "That your Goat over there, mister?"

The police car had cruised past and out of sight down the street. "Yes," he said.

"They're the best. It never really happened to me, it happened to my brother." She smiled. "But he was like a god or something. I was just a kid when he bought a Goat and drove out to California to live. He wrote me that he got it up to ninety-five going through Kansas."

"And nobody stopped him?" Lasari said.

"Not that he told me," the waitress said. "He's down near

San Diego somewhere, working in avocados. He's still got the car.''

Lasari sipped the black coffee, the cup sending warmth through his stiff hands, content to sit at the counter, listening to the waitress with her thoughts about a fabled souped-up car and a godlike brother she hadn't seen in years, delaying the moment he'd have to leave this warm place and walk back to the Veterans' office and tell them about what he had done.

# Chapter Two

THE GREYHOUND BUS station near Van Buren and Randolph streets on the north side of the Loop was cold and windy and smelled of worn luggage and discarded cigarettes. An old man in overalls was mopping the terrazzo floor, a bucket of hot water steaming in the chill air.

Only one ticket window was open and the clerk was reading the sports page of the *Tribune*. A pair of Military Police, big young men with white helmets and shining leather hip holsters, stood beside the glass doors leading to the ramps for loading and departing buses. All the parking bays were empty. The last buses from O'Hare and Midway had come in more than an hour ago, quickly emptying civilians and soldiers with duffel bags before pulling away to the garage behind the terminal. Most of the exhaust fumes had blown away by now, and the air around the loading ramps was brisk and cold with the wind off the lake.

Mrs. Amanda Lewis sat alone on a wooden bench and wondered what she should do next. Randy hadn't been on the bus from O'Hare, as he'd written he would, and now there wouldn't be another bus until seven the next morning. All the way from Germany, she thought, and here she'd missed him right in Chicago. Her skin was the color of milk chocolate and so smooth that even her ready, quick smile hardly creased it. She looked respectable, even old-fashioned, in a neat brown coat and a hat with a brown feather that lay on her cheek against her graying hair. But her eyes reflected her worry, her

7

uneasy concern. Amanda Lewis had not made a trip to downtown Chicago for years and found it challenging and foreign terrain. She'd made a note of the date on her kitchen grocery pad the day Randy's letter came, but now she wasn't sure if it was A.M. or P.M., when his flight was due in from Frankfurt. And somehow, she'd lost or mislaid the letter.

Amanda Lewis, who was Randy's aunt and only living kin since her sister had gone, had arrived at the bus station before nine that morning and stayed all day and into the evening to watch the buses coming in from the airports.

His mother had been dead only a month, sick from alcohol and buried in their hometown of Barlow Bend. Randy wrote he wanted to see his aunt in Chicago before he went on home to that empty house in Alabama, and Amanda planned to cheer him up, to show him a real welcome home. She'd borrowed fifty dollars from the credit union so they could go somewhere nice for dinner and maybe hear country music.

Randy was kind of wild, never having a father to raise him and Missy Jane always blaming herself and the bottle weakness. But maybe he'd be all right. His letter had been serious. He wanted to see Aunt Mandy, he wanted to talk to her, he said. He was planning to make something of himself when he got out of the Army. And he was bringing presents, or maybe he'd mail them, German stuff he'd picked up. He hadn't asked for any favors, didn't go to the Red Cross or anything, but a sergeant had heard about his mother's death and arranged for him to leave for the States early, even fixed the stopover in Chicago.

"There are some fine people in the world," he'd written, "people who don't mind helping us get ahead if we cooperate."

If you could use such a word about Randolph Lewis, then he had matured, she thought. The big crazy kid, with all his Southern boy tricks and meanness, had sounded grown up for once in his life.

The MPs, the military police, they'd been real nice. One of them was named Homer Robbins, she saw that on his nameplate. He'd told her the best thing to do was to find that letter, come back tomorrow. Maybe she had the wrong date, Robbins said, or maybe her nephew missed his flight and was a day late.

The old man mopping the floor said she could call Missing

Persons, but they'd probably tell her to wait a week or so. Then the clerk at the ticket window suggested a soldiers' place he'd read about, over near Diversey about twenty blocks from here, open twenty-four hours a day. They answered questions for servicemen and their kin and didn't ask too many of their own, that's how the man put it. They could make a few phone calls, advise her. Mrs. Lewis knew she'd rest better if she could tell someone about her nephew, so she took down the address, stepped carefully around the wide, wet swaths of suds on the floor and went outside.

A few lights shone from nearby bars and from a small, four-story hotel, but all the brighter lights seemed on the far horizon, the big hospital and the rows of tall apartment buildings along the lake shore. Nobody is on the streets this time of night but fools like me, Amanda Lewis thought as she got into her car, locked the doors quickly and started the motor, letting her breath out as the motor caught.

A sound like a faint human scream or a cat in heat came from a building down the block, an unlit warehouse with corrugated metal doors and windows. Mrs. Lewis's heart beat erratically as she pulled away from the bus station and out into the dark street.

Turning north on Dearborn, she began to count off the blocks to Diversey Avenue and arrange her thoughts. "Private Randolph Peyton Lewis, twenty-two next New Year's Day, enlisted out of Montgomery, Alabama, just finished up a one-year tour of duty in Germany". . . that's about all she could tell the soldier people.

In a recent article for the *Tribune* on the opening of the new Veterans' Assistance Service, Bonnie Caidin had written:

American soldiers who fought in the Vietnam war represent a largely anonymous concept to many fellow Americans, particularly those who viewed that distant slaughter as a kind of impersonal political entertainment on their pre-dinner TV shows.

That war is *over*, but it is not *done with*. Those veterans are real, they are our own people. *It is time we welcomed them home*. This is the opinion of Dr. Irene Kastner, director of this city's newly opened Veterans' Assistance Service, a nonprofit organization, volunteer staffed and funded, and located at 400 Diversey Avenue.

Dr. Kastner, the first black woman to receive a doctor's degree in both medicine and psychology from the University of Chicago, made her remarks at a sparsely attended ceremony at the service offices on Monday night.

"The emotional and social dislocations of these veterans must be treated on a continuing therapeutic basis. Whatever their problems, we will give them love and acceptance and assistance, with a guarantee of compassion and privacy. We will be here to listen, understand and resolve, never to interrogate or interpret," Dr. Kastner said.

Bonnie Caidin's article featured statistics on the number of Illinois veterans who had served in Vietnam, references to various existing state and federal services and budgets, and ended with a statement from the mayor commending the Veterans' Assistance Service on its aims and stating that if the service were ever short of help, the mayor's staff could arrange to put in a few hours per month as volunteers.

The article, with the Caidin byline, ran for two editions in the Sunday *Tribune*, just below the fold, and was then lifted to make space for the story on a shocking and unprecedented act of vandalism, the graffiti spray painting of the giant Picasso sculpture in Civic Center Plaza.

Dr. Kastner had called the newspaper in person to thank Miss Caidin for her fine reporting and Caidin decided to offer her services as a volunteer on the night staff.

After leaving the luncheonette, Lasari circled back to the corner opposite the storefront office. Almost compulsively he found himself mulling over familiar excuses. He had to work tomorrow, another day or so wouldn't matter, he should think his whole story through again. He had just about talked himself into giving up for the night and driving back to Calumet City when an old blue car turned into Diversey and slowed down on the opposite side of the street. Almost simultaneously, a new sound echoed from down the block, a staccato of hard-heeled boots. The three Latinos in baseball caps came trotting along the sidewalk out of the shadows, arms linked, laughing and talking to one another in high, excited voices.

A plump, black woman climbed from the car, closed and locked the driver's side and started to run with heavy steps toward the lighted office.

The three Latinos broke ranks then and rushed the woman like predators, coming at her from the front and from two sides, pushing her screaming and stumbling backward against the brick building. The woman screamed again and hugged her handbag tightly against her brown coat.

Without articulating his thoughts, Duro Lasari knew the lady was his excuse to let loose the rage that fed his indecision, a reason to get to the other side of the street, and finally step into that lighted office.

He left the curb and dashed across the slippery pavement in a half crouch, stopped a moment behind the car, breathing slowly and deeply, flexing his chilled fingers in the pockets of his coat. Then he stepped out in front of the three Latinos, his hands loose at his sides.

"Come on, guys," he said quietly, "back in the woodwork. Let the lady alone."

The three boys were rolling Amanda Lewis's stout body from side to side against the rough brick, pounding on her shoulders and tearing at her crossed arms, thrusting like pack dogs for a grip on the leather strap of the shoulder bag. Her first screams had turned into a moaning prayer. "Don't hurt me, don't hurt me. I can't give you *nothing* . . ."

The door of the Veterans' office swung open and the male clerks stood framed in the light, not speaking, not moving, staring out at the struggling woman, then at Lasari. At a desk inside the red-haired girl dialed rapidly.

It was the insolence, the unearned honor of those baseball caps that first stung Duro Lasari, and then the animal challenge of the three sullen faces turned toward him.

"Fuck off," one of the boys said. "Fuck off, prick, before you get yourself cut."

They were young, twelve or thirteen years old, but slim and wiry and deadly, Lasari judged, with pack strength and pack guts. They had been stalking for prey and they'd found it. The terrified woman's purse belonged to them because they could take it from her; as simple as that.

One of the trio swung around and faced Lasari with an open switchblade. He walked toward him in a crouch, holding out the thin, razor-sharp blade before him, carving out his territory with wide swings of his arm. "You asked for it," he said softly. "I'm comin' into your space."

The shining blade, swinging back and forth, cocked the final trigger of rage in Lasari's head and his speed caught the youth off guard. He feinted left, then right, spun around suddenly on the balls of his feet and swung his right leg in a powerful arc, grunting when the top of his work boot struck the young man's wrist and sent the knife into the gutter, and the challenger sprawling backward against the hood of the car.

A police squad car turned into the block, siren wailing and lights flashing. The three boys sprinted off toward the intersection, one bent almost double to ease the pain in his broken wrist.

Duro Lasari told the battered woman that everything was all right, and when she shivered and stood motionless he moved toward her and put an arm around her shoulders. With eyes shut tight, she was still praying in ragged gasps.

Amanda Lewis could not stop moaning and stammering until a police officer and the woman in the plaid suit took her inside the office, where she sank into a chair, eyes bright with fear, arms still locked about her shoulder bag that held her car keys, wallet and the five ten-dollar bills she had borrowed to entertain Private Randolph Lewis.

# Chapter Three

"I JUST HAPPENED to be walking by," Duro Lasari told the red-haired girl.

She smiled at him. Her skin was smooth and white and probably freckled when she was young, he thought. Under the high neon stripping in the ceiling, her eyes looked dark and shadowed, almost bruised, as if she were overworked and tired. "But what you did, that was very brave, George."

He'd told the police that his name was George Jackson, that he was from out of town and they'd let it go at that, hadn't asked for a driver's license or other ID. Lasari helped to search the street until they found a four-inch switchblade in the gutter.

"You're lucky, pal," the sergeant said. "You don't know this town. Them scumbags are just bucking for a chance to open you up."

The woman who led Mrs. Lewis, followed by Lasari, into the office was Dr. Irene Kastner. She introduced them to the staff and poured cups of coffee. One of the two clerks who had watched the action from the doorway put out his hand and said he was Rick Argella. Argella was slim and youthful in jeans and turtleneck and a pale blue cardigan. "I'd like to apologize for not helping you out there," he said. "I just froze. I just don't cotton to those friggin' *españoles*."

The red-haired girl was named Bonnie Caidin. Lasari took his mug of coffee and accepted the invitation to use the extra chair at her desk.

The office was warm, almost hypnotically bright, an insulated cocoon against the cold, dark streets, and touched with odors of chicory blend coffee and the girl's faint perfume. She sat with him, fragile hands folded neatly on the top of the desk, as if she were resting or taking a break in the night's work. Lasari saw the expectant look in her eyes and was aware of the silence between them. He shifted in his chair, put his coffee cup on the desk and stared down at his tight jeans and his feet in the heavy work shoes, carefully crossed at the ankles. He was surprised to see a slash of blood on the coarse welt of his right boot.

He said then, "As long as I'm here, maybe I could ask you something. It's about some trouble a friend of mine got himself into. Carlos his name is, Luis Carlos."

Bonnie Caidin pulled a yellow legal pad in front of her. "Carlos," she said as she wrote. "Luis Carlos. How can we help him, George?"

"He's a deserter," Lasari said, "but he'd like you to know that he volunteered in the first place, miss. He was nineteen, almost, when he signed up. He was in 'Nam for more than two years, nearly to the end. He got hit twice, the first time a flesh wound in the hand that put him out for a month. Carlos doesn't count that one, but it's on his record."

He forced himself to pause, to slow down the rush of his words. "The second time he got hit twice in the leg. It was bad and took a lot of surgery in Saigon to put it together. That treatment didn't work out right, and he was in a hospital in the States, after the second operation, when he saw the end of the war on TV. You probably saw it, everybody trying to crowd onto planes and get out of Saigon in those last days." He paused and looked at the red-haired woman, aware that she was listening carefully, writing nothing on the legal pad.

"How's your coffee, George?"

"It's fine, thanks, ma'am."

"So Carlos was back in the States when the war was winding down. What then, George?"

"There was a lot of time in Fitzsimons, and things didn't always go right," he said. "Carlos had personal problems, a kind of overload, and he never finished out his time in the service. He just walked away from it all. That's more than ten years ago and he never went back. So he's a deserter, miss, plain and simple. He knows the Army kept records on him, and Carlos would like to get that straightened out."

"We're on a first name basis here, incidentally, George. Except for Dr. Kastner, that is. Only her husband and the mayor call her Irene. I'm Bonnie, if you like." She sipped her coffee. "It's obvious that you and Carlos are good friends."

"That's right. We've been close ever since he came to the Midwest. We both work in the same body shop . . ."

"As his friend, don't you think you should ask Carlos to come in and talk to us in person?"

"I suggested that to him, ma'am," Lasari said, "but he's at the place where he doesn't trust anybody. He doesn't feel he owes anybody an apology. He doesn't feel ashamed or guilty. He got hit twice and he put in all those good years. That should entitle him to something, he figures."

Dr. Kastner and Mrs. Lewis walked over to Caidin's desk. Dr. Kastner said, "Excuse me for breaking in, but our friend here wants to say goodbye to the young man."

When Lasari stood, Amanda Lewis took one of his hands in both of hers and pressed it warmly. "I got to thank you, young man. I was too scared to talk when we first came in. But I'm grateful to you, I surely am."

"Her nephew, Randolph Peyton Lewis, was supposed to leave Frankfurt early yesterday," Dr. Kastner said to Caidin, "on a MATS flight scheduled for O'Hare about eight-thirty this morning. But she hasn't been able to locate him yet."

"Was it a direct flight?" Bonnie Caidin asked. "Do you have a number?"

"Yes, MATS 94, out of Frankfurt," Dr. Kastner said. "But the MATS switchboard is closed for the night. Mrs. Lewis is going home now, so here's her phone number and address in case we hear anything." She put a slip of paper on Caidin's desk. "I told her I think her nephew will probably try to get in touch with her there anyway. No need to presume he's in any trouble."

Mrs. Lewis nodded. "I'll go home and wait by the phone. He's only twenty-two, and I just pray the good Lord the boy's all right. But I had to thank this young man here before I go anywhere."

Caidin excused herself, picked up her coffee and went into a small, dimly lighted storage room behind the office. Supplies were stacked there, boxes of stationery and pamphlets and several five-gallon bottles of drinking water. A counter against one wall supported a mimeograph machine and cartons of paper and a two-burner Silex coffee maker. Bonnie Caidin filled her cup and then walked to a wall phone.

Mrs. Lewis squeezed Lasari's hand again. "You're one of God's own," she whispered as Dr. Kastner took her arm and walked her to the front door.

It hadn't been too difficult so far, Lasari thought as he sat at the desk. The office was quiet except for the occasional sputter of the steam radiators and a rhythmic thumping from a side table where Argella and the other clerk were stapling papers.

He'd spelled it out for the lady as he'd practiced it for so long, keeping his voice easy and casual, like he was talking about someone else, keeping the personal anger where it belonged, so deep inside him that no cracks showed on the surface.

He had told the whole detailed story to Luis Carlos, of course, not once but a dozen times or more, sitting in Mrs. Swade's rooming house, playing dominoes; Carlos, the old Filipino, watching, nodding, sipping dark rum and smoking twisted little brown cigars. It helped that Carlos had little English, didn't understand everything Duro Lasari told him. He listened, that was the important thing, listened with his brown eyes creased against the drifting tobacco smoke, his tired, old face watchful and attentive, and he never showed any recrimination or disapproval for what Duro Lasari had done or not done, letting him decide for himself to do what he was doing now, talking to the lady, trying to find some way to clean up that bad paper with the Army.

The office walls were painted hospital green, Lasari thought, a color that smelled of institutional economy and nursing routines; and pain, the green-gray monotony of military hospitals where he had lain so long, flat on his back with his leg in traction, burdened by thoughts of where he had been and where he was going, and violent memories of Vietnam coursing through his brain again and again. Outside on Diversey Boulevard, a single car sped by, its lights flashing a brief arc of color on the rain-streaked window. Lasari wrenched his thoughts back to the present.

Bonnie Caidin was talking on the phone in the storage room, the door open. She looked comfortable with herself, he thought, sipping coffee, the phone wedged between her chin and shoulder. She wore a beige sweater, a pink shirt and a gray skirt, and she leaned back against the counter, one slim ankle swinging idly. He could hear the low, soft murmur of her voice but the words were indistinct, and there were long pauses while she listened thoughtfully to whoever was on the other end of the line.

Lasari sat up straight when she walked to her desk, as if she were a teacher returning to a classroom.

"I hope you'll excuse me," she said. "That was a call I had to make about another matter." She put her coffee cup on the desk.

"Now. I'd like to get all the details you can give me, George," she said. "I won't use your friend's name, of course. That's policy here. I'll make out a card and we'll refer to him by a case number. You can assure Luis Carlos there won't be anything in our files that can be traced to him. Whatever you tell me will be kept in strictest confidence and all the references will be coded, so there can't be an accidental leak."

She picked up a sharpened pencil and dated her note pad. "First of all, I'd like to review Carlos' service record—where he was inducted, his tour of duty, rank, decorations and medals, if any, the names of his superior officers, his family and civilian contacts, educational background, whatever might be helpful if we want character references and so forth."

"You really need all that, a complete profile, Rorschachs, sex kinks, everything?"

Bonnie Caidin's smile was polite but it didn't touch the cool appraisal in her eyes. "George, the Army holds all the aces when it deals with deserters. They made the rules, Carlos broke them. The Army controls all the options. If your friend hopes to clear his record, to be allowed to serve out his time, he's got to convince them there were extenuating circumstances for his desertion, that he's a good and loyal risk for any further investment they have to make in him. So it's necessary for us to have all the facts before we can advise Carlos. Because, and we should be clear about this from the start, if the Army *rejects* your friend's application of reenlistment and/or an honorable discharge, the alternatives can be pretty severe."

"A hitch in a federal prison, is that the alternative?"

"That's one of them. Sometimes the Army likes to let a desertion charge drop. They examine the case, decide to issue a discharge without honor and sever all connections with the ex-soldier. But the Army *does* have the option of sending a bona fide deserter to a federal penitentiary for two years or even longer, plus a dishonorable discharge."

"Okay, I'll tell you what I know about Carlos," Lasari said. He fixed his eyes on a wall calendar a few feet away from where Rick Argella was sorting papers. He kept his tone casual, but careful, every word measured before he spoke.

". . . Raleigh. He enlisted for four years and entered the Army at Raleigh, North Carolina, that was in 1970, May twenty-second. He was out of school and working in a gas station, eighteen years old, a few months shy of nineteen. He'd had some sports interest but that didn't pan out. Carlos had a low draft number, but he decided he ought to go.

"After basic training he was sent to Fort Bragg for awhile, then he was assigned to canine training in a semiamphibian operation in Virginia—Norfolk, the Navy base there. It was a joint training operation," he explained in reaction to Caidin's puzzled expression. "The men trained and jumped with dogs, Army shepherds, from the fantail of Navy seacraft. Units were trained to work as teams, to see how the dog might coordinate in beach assaults. It was an experimental program, and Carlos was part of it while it lasted.

"Later he was sent to Vietnam with a regular infantry unit. He got hit first in the hand, I told you that. The big hit came ten months later, hip and thigh and a lot of torn cartilage in the right leg. Like I said, he had surgery there and then surgery again and therapy in the States, in and out of hospitals for nearly two years, twenty months all counted. And he was in the hospital Stateside when the war ended."

Duro Lasari talked for another ten minutes, filling in, backtracking, encapsulating those years of his life, years of endurance, confusion and ultimately angers and doubts so deep that even now, when he was at Mrs. Swade's or walking the streets of Calumet City, he sometimes had to stop and grip something solid, a telephone pole, a mailbox, or even Carlos until the spasms of rage ceased and he could breathe normally again.

Bonnie Caidin took careful notes. Her handwriting was tiny but legible and she was fast. Several times she erased a word or phrase and substituted something else, determined to get his meaning down as accurately as possible.

"Decorations?" she asked.

"My friend got the Purple Heart twice, a Bronze Star and a lot of those ribbons that just mean you've been there, like buying a T-shirt at the Grand Canyon to show you looked but didn't fall in."

Caidin smiled, her pencil poised, her eyes watching him impersonally. Lasari frowned. "What bothers Carlos is—if he was going to desert—why he did it when he did. His record was good, he was still in the hospital, but the leg was healing and he was going to be one free civilian. In basic, when the going was tough, and in 'Nam, which was a real firefight, why didn't he try to desert then?"

"Did he explain that to you?"

Lasari shook his head. "He's not too much for talking, really. He says he needed time to make sense out of the whole thing. In the hospital he did a lot of reading, books, magazines, newspapers. He told me he didn't know if that made him smarter or more scared. He told me the happiest guys in the wards were the paraplegics, the guys who would never be released, didn't have to figure out what to do with their lives. They had all the answers spelled out for them."

She was writing rapidly, and he stared at her bowed head. "I don't think *why* is the problem, ma'am. It's the fact that he *did* it. He packed it in, just walked away. So he's a deserter."

Her pencil was poised over the yellow lined paper. "You mentioned that his last treatment, before he walked, was Fitzsimons. Is that Fitzsimons Army Medical Center in Denver?"

For the first time Duro Lasari felt a flick of caution. ". . . we won't use your friend's name . . . that's policy here . . . there won't be anything in our files that could be traced to him . . ."

But dates, place names, sequences, that could make a traceable map. He thought suddenly of the years of lying low in Jackson Hole, the peace and anonymity of the Wyoming countryside, and then the suspicions and panic that sent him hitchhiking in a frantic, broken path from the west to the midwest and finally, for the last two years, hiding in a safe Calumet City body shop, with a bedroom and shared bath in a fifty-dollar-a-week boardinghouse.

"He didn't tell me everything, ma'am. I think he was in a

number of hospitals. I don't know exact dates at Fitzsimons."

Bonnie Caidin put her pencil aside and tilted back in her swing chair. She clasped both hands behind her head, turning her neck as if to relieve tension, then said, "Your friend, Carlos, was he on drugs in Vietnam?"

She had shifted moods and topics suddenly, almost making him forget the role he was playing.

"I don't think so, ma'am," he said carefully. "But he told me once that the stuff was everywhere, joints, Mao's one hundreds, speed, morphine. There was heroin so pure you didn't have to cook it, just mix it with cold water and bang it. Carlos said you could get anything you wanted, any time and at the right price. That's what he told me."

"But Carlos himself wasn't a user?"

"Joints maybe, nothing else."

"Was he involved in dealing or pushing? I've got to know these things, George."

"He knew what was going on. You'd have to be blind not to, but he wasn't into that scene."

"So Carlos told you, in substance, that he'd been a good, responsible soldier, and you believe he has been telling you the truth about all this, George?"

"About being a good soldier? Who knows? If he'd thrown away his rifle and refused to fight, a lot of Americans would have thought that was just fine. But he didn't do that, he stood his ground, and I've seen the scars on his legs to prove it. He's not lying about that."

"I'm trying to get at the heart of the matter. Why do *you* think Carlos deserted when he did?"

Duro Lasari shrugged, his eyes became still in his dark, narrow face. He looked at her with defiant appraisal. "Maybe I walked into the wrong office, lady. '. . . we will be here to listen, understand, and resolve never to interrogate or interpret.' Isn't that what you wrote in the newspaper article on this place?"

"Yes, I did," Bonnie Caidin said. She tapped the tip of her pencil against her teeth. "You understand, I mean *your friend* understands, that when he turns himself into the Army . . . if that's what he decides to do . . . what happens next is out of our hands. This office can advise him, make an appointment with the right person at the right time. But by deserting Carlos broke his contract with the Army, and the Army still owns him. That doesn't leave him much to bargain with.''

"He knows that," Lasari said. "This guy's at a point of no return. He can't go forward till he goes backward. Maybe it's the symbiotic relationship between the outlaw and the system. He'd like to serve out his time and be the best goddamn soldier ever, just as long as there's hope he can walk out at the end of his tour with a clean discharge. He'll pay whatever it takes to get that.''

The clerk, Argella, walked over to Caidin's desk, buttoning a leather jacket over his blue sweater. "Excuse me, Bonnie," he said. "I'm taking a snack break." He looked at Lasari, his soft brown eyes friendly. "Maybe I could feed a dime into the parking meter for this gentleman here.''

Lasari explained he was parked in a free zone in the next block. "Thanks anyway, *amigo.*''

"*Por nada, compadre.*''

As Argella left, a cold wind from the open door surged around their ankles and fluttered papers on desk tops.

"I'm going to check out every Army regulation on desertion and/or reenlistment, of course," Bonnie Caidin said. "But the best advice I have right now is that Luis Carlos come here in person and let us prepare a complete file on his service record and personal background. Will he do that?"

"I can't guarantee anything, but I'll ask him.''

"One thing that will be of prime importance in this case is *intent*. If Carlos turns himself into the military authorities *voluntarily,* that could be the best thing going for him. But if someone else turns him in, such as an informer, or if he's picked up by Military Police, well, I wouldn't count on the Army *believing* his good intentions.

"The Army doesn't want 'bad apples'—that's their phrase, not mine, and they're not in the rehabilitation business. If Carlos is heavily in debt, has bad gambling habits, if you're wrong about his drug use, or if he's got deep legal problems, like serious arrears in wife or child support, I think you know what to advise him to do.''

"Stay away from the Army.''

"I can't say that on my own authority, George. We just want your friend to know what he's up against. And we'll do everything we can to help him, that's a promise.''

Lasari stood and zipped his windbreaker. "I'll tell him. I appreciate you giving me this much time, ma'am."

It was strange, he thought, he was almost sorry it was over. He had felt good here, the warm, bright office, the fragrant coffee, this thin, pale woman so willing to listen.

She picked up a raincoat with a wool lining from the back of her chair. A round plastic PRESS disc hung by a thong from a buttonhole. "I need a breath of fresh air," she said. "I'll type up our notes before I check out."

The rain had stopped but the wind was high and they stood close, lifting their voices above the chill gusts. "I was a senior in high school when it was winding down," she said, "not quite eighteen. I marched and demonstrated and carried placards. I sent letters to the editors, and I wrote things for the campus newspaper. I hated that war and didn't believe any American soldier should be in it. What does your friend Carlos think about people like that?"

"They don't bother him."

"You said he was angry."

"There are a lot of things to be angry about." He stared down the street. " 'Civilians get the kind of Army and the kind of wars they deserve.' I read that somewhere, and I'm still trying to figure it out. If it means what I think it means, I was in 'Nam for all the wrong reasons. That can make a guy angry."

"You waited three nights before you came in," she said. "What made you decide?"

He looked at her in surprise, then at the shadowed doorway across the street. "You saw me over there?"

"I'm a reporter. I'm supposed to notice things. What made up your mind?"

"Nothing you'd understand probably. It was those damned baseball caps."

"You don't like baseball?"

"I love it, Miss Caidin. It's just another game I'm not very good at."

As the low roar of Lasari's GTO trembled through the silence, Rick Argella stepped from the darkness of an alley. The glow from the rear lights clearly revealed the license plate.

When the car pulled away from the curb, Argella crossed the street to the all-night luncheonette.

The waitress smiled and brought him his usual order, a glass of milk and two sugar doughnuts. "Some fancy car, Millie," he said, nodding in the direction of the fading reverberations. "Them power cars are collectors' items now."

"My brother had one," she said. "The fellow who owns it was in here and I was telling him about it. Nice Italian type guy."

Argella licked the sugar from his fingers and went into the men's room at the rear of the restaurant. He slid the door bolt into its hasp, put some coins into the wall phone, dialed the detective division of a south-side precinct and asked to be connected with extension 400.

When Detective Frank Salmi picked up the phone, Argella spoke without identifying himself.

"I've got one for you, Frank. A 'Nam vet came in tonight, went AWOL a few years back and he's nervous. Good record, he says, no habit, no drug busts but talks like he knows the scene. Says he wants to clear his record, re-up if necessary, that shit. Alley smart, if you ask me, a tough fucker. I saw him fight."

"Got a name?"

"He calls himself 'George,' made out that he was asking information for a friend. That *Tribune chica* talked to him. He opened up to her some, but he was careful. No way I could move in or push it."

"A deserter with a good record? A spade?"

"No, he's pure honky, man. Maybe Italian."

"What the fuck good is it without a name?"

"I got a plate number."

"But is it his car?"

"*Claro*. I checked that twice. He told me where he was parked and he talked to a waitress."

Argella gave Detective Salmi Lasari's license number in spaced intervals. "Seven—four—bravo—six—dancer—nine."

Salmi read it back. "74B6D9?"

"*Correcto, compadre*. You'll tell Sergeant Malleck where you got it?"

The phone clicked in Argella's ear. He gave the hook a final shake, checked the coin chute automatically and returned to the counter. He told Millie the coffee was cold and that he'd meant he wanted the doughnuts with the coconut sprinkles.

Argella lit a cigarette and looked with sensuous contentment at the curve of the waitress' hips as she reached to get the doughnuts from a shelf over the coffee urn.

# Chapter Four

CENTRAL POLICE HEADQUARTERS, the official nexus for crime analysis and all phases of major criminal investigation in the city, is located on Chicago's south side on State Street between Eleventh Street and Roosevelt Road. A thirteen-story building with a glimpse of Lake Michigan from its upper floors, Central Headquarters stands on the east parallel to State Street in a borderline area between the Loop's business districts to the north and deteriorating sections spreading south and west, into neighborhoods dominated by ethnic groups, black, Asian, and Hispanic, migrant southern rural whites, and by the city's highest crime and poverty statistics.

In his office at headquarters, Homicide Detective Lieutenant Mark Weir considered the information he had received earlier by phone from Bonnie Caidin.

On a notepad he had written the name Private Randolph Peyton Lewis, underscoring it with three heavy pencil strokes. He had added the notations: Age 22, black, en route to O'Hare on MATS Flight 94, departure point Frankfurt. Reported missing by aunt, Mrs. Amanda Lewis, 4800 South Halstead Street.

Sergeant DuBois Gordon, who reported to the lieutenant, was already on his way to talk to Mrs. Lewis, and the lieutenant himself had made a number of calls to contacts around the city.

Weir was in his mid-thirties, tall and rangy, with a wide, square face and sandy hair. He stood now and stared out at the lake which sparkled dully in the early dawn. At this distance, the water looked heavy and lifeless. Weir sipped coffee from a wilted carton and looked uncertainly at his phone, reluctant to pick it up and call his father at his farm outside Springfield. He justified his procrastination by running once again over what information he'd collected so far on Private Lewis.

MATS Flight 94 had arrived on schedule at O'Hare International, carrying two hundred military personnel from various cities in Germany. According to the roster and what they knew at present, Private Lewis had been aboard. He was logged in at Health and Immigration, and then cleared routinely through Customs.

Yet, according to skycaps, cab starters, bus-line clerks, rental car agencies and even private limo chauffeurs, there was no evidence that Private Lewis had left O'Hare International after he had deplaned from MATS 94—at least he hadn't left on a conventional carrier, and it wasn't likely he'd tried to hitchhike into town, not with bad weather and his military gear.

Lieutenant Weir jingled the change in his pocket, then spread it on his desk. Four quarters, three pennies and a nickel, and a metal ring with his apartment and car keys. He studied the coins a moment and returned them to his jacket. He would have preferred to make this call privately from a pay booth in the lobby.

Weir lifted his desk phone and told the switchboard operator he wanted to place a call to Springfield, Illinois. Finishing the last of the coffee, he dropped the carton into a wastebasket and, without being aware of it, stood straight and squared his shoulders to prepare himself for the sound of his father's voice.

To his relief it was Grimes who answered. John Grimes, his father's former corporal, who had followed General Weir through a dozen posts, two major wars and, ultimately, into shared retirement on a farm in downstate Illinois.

"Mark, this is a helluva surprise, a damned treat," Grimes said, his voice hearty. "It's fine to hear from you. You okay, son?"

"Things are about as usual," the lieutenant said. "How about yourself?"

"I'd be lying if I didn't admit I'm stiff and lazy some of

these cold mornings.'' Corporal Grimes laughed. "But you know your father. We don't exactly stand reveille, but there's work to be done on this place. What can I do for you, Mark?''

"I know you weren't expecting this call, John, but I'd like to talk to the general.''

"I'll try to corral him for you, Mark,'' Grimes said, the tone of his voice unchanged. "Give me a moment, will you? Either he's working the dogs or he's in the barn with the tenant farmer.''

As he waited, the lieutenant unlocked a desk drawer and took out a file which contained the names and addresses (conditional in one instance) and various biographical information relating to three United States Army soldiers who had been found dead on the streets of Chicago in the last six months; three black men, all privates with borderline service records, infractions ranging from drunkenness to insubordination. All three had been in their early twenties, and all had been knifed or shot in slum neighborhoods, with high traces of narcotics and alcohol in their bloodstreams. Privates Cullen, Baggot and Jones.

The three homicides were carried in the various police districts in which they'd occurred as open, unsolved crimes. As yet the killings had not been grouped under a single case number or tentatively identified as the work of a single person or persons.

Lieutenant Weir was first alerted to the possibility of a relationship between the slayings from Bonnie Caidin. She had called from her newspaper office with certain questions when the second victim, Will Baggot, was found in an alley behind a bar near Garfield and South Washington. Army privates, both recently back from Germany . . . And she'd called Lieutenant Weir again when a third military victim, Private Titus Jones, was discovered in a trash-littered lot near Washington Park.

Corporal Grimes' voice sounded in his ear, "Mark, you there?''

"Yes, of course.''

"Your father's just left for Springfield with the farmer. He don't like the load of feed they delivered last week. You know how the general always was. Troops and livestock get fed before the officers.''

"It's a little early for feed marts. He's there but he won't talk to me, is that it, Grimes?''

"Don't take that tone, Mark. You think he's stiff-necked, but he was pretty damned hurt, you know. You can't rightly expect him not to be."

The lieutenant felt some of the old angers and frustrations pulling at him. "Grimes, I need to talk to my father. It's not personal."

"Give him a little time, son." Grimes' tone became conspiratorial. "I'm roasting a pheasant tonight, the general's shot a freezer full. After dinner I'll mix him a little malt whiskey and ask him to get in touch with you. I'll make it a direct order if I have to. Hell, it's all gone on too long. Where'll you be tonight, say around eight-thirty?"

"Grimes, I need to talk to my father *now*. I told you this isn't personal. I'm a cop, and I need a professional evaluation from him."

"I said he went to town, lieutenant," Grimes said flatly.

"All right, Grimes, but do this much," Mark Weir said. "Take down three names, three soldiers who shipped out of Germany within the last six months. Ask my father if he'll run a check on them with his contacts in G-2. See if there's any relationship between them and the fact that they were all murdered in my city after they returned from service abroad."

"These soldiers are dead you say? All three of them?"

"That's right. So far they're being treated as separate, unsolved homicides. I've kept the lid on with the Army because there's nothing obvious or logically military to move on. These soldiers were on leave, off duty, drugged and drunk and in bad neighborhoods. But they were soldiers, and they did serve abroad. If the general is willing to cooperate, I'd like him to make those inquiries as discreetly as possible."

"You know Scotty," Grimes said dryly. "Take your chances on how discreet he'll be."

Lieutenant Weir gave Grimes the names of the three murder victims and their Army identification numbers. And one last name to check on, a missing person called Private Randolph Peyton Lewis. Then, unable to help himself, Weir added, "If the old man doesn't want to get involved, if he doesn't want to talk to me or help me, you can tell him for me where he can stuff those four silver stars of his."

"You're out of line, Mark," the man said. "I'll skip that part of your message."

Mark knew Grimes well; the corporal had almost raised

him, but Grimes had never understood the issues between Mark and his father, the gulf that separated them like a lethal moat. It wasn't only a matter of bands at dockside for returning GIs or patriotic bunting on main streets across the country. Most of the differences between himself and his father were generation problems, philosophy gaps, definitions of "a just war" and "other wars" and the inability to talk sanely and quietly about any of it. And there was something else, too, something wounding and estranging that had come between them after his mother died.

The lieutenant looked at his watch. He was waiting for Sergeant Gordon's call and only half listening to Grimes now. ". . . he's not made of granite himself, Mark, never mind the public image. He can be hurt, too, you know."

It was true, of course, the lieutenant thought, watching the surface of the gray lake begin to glitter. A fog had come in and the sun broke through in dappled patterns. A light glowed on the base of the phone.

"Grimes, do your best," Weir said. "Tell my father those dead men on my turf mean as much to me as the casualties at Bastogne or Pork Chop Hill or anywhere else on *his* terrain. I need him to locate the enemy . . ."

The lieutenant broke the connection, pushed a button and Sergeant Gordon came on the line. He was calling from Mrs. Lewis's apartment.

"We found the letter and Mrs. Lewis was right about dates and times. Nothing much else in it except stuff about presents and wanting to make the big time in life. Nice, kind of hopeful, but nothing for us to go on. Mrs. Lewis almost got mugged tonight near the Vets' Aid on Diversey, by the way. Some stud with balls saved her ass. She's making us tea right now, and I'm going to look through a stack of letters from Randolph's mother, see if they give us something. Anything at your end, lieutenant?"

"I'm trying a new approach," he said. "Suppose you pick me up at Congress and Michigan in about an hour, okay?"

"Will do, lieutenant."

Mark Weir lived on the near north side in a block of renovated three-story brownstones. His was the basement apartment, running the length of the house, four rooms and a bath, with barred windows, front and back, opening on shallow courtyards. In summer there were potted geraniums on the front sills, and he resolved that if he ever got a cat, he'd keep a catnip tray growing in the kitchen bay.

At home he changed into track clothes, left his apartment and jogged east to Michigan Avenue. He continued over the bridge that arched the river, past the Tribune Tower to the stretch of shops and the apartment buildings and hotels that faced Lake Michigan.

The lieutenant alternated his route every other day. He ran in Lincoln Park often, and sometimes took Delaware or Oak to the Outer Drive and along the lake to Navy Pier. From there, if he had time, he usually jogged back toward the El, the elevated transportation route that circled the town's original business district. He liked the narrow streets in that area, slatted and shadowed from overhead by the structure of train tracks, the satisfying Chicago sound of old El cars rumbling and screeching above him.

This early frosty morning the lieutenant wore a gray wool cardigan over his jogging suit. Beneath the sweater a .32 caliber revolver in a spring clip was looped to his belt, and under the leather were secured his ID and gold badge. A wristwatch with a small receiver gave him contact with Homicide Central.

Traffic on Michigan Avenue was still light, only a few cruising cabs, morning-shift doormen walking to clubs and hotels and old women from downtown cleaning crews moving wearily toward bus stops and El stations.

From here the lake stretched away from the city like a flat silver platter, the thin sun spreading through the mists. A wind scattered dirt and damp papers in the gutter and ice in the hollows of the sidewalks glittered like bits of broken glass. Street lights were still on, he noticed, their glows paling in the rising daylight. Weir paced himself to the echo of his footsteps and checked his watch as he passed the Art Institute with long, rhythmic strides.

For the last ten years there had never been a cease-fire between himself and the old man, no area of accommodation, not even a no-man's land where they might have met under a flag of truce to reestablish lines of communication. Yet even for a long time before that something had been missing between them, or maybe missing in *himself,* he often thought. He remembered his feelings as a kind of emotional overkill, a demand for more love than seemed to be in supply. As a young boy he sometimes felt lonesome for his father, even when they were together on the same Army post, in the same house, sometimes even in the same room. It was an ache he felt acutely but never understood.

General Weir was stationed mostly in Europe and Washington during his son's teens and university years. Mark had managed a student draft deferment until graduation, then volunteered for service for two years. He went into the Army a private and came out a private. He applied for and received specialized training in communications. He spent a year and a half on various Stateside assignments and the last six months in a suburb of Saigon. Except for basic training, Mark Weir never handled or fired a weapon.

Mustered out of the Army at twenty-three, he transferred his Army savings to a Chicago bank, moved into a small efficiency apartment near the Loop and joined a Veterans Against Vietnam group to publicly protest U.S. military involvement in the war.

A student group at New Trier High School had asked him to speak, and it was there he first met Bonnie Caidin. He allowed her to tape one of his speeches, and some months later agreed to have it printed as a pamphlet for the antiwar student group to stuff in Evanston mailboxes, pass out on downtown street corners and send to the opinion page of the Chicago newspapers and the New York *Times*.

Mark Weir was never sure exactly what had triggered his final anger or flawed his judgment, or why he wanted to hurt his father so directly, but he had instructed Bonnie Caidin to identify him in the introduction to that pamphlet as the only son of Lieutenant-General Tarbert Weir, United States Army.

Even now, at thirty-four, Weir felt an almost crippling chill as he remembered his father's rage and scorn. The Pentagon had sent one of the pamphlets to the general in Paris. He had initialed it and sent it back to his son with the scrawled comment: "High-class rhetoric, I'd say, persuasive to cowardly hearts and immature minds but damned close to treason in my judgment. *Have I raised a turncoat as my son?*"

Mark had written a heated reply: "If civilian criticism of government policy is treason, how would you describe the government's current lies to its citizens? What would you call our faked casualty reports, unreported bombing raids on a neutral country, deliberate underevaluation of enemy strength to keep this war alive? Is that legitimate representation, or none of the country's damned business? I kept my mouth shut while I was in uniform, but I will no longer do that. By your own choice, you have been in uniform most of your adult life, and you don't speak out. By staying in uniform, accepting its powers and privileges, your silence abets the lies of the Vietnam conflict. *You* are committing the ultimate treason. You are not true to yourself."

Coincidence or not, Mark never knew, but less than two years after that letter General Tarbert Weir resigned from the United States Army and moved permanently to Springfield.

Running smoothly now on the hard pavement, Mark Weir crossed the east-west streets named for Presidents Adams, Jackson, and Van Buren, his thoughts as insistent and rhythmic as his stride.

In the post-'Nam years, some of young Weir's angers were eroded by civilian life and simple reasoning. His father had not made policy, had not been a commander in Vietnam or had any part of it. When he applied for Police Academy and was accepted, he wanted his father to be proud of him. He had written him the news to the farm but that letter was never answered.

It was not the accusation of personal treason that had hurt his father so deeply, Mark Weir knew that. Angry words can be forgiven and forgotten. It was the mutilated picture he had enclosed with that final letter. He had literally torn his father out of his life.

It was a snapshot taken the last time they had been photographed together as a family, one mild winter day in Wiesbaden, right after Colonel Weir had come back from two weeks of maneuvers on the border between Czechoslovakia and West Germany. Grimes had snapped the picture of the trio, their eyes squinting against the winter sun, arms around each other. At the last moment his father had taken off his Army cap and put it on his son's head. The cap slid over the boy's fine, sandy hair, and all three of them had laughed into the camera.

His mother had died a month later of lobar pneumonia, complicated by an atypical lung collapse. They had gone for a long weekend together in the Bavarian Alps, but Grimes had shown up unexpectedly to take Mark back to the base on Sunday night. His father said he did not want Mark to miss school, so the boy had not been with his mother when she died.

After crossing Harrison, the lieutenant slowed to a walk and stopped in front of the Blackstone Hotel. In spite of the cold, he was sweating, his hair dark and damp at the temples.

He had torn that picture in two, so that his mother and the boy in the officer's cap were on one side and Colonel Scotty Weir was separated from them completely. But there was still the outline of his father's hand as it rested on young Mark's shoulder.

Mark Weir had carefully picked at the shiny surface, lifting off the flakes of photograph that recorded that hand, and dropping them into the envelope.

Symbolically, and then in fact, he had torn his father out of his life. John Grimes sent an occasional brief note and always a handwritten message at Christmas, but Mark Weir had known for some time that his father did not know how to forgive him, and he had never quite forgiven himself.

But he hoped the general would at least care about the three dead soldiers.

# Chapter Five

A BLACK SEDAN traveling north on Michigan Boulevard made a sharp U-turn, sending up spurts of grimy water, then braked to a stop in front of the Blackstone Building. Lieutenant Weir got into the front passenger seat.

The sergeant at the wheel turned north on Dearborn and drove past the Dirksen Courthouse and then past the Picasso masterpiece, a flaring sculpture of curved iron arches and a facelike flange that reflected in a soft glow from the glass windows of the buildings around it.

"It's all strange to my daddy," Sergeant Gordon said, nodding at the giant artwork as the car angled past Civic Center Plaza. "He says it's the spittin' image of Picasso's mother-in-law."

Gordon was a plump man of about forty with fine, smooth skin, light brown, and the habit of laughing softly in varying pitches to emphasize what he was saying. His eyes were cool and watchful, but bright with a sense of amusement. Only the patchy gray of his sideburns, like clumps of steel wool, gave away his age.

"And my daddy hates all those fucking glass buildings in the Loop. He liked it when everything was brick or brownstone and the streetcar tracks went down the middle of the street," DuBois Gordon continued with a burst of laughter. "It's always the Outer Drive to him, none of that Lake Shore Drive shit. Marina Towers, Daley Center, he won't have 'em. Thinks we went wrong when we took the Pullman sleepers off

34

between here and St. Louis. My daddy still likes to tell kinfolk that Chicago is Indian talk for wild onion . . ." He glanced at the lieutenant.

"Okay, boss, so we're working," he said. "I didn't get much from Mrs. Lewis. Nothing solid. She didn't know her nephew well. Before the Army, she told me, he was always in some sort of trouble, but he never hurt anybody, had a good heart. She never had kids of her own."

At the lieutenant's instructions, Gordon drove across the river and continued north toward Bonnie Caidin's apartment building.

"Here's what I got hold of so far," Weir told the sergeant. "It's just a lot of hearsay, none of the usual sources saw anything, but a clerk at the Traveler's Aid booth said a Hare Krishna disciple had stopped by to get some ointment for a split lip. The Krishna said he tried to intervene when a pair of military police were manhandling a soldier in an O'Hare parking lot. He said the MPs told him the man was drunk, and they were taking him in for his own good. They tossed the soldier and his gear into a closed jeep and took off."

"Did you check with the military?"

"I got the airport to do that, without using my name. They say the regular army MPs reported no trouble at the airport, but the other MPs, the new special cadre that works out of the west armory, they could have been responsible for the action. They're a fairly new and experimental unit, operating only in urban areas. They've been given liaison responsibility between men in uniform and ordinary citizens. If needed, they've got the right to act in civilian areas, like the airport. That cadre reports directly to a First Sergeant Karl Malleck, and that's a call I'm trying to make up my mind about."

"You saying that Lewis could be sleeping off a drunk in an Army brig right now?"

"Let's say I hope he is," the lieutenant said.

Sergeant Gordon pulled up and stopped in a parking place beyond the canopied entrance to Bonnie Caidin's building.

"How long do we sit on it, lieutenant? Three soldiers murdered, one missing and suspicious . . . are you and me just keeping score?"

"The stats aren't out of line." The lieutenant looked at his watch; he still had a few minutes. "I've checked, Doobie. New York, Cleveland, Denver, San Diego—three unsolved dead males over a six-month period doesn't make a blip on the homicide curve.''

"Dead soldier boys?"

"Not far from the national average either. Servicemen are usually young, have money to spend, like to drink, try drugs and raise hell, and they look for hookers in dangerous neighborhoods.''

"Mostly black soldier boys? All with fucked up service records, alcohol on duty, insubordination, shit like that?"

"What good is guessing? We can't make a case on what we've got, period. It's only a series of coincidences at this stage.''

"And we can't lean on Malleck?"

"No. It would be out of line for Homicide to inquire about a soldier who isn't even officially classified as missing. If Malleck is involved, or his special cadre are in on it, it would only tip them off that we're on to a developing pattern.''

Sergeant Gordon smiled without humor, the early morning light shining on his high, flat cheekbones. "You're gonna ask Miss Bonnie to check out the Malleck angle, is that right?"

"She can do it legitimately, as part of a feature," the lieutenant said. "Bonnie met this soldier's aunt last night in a perfectly routine fashion. A follow-up inquiry to Malleck's people isn't out of line.''

"But she'll have to tell him the police heard about a drunk soldier being hauled from the airport by MPs, right?"

"She can say her city editor picked up the tip in a massage parlor or bar, or whatever. 'Your boys happen to pick up a soldier named Randolph Lewis, sergeant?' That's all she has to ask, for Christ's sake.''

"Well, then why the hell you so edgy about it?"

"What's been going on here has been going on for too long, that's why.''

Gordon chuckled but there was a bitterness to his laugh. "Us black folks, we never did like the military helping out the police, not since Civil War days, boss.''

"Look," Lieutenant Weir said. "I know you've got a masters in Public Administration, I know you're taking courses toward your doctorate. You're going to wind up a big shot in City Hall with more degrees than a thermometer, but I also know that when you go darky on me, you're holding back or are damned worried about something . . .''

Sergeant Gordon shrugged. "Tell Bonnie to watch herself, boss. A detective named Salmi, Frank Salmi, is pretty close to Malleck. I've known Salmi since the Academy. He works out of Southside but he's just been assigned to Central two days a week. I saw his name on roster. If Malleck's anything like Salmi, then he's tough as whale shit. Clean that up and tell Bonnie I said so."

In a leather booth near the back of the coffee shop Bonnie Caidin sat alone, sipping black coffee and leafing through an early edition of the *Tribune*.

Mark Weir slid into the padded seat opposite her and signaled the waitress. "I'll have coffee, toast, scrambled eggs —and, miss, ask the chef not to put any of that sliced fruit stuff on my plate. I don't like things that run into my eggs."

Bonnie folded the newspaper and put it on the seat beside her. She lifted her red hair off her shoulders with a quick, absent gesture. Cones of light from the overhead lamps shadowed her eyes and made half-circles of blue above her cheekbones.

"You look a little tired," the lieutenant said.

"It's just because it's winter. I should get myself a sunlamp. How about you, Mark? No orange juice? You need that Vitamin C."

"I take tablets when I think of it," he said. "I'm off the orange juice because I don't have a decent refrigerator in my apartment at the moment." He sat up straight as the waitress put a paper napkin and silverware in front of him. "If you're so worried about my vitamins, you could have married me," he said. "How many damned years did I wait around hoping you'd change your mind?"

"Oh, Mark. Vitamins have nothing to do with it. I was seventeen years old when we met. I wasn't ready for marriage then any more than I am now. And if it makes you feel better—well, I loved you enough to think you could stand being hurt a little."

"Thanks," he said dryly. "I'm glad you don't look back on me as a one-night stand."

"I was counting," she said. "We made love every chance we got for more than two years, two years and four months exactly. Not counting that lovely, strange weekend in Fond du Lac last spring."

The waitress set the coffee and toast to one side and put the plate of scrambled eggs in front of the lieutenant. "I told him about the fruit," she said, "but I hope you don't mind that he put some parsley on. He used to chef down at Boca Raton."

"It's all right," the lieutenant said. "Tell him one of Chicago's finest says okay." He took a sip of the steaming coffee.

Bonnie Caidin reached over and put her hand on his. "I don't like it when you go sad. Believe me, Mark, you were the best thing that ever happened to me. I really loved you, and that's not easy to say. We were the *right* people at the wrong time. But I never regretted it."

"I wish I could say the same." Lieutenant Weir pulled his hand away gently. "Just touching you brings it all back, Bonnie."

"All right," she said quietly. "Shall we talk about what we came to talk about? Do you have anything on Private Randolph Lewis?"

The lieutenant told her what he'd told Sergeant Gordon and when he finished she said, "I'll call Sergeant Malleck, but I don't understand why you or Doobie don't do it."

"It might rustle the bushes, Bonnie. I don't want to make cop noises till I know what we're up against."

"All right," she said, "I'll handle it as a routine check, like I'm doing some kind of feature. I'll tell Malleck some do-gooder called the city desk about the Hare Kirshna, sort of a citizen's complaint, religious freedom in our streets, something like that." She leaned back in the booth, the lights deepening the blue shadows under her eyes. "Whatever we find out about young Lewis, I can't hold back my story on those GI murders much longer, Mark. You've got to realize that."

He shrugged and stirred his coffee. "What story? We've got three isolated murders over a six-month period, no relationships, no motives, no connection except uniforms. The *Tribune* ran a page-three paragraph on every one of them, and that was the extent of their interest. So far it's random violence, typical of any big city in the country."

"They all saw service in Europe, Mark."

"Damn it, Bonnie, on any given day the United States has more than three hundred thousand men in uniform in Germany alone and they've had men there by the thousands for nearly forty years."

She said with finality, "If Private Lewis doesn't turn up safe and sound within the next twenty-four hours, I'll have to turn over my notes. My editors have got to be told. I can't decide on my own whether or not to sit on this information."

"Doobie Gordon told me about the man who saved Mrs. Lewis last night. Does he fit into the story?"

"I don't think he does. He was across the street three nights running, trying to work up courage to come in. Those Latino turkeys who tried to zap Mrs. Lewis gave him an excuse."

"It wasn't an act? He wasn't tailing Mrs. Lewis?"

"No. I'd been aware of him for three nights."

"What was he so shy about?"

"I'm as bad at cocktail psychiatry as most amateurs," Bonnie Caidin said, "but here's my thumbnail analysis. George Jackson, which probably isn't his name, is carrying a double guilt load, first because he was *in* the Army and secondly because he *ran away* from it. He doesn't quite see himself in either role.

"He's about thirty or thirty-two, blue collar, high-school education and then something extra. Did time in Vietnam, wounded twice. A private sort of person but street smart, a little touch of the old South in his voice. He's good-looking in a *macho* way, maybe Italian, and he's ballsy, we know that from how he fought for Mrs. Lewis."

She finished her coffee and put the cup down with a decisive click. "He let a little something slip. He talked about 'the symbiotic relationship between the outlaw and the system.' So he's not your ordinary deserter. He's been reading Genet, Fanon, Marcuso, something besides the thrillers and sports magazines you get in a PX or GI hospital. He's been thinking."

"And he came to the Vets' to clear up his bad paper?"

"In a way. He said he came in to get that information for a friend, who wants to get squared away with the system. I felt sorry for this George."

"Bleeding heart sorry or person-to-person sorry?"

"Person-to-person sorry, and rather admiring. He's in a kind of agony with his anarchy, whatever you want to call it. He hasn't made your kind of adjustment, Mark. He didn't put down one gun because it was wrong and then pick up another gun because it was right. He just walked away. And he doesn't seem to have a father to play off his emotions on."

Bonnie put the folded newspaper under her arm and pushed

her coffee check toward the lieutenant. "Thanks for breakfast, Mark. I'll give you a ring when I talk to Malleck. And I think we can just forget about my 'George Jackson.' He's got nothing to do with Private Lewis, I'm sure of that, and I've got a hunch he's not going to turn up at the Vets' again. It's probably the end of it."

"Can't you call him?"

She laughed. "It's against the Vets' Assistance policy to interfere or pursue in any way. Besides, do you know how many Jacksons there are in the Chicago phone book?"

"You've already checked?"

"Yes. Five full pages, and thirty-eight of them are named George."

# Chapter Six

Lieutenant Weir paid both checks and pushed through the revolving doors of the coffee shop, buttoning his sweater against the damp cold. The alarm buzzer sounded on his wristwatch.

He hurried to a corner phone booth and dialed Central Headquarters switchboard. Identifying himself by badge number, he asked the operator to patch his incoming call to the public phone.

"It's Springfield, Lieutenant," the operator said. "The party said it was urgent."

Mark Weir used a thumbnail to scrape off a smear of scarlet lipstick that almost obliterated the number above the phone.

"Okay, I got it," he said. "Patch my call through to phone number 636-6103. No, wait a minute. That last number's not a three, it's an eight."

The phone booth had been vandalized. The glass panels, reinforced with wire mesh, were splintered in several places and wind blew in icy blasts through the cracks. Mark Weir began to jog in place, awkward in the cramped space, and rubbed his hands together, holding the phone cocked between his chin and shoulder. He realized suddenly how tired he was, tired and discouraged. It was ironic, he thought, that after all these years he'd still be at a disadvantage talking to his father; the older man confident and comfortable in his country study, with Grimes nearby to pour fresh coffee or put a log on the fire, while he was asking for help, freezing and shifting from

41

foot to foot in a phone booth somebody had recently pissed in.

His rubber-soled shoes made a sucking sound on the slippery floor, and he rubbed a hand over the back of his neck, kneading the muscles that were knotting with tension as he waited for the compelling voice that was always, from childhood on, poised at the inner edge of his consciousness.

"Okay, Mark," General Scotty Weir sounded abruptly on the other end of the line. "I got your message but why the hell is any of this relevant to me? According to Grimes' notes, if I can read his damned handwriting, three men were assaulted and murdered in slum neighborhoods in your town. They're on the books as unsolved homicides. One every couple of months or so, all three black, all in their twenties, traces of drugs and/or alcohol in the bloodstream, and so on and so on. Is that right?"

His father's voice was low and resonant, the lieutenant noted with some surprise, without the tone of acid bitterness he had feared. There was a muted, midwestern ring to it, with no hint of the fact they had not spoken for more than ten years.

"Basically, that's what it is," Mark Weir said.

"It's a damned shame what's happened to civilian safety and decency, but you're talking about Chicago police business," General Weir said, "and I don't see what I can do for you. Hold on a minute though. I can't read what Grimes' got scrawled here . . ."

"My reason for wanting help from you is that these three victims were all GIs, active members of the United States armed forces, all murdered while in uniform. Each man had recently returned from a tour in Germany."

"And?"

"My sergeant, DuBois Gordon, has been working with me on this. We've utilized every checklist, analysis and lab report. Gordon's vetted out rumors, stoolies, raw street information. And we've been pressing on our cops' intuition."

"I'm listening."

"We believe we've got the makings of a pattern but it's incomplete, too many lines don't fit. I'm looking for links between those dead soldiers on the other side of the water, what they were like as enlisted men in Europe, who their friends were, their *frauleins,* where they went on R and R, that sort of thing. I want to know where each one served in Germany, when, where and how long and with whom, if they took part in special maneuvers and where . . . The root of our trouble could be in Europe.''

Mark paused and waited. He could hear his father breathing at the other end of the line but the general was silent. ''We could use help,'' the lieutenant said. ''We don't have access to the intelligence information the Army's got through G–2. You have old friends in service who wear stars by now. I remember General Stigmuller and a half dozen others when they were captains on your staff. They'd be willing to do you a favor . . .''

''What you're speculating, Mark, is that something highly irregular, even criminal, is going on between Armed Forces Europe and Armed Forces Stateside, and perhaps even with our Allies, is that it?''

Mark Weir moistened his lips and realized he had done that once too often today; they felt dry and chapped yet numb with cold. ''Even the word 'speculate' may be a bit strong,'' he said. ''We're still searching and guessing, and I'd like to put some fresh material behind those guesses. Your Army contacts can and should get me that material.''

''I'm not sure the Army would welcome prodding from civilians on how to do its duty,'' General Weir said. ''And I'm not sure you're an impartial judge on military obligations. If anything *is* going on, don't you think the Army can be trusted to wash its own dirty linen?''

''Sir, this wasn't an easy call to make,'' Lieutenant Weir said. ''I don't think what I'm telling you is disloyal or could hurt the Army in the long run. I'm a cop. I'm trying to find the bastards who murdered three GIs in Chicago. I can't countenance killing on my own turf. I'm responsible for it. This has nothing to do with our past arguments. I want you to believe that. This is something else altogether. Put those silver stars to use, lean on your connections—''

''Grimes, though he regrets it, told me what you suggested this morning I do with those stars, but I called you anyway. Okay, I've listened and here's my decision. I'm retired from the Army and I'm going to stay that way, no phone calls to the Pentagon, no favors. I requested this retirement and there was a time when you thought it was a damned good idea . . .''

Lieutenant Weir was suddenly aware of tapping on the door

of the phone booth. He turned his head and saw Sergeant Gordon signaling urgently.

"All right, general," he said. "All right. What you're telling me is that my problem isn't your problem, there is nothing you can do."

"What I am saying," General Weir answered, "is that there is nothing I *will* do . . . there's a difference."

"Yes, there's a difference," Mark Weir said, "but I had hoped it was over, father," and hung up the phone.

Doobie Gordon pushed open the folding door. "Switchboard told me it was Springfield, and I didn't want to break in because I know how touchy you are about your old man." He paused. "Bonnie Caidin called Central and they gave her to me. She said to tell you that she talked to Sergeant Malleck and he never heard of a Private Lewis and his MPs never laid a hand on him."

Sergeant Gordon looked out over the lake and squinted.

"And then the morgue called. We don't have to bother looking for Randolph Lewis anymore. Fingerprints just came in from Washington, and he's the dude they picked up dead this morning over by The Studsville."

"Anybody get in touch with his aunt?" the lieutenant asked.

"No, I thought I'd drive over myself and try to tell her," Doobie Gordon said. "She's a nice lady, this'll hurt her. Come on, I'll give you a lift home. You'll wanna change."

The two men walked down the block toward the parked squad car. "I wish *my* old man would get lost for a couple of decades," Doobie Gordon said. "Tonight I got to take him bowling for his birthday, and after that he's gonna ask to go somewhere for ribs and beer."

"You don't have to be nice to me, Doobie," Mark Weir said. "At least my father returned my call. He didn't have to do that."

Sergeant Gordon stepped to the driver's side of the car, stopped and then slapped the mud-spattered hood sharply with the palm of his hand.

"Damn!" he said. "That makes four soldier boys, *four!* Randolph Peyton Lewis . . . why do you think they had to name that poor, dumb, dead *nigra* after a Pullman porter?"

# Chapter Seven

FIRST SERGEANT KARL Malleck was thirty-seven years old, a "lifer" in Army slang, almost eighteen years in the service, five with line companies in Vietnam, the last three with his current unit, working out of the old Prairie Avenue armory. In three years and six months Malleck would be eligible for retirement with full sergeant's benefits.

His tailored Eisenhower jacket displayed a combat infantryman's badge, two rows of campaign ribbons and six overseas hash marks. A braided gold fourragère was looped under the epaulet of his right shoulder. His hair, thick, black and cut short, grew in a ruler-straight line across a low, rounded forehead. The first sergeant's complexion was dark and ruddy in all seasons, his skin tough as cured leather, with high, knobby cheekbones glinting like copper discs under deeply socketed eyes.

During the week Malleck lived in special quarters in the barracks, and usually woke, dry-eyed and unable to sleep, at about four o'clock in the morning. That gave him three hours for his spit and polish grooming and a couple of warming shots of whiskey before going on duty.

From his desk on the first floor of the armory on Chicago's west side, the first sergeant faced narrow, barred windows streaming with sleeted rain. Through the panes he watched the morning storm, gray skies and gusting winds that sent spits of rain across the bricked courtyard.

Malleck had been alone in the office when the *Tribune*

reporter called him, and his eyes went sharp with suspicion at
the sound of her voice. He had seen Bonnie Caidin twice, once
at the opening of the Veterans' Assistance Center, when he
had mingled with the sparse crowd, wearing civilian clothes
and speaking to no one, and again on a TV talk show when she
explained the purpose of the center.

Malleck had disliked Caidin on sight. There was a quality
about her he found unsettling, particularly in younger women,
a quality of self-containment or arrogance, or a combination
of both. He had watched her in the Veterans' office with the
bright lights, taking notes while the black broad, Kastner, was
making her spiel. In the reporter's delicately arched upper lip,
the sergeant had sensed condescension, and in her cool, alert
eyes, a flash of threatening humor. Malleck disliked humor,
especially in women. In both sexes it was the start of most insubordination, not discrimination, privilege, sadistic cruelty
or even despair. Laughter, that's where it all started, with a
joke, ridicule, derision, disrespect. Once someone could smile
at something, whatever it was, the next step was to stop being
afraid of it. Bonnie Caidin was a smiler, Malleck thought, a
cocky cunt who needed watching.

She told him she was calling about a private soldier, Randolph Lewis. The first sergeant had kept his tone mild, his
answers responsive and courteous, but his caution stirred as he
listened to her questions.

"Our religious editor got a call," she had said, "from a
citizen who wouldn't leave his name. Claimed he'd seen a
Hare Krishna handled roughly by soldiers with MP brassards.
Do you know anything about that?"

"No, ma'am. No such report here."

"I was *told* to check into this," Bonnie Caidin said. "You
understand, I'm sure, sergeant. We have brass on the city
desk, too."

"I'm doing what I can to help, ma'am."

"Then you have no report at all, sergeant, on a Private
Lewis or a disturbance involving the military at O'Hare last
night?"

"No, ma'am. Nothing. And the personnel in my outfit are
pretty strict about their duty reports."

"The soldier's aunt said she'd made an inquiry of one of
your men at the Greyhound bus depot earlier in the eve-

ning—a Sergeant Roberts, or close to that.''

"What was the complete name of that soldier again?" With his thick, muscled knee Sergeant Malleck pressed a buzzer on the side of his desk. "I'm just writing out my own report here."

"Private Randolph Peyton Lewis," Caidin had said.

Malleck's orderly, a tall, bony black with touches of premature white in his short hair, came in and set up a steaming canteen cup of coffee on the sergeant's desk. Private Andrew Scales snapped to attention, his thin hands trembling as he pressed his thumbs tight to the seams of his khaki trousers.

"Excuse me a moment, Miss Caidin." Malleck cupped his hand over the phone. "Nobody asked for coffee, Scales," he said, his voice cold and measured. "You get your ass over to the barracks and tell Robbins I want him. On the double, snap shit!"

"Homer's sleeping, Top. I just—"

Without changing his tone, Malleck said, "That's gonna cost you your weekend, fuck-up. Move! Get him."

Scales left the office at a shuffling run, rehearsing under his breath. "It's tear-ass time, Robbins. Force Ten tear-ass. On the double! Sergeant wants to see you . . ."

Malleck sipped coffee from the canteen cup, watched the second hand on his watch for a full minute and then said into the phone, "My apologies, ma'am, but I'm with you now. And you said this Lewis was expected in from Germany?"

"Yes, sergeant, on MATS Flight 94."

"That hearsay incident with a civilian Hare Krishna at O'Hare you mentioned—my men wouldn't be involved in that kind of thing. They are on special duty. Unless the local law enforcement officers needed manpower in a riot, undue criminal activity or a like emergency of any kind, they wouldn't be involved with civilians . . .

"My own theory, ma'am. Couldn't this Private Lewis be off having a little fun on his own, maybe found a friend and decided to shack up for a while?"

"Not likely, since he wrote to ask his aunt to meet him," Bonnie Caidin said.

Private First Class Homer Robbins hurried into the office and stood uneasily in front of Malleck's desk. His blond hair was tousled, his soft, ruddy face creased and flushed with sleep. With a quick, furtive gesture, he zippered his uniform pants and then tucked his OD shirt under his belt as Malleck stared at him coldly.

"I came on the double, sarge," Robbins said, "like Scales said you wanted."

"Excuse me once again, Miss. I may have something for you." Malleck covered the phone with his big hand. "Tell me, you lard-assed idiot," he said to Robbins, "why didn't you report to me that a black lady was looking for a soldier at the bus station?"

"I didn't think it was . . ."

"You're not paid to think, asshole. If you were, you'd be paid a lot less. Listen good . . . that lady you talked to wasn't worried, you got that? Just wasn't sure of *when* the soldier boy was coming in, got *that?* A case of Aunt Jemima in the big city, maybe a little coon senility, is that clear?"

"Right, sarge."

Malleck took his hand from the phone. "Miss Caidin, I've located the soldier who talked to the Lewis boy's aunt. He's in my office now." He stared at Private Robbins.

"Now, Homer—" Malleck raised his voice. "The lady who approached you was looking for her nephew, is that it? This black lady?"

"Yes, sarge, 'cause she didn't know when he was expected exactly, wasn't worried or anything, just sort of confused. She said he *thought* he might be on a bus and had I seen him, that's all she told me."

"She check with anyone else at the station?" Malleck nodded affirmatively, indicating the response he wanted.

"Sure, she talked to the guy selling tickets. Then she sort of apologized and left." Robbins smiled at the phone in Malleck's hand. "She was a nice lady, sarge, real pleasant—not liquored up, I don't think, but more shy like."

"Miss Caidin, my Private Robbins tells me—"

"Thanks, I heard him, sergeant. And thank you for your time."

"Anything comes up, you want me to give you a ring?"

"I'd appreciate that. Here's my extension . . ."

Malleck wrote down the numbers and replaced the phone. He stood then, spinning his chair with the suddenness of the motion, and walked around his desk, not taking his eyes off Robbins.

Private Scales came to the open door and said, "Sarge, Detective Salmi's here. Want him to come in?"

"Ask him to wait."

"Got it, Top."

Sergeant Malleck was not tall, but he was wide and thick in the upper body, layered with slablike muscle that smoothly filled out his carefully tailored jacket. His waist was narrow and hard, and he moved with economy and precision on powerful, slightly bowed legs. He liked to keep at his fighting weight and strength. He worked out at an Army gym four days a week and kept a pair of heavy, springbound hand grippers on the night table beside his bed.

The sergeant had been light-heavyweight champion of his division fifteen years ago at Fort Benning, losing the Army finals to a tall, black counterpuncher who fought professionally before he was drafted. The spade had taken him, Malleck conceded as he lay awake on sleepless mornings. The other man, shining and greased with sweat, had kept a left in his face for ten rounds and beat him with a sneaky hard right to the gut, knocking his breath away, but Malleck would have killed him in a bar or an alley.

"For your sake, Robbins," he said, "I hope to Christ you don't think this is funny. Is that some kind of shit-eating grin on your face?"

"No, sarge. I was asleep, I was just wetting my lips."

"Good, because you'll be pissing in your pants if I catch you laughing. I didn't put you out on the street in uniform to act like some Welcome Wagon. Next time leave a written report. Anything out of the ordinary—and you know what I mean—put it on my desk before you hit the sack. Now tell me everything that colored woman asked you, every word and syllable."

When Robbins completed his verbal report, he said, "Can I say something, sarge?"

Malleck nodded and sipped the cooling coffee. "Make it fast, Homer."

"I'm sorry I screwed up on this. I'll watch it." Robbins moistened his lips. Malleck studied him and saw something come into his eyes he hadn't noticed before, a dull shine of cunning or greed.

"Thing is," Robbins went on, "I may not be the brightest guy in the world, but I know how to take orders, my daddy taught me that, and I'm better at receiving than I am at sending. What I'm saying is, I don't talk out of school, I can keep my mouth shut. And if there's anything special you need done, sergeant, well, I want to make good with you here . . ."

"You're not too bad at sending," Malleck said, "but I *am* one of the brightest guys in the world, in this part of Chicago anyway, and I don't need you kicking your humble shit at me." Malleck paused, then went back to the big leather chair behind his desk. "We'll see. That's all I'm gonna tell you, kiddo."

When Robbins left, Malleck swiveled the chair around to look at the series of narrow channels of water visible from his side windows. Mason's and Jay's canals they were called, fingerlings of sluggish green wash from the big sanitary canal which flowed westward through the city to join a branch of the Chicago River. No sound or moisture came through the windows of his office but the gray spread of rain was like a curtain of gloom shadowing the room.

Malleck took a bottle of Bushmill's Irish whiskey from his bottom desk drawer and poured two ounces into his canteen cup. Then he picked up the Chicago phone book, with a picture of the old stone Water Tower on the cover. Malleck liked to know where people lived and he also wondered if there was a Mr. Caidin.

He found only one Caidin listed in the directory, a B. Caidin on Lake Shore Drive. A surge of anger swept through him, causing a deep flush on the backs of his hands. Jesus, he thought bitterly, the *Tribune* must pay her plenty to rate an apartment at that address.

Detective Frank Salmi could wait. Malleck needed a little time to think about Bonnie Caidin. The first sergeant knew her story about some religious do-gooder calling the paper was bullshit. She'd known about Robbins and Mrs. Lewis. Why was she interested in some two-bit black soldier? And why was the smooth bitch sending up a smokescreen? Figure he'd be too stupid to see through it? Think again, little girl, Malleck thought. He had a clearer view of things than she could possibly know; this was his operation, his controlled arena.

It was a military axiom that sergeants ran the Army but Malleck knew the only time this was true was in special circumstances, wartime pressures, isolated posts, even superior officers who were flakes or drunks or long-termers sweating out retirement. A first or master sergeant needed to find an irregularity in the chain of command that he could exploit to create his own empire—a company or battery or special unit which by some fluke slipped through the cracks of standing operating procedures, and was lost for a time to the normal scrutiny imposed by the table of organization.

It had been Malleck's dream to find such an outfit and now he had it, the X-14th Company of Special MPs, and it belonged to him, body and soul, with his own selected cadre. He could never have done it without them, wouldn't have tried, in fact. He needed them as much as he needed the overseas contacts, the security on both ends of the arch.

Joe Castana and Eddie Neal had served with him in 'Nam and shared his conviction that they had the right to set up their own welcome home party back in the States. Malleck rapped the top of his wooden desk with his knuckles. So far they had done just fine.

The sergeant pushed the desk buzzer twice and Frank Salmi pushed through the door, followed by Scales, carefully balancing a cup of hot coffee for the detective. Malleck asked Salmi if he'd like a touch of whiskey.

"No, I'm running late," Salmi said. "A kid has to go to the dentist and my wife's working . Lucky I'm off."

"Very lucky," the sergeant said, and added a dash more Bushmill's to his cup. Scales asked if he might have a private word with him and Malleck shrugged indifferently, then joined the man in the CO's cubicle outside his office.

"Top, you was funnin' about me losing a weekend." Scales grinned nervously. "It was a joke, right, Mr. Malleck?"

"I usually make jokes like that?"

"No, Top, you sure don't. But I promised to meet a man who's got something for me."

Malleck studied him impassively, watching the tiny blisters of sweat starting on the man's forehead. "Okay," he said at last. "We'll make an exception this time, Scales. Take your time off, but I want you home till noontime Saturday. It could be mail call."

"Yes, sir, Sergeant Malleck. They know me at the Green. The mail come, nobody touch my stuff."

Sergeant Malleck put out his hand to open the office door, then paused. "I got an extra job I'd like you to do today,

Scales. You know where those two bird noncoms live?"

Scales nodded quickly. "North side, Top, building on Clark near Fullerton. I know the place."

Jane Avers and Coralee Sio were the "bird noncoms," the tech corporals assigned to Malleck's unit as company clerks to make up rosters, payroll sheets, medical reports, and other official reports. They'd been assigned to the armory just three months earlier.

"Take this afternoon off, go clean their apartment from top to bottom," Malleck said. "Tell 'em it's a birthday present from the boss. Shine their shoes, straighten the closets and clean out the drawers. Scrub the bathroom, get a look in the medicine cabinet. Know what I mean?"

"I think I do, Top."

"Don't give me that *think* shit, soldier. You better *know* what I mean. Find out if they've got guys staying there overnight. Use your nose if you have to. If those little ladies are misbehaving, Sergeant Malleck wants names and phone numbers."

"I'll find out, Top. Don't worry none."

"I never worry, Scales, because I'm not paid to. I'm paid to make *you* worry. Now tell Castana and Neal I want to see them in my office right after this fucking cop leaves. And don't forget what I told you about Saturday. I wouldn't want the mailman to mess up on your birthday presents. I figure some stuff is about due."

# Chapter Eight

SERGEANT MALLECK BELIEVED he understood everything there was to know about Frank Salmi except the detective's compulsion to talk about his family, even though Malleck had never met any of them and never meant to, but never even shared a beer or pizza with the detective, let alone gone to his home in Pine Lawn or whatever suburban *barrio* he lived in.

Salmi had five children and a Puerto Rican wife. She wasn't Cuban or Mexican—he'd made a point of informing Malleck about that at their first meeting—although the sergeant didn't see what difference it made; Cuba, Panama, Chihuahua, El Salvador, they were all the same, fine places if you wanted stomach cramps, get your hub caps stolen or shack up with ten-year-olds. But those family photographs were always in the wallet, right next to the payoff monies, Malleck was sure of that. Salmi had pulled out a snapshot once and Malleck had been forced to look at it briefly before telling the man to put the goddamn thing away. It was a picture of five little Salmis, three of them with bows in their hair, standing in a row against a house with a couple of bushes and cracks in the stucco. Malleck's sense of privacy had been as violated as if the detective had asked him to bind up an open sore or tend to some other personal and revealing piece of carelessness or rotten luck. Since then Malleck had made it policy to keep Detective Salmi at arm's length, on edge, subservient, and just a little bit hungry. Paydays were variable, Malleck saw to that, and he liked to wait till Salmi asked for it.

A small man with neat, dark features and liquid eyes, Salmi's thinning hair was wet with rain and he looked hot and uncomfortable in a double knit suit and damp overcoat. In the warm office, the coat—a thick, green tweed—smelled strongly of cigars and cleaning fluid. Malleck did not ask him to take it off.

"Okay, Salmi," he said. "*You* asked to see *me*."

Detective Salmi put a piece of paper on the sergeant's desk. "My nephew, Rick Argella, gave me this plate number. I checked the motor bureau in Springfield on it. His name is Durham Francis Lasari and the address is Calumet City. I called a contact in Calumet City. Lasari lives in a rooming house, works in a big diesel station there. I got both addresses."

"On the pumps? Just labor, a pair of hands?"

"No, he's some kind of mechanic specialist, transmission, brakes, ignition, the works. He owns a car he did himself, a souped-up GTO. That's what he's driving."

Salmi had telephoned earlier with a preliminary briefing on Durham, aka Duro Lasari, a 'Nam veteran, a longtime deserter, a loser unable to make it in either world, a flake who suddenly got religion and wanted clean paper from the Army he'd walked out on. Malleck already had a stomachful of contempt for this shifty ginny bastard, this Duro Lasari.

"This character," he said to Salmi, "he talked to the *Trib* reporter last night, didn't he?"

"That's right. Gave her some shit about his friend Carlos going AWOL, called himself by the name of George Jackson. Rick heard all of it."

Frowning, Malleck reached for Salmi's canteen cup, poured half the steaming coffee into his own, then added another touch of Bushmill's.

Malleck drank steadily during the day, usually small amounts at roughly forty-five minute intervals. He never got drunk, never lost his awareness of what was going on around him. His reflexes were not dulled by whiskey, he felt, but sharpened to keen readiness. There was little in the way of work or pleasure, Malleck told himself, that he couldn't handle with more stamina and efficiency than men half his age. His insomnia, the trauma of broken slumber . . . well, the sergeant liked to think he slept alert, near the surface of consciousness, and when he woke early, irritable or touched by depression, sometimes with his concentration splintered, a shot of Bushmill's was usually all he needed.

But Bonnie Caidin's call had been the wrong way to start this day. Her questions had sent up faint alarm signals, then a roil of anger. He hadn't planned to send Scales out spying on the female tech corporals but the sudden thought that they might be using their billets for sex had angered and distracted him. They all wanted something, not a bitch in the world you could trust.

Over the years Malleck had honed and savored his attitudes toward women. He had no interest in courting them, gaining their confidences, taking them to dinner and the track, keeping their names and specialties in a bachelor's little black book. The fact was that he didn't like close friendships, couldn't stand to share his living quarters with a female. He already owned one luxury seaside condo in Miami but he wanted to purchase a second unit. He could consider a contractual deal with a woman, a car, an allowance, everything on paper so he could break it off when he wanted to without fear of a shrewd lawyer clipping him on a palimony rap. But his bathroom was a personal and important place to Malleck. It would repel him to find a woman's soiled clothes mixed up with his in the laundry hamper, or cosmetics and makeup cluttering up his own neat collection of toilet articles.

Malleck liked a girl who went to bed with him on his terms, eager to please, afraid of failing. In Miami, when he was leading the life he'd earned, that's the way it would be; sex when he wanted it and the kind he wanted, and then the girl back in her own place, everything bought and paid for.

The sergeant felt he knew himself fairly well and was not afraid of his compulsions or ashamed of his needs. Women did not satisfy the deep core of his sexuality, but Malleck had always known the Army would be a risky place to indulge his other preferences. He'd showered often with other GIs, shared bunk dorms, roughhoused with them, but always forced himself not to pay attention to them. He never looked at the smiling youngsters who closed their eyes under the streaming jets of water and got soft erections when they soaped and massaged their slender loins.

In Miami, when he was older, the past over, the present

earned and the future secured, he'd sell that extra condominium and shop around for a houseboy to take care of him. He wouldn't mind that kind of courtship, he'd enjoy it, in fact. He'd find a young stud who was even tempered and amusing and handsome, a boy without family connections, someone he could train, maybe someone with a police record he could use as a leverage for his own protection . . .

"So?" Salmi said. "You listening?"

Malleck felt the heat of anger touch his cheeks. The Caidin woman had done it. Her voice, the memory of her cool bitch face had roused him sexually, had blurred his final concentration.

"Give me that again, Salmi."

"Mr. M. says he'd like a meet this time. He'd like you to make the payoff in person, wants to see you. I don't think you realize what a big man you're dealing with, sergeant. Mr. M. don't like to be a third party."

Malleck stared at the detective for a long moment, then hit the top of the desk with the flat of his hand.

"Salmi," he said, "we've got an S.O.P., a formula for what's working, and we're going to stick to it. Nothing else. Got that? And Mr. M.'s our bankroll, our distributor, and *nothing else*. We don't need a meet and we're not gonna go steady. He's been paid off three times already, and he'll get paid next week. That's our deal, nothing's changed."

"I'm just passing on what Mr. M. told me," Salmi said. "I'm taking a lot of pressure personally, Malleck."

"That's what you're paid for, Frankie," the sergeant said. "I wouldn't have hired a detective badge if I didn't need privilege and protection. You keep Mr. M. cooperative, and I'll run the rest of the operation."

"There should be some way to quit wasting those couriers each time," Salmi said.

Malleck looked thoughtful. "Maybe you're the only one who cares, Salmi. They get ten, twenty guys shot or knifed to death every month or so on the south side. Run more than a paragraph apiece in the newspaper on each case, they'd have no room for the Marshall Field ads. What's one more drunk or junkie soldier dying in the gutter?"

"The city's got some smart cops down at Homicide."

"Your Lieutenant Weir? He's been on those homicides

since number one, Private First-Ass Sammy Cullen, right? You told me that. And Weir's got *nothing*. You told me that, too. So his old man's Army brass, a big hero. Big deal." The sergeant was thoughtful. "They're all heroes after they retire, sitting on their asses in some country club bar."

Malleck looked at his watch, a gold Rolex shining on his thick wrist. It was nearly time to call Frankfurt. Strasser would be waiting at the fucking phone, a glass in one hand and some *fraulein*'s buns in the other, probably.

"Let me tell you something about your Mr. M., Salmi," he said, "your 'big man.' We're one of a kind, the two of us, and that's why we get along; and why we ain't *ever* going to see each other. We're both double-crossers, we're both out to get ours. The Army don't know what I'm doing and you can be damned sure the Syndicate better not find out that their Mr. M's got his own little racket on the side. They'd have his black balls, right? Just like the Army brass would grab mine. So he's going to cooperate with me and I'm going to cooperate with him and we're both gonna stay alive. We don't need to meet. It's easier to respect strangers."

Malleck took a sip of the cold coffee, savoring the strong Bushmill's on his tongue. "Old man Weir," he said suddenly. "I heard of him and he's *got* the medals. Maybe he earned 'em."

Salmi stood, small against Malleck's bulk, an unfocused worry clouding his soft eyes. "I should get that kid of mine to the dentist," he said.

Malleck was looking at the slip of paper with a name and address in Calumet City scrawled on it. "Do what you gotta do, man," he said absently.

"I don't like any of this operation any more," Detective Salmi said nervously. "It's me who takes all the risks. Mr. M. may not know who *you* are, but he knows who *I* am." He paused and breathed deeply. "My wife's a Catholic. Everything's the Church with her, being in a state of grace and ready to die. She knows I'm not ready to die, but she's afraid I'm going to."

"Surprise her then," Malleck said. "Don't. I want a couple of more big scores—nothing real greedy—and then out. Tell your Cuban lady—"

"Puerto Rican, Malleck. Adella's Puerto Rican."

"Okay, fine. Tell Adella to light a candle for both of us and in a few more months we'll be home free, our tickets to heaven bought and paid for."

"She don't like jokes about it, sergeant. That's another thing."

"Then fuck her!" Malleck said. "She must like that. You got five kids, Salmi, you're not firing blanks. So fuck her, Frankie, and tell her to stop worrying about us. Her prayers are making me nervous."

# Chapter Nine

WHEN THE DETECTIVE left, Malleck began pacing in front of windows. He wasn't due for his next tot of whiskey for an hour and he'd already overextended his morning ration. He could feel the muscles in his stomach tightening with tension. It wasn't Mrs. Salmi who stirred him, it was the other lady.

At the left of the main entrance to the armory was an open-air exercise area, used for training parade horses when mounted troops were stationed here. Now it was a personnel parking lot, partially paved over with asphalt, wet, black and shining next to the rows of old brick. The tack room and stables had been torn down years ago, replaced now with barracks and showers. The first floor of the old armory had been converted into a gymnasium with basketball courts, tumbling equipment and a weights room where Malleck worked out.

He opened and closed his hands slowly now, concentrating on the remembered feel of cool, black iron, and the therapeutic, demanding pull that the heavy weights put on his tense shoulder muscles.

Malleck hesitated, then went to his desk for the last of the whiskey-laced coffee and began pacing again, the canteen cup cradled in one big hand.

Only the tall windows were clean. The neighborhood area outside was crusted with industrial grime, the fucking pits, Malleck thought. Hundreds of troops had been housed in this armory during a series of wars but now the building was a near-derelict, bounded on two sides by low income housing projects and on the others by warehouses and run-down river sidings.

Malleck disrespected poverty and despised dirt. He savored the weekends at the apartment he kept on the north side, a supply of Bushmill's, a good steak and, once in a while, just the right company. For next weekend he'd been looking forward to a little something with one of the tech clerks, Jane or Coralee, it didn't really matter which one, but now it all depended on what Scales found out. If he was sharing, Malleck wanted to know who he was sharing with.

Duro Lasari . . .

The sergeant reviewed what he'd been told about the man, trying to fix a psychological image in his mind. Wouldn't admit he was a deserter, start there. Called himself a phony name, said he was concerned about a friend. A plus, Malleck thought. Lasari was covering up, ashamed of what he'd done, wormed away by guilt. They could use that.

And the deserter had guts, a lot of guts, and know-how. Argella reported that Lasari used an expert karate kick last night. A man could pick up the basics of unarmed combat tactics in regular training but it took real guts to use them, three against one and one a spic with a knife.

The deserter was undoubtedly a noncom, Malleck decided, since he hadn't claimed rank for his friend Carlos. From the beginning, even when the operation was just a dream, Malleck had resolved to use only men from the ranks, no commissioned officers. GIs were what he needed, combat-trained men accustomed to taking orders but basically resentful and angry about their backgrounds, about Army privilege, knowing they would never rate the Officers' Club, or even the high-class broads who wouldn't think twice about a motel room when they saw captains' bars.

Sergeant Malleck looked at his watch. It was still a few minutes short of his whiskey deadline but this Lasari character rated a little celebration. With a sigh, almost sensuous, he went back to his desk and opened the side drawer.

Earlier, Private Scales had warned Corporals Eddie Neal and Joe Castana that Malleck had been in a foul mood, so the two soldiers were surprised to find him leaning back in his padded office chair, booted feet on the desk, ruddy face touched with a faint smile. They saluted the top sergeant, then stood at attention, waiting for him to speak.

Malleck was in no hurry. He stared at them coolly, shifting his eyes from one man to another, from their uniforms to their hair to their waxed boots, as if he was examining and evaluating them for the first time.

Corporal Joseph Castana was in his late twenties, stocky, with weightlifter's shoulders that tapered sharply into a flat stomach and narrow hips. His hair was black, cut as long as army regulations would allow, and he wore thick moustaches with drooping ends, clipped off at the exact line of his thin lips. He smiled quickly at Malleck, his teeth strong and white, then rubbed a hand across his hard, brown face, as if to wipe away an unwanted look of mirth.

Malleck shifted his impassive stare to Eddie Neal. Neal was a head taller than the Chicano, a country boy, a rough, down-home type with tousled blond hair, big hands and high color in his healthy cheeks. His expression was respectful and boyishly expectant as he waited for Malleck to speak. But Malleck knew, from long experience with Corporal Neal, that his boyish appearance and manner had nothing whatever to do with what was going on in Eddie Neal's mind. His courtesy, his smiles, his fresh, close shave and his immaculately tailored uniform were camouflage and defense for Neal's surly tempers, his honed memory for hates and grudges, and for the illegal switchblade that was socketed carefully inside his Army boot.

"We got ourselves a new mule lined up, a deserter," Malleck said, "but he may need a little breaking in." He pushed Detective Salmi's note across the desk. "His name is Lasari. It's all there, where he lives, where he works . . ."

Neal started to reach for the paper, but Castana was closer to it. He picked it up and studied it, running a thoughtful finger over an arc of moustache.

Eddie Neal shrugged his shoulders and smiled. "Go ahead and read it, Tonto," he said.

"You want to read it, Eddie? Be my guest." Castana offered the note to Neal, who shook his head.

"No, you got hold of it first. I figure you got that much ABCs. Read it and tell me about it."

"All right, snap to attention, you ignorant clowns!"

Malleck shouted, his voice suddenly hoarse with rage. He swung his booted feet to the floor. "Don't waste my time with your shit!"

The two soldiers stood erect, eyes fixed at an imaginary point on the wall above and beyond the sergeant's head.

"All right, I'll tell you *both* about it and don't forget," Malleck said, lowering his voice. "Start staking out this ginzo tonight. Locate his shop, drive by where he lives, ask some questions in the bars he hangs out at. Wear sport clothes, buy people drinks, make sure Lasari gets the word that somebody's on his tail. I want him windy. If he turns himself in to the authorities, he's got an edge. But I figure he ain't gonna do that. He's waited too long."

Malleck leaned back again and the chair springs creaked under the weight of his powerful body. "We want him to make a break for it, then we grab him. He's a fugitive, a fucking deserter, he's gonna run, resist arrest. Make *sure* he resists, understand? *But wait for my orders.* When the time comes, don't let him bullshit you by putting up his hands. When I say take him, you take him hard, so it looks like he fought back."

Malleck smiled suddenly and the movement hardened the firm circles of flesh on his cheekbones. "We'll show him Army," he said. "This Duro Lasari's ass belongs to us. We can kick it or whip it or hang it up from the rafters to dry out. We'll just fix the paper and send him right to the federal pen if he's too dumb to cooperate."

When he was alone in the office, Sergeant Malleck placed a call to an Army base in Colorado and talked to a tech specialist in Records. Malleck identified himself as a special assignments officer, told the young woman that he needed, by express mail, all records on Durham Francis Lasari.

When the sergeant told him he needed an authorization for a records transfer, Malleck assured her that he knew that and the proper forms were already en route to the Colorado base.

After hanging up, Malleck stood, sucked in his breath and removed a key from the pouch on the inside of his Army belt. He unlocked a bottom desk drawer and took out a metal file box with a combination lock. Malleck opened the box, took out a form sheet and a rubber stamp. Then he typed out, in correct, official language, a request for the service records of Durham Francis Lasari, affixed a colonel's signature to it with a rubber stamp and folded the paper into a regulation air mail envelope addressed to the military records office in Colorado.

The sergeant chauffeured himself through drizzling mist into the Loop, parked his car and walked two blocks to the main post office to mail the letter himself. Then he drove to a German restaurant, the Black Forest, on Quincy Street, used exact change in a public phone booth to put in an overseas call and sat drinking beer at the bar while waiting for the call to go through to Sergeant Ernest Strasser in Heidelberg, Germany.

When the phone rang, Malleck crowded himself into the booth, pulling the folding door shut behind him. He cupped his hand around his mouth and talked to Strasser briefly. "The pigeon's in the coop, old buddy, message intact. Another's on the wire when the weather is right."

Strasser thanked him and assured him that his message came through A-OK. "Birthday greetings from us are in the mail." The sergeant's voice had a distant, tinny resonance but the words were clear. "And we can service your Blue Rock from this side whenever you're ready."

It was all working, Malleck thought, a sense of satisfaction flowing through his body like the warmth of the first whiskey at dawn. And it would work again.

It was early for lunch but Malleck seated himself at his regular table. He ordered another stein of dark Wurtzberg and then told the waiter he'd like roast Thuringer sausage with red cabbage for lunch, and a half slice of Black Forest cake, to be served with a fresh beer at exactly half-past twelve.

He checked his watch against the ornate wooden cuckoo clock on the restaurant wall, the heavy pendulums, carved like long, thick pine cones, swinging rhythmically.

"Your clock's cuckoo, Pops," he said, "five minutes slow. I got twelve o'clock on the mark."

# Chapter Ten

CAPTAIN HAYS "FROGGIE" Jetter, a U.S. Army Intelligence officer stationed in Washington, D.C., sat at his desk in a small, overheated office and looked out at the snow swirling beyond his windows. Jetter wore a business suit and his section was quartered in an old government building which stored census records and a library of rare law books dealing with Civil War reparations legislation. The frosted glass office door was unmarked except for a single word in neat block capitals: PRIVATE.

Captain Jetter had just replayed for the fourth time the taped telephone conversation he'd monitored earlier that day between First Sergeant Karl Malleck at X–14th Headquarters in Chicago and a technical specialist at Records in Colorado. Like an expert reading a lie detector test, the captain listened carefully to everything Malleck said, trying to note hesitancy, blatancy, or an incriminating waver on given words, but the sergeant's voice was casual and controlled, almost jocular. Jetter scrawled three words on a notepad and underlined them twice. *Special Assignments Officer*. In the U.S. Army, the captain knew, there was no such title.

It had been a failure to take action that first alerted Intelligence to ask for a tap on Malleck's phone. Privates Cullen and Baggot, both wearing the uniform of the United States Army, had been killed weeks apart within a twenty block radius of the old Armory and within easy patrol or notification range of

Malleck's unit. Yet in each case it had been the Chicago police who had found the bodies, conducted preliminary investigation and notified the Army.

When the third soldier, Private Jones, was also found dead by civilian police only a few blocks out of the original perimeter, Intelligence asked for and got permission to put a tap on the Armory phones.

Somebody wasn't doing his job right, Captain Jetter knew, and that usually meant that someone was concentrating on doing something wrong.

His mood was somber as he studied the glowering weather. It wasn't the structure or concept of the American military complex that caused the problems. It was the human factor—greed, self-preferment, the Karl Mallecks of the world who spotted a chink in the system and like piranhas went for the smell of blood and profits.

It was fortunate for the Army, Jetter thought, that the majority of first sergeants were industrious, unimaginative and honest career men, efficient, loyal and good middle-level administrators. On a day-to-day level, peacetime or war, it was the top sergeants who ran the Army and within reasonable boundaries could run it as they pleased.

Every decade a bad apple got loose in the ranks. Jetter had been a junior officer, stationed in Vietnam, when the big PX embezzlement scandal broke there, and the press in Saigon got wind of the fraud almost before Intelligence did. A pair of top sergeants in charge of PX supply and procurement had been falsifying inventories and demanding kickbacks from Stateside suppliers and hundreds of thousands wound up in personal bank accounts. It was partly those sergeants, those corrupters, Captain Jetter thought sourly, who had made it impossible for the Army to win that war. Those larcenous first shirts had pulled their scam for years right under the eyes of Army Intelligence, only because they had the savvy and clout of top sergeants.

Captain Jetter collected his files on Karl Malleck (the Siegfried Express was the operation's code word) and tucked them into his briefcase. He pulled on an overcoat, worked a pair of rubbers over his L.L. Bean loafers and tied a wool muffler around his neck. The captain had been ordered to bring his files to Colonel Richard Benton's home in Georgetown. "He'd like to see you around cocktails," was the way his superior Major Staub had put it on the phone; *around,* not *for* cocktails. There was a difference.

It was four o'clock in the afternoon. Captain Jetter decided he had time to stop at the Adonis Spa for a workout, a sauna and rubdown before keeping his appointment with his superiors. He was thirty-seven years old, a seasoned professional in his trade, and an addict about physical fitness. He observed stringent rules about eating and drinking, favored dark suits with pinstripes, worked out three times a week in the gym, but still his physique and his prep school nickname stuck and rankled him.

Captain Jetter wouldn't have minded being called "Froggie" if he'd been a star on the swimming or water polo teams at Choate, but he'd been called "Froggie" because his classmates decided he *looked* like a frog with his thick torso, short bull neck and protruding eyes. Only fastidious personal habits and grueling physical workouts controlled his self-consciousness and made the captain's squat, powerful body acceptable to him.

"Anatomy is destiny . . ." That thought went through his mind for the thousandth time as he walked toward his Mercedes in the parking lot. Sigmund Freud had made that pronouncement and Jetter had read it somewhere.

But it was Lenin who knew that ultimate power rested in the control of the records, Jetter recalled as he put his briefcase into the trunk of his car, tucked it under a blanket, then turned the key in a custom lock. Never mind the generals at the barricades or the orator in the streets, it was the men who wrote the rules and kept the records who ultimately wrote history.

"Froggie" Jetter had read that somewhere, too, probably in college.

After his forty-five-minute workout, Jetter sat in the sauna with a towel around his waist. An attendant had sprinkled wintergreen scent on the hot stones and the room had the sticky, sanitized odor of a public lavatory. Jetter shifted to the top redwood shelf and hunched over ·in the misty heat, breathing in and out of his mouth.

He was puzzled by the sudden interest in this seemingly

minor operation, a maverick sergeant abusing his privileges for unknown reasons. Until today, Intelligence's surveillance had been routine and cursory, and the tap on Sergeant Malleck's phone had netted them nothing suspicious or out of the ordinary. Yet almost immediately after he had messengered the tape request for the service records on one Durham Lasari, plus a call from a Chicago *Tribune* reporter named Caidin—after those routine memos had been sent to Major Staub, an aide from the major's office had called Jetter and told him to hold for the major. It was then that he had been ordered to report to Colonel Benton's home in Georgetown that evening.

A maid took Captain Jetter's coat and muffler, and after he removed his wet rubbers showed him into a book-lined study with a coal fire in the grate. Major Staub was already there, standing by an antique table laden with an array of liquor bottles, a salver of crackers and a silver bowl of whipped cheese. He nodded at Jetter and then helped himself to the crackers and cheese.

Tall and softly padded, Staub was in uniform but the smart olive drab jacket only emphasized the swelling paunch, the rounded, unmilitary sag of his shoulders. In his late forties, Merrill Staub was balding, with patchy tufts of blond hair dotting his scalp. But his eyes were a direct, piercing blue and his air of disarray had a certain elegance about it, suggesting authority and a preoccupation with higher matters. Staub was unmarried, a dogged, tireless worker and destined, according to Pentagon rumors, to follow Colonel Benton to the top of Army Intelligence in a few years.

"You bring everything on Siegfried, Froggie?"

"Everything we have to date, sir."

"Not quite," Major Staub said. "I implemented your information and got a copy of that Lasari service record. Colorado photo-wired it about two hours ago and I had a memo sent to Colonel Benton at his request. He needed an immediate briefing."

Major Staub studied a fleck of cracker that had dropped on the sleeve of his jacket, then flicked it off with a square fingernail. "For what it's worth, Froggie," he said, "Lasari's about thirty-two now but he hasn't been in the Army for about ten years or so. His file is open but inactive. He deserted, where-abouts unknown."

A chunk of cannel coal cracked apart with a pop like a fire-cracker, sending a glowing cinder onto the hearth. Staub walked to the fireplace and kicked the burning coal back into place with the toe of his polished boot. Somewhere in the house a phone began to ring.

"This case is getting complicated," the major said.

The study door opened and the colonel's wife, a tall, pretty woman in a long dress, looked in on them, smiling. "Hello, Merrill, Froggie. My heavens, aren't you drinking?"

"We're fine, Ellie," the major said, "just fine. Don't you give us another thought."

"Richard will be down soon," Mrs. Benton said. "He's struggling with studs or cufflinks, I expect. We're dining at Admiral Wood's and it's black tie. Richard hates that. Excuse me, fellows, okay? My number two child is writing a piece on hospitals and she can't spell 'catheter' or 'cathartic' or some such thing, and I've got to lend a hand."

When she left Staub said sharply, "When you requested a tap on the X-14th, did you tell the FBI in Chicago why you wanted it?"

"No, I told AIC it was a random check."

"Good. The fewer who need to know the better. In this in-stance, it's imperative."

"Major, can you tell me what your problem is?" Froggie Jetter asked. "We've been proceeding on the conjecture that a pair of high placed noncoms may be running a minimally profitable courier service between Germany and the United States. Petty thievery, industrial diamonds, perhaps—we don't even know that for sure, but we conjecture. We've got nothing definitive yet, a tap on a wire but our man's cautious. We're waiting for a wrong move so we can nail him. That's the way I see Siegfried. Has something come up that makes that evaluation nonoperative?"

"Yes," Major Staub said. "The colonel was summoned to an emergency meeting with Senator Copeland this afternoon. Copeland was aware of certain events in Chicago and had some theories on the matter. That came as an unpleasant shock to the colonel. We think we're monitoring a routine, low-grade racket and suddenly House Military Affairs works up its own position paper.''

"What's Copeland got that we don't have?"

Before Staub could answer, the door opened and Colonel Benton came into the study. The colonel was in a dinner jacket with black tie, the rosette of a military decoration gleaming from a silk-faced lapel. He was tall and lean, with thick, gray hair cut short and when he smiled, which was seldom, the effort tightened the muscles around his mouth and pulled and sharpened the angles of his square, aristocratic features. Colonel Benton was often remembered for the strange quality of his eyes. They were a flat, opaque brown; as though he was wearing dark, rimless glasses.

He was forty-two, third generation West Point, a member of the Army's aristocracy, his roots deep in the South and linked by family and marriage to the closest and most influential branches of the military. His wife was wealthy. In Washington the Bentons lived with appropriate austerity, but the horse-breeding farm in Virginia was a showplace, the air-conditioned stables famous, as were the annual yearling sales.

The colonel poured himself a glass of dry vermouth, then stirred in cracked ice and a twist of lemon peel. "Froggie, are you up with us? How much has Merrill told you?" He drank quickly, then looked down at his half-empty glass.

"Only that Senator Copeland . . ."

"I'll fill you in then," he said briskly. The colonel's voice was flat, uninflected but resonant, a voice accustomed to being listened to. "It was goddamn awkward to have Dexter Copeland tell *me* things I didn't know about our ongoing investigations. But you know Copeland. He had to dump on me first with his lectures on the state of the union." Benton began to speak in agitated, mimicking tones.

". . . one million or more young Americans haven't bothered to register for the draft. That's one-sixth of the eligible service pool. They didn't sign up and burn their draft cards, they just said, 'Fuck off, Uncle Sam. We can't be bothered.' '' The colonel let his voice return to normal.

"Then he tells me the Abrams ML-tank came in millions over budget and the fucker doesn't work too well to boot, problems with treads and firing.

"And he did his bit about nuke silos in Utah and all those antisub peaceniks demonstrating along the coastline in Scotland. Finally he got around to Germany, which he wanted to talk about in the first place.

"Copeland is convinced that the Russians have enough firepower on their borders to lob rockets right into the chancellor's office in Bonn."

Colonel Benton walked to the table, put another splash of vermouth in his glass and then filled it with gin. He stirred the mixture absently with his little finger.

"His approach was oblique but the senator had called our meeting to ask me one all-important question. He wanted to know how in hell he could stay in office and get re-elected if Army Intelligence couldn't clear up that problem percolating in Chicago.

"Dexter Copeland is *from* Illinois, you know," the colonel went on. "He's been in office for a long time—some voters think too damned long. So Copeland wants to hedge his bets guaranteeing all the votes he can get, and that includes every black vote from Cabrini Green down to South Cairo."

Benton snapped a finger at Captain Jetter. "What are those names, Froggie?"

"Privates Cullen, Baggot, Jones—" The captain hastily opened his attaché case and glanced at a memo. "The last one was a Private Randolph Lewis."

"Copeland had all those names," Colonel Benton went on, "plus where, how and at what tick of the clock each man was killed. He got his information in a direct, private number phone call from one of his most important constituents, a voter he cannot afford to displease, the Reverend Jesse Jackson.

"Reverend Jackson told the senator in no uncertain terms that four dead black brothers were four dead men too many. And since all of them were in uniform, supposedly fine young citizens in that service of their country, he wanted to know exactly what Senator Copeland was going to do about it."

Captain Jetter stifled a pang of uneasiness as the colonel turned to look at him with a hard stare. "We've had no indication that the Reverend Jackson would involve himself," Froggie Jetter said defensively, "and I can't see why he should."

"I do," the colonel said. "My dear mother, God bless her southern soul, used to like to have me think when I was a boy that she knew everything I did, *everything,* good or bad. When she found me out on something I tried to hide, she'd say, 'God can't be everywhere, Richie. That's why He invented mothers.'

"And that's how I feel about the Reverend Jackson," the colonel said. "God can't be everywhere and that's why He made the Jesse Jacksons of the world, to watch out after all the shat-upon brethren and take some of the load off our shoulders."

The brief moment of softness left the colonel's face. "I spared Senator Copeland that whimsy when he told me what else was on his mind. Copeland wouldn't name his source, but I believe God and the Reverend Jackson know everything. The senator said he had information that the rumor in Chicago, and particularly with the drug operators around black housing developments, is that the caper you've so humorously nick-named Siegfried Express is not just a petty cash, small-time contraband operation, after all.

"What *is* coming in, and from sources *outside* the Syndicate, is pure white heroin, a high-grade, high-cost product. And because many of the customers for this trade and *all* four suspected couriers are black, Reverend Jackson wanted to know urgently just how the good senator was going to handle this malfeasance . . .

"Fortunately," Colonel Benton said, "I had done my homework before the meeting and could convey the impression we were on top of this thing. I told Copeland we believed we could make a direct connection, that we had anticipated the next courier.

"With the materials received from Colorado, my staff had brought the Durham Lasari records up-to-date, so to speak. We knew he was born and enlisted in the North Carolina area, got most of his post-'Nam medical treatment at Fitzsimons in Denver and disappeared from the military in that area. I told all that to the senator.

"My side had attacked the obvious—the local phone directories. Lasari is not a common name, it turns out. There were two in Raleigh, North Carolina, both in the pizza business, no relations. A professor at the University of Colorado, in his fifties, not our man, and a Jane Lasari in Colorado Springs who drives a school bus. We ran a Motors check in each area, four Lasari registrations, no Durham."

The colonel paced in front of the fireplace with short steps, the ice in his glass rattling as he walked. "Who else is currently interested in this Lasari? Sergeant Karl Malleck. So we try the Chicago phone books, Winnetka, Wilmette, Lake Forest, the suburbs. As I said, Lasari is not a common name. There's not one listed in the Chicago directory or thereabouts. So we put a routine call into Motors in Springfield, and there's our man."

The colonel was suddenly thoughtful. "I didn't mention this to Copeland; in fact, it didn't occur to me at the time, but those Springfield records gave us more on Lasari than his car make and current address . . ."

"What is that, colonel?" Major Staub said.

"Well, he changed that registration legally only about four months ago," the colonel said, "did the paperwork, sent a money order for eight dollars and had the ownership changed to Durham Lasari. Before that he used the name George Jackson."

"After ten years he got cocky, never thought we'd still go looking for him, right?" Captain Jetter said.

"Perhaps," the colonel said, "but you miss a subtle possibility, Froggie. The man decided to use his real identity, go on record, be himself again. I believe the deserter may have been thinking about turning himself in."

The colonel stopped in front of the fireplace, his back to the flames. Two spots of color showed on his taut cheekbones and his dark eyes had an almost liquid intensity. "I wonder if Sergeant Malleck knew that," he said thoughtfully.

"Is that implemental now, colonel?" Captain Jetter asked. "If we've found Lasari, we can assume Malleck found him, too, and means to use him. We give them twenty-four hours to make contact, then we move in and close down the operation, here and in Germany, arrange a few therapeutic courts-martial . . ."

Colonel Benton held up his hand. "Quite the contrary," he said, "and both Senator Copeland and I agree on this."

A light tap sounded on the door. "Just a minute, please," the colonel called out. "Our mutual decision on this . . ."

The door opened and Ellie Benton smiled in at the men. "Excuse me, darling," she said to her husband, "but Patty wants you to look at her essay before we go. And we should be leaving soon if we want to make the soup course . . ."

Something in the colonel's face, a rigidity and then an involuntary spasm of anger, caused his wife's smile to fade quickly. "It's not all that important, Robert. I'll just go ahead in my own car if you like."

"Thank you, my dear," Colonel Benton said and stepped over to close the door behind her.

"My apologies, gentlemen." He paused and listened to the sound of the front door opening and closing, then resumed his stance in front of the fireplace. "Our mutual decision, Senator Copeland's and mine, is to put a lid over the whole Siegfried operation, keep it covert and contained. We issue our own pragmatic sanction in this matter. May I summarize my comments to the senator?" Both junior officers nodded.

"Once again it's crux time in international relations," Colonel Benton said. "Our country *needs* and is determined to *keep* the loyalty and cooperation of our NATO allies, particularly in Germany. And we want to keep a friendly status quo for our specialists stationed in Turkey, Greece, Belgium, Italy, The Netherlands and Great Britain, a good part of the civilized world.

"We've had enough of rallies in The Hague and Berlin and Brussels demanding their governments banish nuclear weapons and troops from their soil. We've juggled German public opinion against the presence of troops in their country for more than three decades. The Greens, with their anti-Establishment, anti-American determinations, have already earned themselves a place in the Bonnstag with five percent of the vote. We're damned lucky that the conservatives managed to push Chancellor Kohl into office. He's our man. The Russians don't like that, but we do.

"We win some and we lose some, but the senator and I agreed that this Siegfried thing is one goddamn caper we're going to *win*. Right now our relationship with NATO and/or Germany is in harmonious but delicate balance. What do you think would happen to that relationship, and to the image of Godalmighty America, if it became known that men in the United States Army, compatriots in uniform, were running drugs, pure white, between the United States and Germany?"

The colonel paused as the sound of his wife's car sounded on the graveled driveway. "If a press story broke now, it would be an unmitigated disaster, that's Dexter Copeland's phrase for it. If we went public, the media would have a field day, the Army would be in deep trouble. It would be an international scandal, the kind of propaganda ammunition that could destroy our control of Europe, Germany—all of NATO.''

"So what *do* we do, colonel?'' Merrill Staub said.

"We put a lid over the entire operation, as I said,'' Colonel Benton explained. "My plan—outlined to Copeland—is this. Ostensibly we will do nothing, nothing at all. We'll let the crooked bastards in this operation *do our work for us*. We'll use Lasari, or rather, we'll let Sergeant Malleck 'use' Lasari in whatever way he has planned. We monitor Lasari's movements through regular Army channels, but we let Malleck bring in the contraband one more time and grab him with the goods on this end. We want the contraband, Malleck and any other man in U.S. uniform who's in cahoots with him.

"We're not looking for a cure for this cancer, we're just going to excise the roots. The operation will be speedy, sanitary and silent. We'll make the necessary military arrests, arrange for quick courtsmartial and then throw away the key to whatever federal pen the bastards get sent to. It's an Army problem and we'll keep it that way.''

The mood had changed in the study. It was relaxed, touched with subtle triumph. The colonel pulled down his black tie, then tossed the dregs of his gin into the fireplace and built himself a new drink. The spurt of steam from the hot coals filled the study with the acrid smell of juniper berries.

"It's what the senator and I agree is the best strategy,'' he said. "Water under the bridge, what they don't know won't hurt them, business as usual, that sort of thing. We wash our own dirty linen and we do it in private.''

He gestured toward the table of liquors. "Major, Froggie, help yourselves. It's way past ice time.''

Captain Jetter moved toward the bar but Major Staub stood quiet, his face taut with concentration. Then he said, "Colonel, about this Lasari . . . do you plan to inform him of the role he's playing, the work he is doing for us, as you put it? Longevity doesn't seem to be part of the plan for Malleck's couriers. Shouldn't we factor in that inevitability?''

"I didn't bring that up with Copeland, of course,'' Colonel Benton said, "but I gave it some private thought. The key word is expediency, major, *expediency*. 'All for the greater good,' as the old saying goes. Foreknowledge might cause the man to spook our operation, so we tell him nothing. And Durham Lasari is a deserter, remember that. I don't see that we owe him much of anything.''

# Chapter Eleven

TWICE DURING THE day Duro Lasari noticed a car slow up in front of the diesel station as if it meant to turn in, but both times the driver gunned the motor and drove off. In the heavy misting weather Lasari wasn't sure it was the same car—gray, mud-splashed, a shine to the wheels—but he thought so. Around noon, when the crew was taking a lunch break, a young fellow, curly headed, blond, wearing a brown leather jacket, came in and asked the boss for change for the pay phone. When the boss said they had no pay phone but he could use the one in the office for a local call, the man shrugged, shook his head and went off down the street. It was an hour later that Lasari noticed a car slow up and drive by again.

At the end of the day he decided to do what he always did after work. He waited until the last employee left, then closed himself in the small, grimy lavatory at the back of the garage and worked with cold water and pumice soap until the last grease was scrubbed from his hands. Then he splashed his face under the tap, ran a pocket comb through his thick, dark hair and drove for a beer in a place he liked outside Calumet City. It was near U.S. 94 off Sibley Boulevard, not far from the truck station where Lasari worked with the boss, two other mechanics and a cleanup man, Luis Carlos.

The Alpine House was an old-fashioned bar, dark and clean, windows boarded over with plywood, painted with scenes of lakes and ducks on the wing, and there was a small, slatted dance floor rolled up in one corner, ready for Saturday night.

Lasari stood at the bar and ordered a beer. The bartender served him and said, "I think a couple of pals were in looking for you this afternoon, George; they said they owed you some money."

"Somebody asked for *me?*" Lasari said.

"Well, not exactly. Two guys said they were looking for a *dago* stud who had a souped-up car. No names. I just thought they meant you." The man wiped at the bar with a clean towel. "If they were regulars, they'd know we don't stand for that *dago* talk in here . . ."

"That's all right, friend," Lasari said. "They couldn't have meant me anyway. No one owes me anything."

Lasari took a stool at the far end of the bar and drank his beer slowly. All in one day, a suspicious car, a stranger making no sense about the garage phone and now someone asking around the Alpine about an Italian in a souped-up auto. Coincidence, it probably meant nothing, he thought, no need to panic, to turn paranoid and run.

But in his heart Lasari realized why he had taken a stool at the end of the bar. It was beyond the colored lights of the big juke box, almost in shadows, and the position gave him a good view of the door near the men's room, the one that opened out on the alley.

It was cold and rainy when he left the Alpine. Sibley Boulevard looked like a patch of silver, the pavements freezing over and picking up the reflections of neon from gas stations, and a few dim lights glowing from wire-meshed shop windows.

Lasari ate dinner at a bar and grill a few miles from town, almost on the Indiana state line, crowded with mill workers drinking whiskey with their beers; men alone for the most part, watching the basketball game on TV, and single women sitting cross-legged on the bar stools, their faces illusive and fragile in the flickering light from the overhead screen.

Lasari had been here a few times before and the waitress was a new one, efficient but impersonal. He had watched the flow of traffic behind him all the way from Sibley Boulevard, seeing nothing but trucks headed for the Indiana border and the usual commuters. He ordered the Tex-Mex special with beans and rice, finished the platter slowly, then asked for pie and a second beer and lingered over that. He tried to relax, to make himself feel he was alone and unnoticed, but his right leg began to bother him and he reached down to massage the muscles and scar tissue, first the thigh and then the calf, trying to work away the knots of tension that always tightened when he was anxious. The doctors at Fitzsimons Medical had tried to tell him he'd forget the scars, that they'd get to be a natural part of his body, but they hadn't.

At the rooming house Mrs. Swade and Karen sat in a small living room off the front hall watching television. The older woman glanced up and waved but her daughter didn't take her eyes from the set.

"It could turn to sleet outside," Lasari said. "Driving will be rough later."

"Thank the Lord we're in for the night," Mrs. Swade said. She was a woman in her forties, thin with brightly hennaed hair and a sallow face untouched by makeup. She was bundled up in two sweaters against the chill and wore fleece-lined slippers over a pair of white wool gym socks. A glass of vodka and ginger ale sat on the floor near her chair.

"You do okay on that biology exam today, Karen?" Lasari asked.

"I did all right, I guess," the girl said without turning. Lasari stood in the doorway, puzzled by the fourteen-year-old's passivity. Usually she had something to tell him or show him, excited and flirtatious with his dark, male presence in the house, chattering up at him as he went to his room, standing at the foot with a hand on the balustrade. Always at the foot of the stairs. Mrs. Swade was strict about that, never allowing her daughter to go to the second floor, even to deliver bath towels or clean up after the boarders.

Lasari went to his bedroom and changed into fresh jeans and an old flannel shirt, without turning on the lights. In the illumination from the hallway the room was large and impersonal, without human touches except for a blue and gold baseball cap with a weathered sun peak which hung from the footboard of a heavy oak bed. Duro Lasari could have packed and left that room in ten minutes, without a trace to suggest he'd lived there; no forgotten packet of letters tucked at the back of a shelf, no faded patches on the plaid wallpaper to suggest that family snapshots, class pictures or a school diploma had ever hung there.

Lasari stood beside his window in the darkness and studied what he could see of the street, black trees, muted yellow house lights, a few parked cars, rain slanting in thin, silver lines. Carefully he raised the window and listened. He heard a plane, somewhere over Gary or Hammond, coming in toward Chicago. A series of bright red flares, chemical expulsions from mill chimneys, spread on the horizon and something new mingled with the rain. A wind gusting in burned his eyes like acid. Among the parked cars he could make out, none looked like a gray sedan.

Lasari turned from the window and in the dim light from the hallway caught a quick glimpse of his own reflection in the mirror above the chest of drawers, a ghostly focus, narrow face, shiny black hair and a look of alert suspicion in the eyes—an unnerving experience, spying on himself in the act of spying.

A psychotherapist at Fitzsimons Medical, the third week he'd shipped in, had asked him to write down the ten worst things he'd seen during his tour of duty in Vietnam. Lasari tried to think, to remember other things, but he knew that the single thing that had baffled and terrified him most was the look of disbelief and horror in his own face and eyes in those years.

Lasari had scrawled on the doctor's pad ten times, numbering each word from one to ten: 1. Me . . . 2. Me . . . 3. Me . . . 4. Me . . . 5. Me . . . 6. Me . . . 7. Me . . . 8. Me . . . 9. Me . . . 10. Me . . .

Long after his wounds were healed, Lasari wondered if he still carried a premature scent of death with him. Sometimes, like tonight, when he could catch an almost palpable whiff of his past, and see the furtive look of fear in his own eyes, he knew what feelings were buried in the depths of his soul.

Downstairs the television set was droning. Across the hall, Luis Carlos' door was open and the old man was waiting at a card table with the checkerboard set out and a bottle of banana wine beside it. Lasari joined him and sat down on one side of the checkerboard.

Luis Carlos was in his early seventies, tall and lean with a face as brown and folded with wrinkles as the underside of a mushroom. The old man's English was limited but his eyes were warm and responsive, and his unquestioning calm had made Duro Lasari talk to him over the past two years more freely than he had ever talked to anyone in his life.

The old man looked at him now and said, "You got troubles?"

"You know me, Luis," Lasari said. "You know me through and through. Listen, I've got reason to think somebody's out looking for me. I'd almost quit running, you know that. Last night I went to that Veterans office and now . . . well, I can't be sure."

"Karen look for you," Carlos said. "After school, she go in your room . . ."

"My *room*? She came upstairs? Why didn't you tell me?"

Carlos shrugged. "I no get her in trouble with her mama. She afraid for you."

A draft of air hit the partly opened window, sending the curtains inward, wet and cold with rain. Duro Lasari was silent for a moment, listening to the spatter of drops and the accelerated beat of his heart.

"Carlos," he said, "I need to make a call, but from a pay phone. If there is someone outside, if someone is following me, I want 'em to believe I'm coming back here. I don't want them to think I've spotted them and I'm running, understand?"

"Tell Carlos again," the old man said.

"Come downstairs with me," Lasari said. "Stand by the front door. When I bring my car around, you yell at me to bring you something back from the store—tobacco, *vino,* anything. *Comprende ahora?*"

Carlos nodded and Lasari went to his room for a lined windbreaker. Passing the parlor, he saw that Mrs. Swade had fallen asleep, the glass on the floor beside her limp hand, the TV set blaring. Karen was not in the room.

Lasari turned up his collar and made a dash for his car, parked in the tar-papered garage beside the house. He checked the rear view mirror before backing into the street and gave a gasp of surprise as Karen Swade's head rose from the back seat.

"Jesus Christ!" Lasari said. "What are you doing here?"

"I was listening by the stairs and heard you talk to Carlos. I have to tell you something. I had to wait till Mama passed out because they paid her not to tell."

He waited a moment as a van came out of nowhere and

moved down the street, tires hissing on the pavement. "Tell me what this is about, Karen," he said. "Straight and simple. I don't want any lies."

"Two men knocked on the door this afternoon and asked to talk to Mother. I was doing homework but I listened. They were in ordinary clothes but they showed Mama a paper and told her they were Army MPs, that they were looking for a certain guy at this address. They said they had to find him to pay off a disability claim or something. They asked what you looked like, what kind of car. Mama said what you looked like and that your name was George Jackson. Then they said, 'Sorry, ma'am, we got the wrong person.'"

"That's it?" Lasari said.

"Not quite," the girl said. "They told Mama you hadn't done anything wrong and they didn't want her to worry. They gave her twenty dollars not to tell they'd been there and she took it."

Lasari reached back to open the car door. "You're a good friend, Karen," he said. "Duck in the back way and don't let anybody see you. That'll be the second big favor you'll be doing me tonight."

Lasari put the car in reverse, letting it ease backward down the driveway and into the street. The front door of the boardinghouse opened and Luis Carlos leaned out, cupping his hands around his mouth, shouting, "Hey, Duro! *Mas vino, por favor. Mas vino, amigo.*"

Lasari held his breath and looked up and down the street. There was no movement and no sound except the echo of the old man's voice.

# Chapter Twelve

THE PHONE RANG while she was showering. Bonnie Caidin reached for a towel and hurried to the bedside phone. It was Larry Malloy on the city desk.

"Did I miss something?" she asked, her mind checking over the last story she'd covered that day, a three-car accident near the airport. A private bus carrying an English rock group on its way to a gig at Rosemont-Horizon had been rear-ended by a tailgating limo rented by some groupies. Minor facial cuts for the lead singer, four girls taken to Passavant Hospital with minor injuries . . .

"No, no, Bonnie, you got it although I still think maybe we fell for a publicity setup on that one," Malloy said. "What I'm calling about is that someone wants to get in touch with you. A man called here, asked for your phone number and they switched him to me. I told him that as policy we didn't give out staff numbers. I asked him for his number so you could call back if you want to."

"Let me get a pencil, Larry."

"Don't bother," Malloy said. "He wouldn't leave it. Said to tell you that it was George from last night." Malloy paused. "I didn't know how important that might be to you, Bonnie."

"Not as exciting as you think, old dear," Caidin said. "George is one of the people I talked to at the Vets' Bureau last evening, that's all. He came in for advice. How do I get in touch with him?"

"You don't," Malloy said. "He's going to call me again in

five minutes. If it's okay, I'll give him your number.''

"He gave you no idea where he was calling from, or why?''

"No. I asked but he insisted he had to talk to you directly. If he does call again, what do I tell him?''

Bonnie was thoughtful for a moment, then glanced at her bedside clock. She hadn't had dinner yet but that could wait. "I know you're going to give me a lecture, Larry, but when George Jackson calls back, give him this number.''

"Bonnie, a reporter's home phone number should be as sacred as the Ark. Do you want all the kooks in the world to know where to reach you?''

"This guy is no kook, Larry. I told him I'd help him. Give him the number, will you?''

Bonnie Caidin replaced the phone and put on a blue cashmere robe. She toweled her wet hair and twisted the damp ends together with a rubber band, then took a pencil and notepad from the night table drawer and sat on the edge of the bed to wait. When the phone rang, she let it ring three times before picking it up.

His voice was as she'd remembered it, deep and touched with a southern twang, but strained now, almost a controlled whisper. "Miss Caidin? Remember the fellow who came in to talk to you last night about Luis Carlos? A little after midnight or so . . . ?''

"Yes, yes,'' she said sharply. "Of course I remember you. George Jackson, right? Is something the matter?''

"Why do you ask that? Do you think something's the matter?''

Bonnie felt a stir of irritation, then apprehension. "Listen, I don't think anything's particularly the matter except that you called my office and refused to give a number and now you're calling me at home and playing guessing games on my time. That's all that's wrong. This is your call. If you've got something to say, George, I wish you'd say it.''

The phone was silent for so long that Caidin thought perhaps the man had hung up. She said firmly, "You must tell me why you made this call . . .''

"I made this call to ask you a question, lady, and it's this. Last night, for the first time, I pay a visit to your office and tell you a few things in confidence about an Army deserter, a buddy of mine, right?''

"That's right,'' Caidin said.

"That's last night. Then today—out of nowhere—I get a strong impression I'm being followed, first at work, then at a tavern I hang out at. And I know for *sure* that two men who claim they're Army MPs came by where I live and interviewed the landlady. All this happened since I talked to you. Somebody's *looking* for me and they know *where* to look. So my question is, Miss Caidin, *who* is looking for me and did you set me up?"

Bonnie Caidin drew in her breath, suddenly aware of the chill, empty silence of the apartment. She tucked her bare feet under her and pulled the coverlet from the bed up around her thin shoulders.

"I would never do that, George," she said. "I told you last night our records were confidential, that you could trust me. Whatever you think is happening to you has nothing to do with the Veterans' Bureau, believe me. I never asked for your address, where you worked or *any* identification. It was entirely up to you to get in touch with us again, you know that."

"Then those Army MPs—how did they know where I lived?"

"I don't know. I have no idea . . ."

"Well, I do, Miss Caidin, and I've been thinking about it."

"Yes?" she said.

"That Spanish-looking clerk at your place last night, Rick something . . ."

"Rick Argella. What about him?"

"When I was talking to you, he asked me a very stupid question, or maybe a very smart one. He was going out for a snack break, and he asked if he could put a coin in the parking meter for me."

"Why is that stupid? Or smart for that matter?"

"I told him no thanks, I was down the street in a no-meter zone."

Bonnie massaged her cold feet with her fingertips, then put one foot under the bed to feel around for her slippers. "I don't see—"

"It was after midnight, remember?"

"All right, all right, I get it. It's not necessary to feed dimes into the parking meters after 8 P.M., is that it? And you think Rick Argella had to know that? Aren't you being a little paranoid, Mr. Jackson?"

"With just one question, Rick Argella, your office

*compadre,* found out that I'd come to the Bureau not on foot, not by taxi or the El, but by car and he got a good idea of where I was parked. And when I got *into* my car after leaving your office, somebody stepped out of the restaurant across the street. It was raining and I can't swear it, but it could have been Argella and he could have taken down my plate number. You still think I'm paranoid?''

"I'm listening, George," Bonnie Caidin said, picking up the pencil.

"Either you're in on this or you're not, Miss Caidin. But I believe somebody checked out my license number with Motors Registration and found out who I am and where I live . . .''

"Let me tell you two things, George," Bonnie Caidin said, interrupting. "First, I'm not 'in on this,' as you suggest, not in any way at all. And second, Rick Argella is no more than a filing clerk at our office, a clerk, plain and simple, not even a volunteer. He gets paid by the hour. He would have no authority whatsoever to ask for plate information from Motors in Springfield. That Bureau wouldn't even give *me* that information if I called, which I didn't. That takes an official request . . .''

"I don't want to argue with you, Miss Caidin, but suddenly I'm a hot property. People are looking for me and they know where to look. That's as plain as I can make it.''

"Look, George," she said. "I'm still not convinced that anyone is following you *or* looking for you, not really, I'm not. I think it could just be a normal—yes, a *normal* paranoid reaction to what's been worrying you, to what you started to tell me about last night. And I'm not convinced that Rick Argella is anything but a nice young guy who wanted to do a veteran a favor. But I want to *prove* that to you.

"I've got a friend," she said, "a dear, old and trusted friend. I'll ask him to call Motors for me—he's official—and inquire if anyone put in a request for information on your license plate. Is that okay? Give me till nine and I'll get back to you on this. Where can I reach you?''

"Nine o'clock and then *I'll* call you," Lasari said.

While she was talking, Caidin had scrawled some words on the notepad: "Mark Weir . . . Mark Weir" and "MPs . . ." and then a pair of telephone numbers. After that, as she listened and almost without realizing it, she had made a series of question marks in heavy strokes, underlining them three times. And then the word "Springfield."

She knew she had to locate and talk to Weir now, not from a special reporter's instinct, but from a gut apprehension, a conviction that, as George Jackson had said and whether she had meant to be or not, she might—in fact—be a "part of this."

Bonnie Caidin laid the palm of her hand flat against her robe, between her small, firm breasts, and pressed hard against the breastbone, trying to make contact with what she thought of as the inner core of herself, determined to force the sudden trembling to leave her body and willing her voice to stay firm.

"Is that a promise, George? You *will* call back? Last night, when we were talking—didn't you trust me last night?"

As she waited, Bonnie Caidin flipped to a fresh sheet of paper on the notepad. Finally Lasari said, "Yes. Last night I did trust you and I'll call you back at nine. And my license plate number, it's 74B6D9."

His voice was normal now, low but clear, without the cautious, muting whisper. "One more thing, Miss Caidin, because I *am* trusting you, the car is registered in my real name, Durham Francis Lasari."

"D-u-r-h-a-m. I'm writing that out."

"Right," he said. "It's spelled just like the place in North Carolina. And the last name—that's Lasari with one 's' and one 'r,' okay?"

Bonnie Caidin checked the clock and noted the hands were at 8:10. That gave her almost one hour. She dialed the first of the two phone numbers she'd scrawled on the front of the notepad, then waited while the phone rang six times in Mark Weir's apartment.

She hung up and opened the Chicago Yellow Pages directory, running her fingers down the "Clubs" category till she came to the Illinois Athletic Club on South Michigan Avenue, almost opposite the gray arches of the Art Institute. When a male voice answered, Caidin identified herself and explained she was trying to locate Lieutenant Mark Weir and could he be paged in the bar and the dining room?

Within minutes the voice came back on the line to say that Mr. Weir did not answer the page.

"Just a moment, please, let me think," Bonnie said.

"Maybe he decided to work out before dinner. Can you try him in the gym or the handball courts? It's very important that I find him."

The bedside clock ticked away a full five minutes before the voice said, "I'm sorry to keep you, Miss Caidin, but I took the liberty of checking with the doorman and both the bartenders and the maitre d' and none of them has seen the lieutenant tonight. He didn't answer our page in the gymnasium. Charley in the locker room says Mr. Weir hasn't been in for ten days or so . . ."

"Thank you," she said, "but if he should happen to stop in, can you ask him to call me at home? He has the number."

She hung up and circled the second number on the pad, detective headquarters. She hesitated, and then on impulse ran her pencil in a square block around the question marks and the word "Springfield," and asked information for General Tarbert Weir's home phone number.

When she dialed the number, she heard four rings, then a taped announcement in a deep, masculine voice, curt and brief, asking that the caller leave a message, with date and time of day, and Tarbert Weir would return the call when possible.

Stifling a sigh of disappointment, Bonnie Caidin left General Weir her message. After that she dialed detective headquarters on State Street.

"I know Lieutenant Weir isn't working tonight," she told the switchboard operator, "but could you ring his office anyway? I can't get him at his club or at home or anywhere else."

"As a matter of fact," the operator said, "the lieutenant *was* in until about twenty minutes ago. I put through a call he was waiting for and right after that, he checked out."

"Is Sergeant Gordon in the building?"

"No, ma'am, he went off duty at six o'clock."

"Look, I realize this is irregular, but could you try to rouse the lieutenant on his police signal for me? If he's in the squad or tuned in on his two-way, maybe we can reach him. It's urgent."

"May I ask who's calling, madam, and the nature of your business with the lieutenant?"

"Well, it's rather personal. Just tell him his first wife needs to talk to him."

\*　\*　\*

Lieutenant Weir was alone in the squad car, driving along the lake front near the city limits when the dashboard phone rang. On the tape deck Willie Nelson was singing loudly about "the good times." Weir turned down the volume and picked up the receiver.

"Weir," he said.

"I know you're off duty, lieutenant," the headquarters operator told him, "but the lady insists it's urgent. Says to tell you, it's your first wife calling . . ."

Mark Weir felt a slight quickening of his heartbeat. "Thanks, operator, put her through," he said. Willie Nelson's voice, now in muted miniature, was singing something about "Sunday mornin' comin' down . . ." The inside of the blue and white car with its worn leather seats, the rain-misted windows and the glowing signals on the dashboard seemed suddenly to be the whole world to Mark Weir, enclosed, personal, valuable.

He heard a faint click in the receiver and before she could speak, he said, "Mark here. I'm listening to you, Bonnie."

"Oh, Mark," she said, her voice small and hurried. "There is something I need to talk to you about. Did you speak with your father this morning?"

"Yes. We spoke, but he said he wouldn't raise a finger to help me. That was the essence of it anyway."

"Then that isn't it. I'm trying to consider everything," Bonnie said. "I know I need your help, Mark. Could you give me a ring from a public phone? This may have something to do with that call I made for you this morning . . ."

Weir checked the street signs at the intersection, then looked at his watch. "Listen, baby," he said, "I'm just cruising around waiting for an important call to come in on this line, something about a case I'm working on. I should hear in about twenty minutes, then I can head for your place. I'd be there about eight forty-five, ten to nine at the latest. Can it wait that long?"

"Yes, yes, that's just fine," Caidin said. "But if you're going to be later than ten to nine, call me, will you? That's how important I think this is."

Mark Weir clipped the phone to the dashboard, then snapped off the tape deck. He reversed directions, and began to cruise back to the center of the city. He would have liked to attempt to reach Doobie Gordon again, but he had already tried four different bowling alleys and decided it would be better to leave this line open.

In her bedroom, Bonnie Caidin pulled on a green jumpsuit over a black jersey body stocking and twisted a green scarf around her hair. Then she slipped her feet into the fleece-lined slippers.

She plumped up cushions in the living room and squared off a pile of magazines on the coffee table. The apartment, three rooms overlooking Lake Michigan, was large and sparsely furnished, low couches, lamps of chrome and parchment, bright paintings on the walls and a scattering of sheepskin rugs. The air was chill with winds from the lake. Periodic gusts forced the cold in around the edges of the glass windows, even through the concrete and reenforced steel walls themselves.

Bonnie looked out at the stormy lake, the black horizon edging somewhere into a black sky, the lights of the city just touching the eerie white water that crested on the swells. She lit a half dozen candles on tables and bookshelves, letting the tiny bright stars of fire add a spurious warmth to the room.

In the kitchen she made fresh coffee and removed a rock-hard package of lasagna from the freezer. From a basket on the window sill she took six oranges and squeezed the juice into a tall crystal glass, placing it on the top shelf of the refrigerator.

Bonnie went into the bathroom then, polished steam off the mirrors and shower door, refolded the towels. She plumped up the pillows on her bed and straightened out the quilted coverlet, twisted and rumpled as if two people had been lying on it. How odd, she thought, after all these years she still cared desperately, perhaps childishly, what Mark Weir thought of her.

She poured herself a cup of coffee and brought it to a couch near a big window so she could look out over the lake and down at the bright, pinpoint crawl of traffic on the avenue.

She was aware she had busied herself partly to keep from worrying. Mark was late, she knew that without checking the clock, and her thoughts were touched with a wisp of anxiety. The apartment was so silent, her own breathing so light and shallow that she could hear the sound of traffic rising in a hum from the street ten stories below.

At five minutes to nine Bonnie moved to stand by the phone and picked up the receiver on the first ring. "Give me twenty minutes more, Lasari," she said. "I contacted my friend, he said he'd help. I expect him any minute."

"This isn't working, Caidin," Lasari said, "even though I'm trying to trust you. I'm a clay pigeon, hanging around this phone. Who is this dude we're waiting for?"

Caidin hesitated, then said, "He's an old friend, almost family. It's Lieutenant Mark Weir of the Chicago police . . ."

At that moment the buzz of her doorbell cut through the conversation. "He's here, Durham, the doorbell just rang. Stay there and give me just a little more time."

"Twenty minutes more, lady. That's how long I'll stay put."

Mark Weir's presence seemed to fill the room with a rush of energy, of vitality. His cheeks were reddened from the night wind and his dark eyes unnaturally bright. He pulled off his raincoat and shook off the droplets with a force that guttered the candles and threw shadows on the ceiling.

"I'm sorry, Bonnie, the call I was waiting for came later than I thought it would."

She raised her hand. "I stalled, I bought us another twenty minutes, Mark. And I took out some lasagna. Let me put it in the oven if you've got time."

"Not tonight, Bonnie, but I'll take that fresh coffee I smell."

She hurried to the kitchen and brought a mug of coffee to Weir, who stood at the window looking out at the night. He held the mug in both hands for a moment, turning it round and round, savoring the warmth on his fingers.

"I've seen a nighttime view like this a thousand times and I think I'm lucky every time." He smiled at her. "I don't mind being a little crazy, Bonnie, but I just love this city." His tone changed suddenly. "I'm on kind of an adrenaline high right now. I may be onto something tonight. But you wanted to talk. What do you want to tell me?"

"I've got to make it fast, Mark. This person who's in trouble is waiting in Calumet City at a pay phone."

Weir sipped his coffee as Bonnie sketched out everything she knew of George Jackson from last evening and everything of Durham Lasari from this evening.

When she finished, Weir was thoughtful for a moment. "I can make that call to Motors for you, Bonnie," he said, "but I feel the results will probably be negative. I think you're dealing with a typical sad sack case. You wrote those features on delayed stress syndrome, post-'Nam shock, you've met enough of them at the Vets' Bureau. Why is this Jackson-Lasari character any different? He sounds to me like a hard-nosed loner, more than a little paranoid, maybe even psychotic."

"Don't make me beg for this, Mark. We have too little time."

"Hey, this guy means something to you, doesn't he, Bonnie?"

"I've only seen him once," Caidin said obliquely. "But I promised him confidentiality, I owe him something."

"Your phone?"

"In the bedroom. His full name and license number are on the phone pad."

"All right. I have to make a couple of local calls first," he said. "I'm trying to track down Doobie Gordon. Then I'll call Motors."

He hesitated, his hand on the bedroom knob. "Forgive me, Bonnie," he said, "but I'm going to close this door. I know we're both on the same side, but I'm cops and you're press. If I do reach Doobie, what I've got to say is police business, private. I'm onto something about these dead soldiers. It will be your story first, I promised you that, but I don't want you obligated to Larry Malloy till we've done our police work, okay?"

Bonnie Caidin nodded and he closed the bedroom door behind him. She thought of turning up the kitchen radio but instead she moved closer to the windows, letting the hum of street traffic float up and mask out the drone of Mark Weir's voice in the bedroom.

First there seemed to be two conversations, low and short, then she could make out a longer series of digits being dialed and knew he was calling Motors Registration in Springfield. There were murmurs and pauses, then a longer murmur of Weir's voice and a pause as he listened.

When Weir emerged from the bedroom, his expression was

thoughtful and withdrawn, almost as if she were not in the room. "Something wrong? You couldn't locate Doobie?" she asked.

He shook his head. "No, I couldn't. But that's not what's worrying me." He glanced at his watch, then joined her at the window, putting both hands on her shoulders and turning her slim body to face him squarely.

"Listen, Bonnie, and listen good. I told you I was onto something. Well, Durham Lasari may be part and parcel of the whole thing. I can't explain now, but I want to meet with him. I'll get back here by 6 A.M. That should give me time to do what I've got to do."

As Bonnie began to speak, Mark held up his hand, "You're listening, baby, I'm talking. When Lasari calls you from Calumet, tell him to come here. Tell him not to let anyone know where he's going and to be sure he's not being followed. Keep him here till morning, till I get back to you. Don't go out, don't let anyone in."

"What if he won't come?"

"Convince him, Bonnie, for his own good."

"Then someone *did* check him out at Motors?"

"Yes," Lieutenant Weir said. "A detective from Head-quarters checked the plate this morning, early. I know who this man is and who he pals around with. It's part of a damned jigsaw, but it's falling into place."

Weir pulled on his damp raincoat. "I squeezed some fresh orange juice," Caidin said. "Want to drink it down right now, Vitamin C and all that?"

Weir shook his head. "I'll have it for breakfast, okay? And Bonnie, once Lasari is here, keep the door bolted from the in-side, understand?"

"I understand, Mark," she said, "but I also understand you're holding out on me. You were on that phone to Spring-field just too damned long. So who else called Motors about Lasari today?"

"I know you're going to have to tell him about the cop to get him up here, but the next one's strictly between you and me, Bonnie. Do I have your word on that?"

When she nodded, Weir said, "There *was* a second call, around 3 P.M., a confidential request from a government agency. I'm not authorized to ask who or what on that one, Bonnie." He frowned. "I sure as hell hope I'm not making a mistake in telling this, even to you, but that call was an A-1 priority level request from Washington. Your Durham Lasari is suddenly a very important person.''

When the lieutenant left, Bonnie bolted the door and went to sit on the edge of the bed. She began to rehearse quickly what she wanted to say when the phone rang from Calumet City. She wanted to get the words right the first time.

# Chapter Thirteen

IT HAD BEEN a pleasant enough day, Tarbert Weir thought, even with Mark's unexpected phone call and the puzzling request for help. Several times the general had tried to reconstruct that conversation, first in his head and later aloud to John Grimes.

". . . all right, general, all right. What you're telling me is that my problem isn't your problem, there is nothing you can do."

". . . what I'm saying is that there is nothing I *will* do . . . there's a difference." General Weir was sure those were the words he'd used, but his son had interrupted abruptly, pained and angry, before he had had a chance to explain.

The sound of Mark's voice, mature, vibrant, had unnerved the general and set loose a flood of memories.

He would have liked to talk longer, find out more about what was troubling Mark. He didn't even have his son's home phone number, but he supposed the lieutenant was listed. There couldn't be more than one Mark Weir in the Chicago police department.

The six o'clock news had predicted rain, possibly turning to snow for the suburban areas, but here the night was clear with the pale winter moon in a windless sky.

General Weir stood on the porch of his farmhouse in Logan County, outside Springfield, and watched the shift of gray light over the cornfields. The stalks had been broken at almost uniform angles by the snow and looked to Scotty Weir like troops lined up in a ragged formation, stretching down to the small lake at the base of the meadow, a black flash of water rimmed by a stand of bare trees. A sparrowhawk circled toward its nest, wingtips white in the gathering darkness.

The general sipped his drink, trying to relish the bite of the whiskey with which he had become accustomed to ending his day. Usually the liquor brought with it a welcomed release, the knowledge that this day had few more hours to fill.

Early that morning he had helped the tenant farmer dig fence post holes and string new wire along the road at the side of the property. Weir expected to add two dozen new heifers to the milk herd in the spring. He had written out checks for winter feed bills, looked over the blueprints for the expansion of the new milking shed and run a personal check on the silo temperature of the field corn and sorghum silage. Before lunch he fished for bluegills and pan bass through the soft lake ice near the springhouse, then took the new Irish setter for a run through the woods.

General Weir liked movement and speed and exercise, and he savored the rough, underfoot resilience of country terrain. It reminded him of army maneuvers, bivouacs in Germany and Korea, his basic training along the piny trails of Georgia. Now he tramped the farm woods in the new snow, even more than he did in the green of spring and summer or in the fall pheasant season. His wife had died because of his love for her, and of snow, but beneath the guilt and pain there was something soothing in remembering Maggie in the whiteness and silence and ecstasy of the last night they had ever spent together, in the lodge in the Bavarian Alps.

Grimes had cleaned and panfried the lake fish, bringing the general's lunch on a tray to his study. Later Weir had driven to the country club where he won seventy dollars playing five card stud with Laura Devers. She'd asked if he'd like to go with her to look over a miniature Shetland she was thinking of purchasing for her granddaughter, but he declined. Mrs. Devers said she'd call about dinner.

He spent the rest of the daylight hours driving on backroads through the flat, snow-streaked Illinois countryside, trying to let the black and gray landscape soothe the unrest, the loneliness which, if uncontrolled, could grow and wrench through his insides like a twisting rasp. Damn Mark's phone call . . .

He had been lonely and poor and hard-worked as a farm boy in this same country before he'd faked his age to join the Army at seventeen. The Army, its disciplines and rewards, had become his mentor and ultimately his life. As a teenager, he had been a quiet but brilliant student. In the Army he studied and broadened his horizons, taking advantage of every specialization program offered, from language school at Monterey through the Army College at Carlisle, Pennsylvania, and administration studies at Indianapolis. There had been deep satisfaction, a strong sense of accomplishment and pride as he worked his way through Army ranks from stripes to stars.

But the only pure joy he had ever experienced, Tarbert Weir believed, a happiness soaring out of the realm of ordinary human experience, had been in the years he was married to Maggie. His bitterness, his hardness after her death came from a conviction that he had been robbed by life, that he had not had her long enough.

As a soldier he had been exemplary, as an individual he had been a detached and introspective loner until Maggie came into his life. He had always felt that her love, her loyalty and the pleasure she gave him was curing him of some deficiency. It was her presence that made him feel complete, a full man, and her mortal absence left a void he refused to allow any other human being to fill.

After his wife's death, a friend had suggested that then-Colonel Weir resign from the Army, find a career as a civilian, care for his young son. Weir had never even considered the suggestion. The Army and Maggie had been the centers of his life. With his wife gone he had accepted the military as a demanding mistress and chose to stay in service.

He could still keep a place in his heart for his young son, Colonel Weir had thought at the time, but there was no point in pretending they were still a family, that they had a home. He had tried for some closeness, summer vacations, weekends together whenever he was within flight distance, but Mark had spent most of his growing years first at boarding school in Germany, then at a military academy in Virginia, finally as a student at several Eastern colleges.

Tarbert Weir believed he was doing what was best for them both. And it was easier for him to love his son at a distance, when he could not see the distinctive bright eyes, the inherited mannerisms, the quick, eager smiles that reminded him so disturbingly of the boy's mother.

Beyond explaining what the doctors at the Garmisch-Parten hospital had said and tried to do, Tarbert Weir had never been able to make himself talk much to his son about his mother's death. It was John Grimes who was closest to the boy in the weeks afterward, held him when he cried, brought him warm milk in the night, but the older Weir had often wondered if he had been less selfish, if he had not insisted that Grimes should take the boy back to Frankfurt that winter Sunday, then Maggie Weir might be alive and standing with him on the veranda today.

". . . what you're telling me is that my problem isn't your problem, *there is nothing you can do.*" It was the last few words that bothered Scotty Weir. His estrangement from his son had distressed him more than he cared to admit. And the phone call had taken him by surprise. He had been thinking more about Mark himself than the words the lieutenant was saying. Momentarily the general's emotions had tricked him, he had spoken as if by rote, almost without thinking. But had not his son, out of the residue of bitterness over Vietnam, from his own strange interpretation of obligation and duty, made up his mind for him, articulated what the general had not truly decided to say?

The sights and sounds of the night, the whiskey, began to soothe him; the look of the lake in the semidarkness, water glinting like tarnished silver beyond the stubbled fields and the rustlings of nature, the frost creak of branches, the scuttle of rodents in underbrush. Headlights from a distant truck flared on the horizon and a jet was circling over Springfield to the south, the only movements disturbing the deep silence around the old farmhouse.

This was the home General Tarbert Weir and his wife had imagined and planned and drawn sketches of in half a dozen countries and many army posts, bundled up at a kitchen table during a Nebraska snowstorm or slapping at mosquitos on screened porches in Georgia and Tennessee and Texas. It was Maggie who suggested they try to purchase something in the area of his boyhood, so they could be together and happy in a place he had once been lonely.

Maggie had found this old house and bought the two hun-

dred acres of farmland in Logan County, Illinois, while Scotty
Weir was at a command post in South Korea. Mark had gone
to first grade at a country school here while the house was torn
apart and rebuilt over two years. But they had all lived
together here for only one serene August before Scotty Weir,
wearing the silver oak leaves of a light colonel, was transferred
again to Germany and took his family with him.

One thing they had never included in their plans and
sketches for this farm was the old, walled cemetery a short distance behind the house, with its moldered tombstones dating
back to before the Civil War. During that hot August when
they had lived here as a family, Scotty Weir had helped local
masons mend the crumbling walls and right the slanting head-
stones, and had stripped to the waist and scythed back rye
grass and clumps of wild and fragrant honeysuckle.

Colonel Weir was putting his land in order and wanted to
show respect and honor for those neglected bits of human
history who now rested within his boundaries. They were all
strangers to him until he retired from the Army and returned
to Illinois to make the farm his home. He knew he wanted
Maggie with him then. He had her coffin removed from its
burial site in Germany and sent to that little graveyard. Only
Grimes stood with him as the men from a Springfield funeral
home put Maggie Weir to rest for a second and final time. It
had snowed later that day, too.

It had been because of a heavy, almost historic snowfall that
German winter almost two decades earlier that the Weirs had
decided to take a three-day winter vacation in the German
Alps. Maggie had always wanted to show young Mark as
much of Europe and its life as possible. The base school allowed students travel days in return for an essay about their
experience.

On Saturday they had done some cross-country skiing,
moving first over high Alpine meadows, then gliding in white
silence through forests of fir, the feathered branches bent with
snow. Near the end of the day, they'd skied holding hands.
When they stopped to watch the sunset as it touched the highest peaks and ridged the snowdrifts with pink and coral, Colonel Weir was filled with an almost tangible sense of serenity.

Then something happened that touched first his thoughts,
then his loins with a sexual stirring so deep that the quality of

the arousal, and his determination to fulfill it, had never left his memory.

Just before dusk, not far from the lodge, Maggie had broken from them, pulled off her skis and shouted to young Mark, "Look, look! Mommy's making angels!"

Then, neat and slim in a red ski suit, she had flung herself backward onto a pristine snowbank, laughing and flailing her arms and legs in arcs on the snow, and when she rose the print of her body looked like a winged and flying angel.

Spurred by her son's delight, Maggie tossed herself into fresh snow again and again, making a frenzy of angel imprints that lined the banks almost back to the hotel.

For Colonel Weir, the sudden, strange beauty of his wife's body against the snow, her vitality, the grace and abandonment of her movements had acted as a new and powerful sexual spur.

That night he lay quietly beside her, awake long hours after his wife had fallen asleep, acutely aware of her presence and also of his son's light breathing on the rollaway cot in a corner of the pine-walled room. His need for his wife was so strong that he forced himself to lie motionless, afraid to feel her warmth and softness with even the slightest touch.

Early the next morning he made a call from the hotel lobby to Corporal Grimes in Frankfurt, instructing him to take a military plane to Munich, then drive to the lodge to pick up young Mark. At breakfast the colonel told his son that a three-day vacation at this time would be a violation of responsibility, no matter what school rules allowed. Mark Weir would be back in school at the Frankfurt base on Monday morning.

That night the colonel and his wife were alone. From the very beginning, Maggie Weir's sensuality, her pleasure in variations of lovemaking, had been a constant, goading pleasure. In the hotel dining room, over dinner and a fine bottle of Rheinhessen Liebfraumilch and an Eis Wein with dessert, Colonel Weir told her what he wanted.

Later they had showered together, embracing under jetting streams, lathering each other with pine-scented soap, leaving the shower door open till every bathroom mirror was misted over, closing them in a warm, muted world of sexual arousal.

Then Maggie had run naked to the snow-covered balcony outside their bedroom, thrown herself into the cold, white blanket, thrashing her arms and legs into sculpturing angels. Her husband followed. They went through this antic arousal half a dozen times before they flung themselves into the bed and under quilted eiderdowns and between sips of warming brandy, made love with an intensity as hot and frenzied as the strange images their bodies had left on the snowy balcony.

When Weir woke in the morning to kiss his sleeping wife, her forehead was hot to his lips. By ten o'clock she had tried strong tea and aspirin but there was a glisten of fever in her eyes and two spots of unnaturally high color on her cheekbones. It was then that Colonel Weir called the lobby desk and ordered a cab to drive him and his wife to the local clinic.

Even excellent hospital care and the strength of Maggie Weir's young body could not fight off the sudden, devastating pneumonia and subsequent lung collapse.

Three days later, when the colonel came back alone to the hotel room to pack their things, he noticed that a light snow had fallen but the deep curves of two bodies were still faintly outlined, almost as if traced in blue shadow, in the snow on the balcony.

The telephone in the study of the old farmhouse rang and the general carried his drink across the veranda and into the front hall. Laura Devers, he thought. She'll be calling about dinner. Good friend that she was, Mrs. Devers didn't understand, in fact, disapproved of the general's need to spend so much time alone.

The phone was still ringing as the general walked into his study. Small logs crackled in the fireplace and the room was lit with light and shadow. The general waited as the phone rang a third and then a fourth time. His own voice sounded from the answering machine after the fourth ring. "This is Tarbert Weir. After the tone signal, would you please leave a message and your phone number. I'll get back to you as soon as possible . . ."

The tone signal sounded and then a vaguely familiar voice came from the speaker. "General, this is Bonnie Caidin, an old friend of Mark's. You may remember me. I'm trying to locate him and have a hunch he may have driven down there." She seemed to hesitate a moment. "Tell him I've got to talk to him. It's urgent. Something abut George Jackson, that soldier. My number is 312-346-7077. And thank you, sir." The tape clicked off and a message button at the base of the machine lit up red.

". . . you may remember me," Bonnie Caidin said. He'd met her once with Mark, after his son came back from Vietnam and before he began making his campus speeches, a tall girl, all white skin and freckles and soft, shining eyes. And so polite to him, the Army officer, the enemy, and yet the father of the man she was in love with. It had been so obvious to him that he'd felt a sharp pang of envy that hot afternoon. All three had crowded into a booth in the Pump Room, gin and tonics in frosted glasses for the gentlemen and a fresh limeade for little Miss Caidin, who couldn't have been more than seventeen or eighteen, sitting so close to his son, her hand touching Mark's broad, brown one on the starched tablecloth. Their eager sensuality and animal warmth was so palpable that General Weir, much sooner than he'd planned, called for the check and said goodbye.

Tarbert Weir had walked with long strides down the three blocks to Michigan Avenue, then zigzagged through rows of heavy traffic to reach the beach walk along Lake Michigan. He positioned himself at the edge of the cement block breakwater, standing close so that the spray of crashing waves cooled his face, soothing his rage and finally admitting, with some generosity, that every man had a right to be loved that way, even his own son.

Little Bonnie Caidin . . . he had thought that was over a long, long time ago, and, yes, Miss Caidin, I *do* remember you.

Grimes appeared then, backing his way in against the study door, two logs cradled in his arms. He put one piece of wood on the fire and the other on the hearthstone. He pulled off his gloves and plaid jacket and said, "I thought I heard the phone ringing, general, somebody leave you a message."

The general switched on the desk lamp. "It rang and somebody did."

"It could have been for me, you know," Grimes said. "I still got some old pals and lady friends who like to keep in touch."

Grimes was short and thickly built, forty-nine, eight years the general's junior, with a head as round and solid as a bowling ball and a complexion weathered a dark brown in all seasons. His eyes were small and blue and he wore his black hair in a crewcut, the same style that had been popular when he was an enlisted man almost thirty years before, assigned for the first time to the same unit as Lieutenant Tarbert Weir.

"It wasn't for you, corporal," Scotty Weir said. "I didn't answer it, but I listened to the message." Grimes waited, studying the general's quiet, thoughtful face.

"Let me fix that drink for you, sir," Grimes said, "and then you can tell me whatever you feel you want to tell me." He took the crystal whiskey glass from the desk and went out toward the kitchen.

John Grimes had asked for and received an honorable discharge as a corporal, his rank for fifteen years, the same month as the general left the Army. Grimes' last commanding officer had offered him sergeant's stripes in his last month in service, a customary promotion among long-termers to insure additional pension benefits and privileges. But taking his lead from General Weir, Grimes declined it.

When he decided to retire early, Tarbert Weir had refused to accept a token physical disability on his record, a popular practice among officers to increase retirement benefits and other perks.

Weir would have found it repugnant to go along with that deceit, with its implication that he had performed at only twenty-five percent of his maximum efficiency. He had enlisted at seventeen, a rugged, determined farm boy in one hundred percent shape, and he insisted on being separated from the service in the same condition he'd entered it.

From the kitchen he could hear Grimes washing the crystal glass under running water, then cracking ice cubes from a tray. It was typical of the man, Weir knew, to wash and shine the glass before making a fresh drink. But Grimes was not always an automaton, the perfect corporal.

Firelight flickered in three empty, glass-fronted cabinets built flush into the study walls, designed and placed on the house plans by Maggie. In one corner of the study stood an old Army footlocker, brass corners gleaming. It had once been Mark's toy box, and they had carried it, filled with trains and dump trucks and tattered children's books, from one post to another. In later years the locker was used to store things Maggie had saved and planned to display as General Weir's career memorabilia—medals, campaign ribbons, newspaper clippings, foreign decorations, letters of recommendation. If she had lived, they might all be displayed now in the empty cabinets.

Once, some years ago, Weir had asked Grimes to consult a local carpenter about removing the glass doors and widening the shelves to hold books, but the corporal had never got around to it. Nor had he gone through the items in the locker, as requested, to arrange them according to dates and places and actions, so they could at least be put away in a closet or storeroom. The collection was still a jumbled mass of colored ribbon and inscribed metal and folds of yellowing paper piled into an old trunk without lock or key.

His son would have little interest in the footlocker's contents, General Weir was sure of that, but if there were grandchildren they might like to look at it some day, not as mementos of blood and glory, but as part of a historical record. General Weir himself was still acutely aware of every decision, every conviction, every ultimate action behind that collection of honors, but more and more, since the break with Mark, he had begun to feel detached and inoperative, a military statistic, an outdated cipher.

One special medal was not in the clutter of the toy box, the one with scattered stars on a blue field, the head of Lady Liberty and the single word: Valor. General Weir kept that hidden in a zippered compartment of his wallet, along with a medallion picture of Maggie and the two initial beads, an M and a W, from the identity bracelet snapped on Mark Weir's wrist in the Paris hospital only moments after his birth.

Tarbert Weir stood and almost reflexively touched the hip pocket of his corduroys to feel the familiar outline of the wallet. Then he walked to the windows, looking out at the darkness through the fire-flecked panes. His hands were clasped behind his back and he was frowning. Although he was standing perfectly still, there was a restless tension about him.

He heard Grimes' footsteps and said, without turning, "Just put the drink on the desk, Grimes. I want you to listen to the phone tape. You'll remember the lady, I told you about her."

He'd help his boy, General Weir was thinking. Mark had called him, he had even told his lady friend he might drive down. He had thought of his father, sought him out and that was the important thing. They were both men now.

The general waited as Grimes switched on the phone tape and listened to Bonnie Caidin's message, once, then a second and a third time.

He had a past, too, Weir thought almost defiantly. Since seventeen, he had lived and learned and believed in the lessons taught by the Army—loyalty, love of country, dedication to other men in uniform, a demanding dictum. Was that code of behavior always wrong?

Weir picked up the glass from the desk and drank it back almost to the ice cubes. Was there anything, he thought, new or revealing about war or life that Napoleon could tell a West Point cadet today? If Hannibal were alive, would he be a man of vision and courage or would he be working in an elephant act at Ringling's?

The general asked telephone information in Chicago for his son's home phone number. When he dialed it he let the phone ring six times before hanging up. Then he called the number Bonnie Caidin had left on his phone tape. That line was busy.

"Grimes," he said. "I want to talk to Mark again. I'd like to find out if he trusts me. I can't really help him unless he does."

"I think you can depend on him," Grimes said obliquely. "You're more alike than you know, sir. A homicide detective in one of the toughest combat zones in the country, that's the duty Mark's pulling, general."

Weir shrugged. "I was never the father that boy wanted to believe in. I was a human being, full of flaws. That's always fatal for true believers. The Army taught me a man has to turn his back on troops to lead them. Mark never understood that, and now I wonder if we couldn't have walked side by side at least part of the way." He glanced at a wall clock. "Call Mrs. Devers and tell her I can't make dinner tonight."

"She'll want details, sir."

"Goddammit, Grimes, you know how an officer puts up a tent, he asks a sergeant. Well, I'm asking a corporal. You tell Laura anything, tell her I'll talk with her tomorrow. I want the lines clear when I try to locate Buck Stigmuller."

Grimes said, "After Mrs. Devers, you want me to bring down the correspondence with Marta Tranchet? You still keep it in the mapcase?"

The general looked at the stocky corporal with frank admiration and said, "Dammit, Grimes, you should be in plans and strategy in the Pentagon. You're right. If General Stigmuller can't help us, then the problem could be in Europe. Young Tranchet-LeRoi got promoted, he's with NATO in Kassell. Marta told me the last time she wrote."

Scotty Weir reached for the phone and said, "First, let me dial that Caidin lady one more time."

Both men waited until a busy signal sounded on the line. The general broke the connection and held up his glass. "Call Mrs. Devers on the kitchen phone, will you, so I don't have to hear your lies. And fill this up, if you please, Grimes. I didn't even taste the last one."

# Chapter Fourteen

"YOU SHOULDN'T BUY this junk food," Duro Lasari said, looking at the tepid lasagna on his plate.

"I usually eat out or have a sandwich at my desk before I come home," she said. She was smoking a thin brown cigarette and sipping red wine. "I'm not into eating, really."

"This wine is different," Lasari said, turning the glass to catch the candle's reflection. "Bardolino is made mostly from Corvina and Molinara grapes, the north of Italy. I know a little something about wine, my father drank enough of it. But I know everything about pasta. You shouldn't encourage them by buying this stuff."

He poured wine into both glasses. "Cheers," he said, "and thanks again for the roof over my head. It was raining like hell in Calumet City."

"You're sure no one followed you here? Lieutenant Weir was adamant about that."

Lasari shrugged. "I drove in on the expressway, changed lanes a few times and did the last five miles on surface streets. My car is parked four blocks from here. I walked over, ducked in the alley behind the basement garage—there should be a lock on that door, by the way—rode up on the service elevator." Lasari took a sip of wine. "I hope I have my priorities right. Maybe I should be worrying more about your boy friend than some bullshit tail. Technically I'm a felon, he's a cop. Maybe I'm the hot hunch he's working on for tonight."

"Mark Weir is a friend, not a boy friend, not for years. And he's a very straight guy."

"If he came out of 'Nam with an honorable discharge, and if his old man's top Army brass, why would he want to do anything for me?"

"He must trust you by intuition," Bonnie Caidin said. "He was convinced the Vietnam war was a terminal mistake and had the guts to say so. Maybe he thinks you protested in a different way."

"Okay, so I buy your lieutenant, a cop with compassion, but what about his father? To any bullshit Army brass, a deserter is about as welcome as dung on the flag."

"General Weir has nothing to do with you or me, or any of this. I just mentioned his name because he might return my call tonight, and I plan to answer that phone. Under the circumstances, I don't want to alarm you by talking to bullshit Army brass, as you call it."

"I never even got within saluting distance of a general," Lasari said. "I was in the arena of noncoms and slopes. But I've heard about Weir, or read about him."

Caidin nodded. "Tarbert Weir always got himself talked about one way or another. He was a kind of folk hero in the sixties for the way he handled an Army division when half the South was practically under martial law. He called in all the northern protesters, the clergy, and the red-necked sheriffs, and the black activists and federal marshals, and gave them a speech that's kind of a classic. Weir said the laws of the land applied to everybody, and if a priest or a nun physically or verbally assaulted marshals or cops who were doing a job, they'd end up reading their missals and saying their rosaries in the stockade. And vice versa. He made himself understood."

"I heard more about his bucking General Westmoreland's strategy, protests against phony body counts, that sort of cover up crap in 'Nam," Lasari said. "Those riots and marches down South, I was a kid back then."

"So was I," Caidin said, "but I checked the clips file at the *Tribune* on the general a few years ago. Up until he resigned, well, Weir's file was thick as a bible."

"You must have thought a lot of the son to check out his old man that way," Lasari said.

"It's how I make my living, listening to people, finding out everything I can . . ."

She snubbed out her cigarette in an ashtray and immediately shook the pack for another, narrowing her eyes against the first puff of smoke. They were seated on suede cushions on opposite sides of a glass coffee table. The candles she had lit for Mark were burning low, and the room had a smoky odor of scented wax. Though the kitchen radio played softly and there was a runnel of rain on the big windows, the apartment seemed isolated to Bonnie Caidin, almost unnaturally still.

At the beginning, when Lasari had knocked on the door, she had felt panicked, wondering what she could talk about or do with this stranger during the long hours till Mark's return.

Lasari, however, seemed indifferent to any social strain. He wore tight blue jeans, workboots and a plaid shirt. His windbreaker was neatly folded on a chair near the apartment door. He was as handsome as he had appeared last evening, Bonnie thought, dark hair, high, prominent cheekbones, and eyes that watched her with a concentrated, opaque intensity that made Caidin aware of the vulnerability of her own slim body, and the glow of warmth touching her skin. Lasari was neither reassuring nor threatening, just a strangely demanding presence in the intimacy of the apartment.

"If you'll carry these plates to the kitchen," she said, "there's another bottle of Bardolino in the refrigerator."

"I'd like that," he said.

Moments later he put the new bottle on the table between them and seated himself, watching her. She smiled at him, but said nothing.

"You're not going to talk because you expect me to talk, is that it?" Lasari said.

"I *would* like to know more about you."

"Okay. You checked out the Weir family tree, so I'll tell you about me, though it's not the same neat and pretty package." He picked up a candle and held it for her as she lit a fresh cigarette.

"I told you my father liked wine, Bonnie. Well, he liked it a lot. Finally he had a liver the doctors couldn't fix, and he died from it. He spent *his* war in the South Pacific and came back with a lot of island crud in his psyche that he never really got over. He was a little guy, scared, pushed around. He always tried to work but too many nights he sat up with the bottle. He never seemed to make up his mind about whether or not he'd been a good enough soldier.

"He worked the tobacco sheds, but his drinking got him laid off. He had a little land, about eight acres his grandfather left him, and he started raising table crops, squash, snap beans, and after awhile he opened a stand in the front yard to sell produce on weekends. He hired a neighborhood kid to run it for him, and they started sleeping together.

"My father was thirty-eight when he got married, and my mother was fifteen and pregnant. She didn't turn sixteen till I was about four months old."

Caidin watched as Lasari's dark, bladelike face turned thoughtful, noticing the hard look of challenge that touched his eyes.

"You won't find Francis J. Lasari on file down at your newspaper. I wasn't more than eight when he died, small and skinny like him, but I loved that man and respected him, no matter what he added up to. Some kind of inverse ratio at work, I imagine. The earlier things happen to you, the longer it takes you to forget them."

"You're full of little surprises, Duro," she said. "First, 'a rebel with discretion,' now 'inverse ratio' . . ."

"I was in a hospital," he said.

"That's a good non sequitur."

"No, it follows. I had a lot of time for thinking, lying in bed, or stretched out on gurneys, waiting my turn at X-ray or therapy. There was an old man, a retired vet who pushed a cart of books around, real pablum—Zane Grey, old mysteries, how to raise mushrooms in your basement. I finally asked him for something else, and for the next few months I got a different menu—opinion magazines, Mark Twain, Marcuse, the Bible, philosophical ideas that maybe I didn't have enough education to evaluate or absorb at the time. It was like stockpiling. I collected information and ideas so I could take them out when I needed them. I began to understand myself. All the years I was in Wyoming I kept reading. So it was like an emotional dam broke inside me when I ran away that last time from Jackson Hole.

"When I found Luis Carlos, the old man I work with in Calumet City, I just talked my whole life out to him. I knew I was ready to quit being George Jackson. I'd named myself that after Jackson Hole and the fact that a lot of the dropouts and transients up there are just called 'Hey, George.'

"I guess I told Carlos everything I'd heard, smelled, seen

and dreamed in my whole life, especially about 'Nam, like I was postdating a diary. Carlos doesn't speak much English, but he knew he was helping me.

"I told you my mother was just a kid when I was born. Well, she stayed a kid all her life, looked like one, acted like one. After my father died, there was always a man, a boy friend from town or hired help for the farm. Two or three of them I liked a lot. They taught me. I learned about dogs, gunning, fixing old machinery, but none of them stayed long enough for me to feel they belonged. I had to cooperate, keep out of the way. It was more like having a crazy sister than a mother. I never did feel right about her back then.

"When my mother came up to camp to see me before I left for 'Nam, she was only thirty-four years old, thin as a bean, blue jeans, boots, brass studs on her jacket. She looked like all the girls hanging around the GI bars that my buddies were sleeping with. I could have been sleeping with her myself if I didn't know exactly who she was."

He poured another inch of wine into his glass. "You want some, Bonnie?" She held up her nearly full glass and shook her head.

"When my mother died, I was still in the hospital in Denver. She was riding home from Durham on the back of some guy's motorcycle and he rammed a truck. I got leave to go home, but I wasn't in uniform at the funeral. Some of the locals said they'd missed me around town. One old timer made a joke out of it, thought I'd been to jail. Most of them didn't know there was a war on.

"That night I went over to Chapel Hill, the University of North Carolina is there, prettiest little southern town you could dream of. The jocks were having a big 'Beat Duke' rally on campus, regional basketball finals or something. I sat in a bar near campus watching a TV news report on 'Nam." He paused. "This isn't just your predictable, burnt-out vet story, Bonnie. Believe me, it happened.

"Everybody around me was talking about the basketball game, and I was listening to Cronkite and watching film clips and almost burning with the heat of those firefights around Chu Lai. I got the damnedest feeling then, this is honest, I didn't know which was for real for a while. I was sure as hell aware of two worlds, but for a finger snap I couldn't tell which I belonged to.

"I don't even remember the plane trip back to Denver, and I didn't feel a damned thing, no sadness, no grief, no sympathy for my mother. But what was really bad was that I was relieved to have her gone. It was like somebody'd shot my head full of novocaine. I couldn't feel pain, remorse, guilt, anger—and I figured that for once that was a plus. I felt dead myself, and I didn't mind feeling that way.

"I left the Army a few months after that. I didn't make a big speech, I didn't punch anybody out, I didn't wait for a dark night. I just went AWOL. I packed my gear, drew my money out of the bank and got a cab to the Denver airport. It was March and there was still snow on the ground, and it was so cold inside the airport, the girl selling tickets was wearing gloves. The next flight leaving the airport was for Jackson Hole, Wyoming, and I took it. We made the trip over the mountains in a Beechcraft six-seater. It was so small and jammed with luggage that the pilot stashed my crutches beside him in the cockpit. It was snowing and early morning when we started to come down over Jackson. We passed over an elk herd, hundreds and hundreds of them huddled together, so deep in the drifts that I thought those antlers were bushes moving in the wind."

Duro Lasari stood and walked to the windows. He was silent for a few moments, looking down at the boulevard and resting his forehead against the damp glass as if he felt fevered. "Those mountains were like walls against the world," he said. "Can you imagine what it's like to unwind in that silence after 'Nam?"

When he spoke again his voice was hard but controlled. "You can tell me to stop talking if you want, Bonnie, but you asked. I don't really expect you understand, but I got myself so damned angry over there, trying to figure out who'd sent us halfway round the world, high school dropouts, Hispanics and ghetto bums fighting for jocks who'd rather stay home and beat Duke. If you think there were a lot of Phi Beta Kappas in my platoon, you're reading the wrong duty roster, lady."

His back was to her but she could see the outlines of his face, rigid with tension, reflected in the window pane. "We had collective IQs that would make good golf scores, in the low eighties. In my first month over there, outside Saigon, twenty-eight black guys took a latrine hostage. They captured it, Bonnie, charged us to use it. Fifty cents to piss, a dollar to crap. Otherwise you could just squat outside in the rain. That's the American flag, the code of honor in action for you. Where the hell were the West Pointers, the brass who were supposed to be running our battalion? There was nothing in their goddamn Articles of War or manuals to handle it. If they'd tried to, they'd of been fragged and they knew it.

"A crazy guy, a recruit from Las Cruces, New Mexico, no older than I was, pulled the pin on a grenade and went in holding it in his hand. He told the black bastards that he didn't think it was right to have to pay extortion for the exercise of natural functions. He shouted that we were all American citizens, all *compadres*. He told them he intended to use the facilities for nothing. If they objected, he said, he'd give them just five seconds to make their peace before they met the Great Mother Fucker in the sky, then he'd roll that grenade right under a commode.

"Okay, those heroes said Las Cruces could use the latrine, but the guy had to get rid of the grenade first. He tried to lob it outside the compound, but it caught the top of the wire fence and killed two native kids hanging on to watch the action. Two dead kids and one crazy patriot serving a life sentence in a federal pen . . .

"That was one of the *funny* stories about 'Nam, Bonnie. I was just a private, but I had to judge 'em as I saw them. If the Pentagon planners couldn't keep the damned privies open, how could we trust them to run the rest of the war?"

He slapped his open palm sharply against the window pane, then turned to look at her. "Delayed stress reactions, you've heard a lot about it. Well, it's real. I figure it's like undulating fever. You believe you're over it, you've got your memories under control and then something happens to trigger the whole goddamned thing over again.

"Do you know what got to me tonight? Do you know what makes me want to get out that door and start running all over again? Just this. Why in hell am I putting my fate in the hands of someone I don't know, some officer named Lieutenant Mark Weir, who out of the goodness of his college-educated, liberal heart is going to help this fucking deserter?"

Suddenly it seemed to Bonnie that his voice, low and harsh now, was vibrating and echoing through every corner of the apartment. As he stood staring down at her, obviously waiting for an answer, the rock music from the kitchen radio sounded ominously bright, an unreal, counterpoint background to this raw anger.

"I can't answer that, Duro," she said. "I just believe that he will."

Duro Lasari began to pace up and down the room, his clenched fists so deep in his jeans pockets that the belt pulled low around his hips, the worn denim stretching tight across his buttocks. He was breathing slowly and deeply as if to calm himself, almost unaware of Bonnie Caidin's presence. Suddenly he turned and looked at her directly.

"I'm sorry I criticized your lasagna back there," he said, his tone almost normal. "For about a year my mother kept company with a man who was a chef in Durham. His specialty was Italian. He made a fine lasagna.

"And about my mother," he said, "I shouldn't have said all the things I did. I got to think differently about her in Jackson. One day, the third spring I lived there, I was out jogging, working to build up those damaged leg muscles, and the sides of the road were full of wildflowers. You get a lot of them in the mountains after all that snow, field daisies, columbine, red gilia. I knew my mother was buried in the Baptist cemetery outside Durham, but in my mind I just brought her up there to be with me, and buried her right there in that peaceful place. I had to be honest with myself. I knew damned well she was nicer to me than most sixteen-year-olds saddled with an unwanted kid. And if I wanted all those flowers for her, I must have loved her, too, wouldn't you say?"

He moved closer to her, bending a little so he could look into her face. "I just remembered," he said. "The name of that special lasagna the guy made is Lasagna *al fiorno,* and the trick is that you use diced chicken livers instead of regular hamburger meat and a special kind of creamy sauce . . ."

"Why are you doing this," she asked.

"Doing what, Bonnie?"

"Why are you talking to me about cooking and wildflowers?"

"Because," he said, "you're so damned scared of me, you're trembling. I saw your reflection in the window, all huddled up like a kid. I tried to stop myself. You're just damned terrified, stuck ten stories up with a strange man you've only seen twice in your life. I didn't mean to start shouting, I didn't mean to do this to you."

"I don't believe I'm afraid of you, Duro," she said. "You made me remember some angers of my own, that's why I'm trembling."

"Those two guys in uniform in the picture next to the radio? Are they your brothers? They look like you . . ."

Bonnie nodded. "They *were* my brothers, not twins, just eighteen months apart. Funny, the taller one was really the younger. They were both in the Air Force and both got killed in training accidents in the same month, one in Florida, and the older one in a special program at Camp Pendleton. When we were a family our dinner table was like a fiesta, night after night. My parents sold the big house almost right away, put me to live with an aunt so I could finish New Trier high school. They moved to a two-bedroom condo in Naples, Florida. The second bedroom is always occupied. It's a kind of shrine to their sons.

"I suppose that's why I loved Mark Weir so fiercely when I did," she said. "He was like a miracle to me, so beautiful. He'd been there and come back. He was *alive*.

"And maybe you wonder why I keep my brothers' picture next to the coffee pot where I'll see it every morning. Well, I want to remember them, to talk to them and tell them day after day after day how sorry I am about what happened to them, to all of them. It's important they understand that. *Bonnie Caidin is sorry.* I wouldn't want them to hate me."

Lasari poured more wine into her glass and moved it toward her on the glass coffee table. "Does your landlord turn the heat down after eleven, or something? It's so damned cold in here."

He walked to the chair near the door and picked up his folded jacket, rubbing it between his big hands for a few minutes as if to work a little friction heat into the fabric. Then he came over to Bonnie where she sat on the floor and draped the jacket over her shoulders. She took the long sleeves and knotted them across her chest.

"No one could hate you, Bonnie," Lasari said.

# Chapter Fifteen

GENERAL BUCK STIGMULLER'S home phone in Georgetown was still busy when Scotty Weir dialed the third time. Stigmuller had married late, an attractive divorcee with two daughters barely ready for kindergarten. Weir had, in fact, been his best man, flying into Hawaii on a muggy July day for the ceremony. Those two daughters must be in their teens now, he thought, but at least the number was current and someone was at home.

Tarbert Weir began to pace his study, attempting to clarify and then marshal the questions he wanted to ask Stigmuller. Birddogging for information was not the way Weir had expected to spend this evening and he felt himself growing restless, even angry, at the busy signals, the delays in his plans. It was his *Army* they were talking about . . . and since he had decided to help his son the general wanted to get the process underway.

As he paced he caught sight of his face reflected back at him from the glass doors of the trophy cabinets and was almost surprised at the hard, intent impatience in his features.

The general's nose was sharply arched, the bridge twisted at the place where it had been broken years ago by the recoil of a misfiring artillery piece. That injury had occurred in Korea, and a medic had set and then reset Scotty Weir's shattered nose at a battery command post, working by flashlight in a snowstorm. The break was clean, there was no infection, but

115

Weir had insisted on going back into action and somehow, in the winds and cold, the bones had mended, causing the general's nose to slant at a crooked angle between his high, strong cheekbones. As a result, his face had a damaged, almost piratical mien, an air of challenge, warmed only by the look of interest and communication in the dark eyes.

Scotty Weir had long enjoyed the battered look of his face; it gave him an edge of authority that had served him well in the military. He never had to give an order twice and few soldiers, from brass to noncoms, smiled at General Weir until they were sure he was ready to smile in return. How much he had changed in body and mind, he thought, since those first fading photographs were taken at the Tranchets' barnyard outside the village of LePont, Belgium, nearly four decades ago.

Grimes had brought down the old mapcase from Weir's upstairs bedroom, and the general leafed through it while waiting to get his call to Washington. The mapcase was of natural pigskin, long and wide enough to hold several folded maps, worn rough at the corners, the leather beginning to darken. It had been a Christmas gift from Maggie the first year they'd known each other. On active duty, at every post, at every battle station, Tarbert Weir had taken the mapcase with him, putting it to practical use and trusting it as a talisman link with Maggie.

In peacetime, on all their leaves and jaunts through the United States, Africa and Europe, often with young Mark in the back seat, they had kept the case in the glove compartment, tracing highways and mountain passes and back roads of their trips in bright red ink, like a vital network of the time and places they were able to be together.

After his wife's death Weir had bound a thick rubber band around all the maps and that packet rested now with other memories at the bottom of the footlocker. Yet he could never quite force himself to discard the mapcase itself and tonight, even under the cured animal leather scent, he felt he could catch the faintest hint of Maggie's perfume.

Now the general used the pigskin envelope as a filing case for his correspondence over four decades with Marta Tranchet, three dozen letters, telegrams of congratulations for his wedding, his promotions, a collection of photographs and—

just last year—Marta's proud letter stating that her only son, Claud Tranchet LeRoi (a full captain now) had been transferred with his Belgian unit to NATO forces outside Kassel, West Germany.

Grimes had brought the Tranchet file to the study on a tray with crackers and cheese, and a tall Scotch and soda.

Weir settled himself at his desk, opened the mapcase and then took a sip from the frosted goblet. The general held the glass, bell clear and etched with fine flowers, carefully in his big hand. It was one of the Val Saint Lambert set, he knew. Grimes was insistent that this farmhouse was the general's home, that all the fine china and silver and crystal the Weirs had collected abroad be put to daily use. But on more than one evening, sitting alone, roiling with both unwanted energies and memories, thoughts intense almost beyond his control, General Weir had inadvertently crushed one of these fragile goblets in his strong hand.

He studied the old snapshot of himself at nineteen, stiff and shy in his private's uniform, young Marta Tranchet standing close beside him, a coarse wool blanket with holes cut for the arms, serving as an overcoat for her thin child's body. The day, the hour, the moment those pictures were taken seemed suddenly as vivid as yesterday to Tarbert Weir. Splash a little whiskey on your memories, he thought, and they flared up with a brilliance and radiance that startled you.

The pictures had been taken after the peace, when he went back to visit, but Private Weir first met the Claud Tranchets near the end of the war when his unit, caught in the crossfire and confusion of the Battle of the Bulge, were cut off and isolated, without orders and food supplies and almost without ammo, on the outskirts of a war-impoverished farm in rural Belgium. His platoon was then only a handful of stragglers, the first and second lieutenants dead and only a buck sergeant, badly wounded, to tell them what to do.

Supporting the sergeant between them, Weir and a buddy, followed by the half dozen other survivors, had made their way across the frozen, rutted mud of the barnyard to a dark and silent farmhouse, windows blown out from artillery fire, walls and timbers pockmarked by rifle shot.

Young Marta Tranchet was there, huddled with her parents in the freezing kitchen, almost out of their minds with cold

and hunger and fear, waiting for the Germans to come down
the hill at first light, waiting to die.

Claud Tranchet, a man in his late forties, had once been a
prominent businessman in LePont, leasing this farm to tenants. Now he was gaunt and dirty, his arm tattooed with a
concentration camp mark for political dissidents, his voice
slurred, his mind wandering with the fever that often comes
with starvation.

Tranchet had escaped from the concentration camp of Le
Vernet in France, hiding for days in the outgrowth of the bar-
riers of hedgethorns that circled the camp instead of barbed
wire. He had made his way up through the hostile French
countryside at night to the Belgian border, and then across terrain he knew well to his own fields and farmhouse and his wife
and child. But in the last half mile he had sighted a tank and
German soldiers, twenty or more, bedded down for the night
two meadows away, waiting for the morning light.

When the Americans entered the farmhouse that December
night they found the Tranchet family crazed by terror, human
beings unable to further absorb or accept or come to terms
with human stress.

Claud Tranchet told the Americans about the German
soldiers, and then put both arms protectively about his dazed
wife and child. They had nothing to fear, he had told his family, and even now, in the warmth and familiarity of his own
study, General Weir could remember the singsong words, the
hiss of icy breath through the Belgian's broken teeth.

The man had become mesmerized by the winter-dead lilac
bush at the side of a stone barn—they could all see it beyond
the broken window—a spray of dark sticks, slick with ice, but
alive and meaningful to Claud Tranchet, a promise of life. It
was a miracle, he told his family that night, a portent of the
spring to come and of many other springs. The bush was filled
with blossoms, he told them. It was a sign to them from God
that they would live. Look, look, he cried, *see it*. The flowers
are purple, they are wet with honey. Smell their fragrance.
Even the Germans will know that our prayers have been
answered, the Almighty has chosen . . .

Marta and her mother, mute and exhausted by fear, were
lulled with these feverish rantings. They became trusting, pas-
sive, huddled together, staring out at the frozen bush, believing the miracle had happened.

Private Weir had waited in the house until dawn. Then he hooked three grenades to his belt, felt his way through a hole in the shattered wall and took off at a crouching run across the fields to where Tranchet had said he'd sighted Germans.

Weir, raised in the rough and snowy fields of Illinois, ran swiftly, moving like a yearling bear, silently, without wasting muscle. He needed the dark to hide him from the Germans, the dawn to show him where to go. A bear in pursuit can catch anything it wants to, he knew, not by running apace, but just by moving the whole body faster. Scotty Weir willed his young body to an almost bearlike speed.

Within minutes after leaving the farmhouse he had stopped behind a stand of trees. The German guard at a machine gun mount had come suddenly alert, swinging the gun position away from the farmhouse and trapped American soldiers and toward the young private crouching in the trees. But the guard's actions came too late. Weir lobbed his grenades into the German encampment, and the three blasts, seconds apart, left little evidence, metal or human, in that huge crater to indicate what had been waiting there, what had terrorized the Tranchets into praying to a lilac bush.

Private Weir was later awarded the Medal of Honor for his bravery. When he went back again to the farm it was spring, and the lilac tree was indeed in bloom, the sweet fragrance a benediction over the scarred and battered farmhouse.

Weir did not know exactly what he expected to find there, but he knew a part of him would be left forever at that Belgian farm. Young as he was, he realized there was a fulcrum for every soldier, a balance point in peacetime or in battle, when he knew the value of his uniform, when he behaved not just as a soldier or automaton, but as a sentient and courageous man. It was then he had decided to become a career soldier.

Over the years Weir and Marta Tranchet had kept in touch, cemented by the memory of fear and trust that for one night had been as strong and binding between them as any physical passion.

Maggie Weir had been understanding, even generous about his friendship with the Tranchets over the years. Weir had been the correspondent, but at Christmas when Marta married and when her only child was born, it was Maggie who remembered with cards and gifts. She had gone with him one winter to the LePont farm, now run by Marta's husband, and stood with Colonel Weir and Marta at the window, looking out at the same lilac bush, fuller, taller, more twisted now, yet alive and greening under its coat of ice.

"I still believe it was a miracle that night," Marta had whispered. "First the lilacs and then the young soldier . . ."

Maggie Weir had glanced down and seen that the young woman's hand was entwined with her husband's, narrow fingers with a gold wedding band, knuckles white, straining with emotion.

"Of course, it's a kind of love she feels for you, Scotty," she had said to the colonel as their Army touring car sped over the dark roads back to Liege. "One can know it just by listening and watching. You were with her at the crisis of her life. I can't allow her to love you in *my* way, but except for death itself, I can think of no emotion more binding than mutual fear. You will always share that, you and little Marta."

General Weir rearranged the letters and snapshots and wondered why he hadn't thought to take a picture of Maggie and Marta together that cold afternoon. No, the mapcase was peopled only with Tranchets and young Claud Tranchet-LeRoi and Tarbert Weir, recorded there in photographs, faded black and white to rich color, boy soldier to full man.

Weir tried Georgetown again and this time Ann Stigmuller answered. "Scotty," she said, "so wonderful to hear from you. Are you in town? Can we see you?"

"I'll take a raincheck, Annie. I'm down on the farm in Illinois. I've been trying to reach you for a couple of hours."

"Oh, dear," she said. "That means the girls have been on the upstairs phone. But at least they're home, and that's something for teenagers these days. But then you never had any trouble at all with Mark . . ."

She caught herself sharply, and he heard her light laugh. "*Damn*, Scotty, I wish you were in town. We could talk and talk. Buck *still* starts every other sentence with 'Scotty always said' . . ."

"If he's there, Annie, I'd like to talk to him."

"Hold on," she said, and lowered her voice. "We have a couple of godawful bores here tonight, Pentagon-type senators that Buck has to toady up to now that he's number one man in Appropriations and Budget. Buck's like you, Scotty, he hates the politics that go with wearing stars. He walked them down to the greenhouse with coffee and brandy. He said he'd show them the cymbidiums I've been cultivating, though Buck wouldn't know his ass from an aster, as our old gardener used to say. Sorry, Scotty. That was vulgar of me. I'll buzz the greenhouse."

General Buck Stigmuller had served as Scotty Weir's aide in Korea for three years, and their paths had crossed again at military college and later in Germany. When Mark was at boarding school in Frankfurt, Stigmuller had often played surrogate at father-son affairs.

When he came on the line he said, "Stigmuller reporting, sir. Give me the number of the hill you want taken and cut me loose. How the hell are you, Scotty?"

"I'll understand if you can't answer me right off, Buck. Ann told me your social situation there. But I need a favor."

"Not a favor," Stigmuller said. "Make it an order and you've got it. What can I do for you?"

"I'd like you to take down the names and serial numbers of four deceased soldiers." Then he told the general about Mark's phone call and his request for help from the Army.

"I'm glad you called me first, and I'll get right on it," Stigmuller said. "You want background, profiles and/or records on these men to see if they interrelate, right? Aside from their uniforms and their deaths, what do they have in common. I gather that's what Mark's after.

"Tell you what. I'll give this information to an intelligence officer I have confidence in. They have the computers for this. You may remember his father, Lieutenant-Colonel Benton, served with MacArthur all through the Pacific. Got killed later in a polo accident in Boca Raton, I'm sorry to say. But Richard Benton II is a comer, Scotty, a very bright and well-connected young officer. Breeds horses as a hobby, married a girl in a million or with a million, which amounts to the same thing, I guess. Tomorrow morning time enough?"

"I'll be sure to let Mark know it was you. Now go take care of your guests, and thanks, Buck."

"Thanks for what? Following orders from an old friend, Scotty? I'll be back to you."

Tarbert Weir put the slip of paper with Stigmuller's phone number in the mapcase. Then he dialed his son's apartment in

Chicago, waiting as six rings went unanswered. Tomorrow
was time enough, after he heard from Washington, but he
needed the excuse to hear Mark's voice again, let him know
the old man could still give orders. On the seventh ring he
hung up.

He replayed Bonnie Caidin's tape message and wrote her
phone number next to Mark's on his notepad. He glanced at
the wall clock. It was nearly midnight, too late to call a young
lady, he decided. Probably she'd located Mark by now,
chances are he might reach them both by dialing the same
number . . . What had she said again? Her phone number and
then the message that she had to talk to Mark about someone,
a George Jackson.

The name meant nothing to Weir, but he wrote it out in
block capitals next to Bonnie's phone number and underlined
it twice. George Jackson . . . he'd tell Mark when he talked to
him.

Colonel Benton's phone rang shortly after midnight. It was
General Stigmuller. Colonel Benton sat upright, automatically
pushing his tousled sandy hair back from his forehead.

"No, sir, it's not the least bit inconvenient. I was just checking through some files here, a little late homework."

His wife turned on her side to look at him, shading her eyes
with her hand, her expression exasperated.

The colonel shook his head warningly at her and said, "Yes,
general, I have a pad and pencil here. I'll take down the
names." After a pause he added, "I'll get my section right on
it, sir. I'll have a report for you and General Weir just as soon
as we have the material collected."

Hanging up, Benton got out of bed and said, "Goddamn
everything."

He went into the bathroom and took a swig of Maalox from
the bottle. When he returned to the bedroom, his wife was sitting up, her bed jacket around her shoulders.

"Well, who was it?" she said. "I live in this house, too, you
know."

"Go back to sleep," he said, and without bothering to put
on a robe went downstairs to his study and placed calls on his
private line to Major Staub and Captain Jetter. When he had
them both on a scrambled conference line, he said, "I just got

a call from General Stigmuller that was about as welcome as a turd in a punch bowl. Stigmuller says that old war horse, Tarbet Weir, wants information on those four military DOAs in Chicago.''

Froggie Jetter cleared his throat and said, "Just off the wall, sir, but couldn't we tell General Stigmuller that Intelligence is aware of the situation, but it's a sensitive area related to national security, and so forth?''

Colonel Benton felt a surge of rage and realized that the stiff drinks earlier in the evening hadn't worked off as much as he thought they had. "Goddamn it, Froggie, talk sense. You don't stonewall four star generals on the grounds of national security. They *are* national security, as they're goddamn quick to tell you. Major?''

"Yes, sir," the Major said evenly.

"Get to work on this, okay? Muddy the waters, buy us time. Don't lie when you don't have to, but put together a nice, tranquilizing coverup for Stigmuller and General Weir. In the terminology of Weir's war, I want a snow job.'' He paused. "As an officer in the United States Army, I'm pledged to obey orders. As a member of Military Intelligence, I'm entitled to decide whether or not I damn well *should*. Our plans of last evening will stand, gentlemen.''

"What do we know about Weir?'' Major Staub said. "Would it be useful to run an update check on him?''

"General Weir is probably just a meddler, another piece of retired brass playing bridge or hacking around a three-par golf course somewhere, wishing he still had some ass to kick. But we'll play it cautious. Froggie, use your classification and pull his file.''

After hanging up Colonel Benton went into a downstairs powder room and took another two teaspoonsful of Maalox from his standby supply. In spite of his disparaging comments to his junior officers, he began to remember things he'd known and heard about Tarbert Weir—General Scotty, the old man had called him—and those memories suddenly stirred and sharpened the unwelcome acid tensions in his stomach.

# Chapter Sixteen

LASARI WALKED ONCE more to the big window, craning his neck as if to look down into the street. Bonnie Caidin said, "Six o'clock is what Mark told me, Duro, and that's what he meant, give or take a few minutes. Time won't pass any faster by watching for him."

"I'm not looking, I'm listening," Lasari said. "It sounds like a cat with its back broken down there." A thin, cracked wail, swelling and growing louder, sounded up from the street. In front of the building it seemed to pause in peak crescendo, then move on.

"That's a police siren, or maybe an ambulance," she said. "I'm never sure which."

"Why would a police car be on this street?"

"They're all over the city all the time," Bonnie said. "Chicago's a lively town. Mostly I don't hear them, we're ten stories up, you know. It depends on how the air carries the sound. In the summer you probably wouldn't hear it. But tonight there's wet pavement and high winds, it's just the combination that does it."

"I'm more accustomed to quiet," Lasari said.

"All those mountains, all that open space. How did you make a living in a little town like Jackson, Duro?"

"It's not that small," Lasari said. "Three thousand or more regulars, but in the winter the skiers come in, in summer there's campers. And then people like me, lots of them. I don't mean deserters, just drifters. It's cowboy country. You can mind your own business, stay just as quiet as you want to be."

"Did you work for someone?"

"I worked a little for everybody. I couldn't come up with ID and I couldn't risk getting on a payroll. First few months I helped out an old hippie, he'd been in Jackson since the fifties. We made polepine and rawhide chairs to sell to tourists. In spring, I'd get on the local work crews to mend the split log sidewalks in town. The wood gets chewed up and warped from wet and cold, and all those cowboy boots all winter. In clear weather, I could pick up work cutting firewood. All you need is a permit to cut all the windfall you can haul out of the woods. Eventually I bought my own chainsaw and I'd go halves with someone who owned a truck. For the last four seasons I worked at ski lodges repairing snowmobiles. I got to be a specialist on Yamahas."

"You make it sound so simple, like a big camp."

Lasari shrugged. "Not really. The first winter in town, I though I'd starve to death. I wasn't in top shape when I left Fitzsimons. I hadn't had enough rehab on my leg. Slogging through snow with damaged muscles, that can make you feel you're wearing solid lead boots. The first few months in Jackson, my leg felt on fire most of the time. I had to do easy things. For awhile I slopped out the Silver Dollar Bar at night. It's in an old hotel. I'd do glassware, the tables and floors, and then I'd polish up the two thousand thirty-two real silver-dollars they've got imbedded in the old bar. These dollars are a big tourist come-on, makes everybody feel rich."

"Did you live at the hotel?"

"No. I didn't make that kind of money. There was always someone in town with something to rent, a house trailer, a room over a garage. I spent the last four winters there in a wooden house right across from the town library. An old lady owned it, Mrs. Snipes, she's from Denver and couldn't take the hard winters in Jackson any more. I kept the house clean for her, it was just a little place, saw that nobody broke in, mended anything that got broken. It was only one story high and every once in a while, when she'd hear about a big snowstorm, she'd send me a postcard to ask me to climb up and shovel off the roof. She was always afraid the old house would cave in."

He paused. "At first I was just able to walk with a limp, then I worked up to running. In the end, I could even ski a little, pretty damned good, actually.

"I bought a pair of Head skis from a friend who was going back to Miami. He'd had special safety clamps put on to hold the boot, took away a lot of the knee strain." Lasari looked thoughtful. "That clamp, which is called a 'Lupo,' had a patent pending number on it, 5885257-019. Funny how unimportant names and numbers like that stick in my mind. Sometimes I think the inside of my head must have tapes like a cash register. You ski, Bonnie?"

"No," she said.

"What I meant to explain was that I was George Jackson up there. I knew in my heart I was hiding but I felt completely free. I didn't feel like I was on the run, I didn't feel like a deserter. I was living as somebody else and, as I see it now, I was healing inside and out.

"There must be a hundred millionaires living on big spreads in that part of Wyoming, cattlemen, oil, minerals, but I got to feeling there was no one richer than I was. It was all one big, beautiful thing. No one owned those mountains or forests any more than I did."

"Why didn't you stay there, Duro? Why didn't you *stay* George Jackson?"

"It happened slow at first, and then it happened fast, and I'm not sure I can explain it, Bonnie. Maybe I wasn't as good at being alone as I imagined, because the more I read, the more I *thought*—the more I got to wondering about Durham Lasari. He had to *be* for a reason. I began wondering whether or not if it wouldn't have been better if I'd been killed in Vietnam, an honorable casualty, not a deserter."

"I can't believe you mean that," Caidin said.

"It was a slow process, like I said, but it was a conclusion I almost arrived at. You see, there's a little park in the heart of Jackson, maybe a block square, with an entrance at each corner. To go into the park, on any pathway, you have to walk under twenty-foot arches of elk antlers all piled up and hooked together, horns shed by the wild elk each spring. Tourists like to have their pictures taken there, but for me that park became an obsession, a magnet. Those gateways, all those gray, twisted, pointed horns were like big crowns of thorns. It was like Christ was there, a suffering place. It got so I'd visit that park every day of my life, even when it was fifteen below.''

He had begun to pace again, his hands pushed deep in his pockets, as if he were keeping them under control. "See if this makes any sense to you, Bonnie. In the dead center of that park is a memorial to all the war dead of Teton County, a base made of big mountain stone and then a four-sided plaque with names on it. At the very top there's a little bronze statue, not a soldier, not a marine, but a cowboy in chaps on a bucking horse and the cowboy has his hat in his hand and his head is bowed. You know he's not going to make it.

"You have to squint to read the names on those plaques because the bronze has gone black with weather. There are three hundred names there, maybe more, veterans who died in Europe, the Pacific, Korea, Vietnam.

"And this is what I wonder if you can understand, Bonnie. That memorial became part of my life. If I had to work late, I'd go there after dark. I memorized every name on that monument like they were my buddies. It was like a spiritual thing, like I wanted to be close to them. Their deaths hurt me. I think I prayed for them. I began to wonder why my life was spared, why I was alive. I didn't know if I should be happy or guilty, but I sure as hell was feeling *something*.

"Then one day it was like a mirage, a trick of the eye. I found the spot on that memorial where my name could or should have been—between LaRue, J. D., Colonel, World War II and Laughrey, T. W., Sergeant, World War I. I could almost read it there. D. F. Lasari, Private, Vietnam . . .''

"I know what you're saying," Bonnie said softly. "You wanted to be accounted for, you wanted to put your true name up there. Durham Francis Lasari, United States Army."

"Yes," he said. "I wanted to be myself. I didn't want to be George Jackson forever. I didn't want to be running scared for a lifetime and I didn't want to be ashamed.''

He looked down at Bonnie intently, not speaking, lost in his own thoughts. She poured the last of the second bottle of Bardolino into the glasses and then bent over one of the low candle flames to light a cigarette.

"You might as well tell me the rest of it, Duro. You left Wyoming almost a year ago, you've been living and working in Calumet for months, and yet you didn't come over to the Vets' Bureau till last evening."

Lasari sat down beside her on the rug, his long legs stretched out in front of him. He pulled at the stiff denim of his jeans with two fingers, loosening the fabric where it stretched tight over his upper thigh. He took the glass of wine she offered and nodded his thanks.

"It wasn't until weeks later that I really knew what happened to me." He reached over and put his big hand over Bonnie's as it rested lightly on the beige carpet. "It was like everything you hear about, delayed shock reaction, flashback anxiety, the terrors of 'Nam, of getting hit, hurting, bleeding, all that self-loathing that built up in the hospitals . . ."

"I'm listening," she said softly.

"It was last March, still deep in winter up there. A friend of mine sprained his wrist skiing so I took over for him. He was night maintenance at the Snow King Resort. The sauna there is open till midnight, so I went in about a quarter to twelve to start clean-up. I had a pail and brushes and antiseptic to sluice down the redwood.

"There was still one guy there, sitting on the top shelf with a towel around him, a big fellow with sandy hair. He was quiet, and it was hot as hell in there, but I could feel him looking at me. I had on a pair of swim trunks, nothing else, and he was watching every move I made. Just another queer, that's what I though at first. A lot of jocks get a kick out of swinging both ways, especially out of town, and I knew that. So I decided to hurry up and cut out of there.

"I started to wash down the shelf just below him. Then I realized what he was staring at was not *me*, but the scars on my leg. On the lower calf, it doesn't show much, just a little zigzag like red lightning. But the big one, the wound that gave me trouble, is high up on my thigh, mostly on the inside; the ammo came in right below the crotch and came out the other side. I remember I looked down at myself that night and saw the heat of the sauna had reddened up the natural skin leg so the scar almost stood out by itself, like purple crayon on paper."

"Which leg was hit?"

He took her hand and brought it onto his right leg. Taking one finger, he guided it to trace his calf, then the outside of his thigh and then the inner side.

"I don't want to hurt you," she said, as she moved her hand over the denim.

"No, you couldn't do that," he said. "As it healed, it all pulled together, the whole area got smaller. Now the big scar is about six inches long and about three inches at the widest part."

He paused and looked at Bonnie's small, pale hand, motionless except for a slight movement at the tips of the fingers.

"Out of nowhere, Bonnie, the man in the sauna said, 'You've healed up nicely, soldier. 'Nam, right? About eight or ten years ago a high velocity rifle, probably an AK–47. It would take one of those to fracture the leg, blow out the muscle, do that kind of destruction.'

" 'Soldier,' he called me. I stood there. I couldn't run *or* answer him. It wasn't just aphasia. The guy knew so much about me, I felt completely vulnerable, like someone paralyzed or dying. He kept talking, told me why the outer ridges were that color, all reddish blue, and the healed, covering skin gray, almost shiny, like you could see through it.

" 'Four pins in the bone,' I remember he said that and then, 'They probably sewed you up too fast in 'Nam and that could cause a deep infection. Who did the final job on you? It looks like Fitzsimons, Colonel Brown's work. Brown could give you a clean leg like that . . .'

"I hadn't said a word, Bonnie, and the man was reading me like a map. He knew what had happened to me. I was sick, I panicked. It was like I was in 'Nam all over again. One of the hardest blows to a soldier, psychologically, is to have to admit he was hit, that the magic didn't work for him. Some people can never face it. A buddy in the hospital had lost both legs to a land mine. He could never say the world 'leg' to me, to the doctors, to anyone. He called those stumps 'the girls.' One leg he called Agnes, the other one Irma. The only way he could discuss treatment, rehabilitation, pain, anything, was to say 'since Agnes left me,' or 'now that Irma is gone.' He could have stood being jilted by women, but he couldn't stand to admit his own body had betrayed him.

"I didn't want the guy in the sauna to *know* about me. I didn't want to admit what had happened. I wanted to shout at him—who are you, how do you know me? Are you Army, somebody they sent after me? Nothing came out but my face must have showed what I was feeling.

"The man said, 'I'm sorry, soldier, I didn't know you felt that way. I'm a doctor at St. John's, an orthopedist. I just wanted to talk to you . . .'

"Bonnie, I threw the bucket of cleaning water onto the coals, made steam all over the place, and ran out. I wasn't even sure then he *was* a doctor, that he wasn't following me. The last thing I remember was the man shouting after me, 'Remember, soldier, you can live with it . . .'

"At six the next morning I caught the first bus out of Jackson. I went south to Phoenix, then west to San Diego. It took me weeks to convince myself the man was a true medic, that he wasn't out looking for me. Eventually, I got to Calumet City and decided I didn't want to run anymore.

"I'd be a fool to get myself a prison sentence if I don't have to. That's why I came to your office last night, to find a solution. The scars on my legs, I'll always have them, I know that. The scars on the inside, well, they're just not as raw as they used to be. I've got myself believing what the doctor said, 'Soldier, you can live with it.' I'm convinced, Bonnie, I can work it out."

Against the rough cloth of his jeans Bonnie's hand looked almost like the hand of a child, the nails rounded and pink, without a trace of polish. Lasari bent forward suddenly and kissed it.

"Except for Carlos, I've talked to you more than I've talked to any person in my whole life," he said.

She sat very still, watching him and the sound of her breathing was light and shallow in the quiet room. "Duro," she said, "I'd like to look at your scars, I'd like to touch them."

"As long as you're not sorry for me."

"It's not that at all," she said, "I want to know more about you."

"Can we go into the bedroom, Bonnie?"

"That's what I meant," she said.

# Chapter Seventeen

LASARI LAY ON his back and watched the pinpoints of light playing on the ceiling. The bathroom door was ajar and the bulbs around the mirror refracted light from cologne bottles on the dressing table, Bonnie's empty wineglass and the illuminated hands of the alarm clock beside the bed. She had fallen asleep in his arms and he didn't want to awaken her. It was almost half-past two.

With a sigh Bonnie turned on her side, away from him, stretching her legs and putting both hands under her cheek. The faint light was white on her shoulders and he could trace the slim, delicately ridged outline of her spine from her neck down to the small of her back. He pulled up the blanket and tucked it around her shoulders.

Her phone began to ring.

"Want me to get it, Bonnie?" he asked, but she had come awake instantly and reached for the phone, her arm like ivory in the dappled shadows.

"It has to be for me," she said, and then, "Hello?"

She listened for a moment and then he heard the sharp intake of her breath as she swung her legs over the side of the bed and pushed her hair away from her face.

"Christ!" she said, the single word straining the muscles in her throat. "Christ, Doobie!"

Lasari snapped on the bedside lamp. Bonnie sat with her back to them, but with her face turned in profile so he could see the stricken look in her eyes.

"Where'd they take him? Where did it happen?"

Lasari got out of bed and reached for his clothes. As he pulled on his jeans, he whispered, "What is it, Bonnie?"

She made a silencing gesture with her hand and shook her head. Tears formed in her eyes. Lasari took her robe from the foot of the bed and put it around her shoulders.

"But he's not dead, he has a chance they say . . ." She listened and then said, "Hold it, Doobie." She swiveled around and began writing rapidly on a phone pad.

Lasari buttoned his shirt and went into the kitchen, turned on the stove under a kettle and opened closet doors. He found instant coffee and two mugs, and when the kettle whistled he poured the boiling water over the coffee. The shower in the bathroom was running.

Lasari carried the mugs of hot coffee into the front room and set them on a table near the door. Then he returned to the kitchen and knocked some ice cubes loose from a freezer tray. The ice had dissolved into slivers in the mugs when Bonnie came into the room wearing slacks and a sweater and belting her raincoat. Her face was white and still with shock, almost expressionless.

"Here's some coffee," Lasari said. "It's cool enough to drink."

"Mark Weir was shot about an hour ago. That was his partner who called me, DuBois Gordon. He wasn't with him. God knows what Mark was doing at Cabrini Green alone. Good God, he should be smarter than that!"

"How bad is it, Bonnie?"

She shook her head. "They don't know yet. He's at Henrotin Hospital." Her lips were stiff, the words slurred as if they were too painful to utter. "The ambulance took him to Henrotin. That's West Oak Street, number one, one, one. It's about eight blocks from Cabrini Green, no more than that. Henrotin . . . emergency surgery."

"I'd better come with you," he said.

"No, no, Duro, please!" she said quickly. "Almost the last thing Mark said was for you to wait here, not to go into the street. I'll call you from the hospital if Mark's going to make it . . ." Her voice was almost a whisper. ". . . or else I'll be right back, Duro."

He touched her cheek gently but his face was hard and

thoughtful. "This changes things, Bonnie. I'll wait here till six o'clock, that's all I agreed on. Your lieutenant's one thing, God help him, but I'm another. I'll do better on my own."

She nodded and said, "I understand. I'll knock three times when I come back, three sharp raps and you'll know who it is. Three, Duro. Don't open for anyone else . . ."

In the elevator to the garage Bonnie felt in her purse for the key ring. She clenched it in her hand, the keys glinting sharply as she checked them through her tears.

Central had reached Sergeant Gordon at home. Mark had been conscious when he got to the hospital, Gordon had been told. Staff had met the ambulance at the emergency entrance with plasma and oxygen. Mark's eyes were in focus, the head nurse reported, and he was breathing on his own when the aides lifted him from the stretcher to the gurney. The doctor on duty asked the lieutenant what happened, who had shot him, but the patient had frowned and slipped into unconsciousness without being able to speak . . .

The sublevel parking area in her building was lighted by a series of overhead bulbs encased in heavy metal frames. A patterned grid of light and shadows was thrown across the pavement and parked cars.

As Bonnie hurried across the garage, separating the car key from others on the ring, a shadow fell across her face and she turned, sucking in her breath. A tall man she did not know was facing her, his arm already swinging toward her face. She had never been struck so hard in her life. The jaw and cheek went numb and her vision was distorted into surrealistic patterns by a pressure that seemed to be exploding inside her head.

She was on her knees, whimpering, the key ring on the cement floor beside her, when the man's hands closed on her shoulders, lifted her to her feet and slammed her against the car.

She thought she heard movement from behind parked cars but could see no one. Sergeant Karl Malleck held her with one hand, putting the bulk of his body between her and the two men standing in shadows.

"Lady, we think you're harboring a deserter," he said. "You cooperate with us, we'll overlook—"

She drew her breath to scream but the man slapped her so hard that the sound died in her throat and blood spurted from her lip.

"Don't give us any goddamn hysterics or heroics, lady." Malleck put a hand in her hair and gripped it tightly, forcing her head back until Bonnie's eyes were staring straight up into the lights.

"All right, I'm gonna ask you just once," Malleck said. "These good men are going upstairs now and get that deserter. You got a signal to alert him, some way to let him know it's his sweetie? Tell us your plan and there won't be no trouble. The boys will knock or ring like you say and they'll take Mr. Lasari nice and quiet."

Bonnie drew a deep breath and fought back hysteria. The pain in her scalp was excruciating. With explosive strength she spat directly into Malleck's face.

He smiled amiably and said, "I like that, ma'am. Shows spirit."

"You animal," she said, "you sadistic, fucking *animal*."

"But I never like a cunt with a dirty mouth," Malleck said his voice almost conversational. "Never. Some ladies think it's smart, a sexy turn-on, but I find it disgusting."

Joe Castana glanced down and saw Bonnie's key ring on the garage floor. He bent to pick it up, concealing the keys in the cup of his hand. He looked at his watch and then at the empty car ramp leading outward to the street.

"You're calling the shots, sir, but we ain't got all night," he said.

"Little lady," Malleck said. "I want to make myself clear. You keep up this dirty talk and refuse to cooperate and the boys will kick in the door to your apartment, then they'll kick the deserter's face in and *then* they'll take him away nice and quiet. You go on being a foul-mouthed cunt and it's gonna cost that ginny his teeth."

"Four knocks," she said. "Four sharp ones. I said I'd knock four times."

Her mouth was so full of blood that the words were muffled and indistinct. "What's that, Miss?" Malleck said. "Speak up."

She swallowed and said, "Four times . . . four knocks, god-damn you!"

"There goes that dirty mouth of yours again," he said. "Okay, boys, you heard her. Go up and get the yellow bastard. Mark the sonofabitch up good, make sure he puts up a fight. We'll want pictures if there's a court-martial . . ."

Malleck's hand was still clutching her hair, holding her head rigid, but Bonnie could hear the footsteps of the two men receding toward the elevator. Before she could try to scream Malleck struck her again with his open hand and she fell to the floor beside the car, her handbag tumbling from her limp fingers. Her hair spread against the oily concrete floor and a ray of light fell across her throat, limning the pulse of her bruised carotid artery.

Malleck knelt beside her, flexing his big hands. He crouched in the half shadow until the floor indicator above the elevator stopped at number ten.

At that moment headlights flashed into the garage and a car came down the ramp from the street level. Malleck moved closer to Bonnie's sprawled figure, concealing her fallen body with his bulk.

The car pulled into a parking slot on the opposite side of the garage. A man climbed out, staggering slightly as he slammed the car door. He tried to lock the car, but the keys dropped from his hand. Twice he circled the car, moving his feet over the floor in a shuffle. Then he laughed with drunken annoyance, left his car and disappeared through a door that led to the street lobby of the building.

Within a few moments the man returned with a uniformed doorman carrying a flashlight. Malleck noted that the elevator had started down, passing from the tenth floor to the ninth, then the eighth, en route to the garage.

The doorman found the tenant's car keys, locked the car door and dropped the keys into the man's coat pocket.

Bonnie stirred slightly. Malleck drew back his arm and waited, concentrating on the pulsing blue vein in her neck.

As the doorman and the swaying tenant went out of view, the doors of the garage elevator slid open and Neal and Castana emerged with Duro Lasari supported between them, his head hanging forward from his sagging shoulder, a bright smear of blood on his mouth and forehead.

Malleck chopped his big hand down at Bonnie's pulsing throat but the delay caused by the drunken tenant had broken his concentration and the knife-hard edge of his hand missed the carotid artery and struck her slender jaw instead, sending a ripple fracture through it with a sound as delicate as a snapping twig.

Scrambling to his feet Malleck ran to his parked car and pulled open the trunk. The two soldiers threw Lasari's limp body inside, slammed shut the lid and within seconds the car had roared out of the underground garage, braked at the street exit, then moved out smoothly to merge with the Chicago night traffic.

# Chapter Eighteen

DAWN LIGHT WAS streaking near the X-14th Command Armory as Detective Frank Salmi parked his unmarked squad car and walked the two blocks to the old building, footsteps echoing in the silence. The man's normally sallow face was pale and he moved with his shoulders hunched forward, as if breasting a cold wind. Outside Sergeant Malleck's office he rapped, then pushed open the door.

Malleck was at his desk, typing out a report, talking aloud as he worked, his voice sounding out over the clatter of the typewriter. Sergeants Neal and Castana stood at ease on either side of the door. Detective Salmi took off his hat and waited nervously while Malleck changed papers in the machine. Without turning the sergeant said, "Well, Salmi, can we say 'mission accomplished'?"

"Yes," Salmi said heavily, "Lieutenant Weir died about forty minutes ago on the operating table."

"He have anything to say, any statement?"

"He never regained consciousness . . ."

Malleck swiveled around in his chair and looked hard at the three men. "Then the lieutenant is no longer a part of our problem, is he?" He stared at Salmi. "You don't know me as well as my men here, Salmi, but I've always been a positive thinker. So now I'm gonna tell you what I *like* about our current situation. We are all in on this and we're going to stick together. Nobody can save himself by second thoughts anymore. Who fired the bullets is immaterial. Might have been

**137**

Neal, might have been the Mex here. They both used imported, foreign-made guns so ballistics can't trace anything back to army issue. But we're all in on it."

Eddie Neal grinned and said, "Let's give credit where credit is due, Sarge. Castana's the hot shot, he won all the medals in the division shootout."

"You shit!" Castana said, staring at Neal. "You red-necked, two-timing *shit!*"

Eddie Neal chuckled in an embarrassed fashion, as if deflecting a compliment, and said, "Kind of hard words you're laying on your best buddy, Mex. I'm not saying for sure it was you put him down . . ."

"Shut up, both of you," Malleck said. "We don't say one more fucking word about this, you understand? I knew it was going to happen, so I'm an accomplice, Frank Salmi set it up . . ." He paused. "*Detective* Salmi buzzed Weir on the police radio, said he was a concerned citizen, that he had a tip on the Private Lewis case. It was Salmi who asked his *compadre* for a meet at Cabrini Green . . ."

"I told him what you said I should, that I was kin to Mrs. Lewis. I thought you wanted to meet the lieutenant to make a deal. That's all I knew."

"Did you go into a bad-ass nigger act on the phone for your buddy, Salmi?"

The detective's face went gray. "I'm not a clown, Malleck," he said. "I'm an officer of the law. I made a certain phone call because you asked for it." He took a step toward Malleck and lowered his voice. "Listen, sergeant, those other wipeouts, you said they were matters of expediency. I understand that. But Weir . . . a fellow officer. You didn't tell me you were blowing him away."

"Spare me your man-with-a-badge shit, Salmi," Malleck said. "You don't give a damn what happened last night just so long as you keep on collecting your paycheck. We both know that."

Malleck took a bottle of whiskey from his desk drawer and poured a shot into a canteen cup, his face flushed with anger. "Like I just said, that part of our operation is over and done with. Weir was getting too smart, he was crowding us. Now we go on to the next phase."

He tapped the paper in his typewriter. "I'm preparing a report to cover Lasari."

He began to read in a mocking, singsong voice. "Our first tip came from Chicago Police Detective Frank Salmi who noted a suspicious car near an unofficial veterans' office and checked plates. Such information was turned over to us and we checked Army reports. Learning the subject was a deserter, currently employed in Calumet City, Privates Neal and Castana, operating on orders from First Sergeant Karl Malleck, went to Calumet City to attempt to locate the deserter, checked place of business, local bars and so forth. Army personnel located subject's rooming house, hoped to apprehend subject and bring peacefully into custody. Subject attempted to elude our surveillance and was declared fugitive."

Malleck looked at the other three men in the room and controlled an almost diffident smile. He was pleased with himself because this was an area of expertise he had mastered and felt at home with—the "truth" of records, the "sanctity" of clerical reports issued in quadruplicate on official paper, fake or real, marked and stamped and sealed with proper endorsement.

"Subject was surveilled from Indiana to state line and then to center city Chicago. Surveillance lost when subject left car. However, acting on an anonymous phone tip, we had reason to believe that the subject had barricaded himself in an apartment rented to one Bonnie Caidin."

Malleck smiled. "I added that little variation of the truth about a tip just to make the civilians look good. We never lost Lasari. When he parked his car in the lady's neighborhood, we knew exactly where he was going."

Malleck sipped his whiskey. "And on and on and so on and so on. When I finish the report, it's gonna read that Lasari resisted violently and had to be subdued with force. That's our story. It's clean, it's legal, and I can swear by these six stripes I wear that it will go down with the brass like a cold beer after a hot march.

"We got him by the balls on this. If Lasari doesn't buy the proposal I'm gonna make him, he's facing five or ten years minimum in a federal pen."

Malleck smiled easily. "Okay, get out now, all of you. Castana, tell Homer Robbins I'll want to see him in about an hour. Salmi, *adios* and *buena suerte.* Neal, go get yourself a real GI haircut and make a request for some new uniforms. You may be doing some traveling. But first, tell Scales to bring

Lasari in here. I want to talk to him alone. I'm gonna take that yellow prick up to the mountaintop and show him the promised land."

Salmi said unexpectedly, "I want to make one thing clear before we break up this meeting. You guys think you got some kind of protection because you wear the same uniform. Well, don't try to double-cross me just because I'm not part of the club. If it ever slips that I fingered Mark Weir—even if I didn't know I was doing that—he's got a lot of friends in this town who might want to shorten my life expectancy. Nobody likes going down alone, just remember that."

Malleck said, "Frank, if there's one thing I got no use for, it's a whiner. As I remember, *you* came to *me* with a sad story, wanting in on this action cause you had contacts with Mr. M. Me and my soft heart, I bought your story—five kids that you want to educate and you gotta keep feeding them first. You don't want 'em on drugs, you don't want 'em turning into the kind of spics that's made this city a cesspool. You wanted to be Santa Claus, the big daddy. You wanted a better shake for your kids. Well, you're going about it in the American way, Salmi. You're *paying* for it."

The report was typed in quadruplicate in stilted Army language on appropriate forms without erasures or strikeovers, addressed to one Lieutenant Colonel Edwin Facknor, Special Processing Department, Fort Lincoln, Illinois. The subject was Francis Durham Lasari.

Seated in front of Malleck's desk, his face and lips dark with dried blood, Duro Lasari read the account of the charge against him. The report was studded with ponderous, quasi-technical jargon—"subject was observed," "surveillance commenced at 1900 hours," "acting on information received" and "subject advised of charges according to Articles of War." It ran four and one-half pages.

When Lasari finished reading the report, he looked directly at Malleck, waiting for him to speak. Lasari had spent the night on the floor of an old tack room at the Armory, a chill, dark place that still smelled of saddle soap and horse leather. About an hour ago, a black orderly had brought him coffee and aspirin and whispered, "I'm not going to wash you up , man. Tops don't want me to do you nothin'."

Lasari was unclear about what had happened at the apartment last night only minutes after Bonnie had left. There had been the turn of a key, the door bursting open suddenly, and the crunch of a zap against the side of his head. He had been aware of two men, but the movement had been so swift he hadn't really seen them. They must have struck him again, adding other injuries after he was unconscious from the first blow. He had been dimly aware of sick, antic laughter.

He was not sure where he was now, but he was well aware of the sergeant's immaculate and perfectly creased uniform, the rows of campaign ribbons and the man's stern and tanned facade, an impeccable but ruthless military facade.

Finally, Sergeant Malleck said, "Lasari, I've looked over your records and you've got a pretty fair IQ, so you gotta know you're into this shit up to your shoulders. Make one little slip and you go all the way under."

"I was planning to turn myself in. I can prove that, sergeant."

"Too bad you never got around to it, soldier."

Although he knew he had little to bargain with, Lasari said, "First off, I want to know how you found me. How did you know where I was?"

"I think this will go faster if you just hear me out." Malleck stood and began pacing, rubbing his big hands together. The movement caused the muscles to flex in his upper arms.

"It couldn't be Carlos," Lasari said flatly.

"I told you the ground rules, soldier. You'd better start listening."

"And it couldn't be the Vets' Bureau. She told me that was confidential."

"Now we got two ways to go," the sergeant said, pausing to look down at Lasari. "You can pretend you didn't hear what I told you and keep up these damned fool questions, but I sure as hell wouldn't advise that. Or you can sit there and listen to what I'm going to tell you about that report on my desk." Malleck tapped the report with a blunt forefinger.

"You're looking at five to ten years in the federal pen, and I don't give a shit one way or the other. I don't like deserters. Not that you're a yellow bastard, you didn't walk out on your buddies under fire, but the reason I don't give a shit about you is because deserting is *dumb*. You're a stupid fucker, a stupid *ginzo* idiot.

"You could've stayed Army, tried stealing from the

quartermaster, made money on the black market or arranged some kickbacks, I'd say fine. You could've used your military career to better yourself, trade dollars for bigger profits, buy yourself some real estate with a slope partner, run some whores, all that can make sense. Or if you lack guts for business, just do your duty, brownnose the officers and wind up with a pension and a one-bedroom condo in Fort Lauderdale."

Malleck leaned against his desk and crossed his arms. He felt an uncontrollable flush on his cheeks and an agitated, heavy stroke to his heartbeat. He would have liked to take a drink of whiskey but didn't dare break his poise.

"Want a cigarette, Lasari? Some coffee? I got a colored orderly makes the best coffee this side of New Orleans. Uses chicory and a fresh eggshell in it."

Lasari shook his head.

"Then let's get down to business," Malleck said. "If I send that report to Colonel Facknor, you'll be shipped out of here in handcuffs to Fort Lincoln, there'll be a court-martial that will last, if things move slowly, about fifteen to twenty minutes. I'll be called as a witness, so will my men, if need be."

Malleck grinned without humor and opened the top drawer of his desk. He took out a small, transparent bag of white powder. "Hell," he said, "we can make that court-martial go even faster. I'll change my report to read that we found contraband drugs right on the deserter's person. We can even have Scales decorate your right arm with a few needle marks. Scales is good at that."

Malleck pressed the buzzer on his desk and immediately the door opened and Private Scales put his head in. He avoided looking at Lasari.

"Bring me a pot of coffee and one cup, Scales. On the double."

When the door closed Malleck resumed pacing, cracking his knuckles and twisting his hands together in the same powerful motion, muscles bunching in his arms and neck.

"I'm going to tell you something about Karl Malleck now, soldier," he said, "so you can evaluate exactly the position you're in. The one thing going for you, and I'm telling you this frankly, is that we share one thing in common. We both got fucked by that goddamned Vietnam war. Sometimes I think the U.S. got into that war just to get rid of a lot of second-class citizens. I was there. Maybe I didn't see the fighting you did, but I was there. I paid my dues. But we were greeted like a bunch of crazy killers when we got home, right? You see any parades, any welcoming committees? I didn't. A bunch of egghead congressmen and gutless generals and mealy-mouthed Jews and Catholic liberals, they saw to that.

"Pretty fucking funny when you think about it. Some guy with a stiff cock just like I got puts his collar on backward or wears a skullcap and lets his fucking sideburns grow and suddenly he's got the right to get on a soapbox and tell the world what immoral fuckers you and me are.

"A lot of poor slobs cracked under that. They missed those bands playing, thought they'd earned it. But I don't have much respect for them either, Lasari. Most of them are a bunch of fuckups. They crept home with their tails between their legs and hands out like trained monkeys for G.I. rights, disability payments, psychiatric treatment, for Christ's sake, pissing up a storm for ramps and handrails for their goddamn wheelchairs, whining about 'delayed stress syndrome,' like they were the only fucking generation that ever fought a war."

Malleck hesitated a moment, then opened a desk drawer and poured two inches of whiskey into a canteen cup and sipped it greedily, running a rough, red tongue over his lips.

"When I point out we got something in common, that means I may *sympathize* with you, but it doesn't mean I *respect* you." He pointed a thumb at the three rows of service ribbons on his chest. "I respect men who *take* what they deserve, even if it means making up their own rules. That's what I've done with this outfit. We formed our own kind of welcoming committee, we reward ourselves. If life ain't drained all the guts and manhood out of you, you can be part of it, Lasari. Battles aren't fought on maps, you and I know that. Sure, I went over your combat record, but that's ancient history. It's what the Army's gonna know about you *now* that counts, what's on that report you're looking at. Typed up on the right forms, initialed in the right places, endorsed by the proper stamps, that's the paper truth this man's Army runs on.

"So here's the deal. I can take that report back, tear it up and write something else . . ."

"*Whatever* you write about me is the truth, is that what you're telling me, sergeant?"

Malleck shrugged. "What I write is *accepted* as truth, so what the fuck's the difference?"

Private Scales entered with a pot of coffee and a single cup and placed them on Malleck's desk next to the small packet of heroin. Scales looked at the sergeant for a moment and then Lasari, his face and eyes impassive. Leaving the office, he closed the door carefully behind him.

Malleck lifted the pot of steaming coffee and poured some into the cup of whiskey. "I like a little pickup," he said, "because I don't take sugar and cream. Sure you won't have some?"

Lasari shook his head. "I don't want to jangle my nerves," he said dryly. "I think you're about to make me an offer."

"Okay," Malleck said, "this is it. We want you back in the Army but only for a limited engagement. I do the paperwork, send it to the right desks, make a phone call or two, and you'll be sent for duty with an army division on a ready-alert status in Colorado. I work fast, you catch up with them. It's an out-fit that's scheduled for an airborne trip to Germany, some field work, then some action in an integrated NATO field exercise on the Czech border. You're gonna be our new pigeon. For now, Lasari, that's all you need to know and that's all you're gonna know. The right people will contact you at the right time and tell you exactly what's expected of you. When it's over, you're on your own."

"What makes you think the Army computers won't cough up the truth about Durham Lasari?"

"Because this is one trip Lasari ain't gonna take," Malleck said. "You're going back into uniform as a man with a good, clean record—George Jackson."

"Yeah, but I have only your word that I get out of this a free man."

Malleck shrugged and held the canteen cup close to his face, sniffing at the warm fumes of whiskey.

"You're between a rock and a hard place, soldier," he said. "You got only one friend left in this world and you're looking at him. Maybe 'friend' is the wrong word because we both know I wouldn't give you a glass of water in hell if you couldn't pay for it. You take the offer I just made you, or you pick the federal slammer, peddling your ass to horny blacks just to keep alive and get cigarette money. Make up your own mind. Don't come to me for sympathy. If you're looking for sympathy, it's between 'shit' and 'sweat' in the dictionary and that's the *only* place you'll find it. But I'm willing to help you, Lasari, because you can help me. Everybody else has already fucked you over good."

. . . "*everybody else has already fucked you over good*" . . . Lasari felt a tightening of rage and emotion in his throat muscles so strong that he could barely speak.

"That brings us back to our first question, sergeant. I want to know how you found me . . ."

Malleck shook his head in mock sadness. "Why don't you *use* that bright IQ of yours, soldier? The little newspaper cunt has been on my payroll from the beginning."

As he came out of his chair, Lasari was sure of only one thing, to touch Malleck violently, to make a connection between their flesh, to hurt him as he'd been hurt, and he did that by swinging his foot high and arched over the desk, catching the sergeant squarely in the stomach and knocking him to the floor.

Lasari scrambled across the desk, scattering files, and grabbed the neck of the whiskey bottle. Leaping toward Malleck's back, he swung the bottle toward the big man's head, but Malleck jerked an elbow into Lasari's face, knocking him aside and sending the bottle shattering against a wall.

Standing now, his face tight with anger, Malleck drew back his foot and slammed it into Lasari's side. It was a potentially murderous kick, even fatal if the victim tried to roll away from it, exposing his kidneys, spleen and testicles. But Lasari was trained in unarmed combat and he swung the full weight of his body forward into the force of Malleck's swinging leg, blocking its destructive power and toppling the sergeant off balance.

Castana and Homer Robbins burst into the room, with Eddie Neal just behind them. Neal pushed the other men aside and said, in his honeyed drawl, "You all let me have him, sarge. You don't have to take this shit."

"Stay back!" Malleck shouted at the man. "Don't come near this ginny bastard!" The sergeant locked his hands together and brought them down like a swinging axe against the back of Lasari's neck.

Lasari fell to the floor, his cheek wet with his own blood,

whiskey stinging the cuts in his face. He knew that Malleck was going to kick him in the ribs and there was nothing he could do about it. He experienced a curious, almost therapeutic disorientation. He knew he was alone again, he had always been alone, alone in his childhood, alone in 'Nam, alone in Jackson Hole, and now once again. That's what Malleck wanted him to know.

The sergeant was panting heavily. "You just don't think good, ginzo," he said. "You hear any knocks last night? You were waiting for knocks, weren't you? My men opened the door and walked right in, don't you know that?"

Malleck kicked him in the side and Lasari began to retch, feeling the acid bile rushing into his throat.

"Who do you think gave us the fucking key, you ginny bastard?" Those were the last words Duro Lasari remembered hearing.

# Chapter Nineteen

EVEN THOUGH HE had not gone to bed, Scotty Weir went through the motions of waking up to a new day. The logs in the study fireplace had long since burned down to a white ash and he knew by the chill in the room that there would be a frost on the fields, some ice on the backroads.

He made coffee in the kitchen, careful not to wake Grimes, then showered in his upstairs bathroom, put on his jogging clothes and spiked running shoes, and went back to the study.

The general opened the gun cabinet and took out a Winchester and a .410 Purdy that had been given to him by a British captain he'd served with during the early years of the German occupation. After his run he planned to call Laura Devers to ask if she'd join him for a few hours of pheasant shooting on the grounds. Maybe they wouldn't shoot at all, much as he loved to kick up a few pheasant from the bramble bushes, but a walk through the fields might soothe his restlessness. He could circle back to the house around lunchtime to check Grimes on whether Stigmuller had called in.

Scotty Weir hooked a flashlight to his waistband and poured himself a half mug of coffee, letting himself out the back door to walk along the graveled driveway toward the entrance gate. He paused there, sipped his coffee and listened to the silence of the predawn day.

From the direction of the house he thought he heard a phone ring and stopped to listen, but he heard nothing.

147

Scotty Weir hung his empty coffee mug on the branch of a wineberry bush and set off jogging down the road, the flashlight throwing bouncing circles of light to guide his footsteps.

When he turned into the gate again an hour later, the dogs were at the end of the drive to greet him, barking, tails wagging. That meant that Grimes had been up to feed them and open the gates of the kennel run. But it was the sight of John Grimes himself, standing halfway down the drive, that sent a chill of premonition through Scotty Weir's body.

Grimes was waiting for him, without coat or jacket, head bare to the winds, his face broken and collapsed with emotion. Weir ran toward him and then stood still, hand on the dogs' heads to quiet them.

"Something's happened to Mark, is that it, Grimes? Tell me yourself. I don't want to hear it from strangers."

"He's dead, sir. He was shot last night, somewhere in the city."

Weir put a hand on Grimes' thick, hard shoulder and gripped it hard. For a moment the two men stood on the open ground between the old farmhouse and the rimed fields, faces firming and hardening gradually, by training and habit, into acceptance of what could not be changed. The hurt and loss and real pain would come later, the general knew, but still he allowed himself a moment now to imagine what this day could have meant if Mark had driven down to see him yesterday as Bonnie Caidin had suggested.

"Grimes, pack me a bag for a day or so, and bring the car around. Can you do that for me?"

"Certainly, sir," Grimes said. "And do you want me to call Mrs. Devers?"

The general shook his head. "No, I'll call her myself from Chicago. Let her enjoy the morning. She'll hear soon enough, good lady."

The two men drove to the county morgue in an unmarked squad car, Sergeant DuBois Gordon at the wheel, Tarbert Weir in the passenger seat, his bulky overcoat bunched up on his knees.

"You understand, sir, that I already made the official identification, not that there was any doubt. But I checked the morgue myself right after I called you," Gordon said.

"This is something I *want* to do," the colonel said and paused. "I hadn't been in touch with my son for some time."

"He told me," Gordon said. "He was real glad to talk to you yesterday . . ."

Mark Weir's body was wheeled into the viewing room and General Weir felt a stabbing memory, an anguished moment of comparison, as he remembered the first time he had seen his boy, an infant behind glass in the maternity ward of a hospital in Paris.

Lieutenant Weir was covered up to his chin with a sheet, and his face looked pale but peaceful, almost healthy, like a strong, young man determined to rest and restore himself.

"All the damage was done in the chest area," Gordon said. "Right through the ribs and the breastbone, front to back. There's not another mark on him."

"He was shot in the chest?"

"Yes," Gordon said. "Someone surprised him head on. He didn't even have time to draw his gun."

"And he was alone, you say?"

"Yes. We were both off duty last night but he got a tip and wanted to follow through. He should've waited, but you know Mark—stubborn as a mule. He said he got that from you."

"He told you he was stubborn like me?"

"And damned proud of it, sir."

Gordon reached down and rearranged Mark's hair with one hand, touching him gently, pushing the hair back from the smooth forehead. "We had a laugh about his hair just the other day," Gordon said. "Mark never liked to wear a hat, but I guess you know that, and we got caught outside in a snowstorm over by Navy Pier. His hair was full of snowflakes and he looked damned funny. I told him I knew just how he'd look when he got to be an old-timer." He paused thoughtfully. "I'd like to have had a Polaroid with me that day."

Gordon pulled at the morgue sheet, flattening out the wrinkles where the coarse cloth lay over Mark's chest. Underneath, Weir could see the outlines of heavy bandages.

"I guess I told you last night was my old man's birthday," Gordon said. "That's why the lieutenant couldn't reach me."

"No, you didn't," the general said and turned toward the exit door of the viewing room. He had longed to lift his hand, to touch his son's face one last time, but Tarbert Weir knew too well how the memory of cold, inert flesh can linger on the fingertips.

*     *     *

The aging housing development called Cabrini Green, named after the canonized saint, Mother Cabrini, who had once worked in Chicago, stands stark and forbidding, one-and-a-half square miles of isolated and dangerous real estate in center city, located a few blocks from the picturesque shoreline of Lake Michigan and the elegant, expensive apartment buildings on the city's Gold Coast.

A low-income, low-rent City Housing Authority project, Cabrini Green is comprised of a number of tall, boxlike brick buildings set on broad lawns of black asphalt, faintly traced here and there with the painted boundaries of shuffleboard courts and white free-throw lines facing rusted basketball hoops with tattered nets. The Green is home to more than thirteen thousand people, couples, singles, families and a collection of rent-paying floaters, pushers, junkies or pimps, street people who need a crash pad or a base.

Doobie Gordon nosed his car into a parking space in a row of blue and white police cars, each lettered with the slogan, "We Serve to Protect," and two large, black unmarked vans.

"Mobile labs," Gordon said. "They've been working since we got the call."

He got out of the car, locked his door and walked around to check the passenger side. "It may seem awful quiet around here to you, general, for such a big place. But except for some workers and the school kids, Cabrini is mostly night people and there's nothing to send folks outta sight like a cop killing. Of course, some of them got an early wakeup call from the fuzz today."

"All those squad cars?" Weir asked.

"Yes. We don't take the killing of a fellow officer lightly in this town," Gordon said grimly. "The order came through from the commissioner first thing this morning: 'Everything within the law, but if a knock doesn't open a door, that door comes off at the hinges.'"

Inside the shabby foyer, Gordon said, "We'll walk up to the third floor, then push for the elevator. I like to be sure it's coming up empty before I get in."

The stairs were cement, painted a dark green, steep and narrow, without handrails. "The Authority has given up replacing them," Gordon said. "Those metal handrails can be sawed up and made into street weapons. Same thing is true of the stuff in the laundry rooms. People just took the machines apart, used the pieces for other things. The basement area in every building is boarded up now. Tenants can use the kitchen sink or find a laundromat.''

The two men stepped out into a hallway on the third floor and Doobie Gordon pushed the elevator button. Tarbert Weir was aware of a strange, disturbing odor in the building. He took out his folded handkerchief and passed the clean cloth over his nose and mouth. There was a sensation of tasting the disquieting reek as much as smelling it.

''I hope the tenants get used to it,'' Gordon said, glancing at Weir. ''I know *I* never could. It's a combination of sweat, disinfectants, roach powder, and a little garbage let sit too long. It's a *poor* smell, not country poor or Eskimo poor, or Haiti poor, but American, big-city poor. It's something my people know a lot about . . .''

Little daylight filtered into the long, narrow corridors. Random light bulbs sheathed in wire casing played dim illumination over paint-chipped walls and hallways of closed doors, several covered over with accordion-steel meshings, reinforced by padlocks.

''It's legal,'' the sergeant said, gesturing at the heavy door protections. ''Either they're trying to hide something inside or keep someone out. But it's their space, the Authority respects that.''

The elevator, with a floor base no more than three feet by five feet, lurched to a stop and Sergeant Gordon slipped open the door, looking down to examine the floor before he said, ''It's okay, general. Sometimes there's stuff in here you wouldn't want to step in.''

On the seventeenth, top floor of the building, two policemen stood on either side of an apartment door. One of them nodded at Gordon, pulled a tagged key from his pocket and unlocked the door. Tarbert Weir and the sergeant stepped into an empty apartment.

It was a small layout, with low ceilings and squared corners, a living room and adjoining kitchen, two bedrooms with a shared closet and a bathroom with a stall shower. In the bathroom there was a toilet and a sink with a mirrored medicine cabinet, but the kitchen had a ravaged look, as if it had been gutted, the appliances wrenched out of the walls. The rooms were painted green and yellow and pink and the windows of the living room, two of them broken and jagged, looked out over Chicago's crowded inner city streets, narrow concrete canyons that ran through to Lake Shore Drive.

"Let me explain something to you," Gordon said. "No one lives on this floor. The Authority agreed to clear everyone out more than four years ago. It was a trouble area, just too high up. Any sign of trouble, the tenants could throw things down on the police cars. If the elevators jammed, it was a hell of a long run up those steps for a cop."

"Yet someone asked Mark to meet them here?"

Gordon nodded. "This address and apartment 1710, top floor, that's the numbers we took off Mark's radio tape."

"And Mark would follow up on a tip like that?"

Doobie Gordon looked thoughtful, then nodded. "It must have sounded kosher to Mark. It was a man, nervous, sloppy talker, no name, just said he was kin to Mrs. Amanda Lewis and she'd asked him to call. They had something to tell us about how her nephew got killed . . ."

"And what does this Mrs. Lewis say?"

"She's scared shitless, general, and that's the truth. Some of those small-town southerners never adjust to the big city. She's down at Central now with one of our matrons, trying to see if she can remember anything for us. And a couple of men are going through her apartment right now. Mrs. Lewis says Randolph Lewis was the *last* of her kin." Gordon swallowed hard, then wet his lips. "She's an old-fashioned lady, a Bible Baptist, and we'd *asked* her to call us. I think that's what suckered Mark last night . . ."

General Weir turned his eyes to the floor, forcing them to see what he knew he would find there—the outline of Mark's fallen body, traced with heavy white markings. The shape, legs sprawled, arms outcast, looked strangely diminutive to the general, as if a child had fallen there.

"You sure you want to be up here?" Gordon asked quietly.

"I want to know exactly what happened," Weir said.

"We don't know for sure yet," Gordon said. "We're building it. Everything's been dusted for fingerprints but we lifted dozens of them. The bullets were sent to the lab, they were fired from a Luger, that's a German-made gun with—"

"I know what a Luger is," Weir said.

"I know you do, sir. The guns that got Mark are 9mm Lugers, we're not sure of the model, hollow point ammo. The ammo tells ballistics both guns are clean bore, no flaws, no scratches . . .''

"How many bullets?"

"Two. Both through the front chest but from different distances."

"How could anyone get the jump on an experienced police officer in this small space?" Weir asked. "There's nowhere to go, nowhere to hide."

"Yes there is," Gordon said. "Look at this."

He stepped across a narrow hall to the bathroom and put his hands on either side of the mirrored medicine cabinet above the hand basin. He wiggled the mirror slightly and the motion made no sound but the whole cabinet came out in his hands.

"Look, sir," he said.

Scotty Weir stepped up to the neat, rectangular opening in the wall and looked through it. He experienced a tug at his senses, a deep feeling of disorientation. He found himself looking into the next apartment, and the next and the next, down six empty apartments, right to the end wall of the building. Every medicine cabinet had been removed.

"Here's how I see it," Gordon said. "Mark came upstairs alone last night, switched on the lights, saw the place was empty. He checked around the rooms, of course, thought he was early and alone and decided to wait.

"We figure there had to be a couple of guys staked up here. One of them lifted out this medicine cabinet from the next apartment—it comes loose both ways—and then the aim at Mark was like a shooting gallery from any apartment on this floor. Those openings in the wall are on an absolute plumb line. All they had to do was wait until he moved into position and call his name . . ."

Scotty Weir felt a sudden choking sensation of rage, then the unfamiliar feeling that he might black out. "Why is it so hot in here?" he said.

Gordon shrugged. "The Authority likes to keep the temperature at eighty-two degrees, seems to suit the folk who live here. Lots of white people'd tell you that the jungle bunnies are used to it, it's like the jungles in the old country. I think different. To me, it's a sop, a placebo. Overcrowding, roaches, night noises, well, nobody can ever complain they're *cold* in here."

"Everybody in Cabrini is black?"

"No, that wouldn't be democratic, would it?" Gordon said. "We've got a few whites but not many. One couple, real old, brother and sister, and he's in a wheelchair. She says she feels safer living right with them than getting mugged in a white neighborhood. Now the man who called the police last night, he's black, black as I am. Lives right below in 1610, full-time warehouse worker with a wife and four kids. He heard the gunshots and did what a citizen should. He called the police and he had to run four blocks to a pay phone to do it."

Tarbert Weir walked to one of the broken windows and leaned toward it, trying to breathe in fresh air. The breeze off the lake was cool and moist. There was a strange sound in the vacant apartment, almost like light music. Maybe that was what had distracted Mark last night, put him off his guard, Weir thought, the rumble and honking of street traffic below and up here the high, thin singing of wind as it came through the sharded glass.

"I really don't understand," he said wearily, "why these windows are smashed when no one lives here."

Gordon looked at him carefully. "I know all about your distinguished record down south during the days of the Freedom Marches. Mark was proud of that, too. I think you'll understand, general, a phrase some psychologists use—'the applause of objects.' Breaking glass, a farewell gesture of defiance, sometimes it's the only thing a black man has going for him."

The two men sat quietly in the third floor waiting room in Henrotin Hospital while the floor nurse made a call to check with Bonnie Caidin's doctor.

When she was brought into the hospital in the early morning, Bonnie Caidin, battered and savagely bruised, her eyes glazed with shock, had scrawled Sergeant Gordon's name on a piece of paper. Staff had summoned the sergeant from an emergency room downstairs where he was waiting for word on Mark Weir.

He'd called Miss Caidin, he told the general, because he felt Mark would want her there; they'd always stayed close. She was mugged and beaten in the basement garage of her apartment building. A tenant parking his car had seen her on the ground, called the police. Her assailant was white, big, that's all she could tell the responding officers. Her purse was found beside her, money and credit cards intact, but no keys. If robbery was the motive, the attacker must have been scared off.

He had lied to the young woman easily, he explained to the general; he had told her Mark was getting along fine.

"There's a fracture line in her jaw," Gordon told him. "She can write just a little and talk with her eyes. She put down her address for me and a name—Durham Lasari. I asked her if she wanted me to go there and she nodded. Then she wrote, 'Tell Mark—the *soldier*.' After that, they wheeled her away.

"I went to her apartment around eight this morning. There were coffee cups, dishes in the sink. The bed had been slept in. The whole place looked kinda messy but then maybe she's not a good housekeeper. There was nobody there."

"She said—'Tell Mark—the *soldier*'? Durham Lasari?"

"Yes."

"You sure she didn't say George Jackson?"

"She didn't *say* anything, general. She wrote it out—Durham Lasari. There's no mistake about that."

The floor nurse came back to say the doctor preferred Miss Caidin not to have visitors. She was heavily sedated and still in shock.

"Has her family been here?" Scotty Weir asked.

"No, her employer has been notified," the nurse said, "but it's our understanding that there's no immediate family nearby." She hesitated. "I can't go against doctor's orders, but if you gentlemen would like to look in on Miss Caidin from the doorway, I can tell her that when she wakes. She's been through a lot."

"Thank you, we'll do that," Tarbert Weir said.

Moments later, in the main lobby of the hospital, Weir said to Gordon, "I don't expect to be here for the funeral, so I'll want a moment alone now. I want to see where he died."

The two men walked around to the emergency entrance, a side doorway covered with a portico of squared glass. "They were ready for him here," Gordon said. "Started work right away. He was on oxygen and plasma before they wheeled him into emergency.

The emergency room was vacant. Three gurneys, in white

sheeting, stood in a row ten feet apart, every inch of the wall
behind them arranged with the tubings, masks, and rheostats
of life-saving equipment.

"Mark was there," Gordon said, pointing to the third
gurney at the far end of the room. "I'll wait for you outside."

General Weir walked to the empty gurney and stood beside
it, his eyes closed, his head bowed, trying to make a commun-
ion with his son, willing himself to accept the fact that on this
spot, breathing this same antiseptic air, Lieutenant Mark Weir
had ceased to be.

A voice behind him said, "Can I help you, sir? I'm the
nurse on duty here."

The general turned to see a stocky, fair-haired man, about
thirty-five, standing near the door. Weir introduced himself
and explained why he was there.

"I wasn't on duty when the lieutenant was brought in," the
nurse said, "but I read the records this morning. Everything
medically possible was done, sir, please believe that, but there
was little chance. The bullets had penetrated the back and
traveled through the lung cavities. There was bone splinter,
torn tissue, heavy bleeding. Your son was unconscious, sir, if
that helps. He didn't suffer after the first few moments."

Sergeant Gordon was already behind the wheel in the
hospital parking lot when Scotty Weir slid into the passenger
side.

"You lied to me, Gordon," he said. "Why in hell would
you lie to me about something like that?"

Gordon tightened his hands on the steering wheel until the
knuckles turned nearly white. "Would it occur to you that I
didn't want to *admit* that my buddy was shot in the back when
I wasn't there? Does it occur to you that I didn't want to even
*say* those words?"

The sergeant turned the key in the ignition, made a sharp
right and then maneuvered the car through the parking lot out
to West Oak Street. He said, "Well, are you glad you know?
How do you feel now that you know that Mark was bush-
whacked, that your boy didn't even see who shot him?"

"I feel like hell," Tarbert Weir said. "Or I'm *in* hell. I think
they're the same thing."

# Chapter Twenty

COLONEL BENTON SAT in his office on the fifth floor of the Pentagon Building, tapping his pencil on the report fanned out on his desk.

"How did General Stigmuller react?"

"He wasn't at his best, sir. The Weir murder in Chicago seems to have hit him pretty hard, personal friends, you know. As you suggested, I delivered and analyzed the report for him in person," Major Staub said. "He told me he'd relay our conclusions to General Weir. He's been trying to reach him himself all morning."

"Would this report have helped the lieutenant if it had reached him earlier?"

"No, not with the material we fed into the computer, sir. From official records and official Army papers, there *is* no connection between these four GIs. They served in different outfits, in different locations, and at different times. They all did leave West Germany on varying dates by way of the Frankfurt Main airport, but that's routine, the country's busiest point of egress, nothing to comment on there."

"And yes, they were all black, all in uniform, and all ended their lives in Chicago," the colonel said. "But we've got more than a third of a million troops in Germany and, as I reminded General Stigmuller, a lot of them are black, a lot of them are from Chicago. Coincidence perhaps, but not a pattern. I gave Stigmuller everything I could jam on those pages, right down to the demerits and good conduct ribbons—only one of those, incidentally—but there's nothing there that ties the four men into the operation in which we're interested.''

Major Staub was seated on a leather-cushioned window seat, a bright morning sun warming his back. ''Colonel,'' he said, ''what do we know about Mark Weir's death?''

''I've talked to Police Superintendent Clarence McDade in Chicago twice this morning. Weir was a service veteran, you know, but our interest in the matter is the welfare and sensitivities of his father, General Tarbert Weir, retired. McDade understood that, of course. There are no suspects as of this hour, but McDade's people are exploring every angle. They're taking a special look at recently paroled criminals, old arrest sheets, anything that Mark Weir might have worked on that would indicate a grudge killing . . .''

He paused and looked intently at Staub. ''And to answer what is your *real* question, Merrill—no, we had nothing to do with it.''

He turned his attention to Captain Jetter. ''And Froggie here has been keeping abreast of our other interests in Chicago. The picture is developing as we saw it. Sergeant Malleck has been his own efficient self. He made a few specific phone calls, we audited them. The new courier designate is now part of the operation, he is on schedule. We will continue to proceed as planned.''

Captain Jetter nodded and said with a slight smile, ''And I'd like to add, sir, that sorry as I am for the young police officer and his family, I surmise the death of his son might just take General Weir off our backs.''

Benton turned to stare at the captain and all the manifestations of his hangover, the pulsing capillaries, the cold sweat, the sting of his reddened eyeballs, seemed to multiply.

''You *surmise*, Froggie, you're telling me you *surmise?* You are 'inferring on slight ground,' you are 'imagining without certain knowledge'? By definition, that's what the word 'surmise' *means*. That word certainly doesn't belong in any vocabulary used in this office, and sometimes I don't think you do either.

''His son's death, goddamn it, does *not* take General Weir off our backs. I *surmise* it might even jam him down our throats. He's in Chicago now, according to McDade, at the

Holiday Inn on Lake Shore Drive, and from this instant on, I want you to know where that man is every moment of the goddamn night and day until what we're fostering is over and done with. Jesus, Froggie, *grow up*. Don't ever *surmise* about Tarbert Weir, understand me?''

Sergeant Gordon ignored the uniformed doorman's whistle and pulled his car into the no-parking zone under the canopy of the hotel. He pulled out his wallet and flipped to his badge.

"Gimme ten minutes," he said to the doorman. "This is official business."

He followed General Weir into the lobby, then down a hall to a bank of elevators.

"You'd probably have liked the Ambassador East or the Sheraton Blackstone," the sergeant said, "but there's a convention in town, fashion wholesalers, and they tied up all the good stuff."

"This is fine," Scotty Weir said. "I dropped my bag off in my room this morning and everything looked just fine."

Electronic arrows above the elevators indicated a car was approaching lobby level. The doors slid open but Doobie Gordon put a hand on Weir's arm and said, "I didn't get an answer to my question, sir. Do you want me to pick you up in about an hour, or would you rather have Superintendent McDade meet you here?"

"Just tell the superintendent I appreciate his concern and I thank him," Weir said.

"I couldn't do that," the sergeant said. "I'm under orders to arrange a meeting between you two. It's much more than a public relations thing, sir. He's almost as badly hurt as you are about Mark's death. Being Army, you should understand. The lieutenant was one of our comrades. That's what the superintendent wants to tell you, and he also wants to consult with you about funeral arrangements. It should be an impressive affair. The superintendent suggested some variations, but Mark filed his burial wishes with the department a couple of years ago."

"Mark was thinking about dying?"

Gordon nodded. "Not morbid, just realistic. Every policeman thinks about dying."

The elevator doors closed automatically and Weir watched

the flickering indicator tracing upward to the penthouse floor. A man in a business suit and briefcase came out of the lobby and pushed a button. He stepped a few feet away and began to read a folded newspaper.

Gordon lowered his voice. "What I mean to say, sir, is that Mark asked for a regulation service funeral with the police chaplain to speak and burial in the police cemetery. Superintendent McDade wants your permission for an honorary motorcade, a graveside presentation of the Medal for Bravery. He'd like to invite the Cadet Glee Club to do background music, selections of your choice, or what you think Mark would like. And, of course, you should be there for the flag folding ceremony and the presentation of the honorary flag to next of kin."

"I told you earlier, sergeant, I won't be here for the funeral. Tell your superintendent to proceed as he sees fit and a John Grimes will be present to represent the family. He'll understand about the flag."

The elevator doors opened again and the man with the newspaper stepped inside. Tarbert Weir noticed to his surprise that the black sergeant's eyes were moist, almost tearful.

"I'm sorry to have to press you at a time like this, General Weir, but I'm on orders. The superintendent asked to see you personally. He's adamant about that. He needs your permission to televise Mark's funeral services live. After what's happened, he believes the city needs a show of unity, a catharsis for its emotions."

"*What?*" Weir said.

"Expediency, sir. This is definitely a two-toned town. A white cop was murdered at Cabrini Green . . ."

"Look," the general said, "I won't *have* a circus, I won't *have* a political sideshow made out of my boy's . . ." He stopped and willed himself back into control. "Sergeant, I deeply appreciate everything you've done and told me this morning. Yes, I'll reconsider what I just said. You can pick me up in about an hour and we might just drive downtown to see your Clarence McDade."

"Thank you, sir. I don't want to seem presumptuous or out of line, but we—the department, that is—think a little pomp and ceremony may make you feel better about your son. The idea is—we want to honor him, I mean."

*     *     *

The general's room on the sixth floor was a conventional cubicle with brown and white striped wallpaper, twin beds covered in a gold floral print, and a round table with two padded leather chairs. The general's overnight bag lay on one of the beds, where he'd tossed it a few hours earlier.

A barrage of emotions was surging through his mind so that for the first time this day he felt the sting of tears in his eyes. It was Mark Weir they had been making plans for, folded flag, television, choral dirges. The dread, the unthinkable had happened and he hurt, the loss was beginning to be real.

The message button on the base of the phone was blinking but Weir went first to the hallway door and set it ajar, then dialed room service for a pot of green tea and rye toast with jam. He wanted to order a double brandy and soda, but he knew his day, and his strategy, had just begun.

The message desk reported five calls, one from Laura Devers, three from John Grimes and one from Superintendent Clarence McDade's office. Weir wrote the names out in his square, neat hand.

In Springfield, Grimes must have been waiting near the phone because he picked it up on the first ring. His voice was emotional but subdued.

"The phone's been ringing all morning, sir, but I put everyone else on the back burner. Mrs. Devers is pretty upset. She heard about Mark first thing. She sets her radio alarm clock to the seven o'clock news. Do you want her to drive up there? That's what she wants. She says she'll do anything . . ."

"Grimes," he said, "tell Laura I'm all right, tell her to stay where she is. I don't need her quite yet . . ."

"And General Stigmuller has a private number he wants you to call on. He's phoned here three times and I told him I'd get through to you. Here's the number, sir."

When General Weir didn't speak for several moments, Grimes asked, "Are you all right, sir?"

"I'm trying, but they shot him in the back, John. I can't forget that . . . but thanks, I've got the numbers."

General Weir replaced the receiver, then gave the hotel operator the Washington number. He was connected directly with Buck Stigmuller.

"By God, Scotty, I'm so cut up about this I can't think

straight. Where the hell are you, man? Why couldn't I reach you?''

"I'm in Chicago, Buck. I drove right up.''

"What are we going to do, Scotty? I mean, what the hell is this all about? Mark, of all people . . .''

"It happened, Buck,'' the general said evenly. "I've seen him. It happened.''

"Benton's been on the phone half the morning,'' Stigmuller said. "He wants to alert the Arlington Committee. He thinks Mark should be honored that way.''

"He's going to be buried in the police cemetery, with fellow officers. That's what he wanted.''

"And Benton's got his hackles up about how and where you are, Scotty. He thinks you shouldn't be alone at this time. He wants to notify someone in Army to fly out there. Not a chaplain, for God's sake. Just someone to help out with planning, get the names right on phone calls—there's a lot of people don't feel good about this, Scotty. The brass wants to know what you're doing, how you're taking it.''

Weir was silent until Stigmuller said, "We're not cut off, are we?''

"No, I'm here,'' Weir said. "I'm just a little surprised at Benton's concerns. Except for my pension check, the Army hasn't paid much attention to me in years.''

"That's the way you wanted it, Scotty, remember that. Your decision, not ours.''

A waiter tapped on the half-open door and Weir signaled him to come in. The man set the tray on the table and brought over a check and a pen to sign the tab.

"Hold on, Buck,'' Weir said into the phone and reached for the pen. A fragmented concern made him pause. ". . . . *there's a lot of people don't feel good about this, Scotty.*"

He put his hand in his pocket and took out a ten-dollar bill. "The change is for you. I don't want charges on my bill.''

The man smiled his appreciation and when Weir heard the door close behind him, he said into the phone, "What about the matter I called you on last night, Buck?''

"Yes, yes. I wanted to tell you about that. Benton put his Major Staub on the job. Staub ran a check and made out a report—twelve pages—and brought it in himself this morning.

"I've gone over every detail and gave it my own evaluation,

Scotty. There is no discernible pattern in the background, assignments, performance or psychotypes that links those four dead GIs in any way. They were in Germany, yes, but at varying times and in varying areas. And as Staub pointed out to me, we have about a third of a million men over there, a lot of them are black, likely to end up in trouble. I'm being as frank as I can, Scotty. I don't think those four Chicago murders are connected with the Army in any way.''

"Five murders, Buck. Somebody got my boy last night."

He heard Stigmuller's sharp intake of breath. "Tarbert, listen to me. You're upset and you have every reason to be. But I know you. I can tell from that goddamn steel in your voice that you're not saying what you really want to say. I'm shocked, Scotty, shocked. Let me answer your question for you.''

"You know my question?"

"Yes, and here's my answer. Get that damned idea out of your head and keep it out. The Army doesn't kill that way and you should damned well know it.''

"Buck," Weir said, "I'm going to be in touch with you again before the day is out. I'll call you back when I can. And in the meantime, I want you to do something for me. I'm going to give you a name, a soldier to check out. I want all the information you can give me. And do this on your own. Don't go through Benton's office on this one, got that?''

"You have my word, Scotty."

"All right. The name to check out is Durham Lasari."

"I've got that," General Stigmuller said. "I'll have a record on him, if there is one, when you get back to me. Anything else, Scotty? You name it . . ."

*Put those four stars to use, lean on your connections . . .* Those were almost the last words Mark had said to him.

"In a day or two, Buck, I'm going to ask you for something, something *very important*. You make up your own mind, but as far as I'm concerned, it will be a direct order."

"I stand alerted, sir," General Stigmuller said.

"And here's a hunch, Buck, just a hunch. When you're checking on Durham Lasari, see if you can find me a readout on George Jackson. Got that? George Jackson, no middle initial that I know of.''

Weir hung up the phone and poured himself a cup of

tea, then looked down at the slip of paper still in his hand. Laura Devers . . . John Grimes . . . Superintendent Clarence McDade . . .

The general tore the paper into bits and threw the scraps into a wastebasket. Then he checked his watch and gave himself five minutes for the tea and rye toast.

He went into the lobby with his overnight bag, told the desk clerk he wouldn't be staying for the night after all, and presented a credit card. As he went toward the revolving doors, Sergeant DuBois Gordon raised himself from a leather chair and fell into step beside him.

"I knew you didn't plan to see the superintendent, general," he said, "so I waited to say goodbye."

General Weir gave his license number to the doorman who jogged around to the hotel parking lot. The two men stood in silence until the doorman brought the Mercedes up under the canopy. Sergeant Gordon swung the single piece of luggage into the back seat, then went around to the driver's side and tapped on the window.

When Scotty Weir rolled it down, the police sergeant leaned his elbows on the door and said, "If there was anything I could do that would bring Mark back, like cutting off my right arm, I'd do it. But I don't want you driving off thinking you're alone in this, general. We're going to find who did it."

A car behind the Mercedes honked and Gordon said to the doorman, "Explain to that gentleman that this is police business."

When he turned to the general again, his dark eyes were moist with tears. "I'm mad, too, general. Different things get different people mad. My grandfather was pretty senile when they brought him up from Alabama to live with us. He got my bed, I got a cot in the corner. I soon learned what got him mad. There was a song down South in the old days called 'What Makes a Nigger Prowl,' a real catchy thing about watermelons and breaking into chicken coops. Little white kids got to sing it at school, sometimes they'd just shout the words at my granddaddy when he was walking down the road. That's what got *him* mad. That's what he'd rant and curse about at night when I was trying to sleep.

"Well, Doobie Gordon's got something different on *his*

mind. I've been black all my life, general. I don't need ethnotherapy. I know *who* I am, what I see and what I hear. And that voice on Mark's squad car tape last night, that wasn't Martin Luther King—that was a honkie setting Mark up. And that's what gets *me* mad, some bastard pretending to be kin to Mrs. Lewis, trying to dump the killing on my people. But I'm not helpless like my granddaddy. I don't have to take it. I got a badge that says I can fight back. So you're not alone in this, general, remember that.''

# Chapter Twenty-one

TARBERT WEIR TALKED over the items on the list with John Grimes and decided to take care of the first one himself. It was ten minutes to ten in the evening, nearly closing time, when he dialed Log Cabin Liquors, the store that catered to this stretch of privileged countryside, and gave an order for a case of J and B Scotch, four bottles of Bombay Gin, some mixers and half a dozen liters of Martells cognac.

When the owner said the order would be out first thing in the morning, Weir protested; it was imperative that the order be delivered that night. After a pause the man said he would make the delivery in person as soon as he locked up for the night, and then added, "Mr. Weir, sir, you have our condolences, my wife and I, our whole staff, sir."

The general sat in the study, lights off, until he heard a knock on the back door and a murmur of voices. He listened as the delivery truck left the graveled drive and Grimes' footsteps sounded on the stairs. Then Weir went up to his own quarters.

There was a pale moon that laid squares of silver light on the carpet and gave the room an ethereal look. The general lay flat on his back, staring at the ceiling, forcing his body into repose long before he could silence the rush of his thoughts and the words he had spoken to Grimes earlier. ". . . . *I have no choice but to go on and do what I know how to do best. Not the thing I'm proud of, but the thing I do.*"

*       *       *

The next morning Weir jogged longer than usual, the dogs at his heels, then spent the morning in his study checking the contents of his wallet, bringing his pocket phone directory up-to-date, looking over his travel kit and studying the weather charts in the Springfield *Journal-Register*.

His call to Henrotin Hospital brought the kind of answer he expected. Miss Caidin's condition was guarded but she had had a moderately restful night. It would be some days before the fracture and swelling in her jaw would allow her to speak. Yes, the nurse would definitely tell her that Tarbert Weir had called.

The phone rang every five minutes or so. Grimes took the calls on the kitchen extension and Weir could hear the tone of his voice but not the words, a low, respectful murmur, courteous but brief.

When Laura Devers called, Weir agreed to speak to her and knew from the broken, throaty quality of her voice that she'd been crying. Mrs. Devers and Mark Weir had never met but she and the general shared an easy intimacy that put Mark well within her sphere of caring. Weir told her that he was all right and, yes, there *was* something she could do for him. General Weir told her of his plans, at least as much as he wanted her to know.

Around noon the young assistant pastor from St. Durban's came to call and the general talked with him in the study. Weir was not a Catholic and did not know Father Keene, so he was mildly surprised when the young curate accepted a glass of Jerez sherry and then, in a rush of information, began to tell the older man about himself, his life back in County Tyrone, Northern Ireland, and his concerns and misgivings about having accepted an assignment to an American pastorate.

He could not have been much older than Mark, the general thought, but slim and tentative, the morning sunlight haloing his red hair and highlighting the balding spots on his receding hairline.

American customs were not quite within his grasp, he told Weir, but in Ireland, in the case of a death such as his son's, the neighbors, all of them, would rally round . . . When he asked General Weir's permission to dedicate his early Mass tomorrow for the peace and salvation of Mark's soul, Weir said yes, and when the young priest left, he told Grimes that he would see and talk to no one else for the rest of the day, unless

General Stigmuller or DuBois Gordon called.

In his bedroom he tried on several of his uniforms which hung, cleaned and pressed, in pine-scented clothes bags. He selected two and tried them on again, pleased to note that the fit was exactly as he liked it except for a break in the line of the trousers, where the cuff edge touched the top of his Bean's loafers. He wondered with a flash of irritation if his height had been affected by the shrinkage of age. Then he put on a pair of buffed army boots and saw in the full-length mirror that his uniform was as straight and creaseless as if he were about to stand parade.

John Grimes left a sandwich and coffee on a tray in the study, set the phone to the answer tape, and drove the Mercedes to a local garage for a complete engine check, two new front tires, a fill-up and a lube job. The car was to be delivered to the farm that evening since the general would be using it the next day. To the mechanic who drove him back to the farm, Grimes explained in some detail that the general was taking his son's death pretty hard, was depressed, had to get away.

Later, Grimes drove to the country club, pulled in front of the pro shop and shouted to the golf pro to locate General Weir's and Mrs. Dever's golf clubs and load them in the back of the station wagon, along with four boxes of new balls. They were going away for a couple of weeks, he said; the general wanted a complete change of scene, they were driving down to the Greenbrier in White Sulphur Springs.

Grimes went into the club lounge and took a stool at the end of the bar. There were male foursomes and a scattering of couples, sitting at tables with sandwiches and coffee, watching a track meet on the TV screen. A man in a sports shirt and plaid golf shorts was sipping gin at the bar. For a moment Grimes wondered if the solitary drinker was staring at him, then decided it was an illusion created by the man's oddly protruding eyes. Tony, the bartender, brought Grimes an ale and asked with genuine concern how the general was doing. Not too good, Grimes told him. He himself had stopped at the club just to get away from the melancholy of the Weir household. It was unlike the general, as Tony would know, Grimes said, but brave and strong as he was, he'd been doing some pretty heavy drinking . . .

It was Tarbert Weir who was up and about first on the day

of Mark's funeral. He made coffee and toast, scrambled some eggs, and brought a tray to Grimes' room, leaving it on a bedside table when he heard the running shower. Ten minutes later he brought around the station wagon and waited beside it, motor running, when Grimes came out the back door.

Grimes' face was flushed with both emotion and a close, straight-razor shave in the hot shower. His body looked constricted and bulky, encased in a new black suit, and there seemed to be no energy in his movements, no trace of hope in his face. "I'm not sure I can do this, sir," he said, his voice shaking.

Weir put both arms around the man's shoulders, embracing him and patting him on the back, as if he were comforting a distraught child.

"You can do it, Grimes," he said. "We both can."

At eleven o'clock the general switched on a television set to an upstate channel. The weather in Chicago had cooperated, Weir thought bitterly; it was appropriately dismal for the funeral of his son, swirling snow alternating with sleeting rain that struck the funeral cortege like flails. A motorcycle drill team preceded the two hearses, the first limousine carrying floral tributes and then the coffin limo itself, flanked by an honorary guard of marching policemen. The side curtains of the car were drawn back with black ribbon to reveal the coffin itself, draped with an American flag.

"*. . . definitely a two-tone town . . . the superintendent believes the city needs a show of unity, a catharsis for its emotions.*"

Tears of rage clouded the picture for Weir. He snapped off the TV set abruptly and went to the gun cabinet to take out a pair of .22 target pistols and several boxes of ammunition.

Outside, the weather was dry, but cold and almost windless, with a frozen crackle of breaking brush under every footstep. Weir walked away from the house and into the deep woods, grateful for the cold air that nipped his cheeks and filtered through his cashmere sweater.

He took down a couple of log rails to make an opening in the fencing and walked to the outdoor shooting range he and Grimes had set up years ago. It was a two-lane, thirty-foot clearing in the trees, with a rough wooden counter for resting guns and ammo at the top and a straight, open gallery running twenty-five feet ahead. The end of the range was backed by a ten-foot-high wall of wire-baled haycocks and two black and yellow targets with scarlet bull's-eyes. Beyond the targets lay several more acres of pristine, fenced-in woodland of the Weir property.

General Weir laid out the pair of .22 target pistols and boxes of ammunition with precision, as if awaiting a signal in the championship meet.

He loaded each pistol and began to fire them alternately, left and right hand, the shots cracking out in the cold air. He reloaded and fired again and again for almost an hour, cleanly, rhythmically, feeling the air cool on his fiery cheeks. When he finally put down the pistols and walked to the end of the firing range to look at the targets, the air was thick with the smell of cordite, the circular targets were tattered, with the red bull's-eyes shot completely away and the hay bales looking as though they had been clawed by a frenzied animal.

They did not wait for John Grimes to get back from Chicago. At a quarter to three, Tarbert Weir went into his bank and converted ten thousand dollars from his account into travelers checks. He told the cashier, whom he knew well, that he was taking a trip down south and she put her hand out from under the grille and touched his hand as he signed the checks, patting it softly, then made a little pursing movement with her lips, a silent kiss of understanding. Weir nodded and thanked her.

Within twenty minutes the big Mercedes left Springfield and moved out into the traffic of the interstate highway, headed across Indiana to Ohio and then down to White Sulphur Springs on the eastern border of West Virginia, a town of less than three thousand people, two hundred and fifty miles from Washington, D.C.

General Weir sat slouched down in the front seat, head thrown back against the leather cushion, as if he were exhausted or emotionally drained. Laura Devers was at the wheel.

# Chapter Twenty-two

AT SERGEANT MALLECK'S request, a military intern stopped by the Armory to examine and treat injuries to the face and torso of one Private George Jackson. The young doctor cleaned and bandaged cuts on the face and forehead, treated deep bruises in the rib and groin areas and administered nine stitches to close a gash that ran from the soldier's left eyelid up through the eyebrow to his temple. Then he medicated and taped the battered rib cage.

"I don't know what gets into you fellows," the doctor said to his silent patient, "riding those choppers without a helmet. Look at yourself. You could have lost the sight of an eye if that cut had gone half an inch lower. I did some motocross riding in college and I never got on a bike without a helmet *and* goggles."

"You know how it is," Malleck said easily, "some smart-asses are just too smart to take advice."

Lasari spent the next forty-eight hours on a cot in the locked back room and then, on orders cut by Malleck, shipped out on a civilian aircraft to Boulder, Colorado, where he and his traveling companion, Private Homer Robbins, were met by military jeep and transported to the bivouac area of the division to which Private George Jackson's orders assigned him.

Code-named Lucky Thirteenth, the unit was a mobile armored division scheduled for maneuvers in Germany. It would be flown by cargo plane in a twenty-four-hour relay from Colorado to an assembly area between Munich and Regensburg, from which its components would be trucked to an eight-mile defense position in the Bavarian forest adjacent to the Czechoslovakian border.

When the last soldiers had been grouped and deplaned for Europe, with George Jackson on the roster, Private Robbins telephoned Malleck at the Armory, spent one night drinking in the bars of Boulder, then took a flight back to O'Hare.

Following Malleck's threats and instructions, Lasari had been an unobtrusive but cooperative member of the Lucky Thirteenth, made no friends, and revealed nothing of his former military background.

On a raw March afternoon, two days after leaving Colorado, the soldier listed as George Jackson, PFC, traveled on new orders cut for him by a First Sergeant Jacob Jens, orders sending him from Regensburg to Heidelberg. The papers provided him with transport authority and a per diem allowance for a twenty-one day transfer to Master Sergeant Ernest Strasser's headquarters battalion, attached to the Seventh Army at Campbell Barracks outside the medieval town of Heidelberg.

Lasari traveled alone in an autobus that sped at ninety kilometers on a highway linking the two cities. At the bus station he swung his duffel bag over his shoulder and took a cab to Sergeant Strasser's apartment.

Sergeant Strasser lived in suburban Heidelberg on a pleasant, beech-lined street, the newer buildings designed to blend with the slant-roofed and *gemutlich* architecture of the older part of town.

The apartment was on the second floor, with a decal of an American flag above the doorbell. A blonde girl in black slacks and a red turtleneck sweater answered the first ring.

Lasari identified himself as Private George Jackson and the young woman said simply, "I'm Greta."

Putting on a heavy coat and picking up a string shopping bag, she said with a wide gesture, "There are things to drink behind the bar, and cigarettes if you like." She extended her hand and shook formally with him. "Goodbye now, perhaps I will be with you for dinner."

Lasari placed his duffel bag on the floor, then put his hands at his sides and stood at near attention inside the door. He saw the oaken bar in the corner with a pair of cowhide stools and near it a large TV set, draped with a crocheted runner. The room was overheated and smelled strongly of pine-scented air freshener.

Around the room, two feet from the ceiling, ran a shelf lined with ornate beer mugs, ceramic figurines shaped like trolls, dwarfs and comic bears in Bavarian costumes.

A half dozen intricate cuckoo clocks, designed like cottages, hung from the walls. None seemed to be ticking at the moment and their pendulums, shaped like pine cones, hung heavy and still. Except for an inlaid chess table and a red leather ottoman which looked Moroccan, the rest of the furniture was sturdy and functional, thick nylon carpets, sofas and chairs in russet tweed, holders jammed with American magazines and a coffee table with a bowl of wax fruit and a compote dish of gumdrops.

A faint hiss of heat came from the radiators, and in the stone fireplace another heater glowed behind a screen etched with logs and imitation flames. Lasari's uniform felt rough and scratchy against his damp hands, and he was aware of sweat forming around the scar tissue on his forehead.

He heard a man's voice say, "He's here now, I'll get back to you." Then a phone was replaced and Sergeant Strasser walked into the room. He stopped and looked at Lasari appraisingly.

Ernest Strasser's hair was gray, cut short, and his light complexion was emphasized by clear and pale blue eyes. He wore civilian clothes, slacks, a gray sweater and plaid sport shirt.

He was a small man, several inches shorter than Lasari, with a corded neck and wide shoulders and a springy, muscular tension in his movement. Yet there was a nervousness in the man, a shifty sense of insecurity that was at variance with his cold eyes and weightlifter's shoulders.

"Let's get a couple of things straight, Jackson," he said. "I'm boss this side of the water. I got you sprung from Lucky Thirteenth and you're gonna train some dogs here where I can keep an eye on you. But there won't be any buddy-buddy shit between you and me. I'm Sergeant Strasser and you're an Article 15 fuckup and don't ever forget it."

"I understand, Sergeant Strasser," Lasari said.

"That's another thing. Don't be so fucking quick to understand me," Strasser said. "I'll do the thinking for both of us.

"Tomorrow, first thing, I'll take you out to the barracks. My CQ will do all the paperwork on your transfer, payroll, temporary quarters and so forth. Put it down kosher. You'll be living off base, right here in this apartment, a bedroom back by the kitchen. It's small, used to be the maid's room, but you're lucky to get it. Housing for GIs off base is tight as a witch's cunt. Like telephones, insurance, a new car, like everything else in this country, it costs too much. Unless you've got connections with the right Krauts around here, you'll wind up a fucking paraplegic. If you want something, they charge you an arm and a leg."

"Why dogs?" Lasari asked.

Strasser shrugged. "Malleck filled me in. You had some training in dog handling back in the States, before 'Nam, right? If that hadn't showed up on your record, I'd have found something else for you to do. You're a mechanic, played a little semipro ball, got some rank in unarmed combat. I could of made use of any of that shit. One of our corps commanders is a baseball fanatic. Another thinks he's a fucking Bruce Lee. But it's dogs. I want you to fit in where you look natural."

As he spoke Strasser walked around the room, squinting up at the beer mugs and trolls, touching the pine cones of the cuckoo clocks in a curiously possessive way, as if he was evaluating them.

"Yeah," he said, "the dogs work best for us. Besides, I don't want you talking to anything that can talk back. A colonel in ordnance breeds German shepherds and Dobermans. He's got kennel runs behind his place, fucking platoons of attack dogs behind electrified fences. Some of the best championship bitches from Germany and Austria. His tour of duty is up in six months and he's shipping them back to some spread he's got in Michigan. He'll have the seed and breed dogs for one of the biggest attack-and-guard dog ranches in the country. He's thirty-nine years old and says he'll be a millionaire by the time he's forty-five."

The sergeant pulled an overstuffed chair closer to the wall, stood on the cushions and realigned a row of beer steins on the shelf, measuring the distance between them with his thick fingers. Then he replaced the chair.

"The U.S. taxpayer is putting the fucking colonel into the

guard dog business, you know that, Jackson? His dogs get free vets' care here, he orders their chow through the PX, and the mutts get shipped home free as part of his household goods. Pretty fucking smart deal.''

"I guess you're right,'' Lasari said. "Sounds like a smart deal to me.''

"That's another thing, don't do any fucking *guessing*,'' the sergeant said. "A lot of things are gonna happen that you don't understand, but there's no point *guessing* about them. I can tell you something else, Jackson.'' Strasser turned to glare at him, taking a deep breath so that his powerful shoulders and chest filled out. "There are things even *I* don't bother guessing at. So you better keep that in mind if you want to have a happy time around here.''

"I'm here to do what I'm told, sergeant,'' Lasari said. "I'm a mechanic, know some karate, and how to go into the hole for a ground ball, which adds up to being an Article 15 fuck-up. You're going to tell me about the dogs I'm supposed to train and that puts us in business. I'm not here to understand things or to make any guesses. That about sum it all up?''

Strasser raised his hand in mock protest and smiled. "Okay, okay, Jackson. I'm not a professional hardnose. You can't be one in this fucking man's army. We got everything now but a goddamn union to contend with. You forget yourself and call some stupid black slob a 'burrhead' and he doesn't go sulk behind the latrine, he calls a meeting and they start sending wires to their congressmen.''

He shook his head as if unable to understand, then said, "Now to the business of Private Jackson. The colonel's name is Warneke. He's got two seven-month-old German shepherd pups he wants to keep as pets for his daughters. They'll live with the family so they gotta be toilet-trained and he wants them to go anywhere, even in traffic, with or without a lead. He doesn't want any snapping, roughhousing or fear-biting. He doesn't want them to take food from strangers because there's so goddamn many kooks in Germany from Turkey and the Middle East and he's also worried about terrorists trying to poison GI dogs or maybe even his kids.

"The colonel lives near the river by a big park, St. Hubert's. My driver will drop you there in the morning, pick you up at night after you get the dogs back. You got twenty-one days at this locale, then we cut your new orders."

Strasser stopped in front of Lasari, then circled him and looked him up and down from all angles. "You got some decent civilian clothes in that luggage of yours, soldier? The colonel don't want his dogs to have a military complex."

"Just slacks and a windbreaker."

Strasser took a roll of German marks from his pocket and counted out a thick pack. "Get something to work in. And buy yourself a suit, some shirts and a tie. We're going to be having dinner with some important people in a couple of nights. One guy from Yugoslavia named Vayetch, Pyter Vayetch. He spells the 'Peter' with a 'y' and he's particular about that. You'll be carrying something for him one of these days, so he wants to check you out. Just remember the rules, don't bother guessing about any of it. You drink, Lasari?"

"I don't need to, if that's what you're asking. Some red wine now and then, that's about it."

Strasser walked to one end of the bar and picked up an object in carved wood about two feet tall, a miniature mountain man with chiseled shirt and lederhosen, cocked hat, walking stick, and a simpleton's smile. It had been beautifully crafted, with even the mock leather stitching on little britches defined. After studying it for a few moments, Strasser put the figure back on the bar, patting the head absently, as if showing affection to a child.

Without looking at Lasari, he said, "You met Greta, didn't you?"

"The girl who was here? Yes, I met her."

"She'll talk your socks off about American television," Strasser said. "Starsky and Hutch, Wonder Woman, Kojak . . . She calls him 'my bald one.' She thinks she means one-balled or eunuch or something like that. I can't understand her when she goes off in German. Her favorites are Charlie's Angels. She keeps scrapbooks on them and she's got her hair cut like Farrah's, you notice. Now she wants a motorcycle. She wants me to buy her one so she can ride up in back of me and wear white cowboy boots. She's like every goddamn German I ever met. That's all she thinks of—getting *more*."

Strasser turned and looked steadily at Lasari. "She's twenty-four years old but she's just a kid. She may sound stupid, but she's important to me. You understand what I'm telling you?"

"You told me not to understand things too fast," Lasari said. "But if I'm going to be here three weeks, we'd better get this out in the open. There's only one person in this setup who can keep the girl in your bedroom, Strasser, and that's you."

"But you're the one who's gotta walk easy. *You're* the fucker Malleck has a file on."

Lasari picked up his duffel bag and slung it over his shoulder. "Show me the room you've got for me and I'll unpack."

He followed the sergeant down a narrow hall till the man stopped at the doorway of a small room. "In here," he said.

"Before you go, I want to point out something to you, Sergeant Strasser," Lasari said. "I've got a lot to lose in this deal, I know that, but I've already lost a lot, haven't I? So that gives me an advantage. I no longer have *everything* to lose but you *have*—and everyone better keep that in mind."

# Chapter Twenty-three

By DRIVING THROUGH Indiana and Ohio at night, with only heavy-duty truck traffic, General Weir and Mrs. Devers pulled up at the triple-arched portico of the Greenbrier shortly before twelve noon the next day. Daffodils and grape hyacinth bloomed in the flowerbeds and the giant fir trees were already touched with the pale finger growths of a southern spring. There were traces of snow in the high, wooded areas of Greenbrier County, but here in the Allegheny Mountain valley, the air was mild, almost warm.

"Our man will take your luggage around to your cottage, sir. How many pieces do you have?"

"Six and two sets of clubs," General Weir said as he filled out the registration blank in the opulent lobby. "Mrs. Devers and I will be staying with you for a while."

"Good," the desk clerk said. "I've taken the liberty, General Weir, of putting your party in D guest house in South Carolina row. That group was built more than a hundred years ago, but of course they're completely up-to-date. Carolina Row was a favorite of Curtis Lee, the general's oldest son. You have two bedrooms and the lady has a dressing parlor."

"That's fine," Weir said. "Is there some kind of bar set-up?"

"Yes," the man said. "There is a pantry next to the dining room and the hotel can send your meals over. And of course bar service is available by phone twenty-four hours a day."

"I'm sure we'll be comfortable," Laura Devers said.

178

"And may I also point out that we have a fine military history here. Not far from you, on Baltimore Row, is the guest house that General Robert E. Lee once used as his summer retreat. I would have given you those quarters but they've been reserved by a honeymoon couple. It's a second marriage," the clerk added.

In their spacious, sunny quarters, Mrs. Devers sprawled into a leafprint chair and put her feet on an ottoman. "God, Scotty," she said. "Must we start before lunch? Can't it wait at least until tomorrow morning?"

"Laura," he said, "for the appearance of things, I'd like to have you along. We'll take a golf cart, but I want to play the Lakeside and Greenbrier courses before dark tonight. Do one of them with me. And I'll play Old White myself tomorrow if you want to sleep in."

"Scotty, I don't want to argue with a great military mind," she said, "but I don't see *why* you have to do it this way. The Valley Airport is no more than fifteen miles by car, and Piedmont Airlines can fly you most anywhere."

"All right then, we won't argue," he said. "I'll just proceed as planned. I'm depending on you." He walked into the small, efficient pantry, opened the refrigerator and called out, "Laura, we're in luck. They've already stocked the bar. Will a Bloody Mary do you instead of lunch?"

All three resort golf courses began and ended at the clubhouse and after playing the eighteen holes of the Lakeside course, Scotty Weir dropped Laura Devers at the club and went off alone to play the Greenbrier.

It was after six when he crossed the veranda of the guest cottage, the red and white striped awnings fluttering, a smell of early lilac scenting the breeze. He had called the stables from the clubhouse and asked that a horse be brought round for him as soon as the sun was up.

Through the window he could see Laura Devers moving around the dining table. She had ordered their dinner from room service, two places were set and she was stooping to lower the sterno lights under the food trays. There was an uxorial feeling about the scene, almost as if they really were lovers on vacation, and Scotty Weir wondered briefly if he had been wise to involve Laura Devers. He had become so accustomed to functioning alone.

After dinner they brought their brandy and coffee out to the wicker chairs on the veranda. A new arrival was checking into the guest house next door. In the dim light they could see a single man, followed by a bellboy with two pieces of luggage. There was a murmur of voices as the bellboy opened the door, snapped on lights, accepted a tip and then walked back to the main hotel, whistling softly.

"I wish you'd say something," Laura Devers said a few minutes later. "Really, I think it might do you good to tell me what's in your head."

"I don't think you'd understand," he said, "and there is no reason to expect you to."

"Try me."

"It's an introspection that's dogging me. I can't seem to avoid it. First I start thinking about how the hell a farm kid wound up wearing general's stars. I try to see myself as a professional and do I still have the guts I once had to earn that medal and was I worthy of it. You know, Harry Truman once said he'd rather have it than the presidency."

"In all the wars, all the branches of service, out of the millions in uniform, only three thousand Americans were ever awarded the Medal of Honor. *You* told me that, Scotty. That should prove something to you about yourself."

"Laura, the new angers and hurts are what's goading me. What I'm thinking now, and I'm thinking it with my guts and balls as well as my brain, is that whatever or wherever or whoever decided that it couldn't let Mark live, I'm going to find that thing, I'm going to take that hill my son died trying to take, and maybe when it's over they'll wish to Christ they'd let *him* do the job. They didn't have to cut him down like that, Laura, not Mark or those other murdered soldiers either, if they're part of it."

Laura Devers put her coffee cup down on the saucer. "We're just friends, I know, Scotty," she said, "but I can't help caring. Be careful, be clever about what you plan to do. Use your head, your skills. It was sheer guts and bravery that got you that medal but it was brains that earned those stars."

A short time later Weir excused himself and went into the guest house to dial room service. He gave an order for a dozen bottles of liquor and added loudly that he wanted the items sent over immediately. He hung up and then, with a swipe of his hand, knocked the brass-based lamp next to the phone onto the floor. He replaced it, snapped the light switch a couple of times, then cursed when he saw a tear in the green silk shade.

Weir walked to the bathroom and flushed the toilet. He ran a stream of cold water into the basin and splashed his face, patting his cheeks vigorously and massaging the taut skin at his temples. He looked at himself in the mirror. His hair glistened with drops of water but his face was calm and resolute, and there was defiance in his gray eyes. He flushed the toilet a second time and slammed the lid.

Moments later, when the wicker service cart came creaking up the walk, Weir greeted the man with a slurred, " 's about time," then asked the waiter to recheck the order.

"And you brought four Tequila Gold, right?" Weir said.

"That's right, sir."

"Put the order in the bar and set the four Tequilas in the refrigerator. I like the stuff cold." When the man did as he was asked, Weir signed the service slip and added a ten-dollar tip.

As the sound of the cart faded away Scotty Weir moved to stand behind Mrs. Dever's chair, tracing a finger over her cheek, then down the soft curve of her neck to the pulse beating rapidly at the base of her throat. He bent and kissed her fine gray hair.

"More than just a friend, Laura," he said in a muted voice. "My God, so much more."

Before going to bed, Weir pulled wide the bedroom draperies and raised the windows. It was before six o'clock in the morning when the changing light wakened him and he went into the sitting room, picked up the extension phone and dialed Springfield.

Grimes answered at once. "I hope you've got a cup of coffee, sir. This list is rather long."

"I'm all right," Weir said.

"There have been a lot of calls, some of them dating back to schooldays on Maggie's side. I've got them written. Shall I read them off to you?"

"No, no," Weir said with some impatience. "You know what I want, Grimes."

"All right, here we go. Colonel Richard Benton called late

yesterday evening and he was on the tape twice earlier, too. He wants to offer his condolences directly. I did as you said, told him you were at the Greenbrier with a lady friend, didn't want to be disturbed."

"And?"

"And he said he understood. General Stigmuller called about eight last evening, said to tell you he'll be at that private number after four o'clock today. He's got part of what you want, but not all of it."

"The Caidin lady?"

"I checked Henrotin when I got back from Chicago and then again yesterday. That head nurse is getting to know me. She says the lady is getting along as well as can be expected. She's been given our messages."

"Has she had other guests?"

"The nurse says still no visitors but she's received a lot of flowers and her boss from the paper stopped by and was allowed to wave from the hall."

"And DuBois Gordon?"

"No word from him, sir."

"All right, Grimes, and thanks. Anything urgent, ring me here. Otherwise, I'll be checking back with you tomorrow."

"Sir? One last thing I'd like your judgment on. I've brought Mark's flag back from Chicago with me. What I don't know is what I should do with it. It's on a chair in the front hall, but that seems so impersonal . . ."

Weir was silent for a moment, then said, "In my study, Grimes, that footlocker with my ribbons and citations and things?"

"Yes, I know."

"Take the flag as it is, leave it folded and place it on top of that locker. All those things really belong together."

"I'll do that, sir."

"And, Grimes, something's bothering me. Not today necessarily, but in a day or two, ask that head nurse when Caidin can leave the hospital. She doesn't have her own people there in Chicago and I'd like her to come to the farm to recuperate. Find out if she'll do that. It means you'd have to drive up and get her. And be sure that Sergeant Gordon knows she's with us."

"I'll check it out, general. And I'll pick her up if that's how it works out. Where shall we put her? Should I get things ready in Mark's old room?''

"No," Weir said. "It just wasn't that way with them, Grimes, at least not for a long time." He was thoughtful for a moment. "Put her in the room next to you, John, that's best. Somewhere you can watch out for her. That young lady was on her way to be with Mark when she was attacked. I never quite believed the random mugger theory, too much of a coincidence for me.''

The Greenbrier stables had brought round a dun mare and tethered her to an iron jockey in front of the guest cottage. Weir mounted the horse and moved out, savoring the warmth of the animal's flanks and the movement of its muscles between his thighs.

He guided the mare along the trails for several miles and then, pulling the reins up short, struck off through the woods, keeping an eye on the shafts of the rising sun where it touched the treetops. The general could sense the increasing elevation and feel the morning air, cool and thinning in his nostrils.

At length they came to a wooded crest, high above the sprawling valley. Down below him, spread out as on a relief map, Tarbert Weir could see the elegant white Greenbrier buildings, the green rectangles of tennis courts and the sparkle of the outdoor swimming pool. The three golf courses were spread out in cultivated precision, beige sandtraps and dozens of smooth greens, bright against the rough fairways, and a sprinkle of hole flags, fluttering and birdlike at this distance.

Weir spent forty minutes surveying the scene, making mental computations, measuring with his eyes. It would work. When the time was right, when he received the information he needed, he was ready to give the necessary instructions to General Stigmuller.

# Chapter Twenty-four

PRIVATE ANDREW SCALES scrubbed the floor of First Sergeant Malleck's office on his hands and knees. Earlier he had washed the area with a mop and pail, then took a nail file to scrape dirt and dried blood from the joints of the planking. Now he used strong soap and a stiff brush to work up a lather. It was Malleck who had noticed the shading where the blood from Duro Lasari's beating had left its marks. Malleck had cursed and ranted and told Scales he wanted the place cleaned up before the orderly checked out for the night, otherwise they wouldn't be doing business as usual, and Scales could count on that.

After mopping up the suds, Scales began to rub down the floor with a chamois cloth, muttering as drops of sweat fell from his forehead to the boards. His nerves were frayed and tender, but he knew Malleck would stick to his word.

When Detective Frank Salmi and First Sergeant Malleck arrived, their footprints stood out clearly on the damp, clean boards. Malleck nodded with approval. "Go out and do the goddamn reception room now, Scales."

"Right, Top. That's what I'm fixin' to do." Scales collected his brushes, cloths and bucket, scrambled to his feet and after nodding at the detective, started on the floor of the outer office.

Malleck put his hand on the desk drawer where he kept his whiskey bottle, then changed his mind. His spirits were ebullient, he felt high and confident enough without booze to celebrate and taunt Salmi.

"It's working, Frank," he said. "He cleared Colorado, he cleared Regensburg and Strasser's got him right under his thumb in Heidelberg. Our pigeon took off right on schedule and we got him roosting right where we want him till we're ready."

Salmi shook his head and looked dour and worried. "I've been keeping Mr. M. abreast of things, but he's restless, Malleck, let me tell you. He wants more say in the deals. He says he trusts you so far but he don't feel too good about putting his trust in a deserter. Mr. M. is quite a patriot in his own way. He'd of liked to check out this Lasari himself . . ."

Malleck raised a hand. "Not to worry, Salmi. Our partners in Europe are going to put the okay on Lasari themselves, yes or no. You tell *that* to your precious Mr. M. If Lasari passes muster, then the rest of the transaction is purely logistical and fiscal. Strasser waits till the right time, then gets orders cut to send the pigeon back to the Lucky Thirteenth right on the Czech border. A certain party hired by the partners passes the goods to Lasari, he checks back with Strasser . . ."

"Where's Lasari coming in?"

"That's something you don't need to know," Malleck said. "And how he's carrying the stuff, you don't have to know that either. Mr. M. is going to get delivery, just like the other times. He can cut it with powdered milk, up the street price, do what he wants with it as long as he gets my payoff to the right account at the bank. I get Strasser his share, plus the payroll, and he pays off everyone on that side of the ocean. Nobody works on credit, Salmi. When I get paid, you get paid. This operation is strictly cash and carry, so nobody's got any complaints. That's how we all stay friendly."

"I'd still like to know how it's coming in."

"As long as it gets here, why should you worry? How many million travelers do you think come into American airports each year? I can't answer that either but I know it's too god-damn many for the customs agents to handle; they don't have the manpower to fine-tooth everybody. False bottom in a shaving kit, inner soles of ski boots, hollow statues from Lourdes, transistor radios, golf club covers, candlesticks from the Bridge of Sighs, razored out spaces in Gideon Bibles . . .

they've all worked. It's nothing you've got to worry about, Frank."

"I might as well tell you, Malleck, that Mr. M. has some suspicions that you're holding back on him . . . that his money is buying more horse than you're accounting for. He thinks you're making something extra for yourself on the side."

Malleck looked steadily at Salmi, keeping his thoughts under control. He refused to let anger or doubt disturb his euphoria. He had waited too long to be top man to let insult or innuendo blight this success.

"Of course, I am, Salmi, but that's just between you and me, or you're a dead man, right?"

"I got a right to know what's going on. I'm the go-between . . ."

"Look at it this way, pal. I'm a realist, and a couple of factors happened to operate in my favor. Take politics. All the warring and infighting going on in Iran, Iraq, Turkey, even Israel, well, that dried up a lot of quality white. The Marseilles Express has stopped running completely. A lot of the poor bastards are trying to make it on Mexican brown. With the right contacts—and that's another factor in my favor, because I've got the right contacts—a smart dealer can bring in a kilo of pure white, almost perfect stuff, worth a million dollars in the street.

"The last factor is straight economics. The dollar is stronger abroad so I'm getting more for my money. It doesn't mean I'm giving Mr. M. any less than we bargained for, it just means that I'm getting more. Lady Luck wants me to have a little something extra 'cause I'm such a good boy, *capeche?*"

Malleck pulled open the desk drawer, took out the whiskey bottle and two canteen cups, poured a short drink into one of them. He sipped it a moment, then lit a cigarette and began pacing the office floor.

"You might as well level with me," Salmi said uncomfortably. "There's something you're not telling me. What don't you like about this deal?"

"Don't put words in my mouth," Malleck said. "I like *everything* about this deal, and the next one and the next one. We've been playing for peanuts so far, big peanuts, I'll admit, but nickel and dime stuff in comparison to the world market. Think what's out there for the taking . . ."

The floorboards were still moist and slick from Scale's

vigorous scrubbing and the soles of Malleck's boots made a sucking sound as he paced. He could hear the black private still working in the reception room, humming and chuckling and talking to himself.

Malleck sipped his drink and knocked a long ash from his brown cigarette onto the floor. It was not a derisive or sadistic act, but the therapeutic flick of contempt he believed the black soldier needed. The man thrived on it, the sergeant was convinced, Scales needed contempt as a flower needed water.

The black man laid out three changes of clothing for the first sergeant every day, whether the schedule called for them or not, starched and perfectly ironed khakis to start the day, Class-A uniforms with service ribbons and decorations for formal occasions and plain blue or gray lounge suits for civilian evenings.

After years of operating in a predominantly male world, Malleck considered himself an experienced manipulator, a good judge of character. He had long concluded that if he didn't find something wrong with Private Andy Scales' valet duties or other services, it seemed to disappoint the man. A speck of dust, a particle of rust on a belt buckle, any mistake at all was enough to send Scales into his grinning, self-rebuking but submissive attitudes which formed the defensive core of his character.

"You're right about something bothering me, Salmi," Malleck said. "On the first four loops we got along just fine. Goods picked up, paid for and delivered. We had our formula. Why did it have to change? I'll tell you why. I think Mr. M.'s got a cob of racial pride up his ass, wants to know what the fuck I'm up to, wants a face-to-face meet, is ready to prove to me he's the Big Tom here in Chicago. Isn't that right, Salmi?"

"That's roughly the word he gave me," Salmi said.

"He didn't give a shit about sitting down and having a drink with me, talking things over when he first started to bankroll, right? He let me do the planning, put my neck out, take the risks. Now that we're thinking big kilos, going to make big money, he wants to get nosy."

In spite of himself, Malleck heard his voice rising. "Doesn't that boss-nigger know I'm doing him a favor? I got stencils and forms and name stamps and official seals—"

Malleck walked back to his desk, flipped a key from his

pocket and turned the lock on a double drawer and pulled it open. "Right here, Salmi, I got the equivalent of a fucking magic carpet. I can fly that dumb ginzo Lasari anywhere in the world we got GIs. I don't need Mr. M. There's people in Detroit, Newark, Miami who'll finance me, and Mr. M. sure as shit knows that. I'm not just some goddamn Chicago beat cop with his hand out like a trained monkey. I'm his fucking *equal*, doesn't he realize that?"

Malleck looked at Salmi's troubled face, then smiled. "That's what it's about, isn't it? I'm a big man now and it bothers Mr. M. that I don't need him, isn't that it? That we are equal . . ."

Salmi nodded. "I guess that's the way I'd call it, sergeant."

Still smiling, Malleck sat down at his desk and put a polished boot against the drawer. He sipped his whiskey, the overhead lights drawing deep lines in his hard face. "I like that, Salmi. I like having the big buck figure I'm as good as he is, 'cause if he's come that far, he's shitting himself into a corner whether he knows it or not. I got the edge now, that's the truth of it."

Raising his voice, he called, "Scales? Get your ass in here. I'm partying tonight."

Scales appeared in the doorway, his teeth opalescent in a wide smile. "Want that new dark blue suit, sarge? That's what I got laid out. You look like a real dude in that one, Top."

"Yeah, the blue suit will do fine, Scales. And I want to see the pearly gates in the tips of my shoes when you get through shinin' them."

Scales laughed cheerfully and said, "And behind 'em, Top, there'll be St. Peter grinnin' at you. I'll take care of it. I'll fix everything up, sarge."

"Be sure you do, Scales. And I want you to do a little pimping for me. Phone those two clerk broads of ours and whoever answers the phone, Avers or Sio, she's the lucky lady. Tell her to meet me at the Black Forest on Quincy Street at seven-thirty. I got an important call to make. And tell her I'm partial to bimbos wearing red."

As Scales turned to leave, Malleck said in a strange, wheedling voice, "You weren't going to let me off that easy, were you, Uncle Andy? You forget to let your old sarge say thank you?"

Malleck took a small plastic bag of white powder out of the top desk drawer and tossed it into the black man's cupped hands. "I never forget a friend, Scales, just you remember that."

When Scales left, Malleck nodded at the bottle on his desk. "You want a belt for the road, Frank? You can afford it, you know. In three weeks or so, you can afford any goddamn thing you want."

Detective Salmi hesitated a moment and then nodded. Malleck put a canteen cup in front of him and leaned forward, carefully filling it to the rim.

# Chapter Twenty-five

IT WAS CALLED Teufel's Atelier, a restaurant-disco on a narrow street leading off one of Heidelberg's old stone bridges. From a revolving bandstand a group in silver tuxedos played soft rock music. Blue and green lights flashing out over the dance floor gave an incongruous modern effect to the otherwise burgherish atmosphere of Germans dining seriously in red leather banquettes. A group of candle-lit tables for two encircled the dance floor.

At the mahogany bar at one side of the room, there was another clash of styles; a plump bartender wore leather breeches, a green vest and a yodeler's hat while the other, a young man with thick blond curls, was outfitted in tight black jeans and a spangled white shirt open to the navel, showing a hairy chest and a glitter of neck ornaments.

Lasari sat with Greta and Sergeant Strasser in one of the banquettes. The German girl wore a white cashmere sweater with a pink scarf and a short white corduroy skirt. Her blonde hair was brushed back from her face and fell smoothly to her shoulders from a ridge of amber combs. A waiter had been standing on one foot and then the other while she frowned and studied the long menu. A bottle of white wine stood next to her goblet. Lasari was drinking beer, the sergeant a citrus soda with Dutch gin.

"Everything they have here is so *German*," Greta said, tapping the rim of her wine glass. The waiter filled it for the second time.

"We have hamburger with *frites*," he said, "and shrimps in dill sauce, *fraulein*."

"That's what I mean," Greta said. "The hamburger will have gravy on it and the shrimps are boiled in beer." She faked a delicate shudder and then said in a singsong voice, "I don't want dumplings or oxtails or sauerbraten, or any kind of apple *Kuchen* or whipped cream or *suppen mit ei* . . ."

"Goddamn it," Strasser said, "then don't order anything. Just drink the wine and have some bread and butter. We're in Heidelberg, Greta, *der Faterland*."

He had been drinking double gins and his voice was sarcastic. "Do you hear me, *dummkopf*? Heidelberg! You think that's Yonkers or East Lansing? This joint's called Teufel's Atelier, heinie talk for Devil's Workshop. You think that's a fucking pizza joint in the Vatican run by cardinals? No offense, Jackson, but we go through this every time we go out. She's pure Deutscher but I'm gonna die of hunger some night while she's wondering why she can't get chop suey or *chile rellenos*."

Strasser put both hands over his heart. "Give us a break, Greta."

Greta decided on an omelet with truffles and the sergeant ordered steak tartare with rolled anchovies and rye toast for himself and Lasari, then waved a hand for more drinks all around.

A half hour later they were joined at the banquette by two men in dark suits who nodded briefly at Greta and then bowed formally when they were introduced by Strasser to "Private George Jackson" as Pytor Vayetch and Herr Manfred Rauch.

Pytor Vayetch turned to Strasser with a fixed smile and said, "No one should sit eating while there is music and a pretty girl. Go on, enjoy yourselves."

Greta hesitated and then said uncertainly, "Ah, yes. We can leave the dessert cart for later. It is exciting to have something to look forward to . . ."

Vayetch looked expectantly at Strasser, but Rauch, a tall, broad man with sallow features and gaunt cheeks, looked solemnly down at his hands. Lasari knew an order had been given and there was an unmistakable weight behind it. Strasser slid out of the red leather booth, took Greta by the arm and led her to the noisy dance floor.

The two men seated themselves opposite Lasari, Herr

Rauch taking the inside seat next to the wall. Vayetch gestured to the waiter to clear the table, then asked for a bottle of Scotch and iced Perrier. Rauch picked up a clean napkin, shook out the folds and tucked a corner into his vest.

Neither man spoke. Vayetch took his time about tapping a cigarette on the back of his thumbnail, then lit it with a gold Dunhill lighter. He was a large man with a round-shouldered plumpness that made him look small next to his rangy, angular companion. His face was smooth and hairless, lightly tanned, so unblemished as to seem poreless, like smooth doeskin across his face. He was perhaps thirty-five with dark eyes and carefully combed dark hair, touched with gray above the ears. His mouth was full, almost sensuous, but Lasari was aware of the tic at the corner of his lip, a quiver that had come alive when Greta was hesitant about leaving for the dance floor.

The men were obviously well known at the Atelier; with the liquor order the waiter brought Rauch an appetizer of chopped pickled herring with onion rings and a bottle of red wine. Rauch began to eat immediately, while Vayetch studied Lasari with his flickering smile, then poured himself a whiskey and Perrier, stirring the cubes with a manicured finger.

"Are you enjoying Heidelberg, Mr. Jackson?"

Lasari nodded. "What I've seen of it is very interesting."

"You like the town clock?" the man asked. "Those droll little figures who come out with sledgehammers and pound the drums to tell the hour?"

"No," Lasari said. "I don't like droll little figures. I like a Timex."

"Ah, you think German culture is too florid, too ornamental?"

"I haven't thought of it one way or the other," Lasari said. "That's not the purpose of my trip."

"I see. You are practical, that is good," Vayetch said evenly. "Let *me* explain something practical then. In about three weeks you will be receiving certain merchandise, delivered to you near the Czech border. Now, in terms of ownership, that particular merchandise will be existing in a state of limbo. You are a Catholic, Mr. Jackson?"

"No, but I understand the term."

"Very well. Limbo is like purgatory, neither heaven nor hell, an in-between, a waiting. The occupants of limbo belong neither to God nor to the devil.

"Until it leaves limbo, money for that merchandise will not be paid to us. In fact, it will not be paid until you have delivered the goods to heaven, the United States in this case . . ."

The waiter was hovering and Vayetch fell silent until the man whisked some imaginary crumbs from the tablecloth. Then he said, "Have you ever attended the celebration of Fasching here in Germany, Mr. Jackson?" Lasari shook his head.

"It's like a pagan explosion. I am trying to pick experiences we can both relate to . . . beer foaming in the gutters, virgins throwing themselves at young men, it's carnival, it's fiesta, just before Lent, before the devil presents his bill for the year's sins.

"But the riot of Fasching is nothing compared to the organized chaos in this country when the NATO games are here, troops from Greece and Turkey and France and others including your country swarming the towns and countryside of Germany during combined military maneuvers."

Vayetch shook his head as if he could not quite believe the vision he was creating for Lasari. "It is like the Tower of Babel, but with military orders. Everyone is in command and nobody knows what the other is doing. It is the perfect climate for us to do business, new faces, new languages, movement and displacement, all official, but here today, gone tomorrow.

"But you must be very resolute while you hold our merchandise in limbo. We all have our jobs to do and Herr Rauch will make sure you have no trouble sticking to yours. If you are tempted to disregard instructions, you can depend on him for support to resist that notion, I assure you. You may not see him, but he will be nearby."

The waiter came forward to remove Herr Rauch's herring course and replaced it with a double steak on a wooden platter, surrounded by roast potato balls and minced parsnips.

"You have no comments, Mr. Jackson?"

Lasari shook his head and shrugged. "I'm a good listener," he said.

Vayetch nodded with an approving smile. "I can see that. And you have direct and revealing eyes. You are allowing me to see your doubts, your caution, your distrust. But what I had hoped to see was greed."

Herr Rauch looked up and laughed suddenly, and a bit of

steak caught in his throat. He hunched his shoulders and coughed, took several swallows of wine in a fast, sucking motion, then returned to his food.

"Eyes, yes . . . you have made me think of something that has often puzzled me," Vayetch said. "That custom of tying a scarf over a man's eyes as he meets the firing squad. What is the purpose? How do you know you are punishing a man if you cannot read the fear in his eyes?"

"The blindfold, the last cigarette, that's to give the condemned man a moment of dignity," Lasari said.

"No, no, it shouldn't be that way," Vayetch said with sudden agitation. "The dignity is in the hand that holds the gun, make no mistake about that, my friend."

Vayetch sipped his Scotch, allowing a calm to return to his face. "I know some interesting things about you, Jackson," he said. "As a youth, you played baseball, you were wounded in Vietnam, but you were a good soldier. You deserted your army and decided to return. That was a mistake. You hesitated, you became a philosopher and now you are in big, big trouble. Fate casts you on our side." He looked thoughtful. "So full a life for a young man."

Greta and Strasser returned to the table then. The sergeant's forehead was blistered with sweat but before he could sit down, Vayetch waved him off. "No, no, go back and enjoy yourself, sergeant. We are just getting to know each other here."

When the couple left, Lasari said flatly, "Unless you ask the right questions, I can't tell you what you want to know."

"Answer me this then. We are sports fanatics here in Europe, you know. We watch Wimbledon, the soccer matches from Argentina, the Stanley Cup finals. We get your World Series by satellite. It took me a long time to understand the philosophy of the 'base on balls.' I'm still not sure I do. The defensive team can refuse to pitch to a strong batter. That would be unthinkable in cricket. Or in a contest of boxers, if one side would refuse to come out for a round because the opponent was stronger. Where is the fairness of *that*?"

"A walk puts a runner on base for free," Lasari said, trying to interpret the opaque face of the man opposite him. Herr Rauch continued to eat steadily, slicing the steak into neat squares, chewing carefully and washing each mouthful down with a gulp of wine.

"A freebie, that's the price the pitcher pays for giving a base on balls," Lasari said. "After that, a runner can steal, advance on a passed ball or a hit, then a single could score him. The defensive team gives up the opportunity of striking out a hot batter, but they must also take the chance he'll score anyway."

"You deserted the army in the United States from a hospital," Vayetch said, "not in the field, not in the face of the enemy. That would be something else altogether." Lasari nodded. "And in baseball," Vayetch went on, "were you a good hitter? Did you have—how do you say—great strength at the plate?"

"I had a good glove, I was better in the field," Lasari said carefully.

Vayetch shook his head. "I do not understand. You were *afraid* of big league pitching? You were *afraid* of being struck by a ball? Is that why you were not strong at the plate?"

"You got it wrong, Mr. Vayetch," Lasari said. "It was the opposite. I disregarded caution, I *crowded* the plate. I made myself a target."

Vayetch nodded, a sudden look of excitement in his face. "I enjoy my holidays in Spain often and I've learned something of the bullfight. Some *toreros* work close to the horns out of courage, others out of fear. But you were not afraid of being hit by the baseball, you are saying?"

"Of course I was *afraid* of being hit, but I didn't *expect* it," Lasari said. "I didn't *wait* for it . . . that's the difference."

Vayetch smiled sympathetically. "Everyone is afraid of certain things, Jackson. Herr Rauch here could break me in two like a stalk of celery, but I'm not afraid of that, because I trust him. But I *am* afraid of misjudging you. A great deal depends on my estimate."

Then he laughed, as if dismissing the subject. "You may consider all this *torero* talk as so much bullshit, if you'll forgive a pun. We are in Heidelberg, not Valencia, after all. We have our reality.

"You'll be training dogs, Sergeant Strasser tells me," Pytor Vayetch said. "Are you good at that, is there some quality of personality that allows you to gain their fear or confidence?"

"A dog is a dumb animal with keen instincts," Lasari said. "A raw canine recruit from the kennels will be trying to figure out what a trainer wants from him. If you can make a dog understand your wishes—and you can do that by your voice, by repetition, by using simple commands and a choke chain—if you can do all that, he'll try like hell to do what you tell him, what you show him you want. Never mix work and play in training sessions. Work an animal only as long as his patience and attention hold, then reward him with food, a pat on the head, tell him he's doing great, and you'll get results. And don't forget the choke chain. A smart dog understands getting his wind cut off once in a while . . ."

Vayetch nodded thoughtfully. "Everybody's in limbo, it seems. The batter at the plate, the bullfighter, the dog on the leash, caught between a heaven and hell they're hardly aware of."

The waiter removed the steak platter and set a bowl of blueberries and cream in front of Herr Rauch.

Lasari sipped his beer and looked toward the dance floor where he could see Strasser and Greta, her shiny blonde head bobbing up and down among the dancers.

"This is a hypothetical question, so perhaps you can give me only a hypothetical answer, but try to be honest. Would you have deserted in a combat situation in Vietnam?" Vayetch said.

"No," Lasari said. "No, I would not."

"Always you would crowd the plate, work close to the horns, right?"

"I walked out of a hospital in the States, but I wouldn't walk away from a platoon in a firefight."

"You're certain of that?"

"Mr. Vayetch," Lasari said, "if you're interviewing me for a job, why don't you come out and ask me what the hell you really want to know. Will I run out on you or not? Will I try to fuck up your deal or not? That's what you're trying to find out, isn't it?"

"That *is* my concern," the man said, and signaled for the check.

"You spelled it out earlier, Mr. Vayetch," Lasari said. "I'm in big, big trouble, and that's why I'm here. So think of me as a dog you're training. Keep your commands clear and easy. I don't want to guess, I don't want to think. I'll do what I'm told, but if I were you I'd keep a choke chain handy. Either you know how to use me or you don't. It's all really up to you."

"It's not that simple," the man said. "The decision is not completely mine." He opened his wallet, counted out a stack of deutsche marks and put them on top of the check.

Herr Rauch had finished his blueberries. He wiped his mouth on his napkin and drank the rest of his wine. Lasari noticed the berries had stained the man's mouth, edging his heavy lips with a faint line of blue. Vayetch glanced at his companion directly for the first time.

"Well, Herr Rauch?"

The man continued to wipe his lips with the napkin. At last he looked at Lasari and nodded dourly. "He is right for us, Vayetch."

Rauch dipped the corner of his napkin in his water goblet, then daubed his cheeks and forehead, as if he felt faint. Standing suddenly, he said, "I'll wait outside for you, Pytor. Even from the dance floor, the whore's perfume spoiled my dinner."

# Chapter Twenty-six

A FEMALE CIVILIAN wearing a striped cafeteria uniform brought a tray of coffee and sandwiches into Colonel Benton's office. The colonel slipped off his military jacket and hung it inside the closet door. Major Staub stood at the window, a half-smoked cigarette slanting in his mouth, watching a squadron of Navy jets heading toward the Potomac.

Benton thanked the young woman and when the door closed, said to the major, "I'm late because Senator Copeland was late, but I wanted to bring him abreast of our operation, convince him everything's under control. He's pleased." The colonel laughed without humor. "In fact, *he* tried to reassure *me* that this is just a small-time operation."

"Copeland is a self-made senile; he was born an old fogey. That man would rather talk than think," Major Staub said. "But in this case, I believe he's right."

"Spare me your amateur aphorisms, or whatever those were," Benton said, "and come over here and serve yourself, Merrill. I'm in no mood to play host."

Staub moved to the desk and lifted a slice off several sandwiches before finding one that suited him. He poured himself black coffee and took his lunch back to the window seat.

"Goddamn it," Benton said impatiently as he rifled the sandwich tray. "I told them no cheese and no egg salad. Whatever happened to watercress and turkey and class? If it isn't one thing, it's another."

"Easy, Dick, easy," the major said soothingly. He paused as the distant jets hit the sound barrier, sending off a rapid cannonade. "At least you're winning the big ones. I feel quite optimistic about the current operation. We've tracked our man every mile from Chicago right through to Heidelberg. Our assignee on that side of the water monitored last night's meet. Private Jackson is part of the loop. For the time being we may be observers, but we are distinctly operative. Patience is the name of the game."

"The point is," Benton said, "I'm cautious both by nature and experience, and I want to *keep* this a small-time action, something within the confines of our jurisdiction, entirely under wraps. I made that clear from the beginning. So Stigmuller's interest jolted me and nobody wants Tarbert Weir sniffing the wind. I don't want to expand our parameters for *any reason*, Merrill, not for any irrelevant bullshit *whatsoever*."

The colonel sipped his coffee and wished he were lunching alone. He picked up a pad and pencil and began to doodle. He would have liked to be in an isolation tank, freed from all external stimuli, disconnected from his own nervous system, from distractions. His nose itched and he momentarily resented even that demand on his attention. His wife's recent attitudes, the deeply personal demands on his emotions were draining the energies he so badly needed for his work. When he thought of her even, white teeth, the strain of her smile, he could feel the muscles in his stomach and groin tightening with anger.

"This morning Senator Copeland referred to our problem euphemistically as 'the minor excesses of a few sergeants,' " he said to Staub. "Let's just hope so. You know my philosophy about rumors—true or not, don't let 'em get started. I'm more concerned about the allover picture, the suspicions and innuendos, the hearsay that might tarnish the image of the U.S. military man. We're stockpiling our GIs on foreign soil just as we're stockpiling nuclear weapons. We've got to keep our noses clean." He sighed. "Now bring me up to date on Stigmuller."

"Buck Stigmuller is a peripheral part of the big picture," Major Staub said. "He accepted my report and interpretation on those four murdered GIs and passed the information on, presumably, to General Weir. Neither had further questions."

"And Chicago, what do you hear from Clarence Mc-Dade?"

"I'm in touch with the superintendent at least once a day. The city gave Mark Weir a hero's sendoff and McDade accepts the fact that the lieutenant's death, in a sense, also happened to one of ours. He shares our stance of antianarchism and prokinship. The murder of a police officer in any city is a grave insult to the entire populace. McDade's people are turning Chicago upside down. So far it's been a dead end, so to speak."

Benton pressed his fingers against his temples and tried to focus his thoughts. His concentration was splintered because, ridiculously, his rich and handsome wife had been refusing root canal surgery for three months. She thought it would be boring and unnecessary. Benton realized his wife had both a terror of pain and a dread of losing her teeth and he had tried everything he could to get her into a dentist's office. Now she faced the prospect of losing a pair of front molars and the possible extraction of her upper front incisors. Translated from dental jargon, that meant Ginny Benton would need false teeth.

She had reacted to the news by extending the daily cocktail hour, Pine Valleys over cracked ice, and yesterday had called the farm in Virginia to cancel the spring yearling sale without consulting the colonel. Last night she had spent several hours crying on her side of the bed.

Christ, Benton thought, looking at the pad on which he'd been doodling. Without realizing it, he had scrawled a margin to margin mosaic of one name: Tarbert Weir.

"All right," he said. "Let's get to our final problem—Weir."

"Of course, Captain Jetter has been in touch with you directly about that," Staub said. "He's checked in with me several times."

"Yes," Benton said, "but I wish he wouldn't be so goddamned pussyfoot about everything. He signed into the guest house right next door, you know."

Staub nodded. "Froggie is very aware. He wanted the perfect vantage point. He reports that General Weir is playing golf, riding, wining and dining in seclusion with his lady friend. Greenbrier registration says they expect the general to be their guest for some time. Jetter's paid off the garage to let him know if the general or his lady calls for the car. On top of that Froggie says he's aware of heavy boozing, a lot of noise and cursing from the general's quarters. In short, Scotty Weir is on a jag.''

"Or he'd like the world to believe that," Colonel Benton said dryly. "I think it would be a mistake to jump to the conclusion that Weir is just one more bereaved parent with normal, sentimental compulsions. He's complex but he's always had the personal drive of a Mack truck. Nothing in his dossier points to evasions, blackouts or buck-passing. Mark Weir was murdered. That's a fact, and I'm concerned about exactly how Scotty Weir is facing that fact.''

"As you say, colonel," Major Staub said, "but at the moment, the subject seems immobile. And there *were* reports he was deep into the booze even back in Springfield. Anyone who drinks Tequila Gold is a lush in my book, or a supermasochist at least. I'll get in touch with Jackson and give him your thinking.''

"I'll call myself," Benton said. "I want to be sure there's no break in our surveillance, none whatsoever. Right now I feel I'm sitting on a pailful of live cats.''

After Staub left, Colonel Benton talked for five minutes to Captain Hays Jetter in guest house E on Carolina Row at the Greenbrier. When he hung up he put his luncheon things on the tray, aligned the files and memos on his desk, then tore off the scribbled sheet from his notepad and threw it into the wastebasket. On second thought, he fished the piece of paper out again and ripped it into a dozen small pieces.

# Chapter Twenty-seven

TWIN TAILLIGHTS ON the Porsche 911-SC blinked as Pytor Vayetch, with Herr Rauch in the passenger seat beside him, braked at the crosswalk, then made a sharp left and turned on a narrow, bricked street.

Lasari and Strasser stood in front of the Atelier, the flashing neon sign above the doorway, a horned devil with trident, coating their faces scarlet.

Greta pushed open the door and joined them. "A big man at the bar stopped me. He asked my name," she said primly. "He thought I was an American girl he knew from Princeton, but it was someone else." She smiled. "I think he just thought I was pretty, but he's too old for me." Strasser ignored her.

"That's a lot of shit, what you just said, Jackson," he said to Lasari. "Get in my car. You're comin' with me and Greta right now."

"No, I'll take a cab later."

"You're not a fucking civilian, Jackson. I thought you understood the ground rules."

"I want to be alone. I want to drink some beer and not listen to anybody," Lasari said.

"If it's me," Greta said, "I won't talk at all. There's beer in the refrigerator and we can all watch television. There's 'Dallas' tonight and that's a good one." She pronounced the name with the stress on the second syllable.

"Goddamn it, Greta, shut up!" Strasser said.

"You're just mad because you had to dance and that makes you sweat," she said. "Mr. Vayetch has no respect for us. I was glad to dance. I would rather watch pigs eat than Herr Rauch. I'm surprised he bothers with a knife and fork. I'm surprised he doesn't sweat when he eats."

"All right, Lasari, go have a beer," Strasser said, his voice tight with rage. "Or take a walk, or do what the fuck you want. But I'll be sitting up till you walk in that door and don't you forget it."

Lasari walked up the slanted street to the bridge and stood on the crest of the old stone arch, hearing the flow of water beneath. He studied as much of the sprawling city as he could see in the thin moonlight, the antique street lights and glowing windows of the old buildings in this part of town.

Heidelberg lies along the Neckar River, a dozen miles from its confluence with the Rhine. One street, the Hauptstrasse, dominates the town, running its length on a parallel course with the river. It is an ancient city of bridges and churches and a picturesque castle on the wooded outskirts of the town. On the other side of the river Lasari could see the outlines of the Bismarck monument, a landmark he had passed in the cab on the way to Strasser's apartment, and that gave him his bearings.

Lasari walked along the Hauptstrasse, listening to the echo of his footsteps on the pavement. He passed several cafes with brightly lit windows, the bar and tables inside crowded with tanned faces and short haircuts. Country western or disco music sounded out into the street.

He stopped at a *bierstube* with stained glass windows facing the street and was surprised to find it crowded inside, damply cool with the smell of beer, and sawdust on the floor.

Lasari sat at the bar and ordered a glass of dark beer. He was near a university, he realized, because several tables were occupied by students, drinking beer and poring over books. Other areas were crowded with older working men, a few playing a game with oblong slates on special wooden tables. In one corner a family of six, four pudgy daughters and their middle-aged parents, were eating bratwurst and watching a game show on the TV at the end of the bar.

Lasari sipped his beer slowly, relishing the coldness against the still-raw abrasions where his teeth had gashed the lining of his mouth and tongue.

A drift of the bartender's cigarette smoke caught in Lasari's throat and he put his hand to his face, trying not to cough. There was still a dull ache in his head from the beatings in Chicago and any quick motion or spasm could bring a burst of pain to his taped ribs. He had walked along the Hauptstrasse faster than he meant to, agitated by his talk with Vayetch, troubled by the dilemma in which he found himself. He realized his body was moist with exertion and tension, the heavy taping on his ribs giving off a sticky chemical odor. Lasari put a hand inside his jacket and touched the bandages through his shirt. They felt thick and layered but even the touch of his fingers sent shivers of pain through his bruised ribs.

The conversation with the two strangers in the restaurant had left him with a terrible sense of inadequacy. They had been briefed, they knew his background, his records and their knowledge robbed him of defenses. What did he know about them?

Somewhere, in the hospital or Jackson Hole, he remembered reading what a logician had written: Survival is knowledge. Examine a trap to learn its dimensions, its properties; decide for what it is designed to lure and snare. Study the bait.

Lasari sipped beer and tried to apply the logician's test. He knew he was in a trap but he couldn't define its true shape or dimensions or how to escape. He wasn't even sure if he was the victim or the bait.

Lasari's thoughts were jarred when someone in the bar laughed, a high, familiar laugh that rang out above the hum of voices. He turned to the German family looking at television, but they were eating and watching solemnly.

If he disobeyed the orders of Malleck and Strasser, and now Vayetch and Herr Rauch, and made a run for it, they could report him and he would be on his way to federal prison. If he cooperated, if he smuggled the contraband into the United States and was caught, the same thing could happen. He had struggled to persuade himself to appeal to the army, to admit to his desertion. Now he had compounded desertion with criminal collusion. Would any Army brass believe otherwise?

A lanky young man in civilian clothes walked behind Lasari and toward the front door. In the reflection of the bar mirror, Lasari saw that he had blond, curly hair and a flickering smile. He did not look at Lasari but gave the bartender a soft salute, calling over his shoulder, "See you all again. You take care, you hear?"

Lasari felt a sudden new pain in his gut, a jolt of fear. As the door swung shut behind the blond man, a draft of cold air from the Neckar swept through the barroom.

Lasari now knew why Sergeant Strasser had allowed him this time alone on the town, because he was not alone. He was being watched. The blond man was Eddie Neal, the soldier from the Chicago armory who had wanted to put the boots to him as he lay on the floor at Karl Malleck's feet. And the laugh, the mocking humorless laugh, was the one he had heard just before he was bludgeoned into blackness in Connie Caidin's apartment.

Bonnie Caidin. . . . *"The little newspaper cunt has been on my payroll from the beginning. . . . Who do you think gave us the fucking key, you ginny bastard . . ."*

Lasari paid for his beer and left the bar. He looked up and down the Hauptstrasse. It seemed to him suddenly more than a strange street in a strange town. It was now a menacing place of dangers, a stretch of lampposts, darkened doorways and shadows . . . a world of watching Sergeant Mallecks, Herr Rauchs and Eddie Neals.

Lasari spotted a cruising cab, flagged it and gave the driver the address of Strasser's apartment.

The apartment door was off the latch and Lasari pushed it open. Greta was sitting on the floor in a blue chenille robe, watching TV with the sound off, a stern man with a goatee reading the late news. Her expression was petulant and her legs were stretched out straight in front of her, slim and pale, in a pose that was childish and defiant. Her high-heeled, ankle-strapped sandals were sprawled carelessly on the floor nearby.

"He won't let me play the television," she said, pushing her thick, fair hair away from her temples. She had pulled out the combs and the soft waves fell to her shoulders. "He's angry with you, so that makes him angry with me." Her smile was sullen and shrewd. "He's drunk, you know, but not that drunk. I got into bed with him and he tried to do something, but he said he was too angry."

Lasari looked around the apartment and then went over to

one of the cuckoo clocks on the wall. With a finger he touched the long pine cone pendulums, sending them swinging back and forth. "Don't any of these damned clocks work, Greta? You'd go to bed if you knew what time it was."

"Of course they work," she said, "but they're not wound up. Who wants to hear cuckoos all day long? And you shouldn't touch those clocks. He won't even let *me* go near them. They're his hobby, he is very proud of them."

"Why does he want so many?" Lasari said.

She shrugged. "Maybe you're just jealous of Ernie because he has something special. He hires my cousin to carve those pine cones, each one separate." She pulled her chenille robe above her bare knees.

"You Americans don't like us because you beat us in the war and you think we're rich again. Let me tell you something, Mr. Jackson. All Germans don't have it so good. Many people have no jobs. My cousin is sixteen. He would like to be a carpenter but his father cannot pay ten thousand deutsche marks to buy him an apprenticeship."

Greta's voice had become soft and petulant, on the verge of tears, as she stared at the walls of clocks.

"That's almost four thousand dollars, those deutsche marks, not much to you rich Americans, but a lot of money for poor Germans. My cousin has no work. That's why the big Ernest Strasser can hire a boy to sit in the cellar and carve things for his silly cuckoos."

The sway and the click of the pendulums seemed to agitate her, so Lasari stopped them carefully with the tip of his finger.

"I think your cousin does nice work, Greta," he said.

"You don't care about my cousin," she said, "and you don't care about me. Do you know what it means for a girl to go to bed with a man and nothing happens? It's not because he's angry, it's not because he's drunk. That's not true. He is very afraid, you know. But if I try to talk to him about that, he goes crazy . . ."

Lasari slid the catch on the front door to lock it and turned toward the hallway leading to his bedroom.

"Can I make some cocoa and bring it to your room?" Greta asked.

"I don't drink cocoa," Lasari said. "It keeps me awake."

"All right! You'll be lonely some night, you cowboy shit!"

she called after him. "You'll beg to stay awake and have cocoa. Don't ask me for it then, Jackson. You can make it yourself then, goddamn you . . . And what did you think, that I would tell him something on you?"

# Chapter Twenty-eight

SERGEANT DUBOIS GORDON paid for his purchases at the newsstand in the lobby. He put candy bars in a jacket pocket and stood peeling the cellophane from a pack of menthol cigarettes, aware of a prickling sensation at the nape of his neck. The first floor of Chicago Police Headquarters seemed to him hyperactive this morning, almost hostile. Gordon felt that he was being watched.

The building had been remodeled some years ago. The lobby floor was now an open space, almost a half block in length, with white marble paneling, terrazzo floors and windows that let in a maximum of daylight.

Gordon stood with his back to a wall and let his eyes travel over the shifting crowd. He saw a couple of plainclothes officers he knew, a reporter from City Press waiting at the elevators, the usual flow of office workers, lawyers, bondsmen and citizens going about their business.

Gordon had felt more comfortable in this building in the old days. As a rookie cop he was excited by the shabby atmosphere of the neighborhood, a tangle of railroad tracks just across State Street and rows of honky-tonk movies, church missions, burlesque houses and pawnshops in the surrounding blocks. That had felt like the real city to him. The railroad yards had long since been replaced by the angular modern architecture of the Dearborn Park condominium development. Between that project and the rows of blue and white police cars lined up at headquarters, the traffic on State Street moved through the area at a horn-honking pace. The neighborhood had become prosperous and middle class.

To Gordon's sharp eye, nothing inside the lobby or outside in the streets seemed out of the ordinary. Then he realized what was tugging at his attention.

Among the glassed-in cases of police citations and memorabilia on the south wall, an addition had been made. Gordon walked to the section marked by a lettered plaque in gold: IN SUPREME SACRIFICE.

To this display, row on row of photographs of Chicago police officers who had lost their lives in the line of duty over the last decades, the Honors Committee, sometime in the last few hours, had added the picture of Lieutenant Mark Weir. The eight-by-ten glossy photo appeared to have been placed in the gallery in haste. All other officers' pictures were in muted color, set off by distinctive, matching frames. Mark's unframed photograph, in full uniform, was in black and white, pinned on a background of dark velvet, his numbered brass badge imposed beneath.

Gordon looked at the familiar face with a new sense of rage and disbelief. In time Mark Weir's likeness might blend and fade into the ranks of honored dead, the sergeant knew, but this morning the glossy photo, the velvet background and the smudge of fingerprints on the glass paneling were as conspicuous as damp soil on a new grave.

Gordon walked to the bank of elevators, picked a crowded car, then pushed the button for the twelfth floor. He kept his eyes on the blinking floor lights above the door, unwilling to make eye contact with anyone else in the car. His frustration, his anger, were so corrosive he did not want to share those emotions with any man.

"Goddamn it, Mark," he thought bitterly, "one thing I am *not* going to do, and that is I am *not* going to mention this to your old man when he calls. You got my word on that, friend, and on everything else that counts. The honored dead is bullshit. The only way to honor a fellow officer is to get the bastards who did it . . ."

Lieutenant Weir's office on the twelfth floor was now the unofficial command post for the investigation into his death.

The desk had been cleared of all Weir's reports and personal papers. They were in a special corner file. Plants from the window sill, his favorite coffee pot, and an oil portrait of a racehorse he'd once owned part of had been removed and sent to his apartment. The desk top was aligned now with a dozen wire file baskets stacked with bound account books. A tape recorder and amplifier had been arranged on a nearby table.

Sergeant Gordon sat at the desk and broke a large Hershey bar into four pieces. The first two pieces would be breakfast, the second two lunch. Mrs. Lewis had offered him coffee and a sweet roll but the overheated atmosphere of her apartment had made him feel confined and thirsty, not hungry. He had asked for a glass of water.

Lieutenant Weir's corner office was one of two on the twelfth floor with a view of Lake Michigan. The water was choppy today and from this distance Gordon could not tell if he was looking at whitecaps or the breakup of ice.

Life was moving too rapidly and in all the wrong directions, the sergeant thought. He would have more of it. He had been up, at work, for hours, but already the clock had ticked past noon and was edging toward tomorrow. Mark Weir had been dead only days, yet every sunset that passed without an answer to his killing seemed a new affront to the victim himself. Before long, the days would lengthen and it would be spring . . .

Doobie Gordon's father liked to fish Lake Michigan in the spring, casting for steelheads and lake trout off the stone breakers that bulwarked the shore. Mark Weir had laughed and said he couldn't believe it when Gordon first told him about the big fish still in the lake, and the very next day the man standing next to Mr. Gordon had caught a twenty-five pound Chinook salmon.

Gordon felt an almost uncontrollable sadness and popped chocolate into his mouth, hoping the sweetness would send a rush of energy through his body.

The sergeant had spent most of the morning with Amanda Lewis in her south side apartment, a third-story walkup in a building so covered with pink and green graffiti, it looked almost tropical. Mrs. Lewis had called the sergeant at the number he had given her. The ring of the phone woke him at home a little before seven.

It was the last letter from Randolph Lewis that had got her thinking. With the funeral of her nephew and the lieutenant's murder, well, she hadn't been concentrating right and that bothered her. She got the letter out and read it over and over again. The reason she had called the sergeant was one sentence she couldn't make sense of. ". . . I'll maybe be sending you gifts, Auntie. I'll know when I see you."

Randy had never sent gifts before, she told Gordon, and, in fact, no gifts had arrived. She hadn't thought too much about it till whoever that was who had called Lieutenant Weir and used her name. She'd felt so badly about that, she'd tried to remember and think of everything. That's when the question of the gifts began to worry her. She'd asked the mailman and he said he'd delivered everything that had her name on it, which was nothing much at all, since that last letter from Germany. She'd bused herself down to the main post office and talked to a lost and found clerk. He'd explained to her that they couldn't put a tracer on a package until they knew a package had actually been mailed. Chicago's was the busiest postal center in the world, he'd told her. It was the mail order center of the United States and more than ninety percent of everything ordered through catalogues went through Chicago. With all those packages coming and going, and the fact that her nephew's letter was so vague . . . well, there was nothing to go on.

The sergeant thanked Mrs. Lewis and told her she was right to contact him and to call again about anything, *anything* that might occur to her.

Now, back in the office, Gordon picked up where he had left off late last evening, and spent the next few hours going over tenant rental records dating back five years for buildings in Cabrini Green, the building in which Mark was murdered and the four others closest to it. He worked deliberately, using a red plastic ruler to slide down under the column entries, studying names, sizes of families, lengths of stay, moving patterns and payment records. Whoever had shot Mark was familiar with the buildings, the apartment layouts, the elevators, the stairs . . .

At a quarter to three Gordon put aside the Cabrini Green files and shut the office door. He told the switchboard operator to hold all his calls except one he was expecting from

Tarbert Weir. Then he switched on the tape from Mark's police car, the tape with the anonymous voice asking for a rendezvous at Cabrini Green. The amplifier swelled the words and threw the voice into every corner of the office.

Sergeant Gordon laced his fingers together over his vest, shut his eyes and tilted back the office chair, almost in an attitude of repose. He let the tape play over and over again, allowing every word, inflection and tone quality stamp its impression into the auditory-response neurons of his brain. He began to wonder briefly if the man's voice seemed familiar because he *did* know it, or only because he had heard it so often that it was becoming routine. No matter, he thought, listening to the repeated tones as intimate as if he held a seashell to his ear, no matter, I will know it if I hear this man again.

DuBois Gordon sat upright in the office chair, frowning with concentration at the paper in front of him. The general's voice and questions were efficient and articulate but cold, almost as if they were total strangers. Person to person, with body language and eye contact, Tarbert Weir had projected as more human, less formidable. Now the conversation seemed one-sided, almost authoritarian, with impatient waits for information, long questioning pauses on the general's end of the line.

It was because he had so little concrete to report, the sergeant realized; the few roads of inquiry the police department had been able to follow had turned into detours or dead ends.

A department message form had been on the desk when Sergeant Gordon checked in. "Tarbert Weir called. Will call again at four o'clock sharp."

When the phone rang Gordon had looked at his wristwatch. It read four minutes to four. Dammit, he thought irritably as he picked up the phone, the blasted thing is running slow on me, I'll have to get my watch fixed . . .

He had made a checklist of points he wanted to discuss with the general and he looked at the paper as he spoke. "The guns, general," he said into the phone, "both Ballistics and Stolen Property have been working on that. Lugers are hard to trace, about the worst. They could have come into the States from Europe or down from Canada any time in the last five years or earlier. Lab's got the report on the bullets. They've got clear calibration marks and could match bullet to gun. We have men checking every pawnshop, gunsmith, collector and hot shop in Chicago and through the state. So far, nothing.''

"I see," the general said.

"The murder site itself, that's still being checked inch by inch. Fingerprints number into the hundreds for the six apartments on that floor and we're running a check on all of them. Superintendent McDade ordered units to work Cabrini round the clock for any fact, rumor or hearsay that might bear on Mark's case. We are getting maximum cooperation, we think, but so far only dead-end leads.

"Every officer in town is working on his private stoolies to come up with something. McDade talked to the press, he talked to the individual districts. We've got the word out on the street that the police department will do a lot of favors, a lot of forgiving to anyone who gives us information on Mark's murder.''

The sergeant paused for a response, but there was none. In the silence he felt he could hear the general's breathing over the miles of telephone wires that swayed and hummed through four states down to White Sulphur Springs, West Virginia.

"Are you with me, general?" he said.

"I'm listening," Weir said.

"All right then. I had backup personnel to check me out," Gordon said, "but I personally went through every scrap of paper in Mark's wallet and on his person. I went through his desk, his files, every report he'd made out in the last year. I came across nothing irregular, nothing that needed any extra explanation.

"And his apartment, general. There's not a drawer, a bookcase, an address book we haven't turned inside out, examined and analyzed. We found nothing there that helped our case.''

Again there was silence.

"I put some of the more personal things aside, sir, things you might want to go through later. As an officer, Mark was the model of efficiency, but he was kind of a packrat about his private life. He hoarded kid snapshots, old plane tickets, every letter you wrote when he was in school in the States . . .''

"Later, Gordon," the general said abruptly. "That doesn't seem relevant now. What else do you want to tell me?''

"A message from the superintendent. Clarence McDade wants to assure you that he is personally in charge of this investigation, that he gets a twice-daily report on all progress."

"Progress?" Weir asked, a touch of irony shading his tone.

"The progress of elimination, if nothing else, elimination of probabilities, narrowing the field of suspects is necessary to any investigation," Gordon said. "Take recent releases or paroles, for example. McDade was emphatic; he wanted those records examined for anyone who might have a blood vengeance or even a death feud against Lieutenant Weir, anyone he'd put in the pen who got out recently. Once again, nothing. Mark was a hard officer, but impersonal in his work, even criminals respected that. Besides, he was a little young to have stockpiled enemies."

"We've got to assume he had at least one," the general said coldly.

Gordon examined the checklist on his desk pad, then made a tick after Mrs. Lewis' name and briefed the general quickly on the woman and her observation about gifts from her nephew, and her concern that no gifts had arrived.

"It's only a hunch on my part," Gordon went on, "but I'm working on the theory that our best clues will come from time and place. Cabrini Green, the place. We're interviewing, we're talking, we're knocking on doors. And we're examining leases and rental records for a name, a combination of names, a coincidence, maybe, anything that will tell us *why* Cabrini Green."

"But it's still a question. You still don't know *why*," Weir said flatly.

"Not yet, sir, not yet."

"In short, sergeant," Tarbert Weir said, "with all the best intentions in this investigation, the police are just about where they were an hour or so after my son was shot."

"The kind of progress we're making is hard to measure, sir, but we're not standing still. Take Mark's phone tape, the one with that last rendezvous call on it. We put linguistic experts on it at once, specifically an authority who specializes in acoustic phonetics. I don't feel free to give you the details, general, but we have a pretty good profile of what kind of person that caller is—sex, age, education, nationality, background. And about *time*, we also know that person was not out duck hunting, he was not farming in Kansas, he was not playing pinochle in Toledo. Five hours before Lieutenant Weir was killed, that man was in a phone booth, maybe in a private home, *somewhere* in the state of Illinois, probably in the city of Chicago, talking to your son. We know that for sure."

He paused. "I've spent hours listening to that tape and I'm adding my personal feelings to what the experts are telling us. I'm convinced that voice speaking is not the voice of a total stranger. It's not necessarily someone I *know*, but someone I ought to know . . ."

"I appreciate everything you people are trying to do, sergeant," General Weir said. The finality in his voice told Gordon this conversation was nearing its end. "And I thank you for it."

"If there's a breakthrough, where can I reach you?"

"John Grimes at my home phone number. You can trust him with anything, Gordon."

The sergeant was reluctant to hang up the phone; he knew there was still something important and unspoken between them.

"General, Mark felt he was up against a stone wall in those murders we were working on, that's why he turned to you when he did. Mark sensed he was out of his depth . . . hell, we both did. Chicago's our beat and yet we couldn't get a handle on what was happening. We had the *effect* here in Chicago, but the *cause*, that's what we couldn't get near. Mark had the impression that the cause might be outside our jurisdiction . . ."

"Sergeant Gordon," the general said, "I've been making some inquiries of my own, as you may have inferred. But to use your own phrase, I don't feel free to give you the details. Just let me assure you I understand what you're saying, that I am aware the trouble could be coming from somewhere else. That was one of the last things my son said to me."

It was nearly midnight when Tarbert Weir let himself out the rear door and set off at a slow walk along the pathway behind the cottages on South Carolina Row. Here and there lights from windows touched the path and lit portions of the groomed, fragrant shrubbery, tipped with new buds. Above the night breezes, there was a faint murmur of voices, the drone of late movies on TV and an occasional clink of glasses.

Weir walked swiftly but easily, swinging his arms and breathing deeply, looking like a midnight jogger in runners' shoes and gray track suit. It wasn't until he was out of the immediate resort grounds, passing behind the shuttered crafts workshop and the Greenbrier museum a half mile from the main buildings, that he broke into a run.

His final telephone conversation with General Stigmuller earlier that evening had been as detailed and grave as a wartime briefing. Stigmuller had said, "I can't condone or even recommend what you're doing, Scotty, but I understand what's driving you and you have my word I'll back you in every way. It's the old survivor's shock syndrome, the way a survivor feels after a battle. You look at the casualties and wish you could be, even *try* to be, part of them in some way. Am I right, Scotty?"

"That's part of it, Buck," the general said, "and I'm not sure yet of the other part. But I'm ready now for what you've got for me."

Stigmuller responded by giving him in detail the Army records of Durham Francis Lasari. "You realize, Scotty, that it's more than ten years since this man was Army. I can't bring you any more up to date than this."

"I understand," Weir said.

"Private Jackson is a different matter," Stigmuller went on. "We haven't been able to locate the original enlistment records under that name, with no middle initial given, but a Private George Jackson was assigned orders out of Chicago about ten days ago and he's been traveling."

Stigmuller summarized the orders that had been cut and signed for Private Jackson, starting in Chicago and delivering him currently to an assignment in West Germany.

Now, as he broke into a trot, Weir ran the facts of both cases through his mind. He kept his footsteps light on the spongy sod, staying close to the trees and hedge line of the Lakeside golf course, watching for the exact stand of pines he had chosen as his landmark to make his break to the right and begin the climb up Old White Course.

Weir's single piece of luggage was there, hidden under a patch of wineberries that edged the fairway. He and Laura Devers had played Old White late yesterday. He had picked up an electric golf cart at the clubhouse, driven round to the back door of the guest cottage. First he loaded a half case of iced beer into the cart. Then he slipped his suitcase under the beer, put two sets of clubs into the cart, and called loudly to Laura to join him.

At the ninth hole, Weir had become aware of a solitary golfer shooting behind them, approaching and playing out each hole in a methodical fashion, never too close to the twosome, but never far behind.

On the eleventh hole Weir had pulled his cart off the pathway into the rough and waited. As the lone golfer drove up in his cart, Weir recognized him as the man assigned to the cottage next to his.

"We're holding you up, friend," Weir called out to the golfer, a burly man with a thick neck and protuberant eyes. "Why don't you play through?"

The man stared at Weir in obvious surprise. "No, no, you play on. I didn't realize I was crowding you."

Laura Devers smiled. "This is a long vacation for us and I'm afraid I'm learning the game as I go. I'll be embarrassed if you just don't play on through."

The man agreed, took a couple of practice swings, then turned for a last look at Weir. He hit a long drive straight down the fairway, got into his cart and followed the ball into the distance.

At the twelfth hole Laura Devers took six putts on the green and Weir waited until the sound of the lone golfer's cart was only a faint whine in the distance. Then he removed his luggage and concealed it in the wineberry bushes.

Now, as the ground began to rise slightly, Weir felt the slip of dew under his feet and smelled the mountain chill in the air. The weather was fair with a few scattered clouds lit by a quarter moon.

Weir had instructed Stigmuller that he wanted an unmarked charter helicopter, not an Army requisition, and Stigmuller understood. Weir then gave him time, location and approximate grid coordinates for the twelfth hole. There would be no radio communications, no ground lights. The time would be exactly 0100 hours and the only signal would be a triple flash from a flashlight on the middle of the twelfth fairway. There would be one passenger and destination would be disclosed when he was on board.

"You don't want to give me a flight plan, Scotty?" Stigmuller said.

"Trust me, Buck," Weir said. "I'll feel a lot more sure of what I'm doing when I get to where I think I ought to be."

Now he stood in the shadows at the wood's edge, suitcase in one hand, a powerful flashlight in the other. He felt the approach of the helicopter even before he saw it, a vibration that seemed to come from the earth and up through the soles of his shoes. Moments later he heard a high, metallic hum and saw a triangle of lights coming toward him across the sky like moving stars.

Tarbert Weir ran out into the fairway, crisscrossed the darkness with three brief flashes from his electric torch, then waited while the machine took its bearings and hovered toward the ground, flattening the moonlit grass with its rotors, and then settled like a trained bird.

Weir ran to the helicopter, slung up his luggage and climbed aboard. The flight to Dallas should take two hours, he calculated, then another flight to Mexico City. By late sunrise he would be on a commercial airline, flying east toward Germany.

# Chapter Twenty-nine

BITTE AND DANKE were purebred Alsatians, intelligent, active, but eager for discipline. Duro Lasari had been working out with them for several days in a secluded promenade in Philo Park. The trees and shrubbery were bare now, held together by a series of winding pathways that led directly to Heidelberg's oldest bridge, a long, graceful stone arch called Alte Brucke. Between the rows of elm and linden the area was alive with strollers, joggers, nursemaids pushing baby carriages, and students on benches, studying with their coat collars turned up against the wind off the river.

Bitte was a cream and silver female and Danke was a black male with huge paws and a thick body, weighing almost fifty pounds. Lasari had been told by Sergeant Strasser that the dogs responded only to German, but their owner wanted them trained to English commands. In the morning Lasari was picked up at the apartment by an armed driver in a military jeep who took his daily orders from Strasser. The training sessions with the dogs were on staggered hours: four hours the first day, then six, then four and so on. At the end of each time period the dogs were returned to the kennels and Lasari was driven back to Strasser's apartment.

Lasari was working with beginners' basics, just as he had learned to dog handle in his early army days. He was training both dogs at once, on a double lead system, walking them back and forth at his heels, left and right with single commands—"heel," "sit," and "stay."

219

He wore civilian clothes, a zippered windbreaker and chinos tucked into short boots. He carried a pair of cuffed leather gloves folded in his back pocket but the dogs did not nip or show a tendency to bite, so he had decided on barehand signals and rewards.

There had been a brief respite in the initial hours under the trees with the responsive animals, but Lasari realized from the first day that he was not alone or unwatched in Philo Park. He heard the sound of a distinctive Southern voice once and spotted Eddie Neal buying a bratwurst from a vendor. Again, taking the dogs for a run, he saw Strasser and Greta having hot chocolate at a terrace cafe and Greta had turned quickly, bending down as if to retie the laces on her white boots. The same middle-aged American he had noticed at the bar in the Atelier was seated on a park bench one morning, reading a German newspaper. A few moments later he strolled off and was gone. There were several persons he saw every day, well-dressed, energetic men, moving as if walking were a serious business, but he could not tell if they were businessmen, tourists or professors from the university on a break between classes. It was Herr Rauch whom Lasari was most concerned about, but he was nowhere in sight.

Lasari tried to concentrate on the dogs, keeping his commands brief and efficient, but his thoughts were splintered. He was preoccupied with the trap he was in, frustrated and sullen that he could think of no way out. In the treadmill of his mind it seemed to him that, either as Duro Lasari or George Jackson, he had no options, no choice in any direction that would not be rewarded by time in a federal prison. There was not even the challenge of a maze to face; behind every closed door or twisted corridor a Neal or Strasser, a Malleck or a military court-martial was lying in wait for him.

On his fourth day in Philo Park, Lasari became aware of difficulties with Danke. The big dog's eyes were alert and intelligent, and he trembled to please and obey commands. But after each workout, the animal became restless, could not hold the "stay" position and turned to Lasari with whining yelps. Lasari reprimanded him with a sharp tap on the muzzle, a stern verbal rebuke. Then he noticed the male dog seemed hot, panting heavily, while the female was calm. Both wore heavy leather collars, studded with decorative brass, but it was

Danke that repeatedly sank back on his haunches, yelped and scratched at his ruff.

Lasari called the dog to him and ran a finger under its collar. The collar was not too tight but at the back, in the area just over the ripple of neck muscles, Lasari's fingers touched a small aluminum microphone. Over the days, in the heat of workouts and sweat, the metallic surface of the detecting device had interacted to irritate the dog's skin. Lasari found a discarded newspaper in a trash basket, tore off a section and folded it under the microphone to protect the dog's hide.

Lasari knew the microphone was connected to a wireless receiver, monitored by someone watching him from the Alte Brucke, the cafe or some wooded corner of Philo Park he could not see. He bent over to pat Danke's head, smoothing his hand over its pointed ears, murmuring words of reassurance and praise to the animal. He was trying to decide whether to remove the dog's collar or simply yank the wires loose, cutting himself free from whatever spies were following him, monitoring his every word. Then he fluffed the dog's thick ruff around the collar and stood upright. He would let the device stay in place, he decided, until he knew why it was hidden there. Maybe the microphone would tell him something about his enemies.

He turned abruptly as someone spoke behind him.

"I've been watching you for a couple of days," the man said. "You're doing a hell of a good job with those dogs, soldier."

It was the word "soldier" and the uncompromising authority in the stranger's voice that sent Lasari signals of alarm. The man was ambling toward him on a graveled path, face open but unsmiling, as if this were a meeting both had arranged and expected.

The Alsatians pulled at the leashes, straining toward the newcomer. "Sit!" Lasari commanded and the dogs sank back on their haunches, watching both men with warm, alert eyes.

"They get confidence doing what they're told," Lasari said. "That's how they're bred."

The man was in his middle years, dressed in a gray jogger's suit over a black turtleneck sweater that showed at the neck and around the powerful wrists. His hair was black and cut short, with thick threads of gray at the temples and a touch of frost through the dark eyebrows. He might have been a fighter at one time in his life, Lasari thought, noting the big-knuckled hands and the broken nose, a powerful, twisted ridge between the high cheekbones and dark, appraising eyes.

"I notice you don't use gloves or a quirt," the man said. "You are not training them as guard dogs then?"

"I'm training them as guard dogs, yes. Attack dogs, no. They will learn to take commands and protect a master. We want them courageous, not paranoid."

The man smiled coolly. "Some Alsatians can be very temperamental, inbred and nervous. And you feel you've accurately judged the potential of these animals in these few days? You just over from the States, right?"

Lasari watched the man's impassive eyes, unwilling to answer either question until he could understand why it was asked. Then he said, "You have a special interest in dogs, mister?"

"I've got hunting dogs on my farm in Illinois," the stranger said. "My dogs will hold point indefinitely if I give the command, even if we kick up a brood. I've had a lot of experience with guns *and* dogs." He paused, as if expecting a response, then said, "I'm General Tarbert Weir, U.S. Army, retired. I thought you might know who I am."

"I don't," Lasari said.

General Weir moved closer to him, his hands at his sides. He was a full head taller than Lasari and the bulk and nearness of his body were more formidable than his words.

"Did you know my son, Lieutenant Mark Weir of the Chicago police department?"

"No, I didn't."

"Then can you tell me why someone would leave a message for my son on my phone tape, asking him to call her about George Jackson?"

The male dog gave a yelp, rose on its haunches and twisted its head within the ring of the leather collar. "Stay!" Lasari said sharply. "Stay, Danke!"

As he spoke to the dog, Lasari took a furtive glance around the perimeters of Philo Park, at the passersby, the distant cafe, the traffic crossing the Alte Brucke. The sudden appearance of General Weir had startled him. He could feel the pounding of his heart, unable to know at once if it was hope or

fear. Bonnie Caidin had urged him to trust her and her friend.
Mark Weir can help you, she'd said. Then he remembered
Sergeant Malleck's derisive words and the brief spasm of hope
was displaced by a wary distrust.

He could spot no surveillance on the immediate horizons,
but he knew that someone would be monitoring and remembering every word of this conversation.

"It's a big world, general," he said, "and I think you found
yourself the wrong George Jackson."

"I don't consider that a responsive answer, soldier," Weir
said. "Let me try you on this one. Do you know a lady named
Bonnie Caidin?"

Lasari answered with a sardonic smile, a shrug. "Now we're
doing business. The lady, as you call her, is a casual friend, a
one-night stand, as the old expression goes. Pretty as hell, but
not particular about friends. She was giving, I was buying,
and that's about it."

He saw the general's jaw harden with anger and his big fists
clench.

"Miss Caidin tried to get in touch with my son to talk about
George Jackson. Then Miss Caidin took a savage beating in
the garage of her apartment when she tried to *go* to my son.
Know anything about *that*, soldier?"

Lasari heard the sharp intake of his own breath, then controlled himself so his answer was even and unemotional. "A
one-night stand, general. I don't think I'd know the lady if I
saw her again . . ."

Weir knew that at the moment his judgment was clouded by
rage, and something besides the soldier's callous denials and
defiance bothered him. He knew men and he knew how they
acted under stress, and he sensed a shift in mood, an almost
animallike wariness in this lean, blade-faced Italian. Even if
the man was lying, and the general firmly believed he was, the
lies did not have the strength of true deception, of venality.

"My son, Lieutenant Mark Weir, was shot and killed in
Chicago a few days ago. He was shot because he knew *something*, or didn't know enough. I think you are somehow connected to his death. I think you can give me some answers."

"Look," Lasari said, forcing anger. "You're coming on
pretty strong. I'm a buck-ass private in the U.S. Army doing
my duty on assignment in Germany. I've got papers and I've

got orders. I don't know you or anything about a man you say got killed in Chicago. I don't know why you're telling me this shit.''

Lasari suddenly jerked on the male dog's lead, and as the dog responded and rose he shouted, "Stay! Stay, goddamn it!" He squatted down beside the dog, holding him by a short leash, forcing him back into a sitting position.

He looked directly at Tarbert Weir standing above him and said, "I know I'm a good-looking guy, so this wouldn't be the first time I got propositioned. Either you walk away from here right now and don't bother me again, or I'm going to yell for the Polizei and report you as a goddamn pederast . . .''

Weir's hand shot down and grabbed Lasari's shoulder with a force that almost knocked him to the ground. The grip was tight as a vise, closing over his bruised flesh with a violence that sent a wave of pain through his whole body. For a moment he thought he would black out.

". . . it's my *son*, my only son, we're talking about, my son and four other dead soldiers, and we *are* going to talk about it. I didn't come three thousand miles to listen to some bastard's lies and disrespect . . .''

Straining against the general's powerful grip, Lasari managed to move his hand toward the dog's collar. He looked up to be sure he had the general's attention. With stiff fingers he pushed the neck fur aside to reveal the cylindrical microphone, shiny and narrow as a pencil. Weir's hand dropped from Lasari's shoulder.

"I can only say it again," Lasari said roughly. "You got the wrong Jackson.''

Both men glanced around quickly. To Weir the park scene was unfamiliar but natural. Lasari thought he might have spotted a warning figure on the bridge—a bulky male was looking their way. It could be Eddie Neal, the man from the Atelier, even Strasser or a tourist. At this distance his camera almost completely concealed the man's face.

When the general spoke again, his voice was without emphasis or inflection. "No need to call a policeman. I've made a mistake and I acknowledge that. They told me in Chicago I was wrong. Understand the strain I've been under . . .''

"Forget it, no harm done," Lasari said.

The general went over to the bitch pup and patted her silver ruff. "Nice girl, nice girl," he said. He turned to Danke and touched the dog's muzzle, rubbed a hand over the head and neck muscles. Then he put his hand over the collar, completely covering the concealed microphone.

"Later, soldier," he said to Lasari. "We'll meet later."

The man ran a few steps in place on the graveled path, then turned and set off at a brisk jog toward the Alte Brucke.

# Chapter Thirty

SERGEANT STRASSER WAS on the phone, face hard and flushed, when Lasari came into the apartment. The sergeant listened, nodded and made a final note on the phone pad.

When he hung up, he ignored Lasari and spoke directly to Pytor Vayetch and Herr Rauch, his voice respectful, almost obsequious. "He did not go to Philo Park at all today," he said. "He had food sent up, stayed in his room. He phoned down to the concierge, booked a flight to Leige. Now he has checked out of the hotel, luggage and all." He glanced at the phone pad. "Lufthansa flight 981. It leaves in an hour. Neal is going to the airport to make sure he's on it."

Vayetch nodded but neither he nor Herr Rauch spoke. Vayetch sat with a drink in his hand and Rauch was at a side table, eating supper from a tray set with Rosenthal china. Strasser turned to Lasari with a cold smile and said, "Your luck is holding, Jackson. Your gumshoes general is leaving town."

Lasari had spent the last two days in the back bedroom with Eddie Neal or Strasser seated at the apartment bar or lounging in an armchair near the front door, on watch at all hours. Greta had brought Lasari sandwiches and fruit and kept a carafe of fresh water on his bedside table. Once she had come into his room carrying her small portable radio, but Strasser followed moments later to take it away. "You're not here for her to entertain, buddy," the big sergeant had said.

Several times Lasari heard the phone ringing, the opening

226

and closing of the front door, and an occasional murmur of voices, the words too indistinct to understand.

It was already dark in the old city when Strasser sent Greta to tell Lasari he wanted to see him. Now, after nearly forty-eight hours of solitude and near silence, Lasari was aware of both the unnatural loudness and bitter anger in his voice.

"You call it *luck*, Strasser? What the fuck's *lucky* about it?" he said. "I never saw the old bastard in my life, that's how lucky I am. Never laid eyes on him."

"That seems likely enough," Vayetch said. "But how do we know the truth about what you *revealed* to him?" Vayetch went on. "It's plausible enough that General Weir checked you out with headquarters in Frankfurt. I can believe *he* found *you*, not the other way around." He shrugged. "But the rest of it, what you talked about, what you let slip—we have only your word, don't we?"

Lasari knew he could not let the heat of his anger warp his judgment, he must not give away the one edge he had, the knowledge that they had taped every word he spoke in Philo Park, even his commands to the dogs.

"As far as proof goes," he said, "the only test is one of logic. What do I gain by lying to you? You're my ticket, my only ticket, out of the spot I'm in. If you honestly think the old man knows how and why I'm connected with you guys, you'd better blow me away right now.

"The man's out for revenge. It has nothing to do with me. He's looking for somebody who killed his policeman son in Chicago. I happened to spend a night with a girl there. She left my name on the old man's phone tape, wanted to talk to his son about me. Maybe a guilt thing, maybe she wanted him jealous. I'd just met her . . ."

Lasari turned to Strasser. "Check it with Malleck, for Christ's sake! That mother knows where I was when his hyenas found me."

Strasser looked at Pytor Vayetch. "The ginzo here's right, Mr. Vayetch. It all hangs together. He was with the chick earlier that night. It was afterward she got herself into trouble."

"Yes. I understand the young lady took a lot of punishment." Vayetch eyed Lasari with a tight smile. "Is this information a matter of complete indifference to you, Mr. Jackson? That this girl who gave you sanctuary, that you'd made love to throughout the night, was beaten bloody only moments after leaving you? Aren't you angry about that?''

A silence settled in the room, broken only by fleshy sounds as Herr Rauch savored the veal sausages Greta had served him. He cut each *wurst* into four pieces, then used blunt fingers to dip the meat into a pot of mustard. After each carefully chewed and relished mouthful, he took a swallow of beer. Vayetch watched impassively as Rauch dipped a corner of his napkin into the beer, then wiped the rim of the stein clean of mustard.

"He's like that from the war," Vayetch said. "There was much starvation in Silesia when he was a boy."

Greta had moved closer to Lasari. "It must be terrible for you about that Chicago lady, George. I remember a 'Kojak' show when bad men kidnapped his niece and threatened to beat her up and kill her. The family was very close, Greeks, you know. Everyone but Kojak turned chicken, like Ernie calls it, and . . ."

"Shut up, Greta!" Strasser said. "Will you shut up and get Herr Rauch a clean glass for his beer?"

"Let me tell you how I feel," Lasari said to Vayetch. "I feel *nothing*. Like I told that old fool, I'm just a buck-assed private in this man's army and I'm not going to screw up now. He was a pretty shrewd bastard. He was trying to work on me about that girl. I told him what I'm telling you. She was a one-night stand. I'm sorry she got herself hurt, I don't get my kicks that way, but I didn't know who she was or what she was. I didn't know she knew the old man's son, and I wouldn't recognize her again if she walked through the front door buck naked. I know I'm up to my ass in trouble and I'm not looking for more of it."

Pytor Vayetch smiled and settled back in his chair, sipping his drink until Greta came back from the kitchen. She bent one knee and touched the hem of her skirt in a mock curtsy. "Your order, sire," she said, smiling at Rauch and putting the clean stein and a fresh bottle of beer on his tray. Rauch grunted but he did not raise his eyes or change his expression.

It was Vayetch who broke the silence. He looked hard at Lasari, then nodded. His tone was formal. "I think we can trust you. I don't think you're concealing anything from us. Logically, as you point out, it is to your advantage not to deceive us, but logic has little to do with human behavior."

Vayetch put his well-manicured fingers together, tips to tips, then stared into the hollow of his hands. "We three gentlemen here, Sergeant Strasser, Herr Rauch and myself, the operative personnel so to speak, are in agreement. We are ready to update our schedule and proceed with plans. Sergeant Strasser has already cut orders for you to rejoin your comrades in the Lucky Thirteenth. Herr Rauch and I will personally drive you back to Regensburg. On the way we will have a little talk. We will let you know exactly what we expect of you. Is that clear?"

"It will be, I'm sure."

"You have no questions now, you do not wonder why you have our trust?"

"No."

Herr Rauch finished his beer and patted his lips with a silk handkerchief. He turned to look directly at Lasari for the first time. Then, with the tip of a big finger, he lifted the lid of a miniature piano on the coffee table, an ornate reproduction of a baby grand, painted a glossy white and etched with gold. Concealed inside was a tape recorder. Rauch pressed a key and a click sounded, then a faint humming. There were background noises from Philo Park but Tarbert Weir's recorded voice sounded as clearly as if he were standing in the apartment.

*"You're doing a hell of a good job with those dogs, soldier."*

*"They get confidence doing what they're told. That's how they're bred."*

Rauch pressed the fast-forward button, passing over a rapid squeal of voices till he came to the words . . . *"I'm a buck-ass private in the U.S. Army doing my duty on assignment in Germany. I've got papers and orders. I don't know you or anything about a man you say got killed in Chicago. I don't know why the hell you picked me."* Then came the sound of Lasari reprimanding the dog.

Herr Rauch manipulated the tape machine and played the same speech over three times, listening intently, narrowing his eyes in concentration. Then he pressed the fast-forward. "Here's the part I admire most," he said. "Clever, deeply subtle, almost Germanic of you, Jackson."

Lasari's voice, recorded close to Danke's collar as he knelt on one knee beside the dog, sounded through the room, hard and sharp-edged. "*I know I'm a good-looking guy, so this wouldn't be the first time I got propositioned. Either you walk away from here right now and don't bother me again or I'm going to yell for the Polizei and report you as a goddamn pederast . . .*"

Herr Rauch snapped off the tape, cutting through General Weir's voice in mid-answer. "You understand now why we believe we can trust you," he said.

Greta was smiling with wonder. "That's the most marvelous thing," she said, "hearing everything they said like that. You could put it in a bedroom some time."

Herr Rauch took the tape reel out of the miniature piano, put it in his pocket and stood to leave. Pytor Vayetch drained his Scotch and joined him at the door. Rauch was frowning, showing displeasure.

"We forget something, Herr Rauch?" Strasser said anxiously.

With an abrupt gesture, Rauch took out his wallet and handed Greta serveral deutsche marks. "For you, fraulein. There is a cologne, made in Berlin, I think, something very clean in aroma, like pine trees and fresh apples. Juni-Wasser, my old nurse called it. I wish you would try it as a favor to me, fraulein, a favor to the world. Unless, of course, you like to smell like soap in a public lavatory."

When they had gone Sergeant Strasser turned the key in the door and put it in his pocket. He went to the bar and poured gin over ice, then shook in droplets of Angostura bitters until the drink was as rosy as red wine. He took the drink to his bedroom, leaving the door ajar.

Greta followed Lasari to his room behind the kitchen, her cheeks red with humiliation, eyes bright with tears of rage.

"That big, fucking farmer! Who does he think he is? Ernest buys my perfume at the PX. You like it, don't you, George?" She blew gently on her wrist, then held it close for Lasari to sniff. "Isn't that like a Hollywood girl?"

"It's great, Greta, just great. A lot of Stateside ladies are wearing that, but on you it smells special."

She smiled at him and said, "No matter what you say about yourself, it must have been terrible to know they hurt that girl. Would you like to talk about it?"

She stood in the doorway, the toes of her white boots on the outside of the door still, as if it were a barrier or a starting line.

A spasm of alarm went through Lasari's warning system. As she reached out to touch his hand, he made an imperceptible move backward. "Greta, it's like I said before—I hardly knew her one way or another."

"I could tell you other things," she said softly. "I know what those big farmers want to say to you on the way to Regensburg . . ."

"I don't think that's what Strasser has in mind for you this evening," he said.

"He's already started to get drunk, George."

"Then you go in and sober him up. That's what he probably wants."

"I know about something else," Greta said. "Something even Ernie doesn't know I know."

Lasari looked at her steadily. "I'm not going to touch you, Greta. I want you to turn around and walk back where you belong."

"I know you like me, George."

"That doesn't matter. Your boy friend is wearing the stripes, remember. I'm just a boarder here."

From the click of her booted heels in the hallway, he knew Greta had walked past Strasser's bedroom. Moments later, he heard the drone of a television set from the front room.

Lasari turned off his table lamp and lay down on top of the coverlet. Outside it had begun to snow and he could hear the click of sleet against the window. He tried to distract himself and then gave in helplessly to memories of another snow, that night in Chicago when he sat opposite Bonnie Caidin. She had been pale and thin, with shadows under her eyes, but her face had been fragile and perfect, without a mark on it.

# Chapter Thirty-one

TARBERT WEIR WAS the last person off the Lufthansa carrier and most of the early morning flight traffic had thinned by the time he picked up his bag from the luggage carousel. The coffee stands were open and the air was filled with the pungence of chicory, fresh rolls and cinnamon.

At the newsstand he bought a day-old New York *Times*, two packages of mint drops and a Norman Katkov novel in paperback. He set down his suitcase, fumbled through his pockets, then asked the newsdealer if he could pay him with a five-dollar bill. The man shrugged, took the money and gave Weir his change in Belgian francs.

At the street level loading ramp Weir walked past an airlines bus marked ''Liege'' and proceeded to the taxi rank. He signaled for the first driver in line to roll down his window. Weir asked what the fare would be to the Hotel du Sud, and when the man told him the general opened the rear door, swung his luggage onto the seat and climbed in beside it. The airlines bus was still taking on passengers and Weir noticed that one of them, a man who had passed his seat twice to visit the lavatory on the Heidelberg-Liege flight, seemed to change his mind suddenly. He walked away from his place in the queue and hailed a cab.

The gray stone hotel faced a bustling, mid-city square surrounded on three sides by banks, office buildings and elegant boutiques, on the fourth by the narrow footwalk and weather-

darkened stone wall and balustrades that edged the River
Meuse, gray on gray.

Weir asked for a double room on the sixth floor overlooking the river, and told the clerk to send up a continental
breakfast with double coffee. An ancient bellman, stooped in
black shirt and trousers with a red and white striped vest,
waited while Weir talked with the concierge.

The general wanted three things. First, a rented Mercedes
convertible brought around to the front of the hotel in exactly
one hour. Second, a ticket, first class, on tomorrow's 6:00
A.M. flight to Kassel, West Germany. And last, he requested
the man to call the Rhein-Baden Hotel Spa in Kassel, ask for
manager Fritz Vestrick in person, and let him know that
Tarbert Weir would be checking in tomorrow.

When the bellman opened the door to his room, General
Weir shuffled through the Belgian francs in his pocket, then
tipped the man with a ten-dollar bill. The man thanked Weir
profusely and peered at him with eyes suddenly attentive
behind the rheumy cataracts. The general knew the Belgian
would remember everything about this generous American, if
anyone should happen to ask.

The breakfast tray was set with fine blue china and the mat
and napkins were damask, worn and laundered to the thinness
of old silk. Weir took a cup of steaming coffee to the French
windows overlooking the square. He had stayed in this hotel
with Maggie the night before they had visited the Tranchets'
farm. It had been chilly then too, and he remembered having
stood with his wife at a similar window, not touching her but
aware of her warmth, her presence as she watched the Liegian
flower vendors wheel their carts into the gray square below,
daffodils, windflowers, carnations and sprays of pink and
white fruit blossoms that stood out against the woody stems of
giant pussywillows.

"I wish Mark could see this," Maggie had said, wistfully.
"When we settle on the farm in Illinois, Scotty, I'm going to
try to grow pussywillows. They don't have to be wild, I'm
almost sure of that."

Now the first flower cart of the day trundled up a side street
and turned into the square, drawn by a Shetland pony with
colored ribbons braided through its bridle. Weir let the curtain
drop back into place and sat in the velour chair next to the

bed. He forced himself to eat a croissant and drink a second
cup of coffee. He felt restless but alive, his body tensed and
vibrant with energy. It was impossible, almost obscene, the
general thought, that with all the emotions, the anguish he had
felt since his son's death, he could still be stirred by an old excitement, the knowledge that he would soon be driving
through historic terrain, that he would again see the Tranchet
farm and the lilac tree.

He looked at his watch, aware that time was moving slowly.
He decided to go down into the square and shop among the
flower carts. He would bring a bouquet to Marta Tranchet.
The little Shetland had been pulling a cart of fresh tulips, Weir
remembered, the flowers brilliant in a dozen colors with petals
as smooth and perfect as candlewax.

A half hour later he was traveling at top speed away from
the outskirts of the old city and into the Ardennes. As soon as
the Meuse River was behind him and the narrow highway
curved into foothills and deep woods, he was already traveling
into higher, thinner air, through stands of firs, with ridges
of snow lining the roads. In the larger cities so much had
changed, the general knew. Malmedy, St. Lô, St. Vith, even
stately Liege, all these had high rises, fast food restaurants and
autobahns with bewildering cloverleaf patterns and flashing
directional signs and signals. But the countryside seemed the
same.

General Weir was indulging himself, he knew, allowing his
thoughts to stray from the mission at hand because his emotions were challenged, because he was traveling through a land
of youth, of ghosts, hallowed ground where justice had once
been served, or so the young men who died there had thought.
Verviers was to the east of him, south were Stavelot, Malmedy, St. Vith. In so many ways, it had been a simple war,
Weir thought, and a simple battle in that last German
counterattack in the Bulge. The issues were clear, right versus
wrong. No one was foolish enough to be eager to die, but a
soldier accepted that as a necessary price. He had never been
able to explain that to Mark. He had never even *tried* to explain it, he realized, because he had only come to understand it
later himself. Tarbert Weir and his generation had believed
that wise and loyal men simply *grew* into the responsibilities of
patriotism, that unquestioning fidelity to one's country was a

part of manhood. As time passed, it was becoming clear to him that what he had so long believed in might not necessarily be true for younger men.

Climbing into the Belgian hills in his rented Mercedes, Scotty Weir could almost imagine again the flash of artillery fire on distant ridges, the pounding of the V-1's and V-2's, the vision of the German attack forces in white, camouflaged by sleet and snow as they milled and regrouped among the snow-whitened trees.

Weir stopped on a crest and looked down into a valley darkened by fog and the woodsmoke rising from a scattering of farmhouses. A pickup truck that had been behind him almost from Liege caught up, swerved around him and disappeared around a bend in the road.

There was too much that succeeding generations did not know or care about each other, Weir thought, and he himself had been part of that conspiracy of silence. He and his compatriots had been better prepared to serve their country than Mark's generation, he knew. Not more altruistic nor courageous, that would be a selfish judgment, but at least they had been bolstered by the support of their own country and the trusted platitudes that made sacrifices respectable, even glorious.

My generation never had the dilemma of multiple choices, he thought. They knew nothing of unemployment insurance, affirmative action, student loans, the politics of protest and confrontation, welfare, housing subsidies, burning draft cards, chanting "traitor" and "murderer" at servicemen in uniform and the country's elected leaders as well.

Scotty Weir drove on into the morning with a feeling of sadness clouding his buoyant mood. He was not thinking of Mark now as a son, that eager little boy, nor as the still lieutenant resting on the morgue slab in Chicago, but as if they were miraculously the same age at the same time, two young soldiers in uniform, side by side, wanting to talk.

"*. . . we thought of our part in that war as an act of humanity, Mark. There was a sense of brotherhood then, I'm sure of that, a continuity of life in what we tried to do . . .*"

Weir's thoughts were so vivid that he felt for a moment he might have spoken aloud, but there was no sound in the Mercedes except the smooth turn of the engine and the hiss of the tires on the snowy road. After crossing a wooden bridge the general made a turn to the left and followed the twisting graveled road leading to the Tranchet farmhouse.

A carved wooden sign at the gate read "LeRoi." When she was eighteen, Marta Tranchet had married Emile LeRoi, a prosperous feed merchant from nearby LePont, a man fifteen years her senior. Both the elder Tranchets were dead by then and though Colonel Weir was unable to attend the wedding, Maggie had selected a silver tea service, Regal Eagle pattern, and Marta had written later that it looked so well, "so American," on a table in the bow window of the old dining room. Scotty would remember the room, she said. She and Emile had decided to make the farm their home, she added. He knew how much the place meant to her.

That fateful rendezvous with the Germans was nearly four decades ago, Marta Tranchet-LeRoi was a wife, mother and Belgian matron, but when Scotty Weir thought of her it was always the frail eight-year-old child with frightened eyes who stood out in his mind.

# Chapter Thirty-two

THE COURTYARD, WIDENED and paved, was flanked by towering junipers. There was no trace of the muddy potholes or rutted cart tracks, the icy ridges crusted like iron, through which Scotty Weir and his comrades had trudged that night so long ago. The old farm buildings, sheds and barn stood as before, but in excellent repair, and a new, rambling wing with bright blue shutters had been added to the main lodgings.

As Weir left the Mercedes the house door opened and Marta Tranchet came running down the steps toward him, a trim, middle-aged woman in tweeds and yellow sweater, arms in an open embrace, face tight with emotion. When the general became aware of the tears streaming down her cheeks, he turned quickly to the car, took from the back seat a bouquet of crimson tulips he had bought in Liege and filled her open arms with the flowers. Marta hid her face in the blossoms, then said, "It's over, Scotty dear. Forgive me. Those were my tears for Mark. I couldn't help it—the sight of you again."

In the fireplace in the dining room logs were lit and the table was set for two.

"Emile is so sorry to have missed you," Marta said, as she arranged the tulips in a crystal vase and put them in the window next to the tea set. "We had your cable from the States, of course, but until you called yesterday we didn't know when to expect you. He is in Antwerp at a distributors' meeting, very important to him."

"There will be another time, Marta."

"Shall we have sherry first and then our lunch before you tell what it is you need, Scotty? And it would make me less sad for you if you told me about Mark yourself. To think, we both had sons, and now there is just one between us . . ."

Weir held the sherry glass in one hand, letting the firelight play through the amber liquid as he talked. He had never told Marta of his estrangement from his son and he did not mention it to her now. He kept his voice low and calm, and he tried to speak without thinking too deeply, so he would not get torn on the shards of his emotions. He told her what he thought she wanted to hear: a loyal father, good son, family devotion, a life too short but well-lived. Details, an honor guard on motorcycle, condolence calls from the United States Army, burial in ground reserved for fellow police officers and the funeral on television . . . That had startled and intrigued her, not the kind of thing one would do in Belgium, she said.

The general felt he was operating on two levels—one the old comrade, benevolent but sorrowing, speaking of his dead son; the other the real Scotty Weir, an angry, agitated and determined man who was willing to play any role to get what he wanted.

He knew the observer at the Greenbrier would have long since decided that he was not out on some distant fairway, chipping balls, and that Laura Devers was, indeed, waiting in the guest cottage alone. At Philo Park, he knew Tarbert Weir had been taped and under surveillance, as well as the morose and stubborn Private Jackson. There had been a blond youth, too, neither quite German nor American, the general had remembered, sitting in the hotel lobby in Heidelberg sipping an aperitif and once again, briefly, at the airport, both places he might or might not have a perfect right to be.

Marta watched his rugged face, aware of the silence. "Poor dear Scotty," she said, "always so brave and now to be brave alone . . ."

They lunched on an omelet with *crepes*, green salad and home-canned blue plums, all foods from the farm, Marta told him. There was a greenhouse off the old kitchen for a salad garden, everyone had them now, she said. Weir had turned down her suggestion that they share a bottle of Beaujolais with lunch.

"I understand," she said. "We aren't celebrating." She poured herself a second sherry and sipped it through lunch.

After coffee Marta Tranchet-LeRoi went to a hall phone and put through a call to her son, Captain Alain Tranchet-LeRoi, on assignment with NATO outside Kassel, West Germany. Weir heard a brief murmur of voices and when she came back into the room, she said, "He asked me to call him when he is off duty, after five o'clock. I have a private number."

"Good," Weir said.

She hesitated a moment and then asked, "Can you do what is necessary without Alain's help, Scotty?"

"The captain can make it easier," he said. "I will tell him as little as possible, so he won't be compromised."

She sighed and her eyes were shining, as if her thoughts were full of tears. "You saved me, Scotty. I thought of that so often when I was growing up, when I married, and I thought of it when Alain was born. Whether it was fate's accident or divine design, Private Weir was not just a *part* of my life, he was *the reason for it*. He let me live."

"Then here are the things I would like Captain Alain to arrange for me," Scotty Weir said, and handed her a sheet of Lufthansa stationery on which he had written his requests. "You can tell him I'll be at his headquarters in Kassel by noontime tomorrow."

Marta Tranchet read the short list in silence, folded the paper and put it in her sweater pocket. "Perhaps it would be better if we walked now, Scotty. We have always done that. You will hardly know the place."

Outside General Weir turned up his coat collar and jammed his hands into his pockets, surprised by the sharp chill in the afternoon air. The sky had turned dark, as if it might snow or send down a cold rain, and the wind had the bite of late frost. When they left the graveled walks around the farmhouse and cut out across the plowed fields, Weir could feel his shoes break the crust of ice on the loamy soil and sink almost to the shoelaces.

Marta had put on a quilted down jacket, headscarf and rubber boots, and she strode along beside him in silence, her bowed head barely reaching his shoulder. She had lived most of her life on this farm, but she kept her head down, watching her footsteps as they walked, almost seeming to count and measure the distance.

"When we first married I wanted to put some kind of

marker out here," she said finally. "Something in stone and brass, just a few words, but permanent." She laughed. "Emile has always been the practical one. He said that if memory is in our hearts, it needs no marker."

After a half hour's walk (had he really once crossed these fields in minutes?), they came to the place where Private Weir's grenades had destroyed the lives of twenty German soldiers and left their armored tank a twist of rubble. The area seemed small now, peacefully rural, neatly fenced. The stand of locust trees, shattered and uprooted that night, had re-seeded themselves into a tidy grove. The deep crater left by his grenades still showed in the earth, the sides and floors marked with the curves of contour plowing, the edges of the furrows marked by snow.

When Marta Tranchet spoke, her voice was so low, so dreamlike and detached, that Scotty Weir wondered if she had forgotten he was there, or if this was a trip she often made in sadness, and alone.

"Your face was smudged with dirt that night," she said. "It made your eyes so white, so staring. There was a rip in your canvas jacket, I remember that, a big, loose tear that went right through to your backbone. One could have touched your skin. It looked warm to me, but I was too cold to move. And your boots were muddy."

Weir's cheekbones felt chapped by the raw wind and he sensed the beginning of a roughness in his throat. The sticky loam had covered his shoes and now added damp and weight to the cuffs of his trousers every time he moved. He took a package of the mints he'd bought at the airport and put two under his tongue.

"Yes, we were a pretty beat up bunch of sad sacks that night, Marta."

"No, no, don't say that! You looked like knights in shining armor to me and my family, don't you know that? You were like white lights, like saviors, and you were that thing I had never known in my young life—a man without fear."

"Then we put up a pretty good front, Marta."

She smiled, slipped off a glove and touched his bare wrist. "You were just children yourselves, what were you, Scotty—eighteen? A child-man, and for your courage, I thought you were a god . . ."

He took her hand in his big one and rubbed it gently.

"Don't talk yourself into anything now because of something that happened way back then, Marta."

She shook her head. "No, no," she said. "I will make the call."

Back at the farmhouse she gave him dry socks and a pair of Emile's slippers while she scraped the mud from his shoes and set them on the hearth. She put the decanter of sherry on the table between them but Weir shook his head when she asked to fill his glass.

"I want a clear head for the trip back to Liege. Those roads weren't quite as familiar as I thought they'd be."

Marta poured herself a sherry. "It is like a holiday for me, Scotty, having you here."

They spent the rest of the afternoon in front of the fire as the apple logs burned down to fragrant ash and the stormy skies turned dark over the countryside. A digital clock, incongruous on the century-old mantelpiece, clicked the numbers rhythmically until the dial showed 4:45. Tarbert Weir forced himself to talk with his old friend, but he was conscious of the growing tension in her manner, the slur to her carefully worded English.

"I wonder, my *cher ami Americain*," she burst out suddenly, "do you know how frightened we are here in Europe? Do even the Russians understand that? More and more of those missiles, hundreds at first, now thousands. They circle our borders and cities, they can be fired from the ground, from cannons on moving railroad trains. The North Sea to the Mediterranean, giant warheads everywhere, ready to fire." She sat rocking back and forth, hugging her breasts. "Poor little Belgium, only ten million souls, all of us. We offer so little, we live on our exports, no natural resources. So what can we give you? Industrial diamonds, a little steel. No, you love us for the pastries we export, our chocolate and hams . . . and space to put your weapons.

"Must we be the prize in your contest for power? We march, we protest, thousands of us in Europe, from Sicily to Amsterdam. In Bremen, there were night-long vigils, people by the hundreds, praying on their knees with candles. Millions marching for peace, *that* is the will of the people. But can we change the man in the White House? Or the Kremlin? What more is wanted of us?"

She had put down her glass and sat staring at him, hands

clasped in her lap now, watching him as if she expected an answer. In the curves of her face, the color high with sherry and emotion, and beneath the coiffed cap of her hair, he saw that her eyes were again like an eight-year-old, pleading and frightened.

"Marta," he said gently. "I will try to understand. You don't want to make the call to Alain."

"You are wrong," she said, standing. "I will call him now. We Belgians are not without honor. If it weren't for you, *le monsieur* Scotty, I wouldn't have a son to be frightened for tonight."

As Marta talked on the phone in the hall, Weir paced the floor of the dining room, trying to drown out the sound of her voice with the shuffle of his slippers. He did not want to overhear. But the loose velvet scuffs with their soft chamois soles made him feel irresolute, almost old. With a spasm of irritation he kicked them off and put on his own shoes, still feeling the stiff dampness as he tied the laces over Emile LeRoi's fine cashmere socks.

He positioned himself at the bow window and looked out past the courtyard to the farm buildings. Through the dusk he saw the storm clouds had parted for a thin moon, a light that glinted on the hedges, the cobbled courtyard and the dark mass of the plum orchard. The barn was as he remembered it, but freshly roofed and tuck-pointed, and beside it the tall lilac bush, graceful and bare now, just as it had been that winter night decades ago.

Marta entered from the hallway and came to stand close to him at the window. Weir put an arm around her shoulders and pulled her close to him, stooping to kiss the top of her hair. It smelled pleasantly of fresh air, wood smoke and sherry.

"I'm sorry for what I said a few moments ago," she murmured. "Alain will be expecting you tomorrow, sometime before noon. He understands, he will be ready."

Scotty Weir kissed her hair again and pulled her close to him, grateful for the warmth of human flesh. He felt a faint sexual desire, something he had never felt for Marta before, and he wondered if she sensed the shift in his mood.

"I was looking at our tree, the old lilac bush," he said. "It is still where it should be. I have never forgotten it, Marta, but it's strange how memory changes things. I had remembered the old bush as more full, and taller, reaching as high as the barn roof, in fact.''

He felt her intake of breath, then a tremor that passed through her body, an almost imperceptible drawing away from his embrace.

"I didn't think you'd notice, Scotty," she said. "It *is* a lilac tree, or bush. The first one, long ago, was a lilac *vulgaris*. My father told me it must be a sport, a stray seed that came in on the wind. He never remembered his parents planting it. It was just *there*."

Weir stared through the darkness, straining for a better look at the tree. No, it was not as tall as it should be, and much slimmer than he remembered. Marta was saying, "I'm trying the species Leon Gambetta this time. It's a double-flowered hybrid and does well in this part of the world."

Weir withdrew his arm from her shoulders and turned her body so he was looking directly down into her eyes. "Let me understand you, Marta. Are you telling me that lilac bush out there is *not* the lilac bush we all looked at the night I killed the Germans?"

"It's a *lilac*, but not the *same* lilac," she said. "The genus *Syringa* is not all that hardy. Besides, lots of natural things have accidents."

"What kind of accidents?"

"The first one broke apart when there was a sudden thaw one year and the snow fell off the barn roof. That was the winter mother died."

"By 'the first one,' you mean our 'miracle' bush?"

"Yes," she said. "The second one was doing very well, it had at least nine seasons. But it got a bacterial blight, little cankers that killed the stems. It's a plant disease that begins with a P—*Phytophthora* is what I think the nursery man said."

"You're telling me now about a *second* lilac bush," General Weir said carefully, his arms stiff at his sides. "I believe what you are saying is that we are not looking at the *first* lilac bush, nor are we looking at the *second* . . ."

"That's right, Scotty."

"And the winter I brought my wife here, when Mark had to stay in school, was that the *original* tree we looked at? Which lilac were we toasting when we all got drunk and sentimental and you brought out champagne?''

"What year was that?"

"You know goddamn well what year it was, Marta, and don't give me any more double-talk about genus and blight spots. What tree was it?"

"That lilac was the third."

"And this?"

She sighed. "Last spring and summer the flowers weren't right. They're supposed to grow in panicles, you know, almost like bunches of grapes, but there were just a few scattered flowers, pinkish, not lilac, and a really bad smell. There were little white meshes on the leaves, like tent caterpillars and . . ."

"Then this is the *fourth* lilac bush, *a complete imposter plant*, I've been looking at like a damned fool? And you let me make that jackass speech about 'our talisman'?"

She shrugged and looked away from him. "I would have waited for spring, but when I got your letter that you were coming, I called a nurseryman in Liege. They cut down the diseased tree and softened the ground with steam hoses and things and planted the new lilac. In fact, they had to put it six feet back so it wouldn't get tangled up with the sick roots. You'd never have noticed the change, Scotty, if it had been taller. It wasn't a matter of money, believe me. That was the biggest lilac bush they had in the nursery."

Tarbert Weir let his breath out hoping the release of pressure would soften the anger that seemed to be swelling in his chest.

"I don't think I did wrong, Scotty," Marta said softly.

He wanted to reach out to touch her cheek, to reassure her, to remember her as a treasured friend, but he felt dread at the thought of flesh on flesh. What else, Weir wondered, had they all been lying about . . .

"Of course you didn't do wrong, Marta. It is a strange kind of falsehood you've kept alive over the years, but I love you for it. It's what a frightened eight-year-old girl would do. It must have meant so much to you, that miracle tree."

"Yes, yes, dear Scotty," she said softly. "It did, it meant so much to me. But you—wasn't it just *everything* for you?"

# Chapter Thirty-three

GRETA STOOD AT the stove, stirring a pan of cocoa. She wore a black crepe slip with thin gold-braid straps, gold mules, and her hair was piled high, tied back with a ribbon.

In the adjoining bedroom Duro Lasari stepped out of the shower, a towel around his waist. The bruises on his chest and groin had turned grayish yellow, the edges marked pink with signs of healing. The deep cut above his eye had healed but the hot shower had turned the welt an angry purple. A private's uniform hung from a wall pole, a pair of regulation boots on the floor beneath. He would be making the return trip to Regensburg in a few hours; Strasser's driver was coming by to take him to the bus depot. Strasser had made that decision in a drunken but defiant phone call to Pytor Vayetch last evening.

"I don't care *what* you gentlemen got planned," he'd said. "My orders come directly from Karl Malleck in Chicago, and he says no pussyfooting GI's gonna be delivered back to his barracks by Porsche. He comes in by bus, he goes back by bus . . ."

Vayetch and Herr Rauch were scheduled to meet with Lasari at the apartment within the hour.

"You want some cocoa or anything, George?" Greta called out from the kitchen.

"No, I'm fine, Greta. That was a great farewell luncheon, by the way. Thanks."

"You can't leave without eating something more, George. The PX will be closed when you get to Regensburg. Too bad

245

we don't have jerky. You know what jerky is? Everybody on the 'Bonanza' show took beef jerky with them on trips, remember?"

Lasari put on his socks first, then pulled on khaki undershorts. "You don't miss a thing, Greta," he called out then turned as he heard the door pushed open.

Greta was smiling, almost shy. Lasari took a shirt off a hanger, put it on and began to button it.

"Why are you putting your shirt on?" she said. "I thought you were talking to me because you wanted me." Her eyes clouded. "Ernie is always drunk and you act like I'm not here. You're putting clothes on. I feel so useless."

She came to stand close to him and raised one slim leg, running her fingers along the curve of the calf. "Did you ever notice I don't shave my legs, George? I don't have to. Blonde ladies are lucky about hair, a nice color. I'm that way all over."

Lasari took his uniform trousers from the hanger, stepped into them and pulled the zipper into place. "Look, Greta," he said, "if this had happened at another time, if we'd met at a bar or a dance, and were both alone, I'd want to get to know you real well. I mean that. But you belong to Ernie Strasser." As she began to frown, he held up a hand. "I don't mean like his goddamn cat or dog, or his motorcycle. Not that. Strasser's your guy, you're his woman, and I think he feels for you."

"Some boy friend," she said morosely. "He can be sweet sometimes but he's drinking like this because he's a born coward. He was always afraid of Malleck and now it's Eddie Neal and those other men."

Lasari had taken his tunic jacket in his hand but made no move to put it on. "Here's how I see it," he said. "Strasser's got some problems, sure, but he's loyal and you've got to admire that. Maybe I'm old-fashioned, Greta, I don't know, but no matter how much I like you and want you, coming between two people who are together, that's not my style. If you and I were alone here, if there was no Ernie Strasser, who knows what would happen? But this way, three people could get hurt."

She was smiling again. "What you're saying, George, is that if it weren't for Ernie being my boy friend, you couldn't control yourself, I wouldn't be safe with you. Isn't that what you're saying? You're crazy and sweet like Brett Maverick when you're like this . . ." She stopped short, sniffing the air attentively.

"Damn! You're right, Greta," he said. "I smell it, too. You forgot that cocoa on the stove."

When she left the room Lasari put on his tunic and walked quickly down the hall.

Lasari found Strasser sprawled in an armchair, breathing heavily and seemingly immobile, but with eyes open and wary. "Don't think I'm drunk, Jackson," he said. "I just want you off my ass and out of here."

Sergeant Strasser had finished all the paperwork at his office yesterday, stamping, initialing and certifying the details of Private Jackson's detached duty time on leave from the Lucky Thirteenth, specifying the assignment for Colonel Warneke in dog training. And he had cut orders for Jackson to rejoin the Lucky Thirteenth outside Kassel in two days.

Greta had prepared a lunch of fruit, headcheese, pumpernickel and canned white asparagus, but Strasser had pushed his half-filled plate away and finished off a bottle of white wine laced with Bols gin.

When the doorbell rang and Greta hurried from the kitchen, Strasser signaled her to go into their bedroom. He turned the radio on the bar to Viennese dance music and opened the front door.

Pytor Vayetch folded his coat over a chair and put his hat on top of it, but Herr Rauch sat with his overcoat on, his big shoulders hunched forward, face impassive, like a man who did not expect to stay long and who had not wanted to make this visit in the first place.

Both men refused Strasser's offer of drinks and Vayetch began to pace back and forth. When he finally spoke, he talked slowly, picking his words carefully, savoring the tutorial role.

"The background of our operations, the financing, contracts, who's who, none of that is relevant to your contribution to our project, Mr. Jackson. Everything is planned to move as smooth as honey, and you have to know only your function, your responsibilities, nothing more." He paused and looked expectantly at Lasari.

"Goddamn it, soldier! Answer the man!" Strasser snapped.

"Yes, sir, Mr. Vayetch, yes, sir."

"Even though you and I are not users, we share mutual knowledge. From your experience in Vietnam, I know you are well aware of how dependent servicemen can become. And our civilian users, too, of course. Worldwide, it is a seller's market. Take Thailand, for instance. It used to be a major export country in our market. But the Thais began to enjoy their own product. Now that country imports more heroin than it exports. There are continuing shifts in both demand and supply.

"Some time ago the reliable Marseilles connection was permanently interrupted. That created a real hardship, especially in the United States, we learned. There are supposedly five hundred thousand heroin users in your country, but I believe that estimate is low by more than one hundred percent. Without Marseilles, the suppliers tried to fill their clients' needs with Mexican brown and whatever medium-quality stuff they could get from South America. My partner and I were not idle." He nodded formally at Herr Rauch. "It took time, but we were able to get our hands on a steady source of white, the finest there is, pick of the world market, worth top dollars. It is a quantity of this excellent product that you will be kind enough to take into the United States for us."

Lasari glanced at Strasser, standing near the bar, and noted the tremor in his hand as he poured gin over ice cubes.

"Yes, sir, Mr. Vayetch," he said again.

"Here is how you will proceed. In about two hours you will be taken to the bus station and boarded. You will be met in Regensburg. Tomorrow, at first call, you and a group of servicemen, regular NATO troops on assignment, will be flown by Army plane to Kassel in West Germany, a few kilometers from the Czech border. Sergeant Strasser has made all the necessary paper arrangements. You will be expected, there will be no surprises.

"The sergeant has requested you be put on the duty roster starting at ten tomorrow night. Your battery, a guard unit, moves out to grid coordinates A–12, a forward observation post. There are nine nations represented in the maneuvers, and one extra soldier in the area will be next to invisible. All you've got to do is keep your eyes open and your mouth shut and follow the scenario we've laid out for you."

He turned suddenly to Strasser. "Turn off that music,

sergeant, if you please. We are men of business here, not senile fools in wigs and waistcoats.''

When the *gemütlich* strains had faded away, he turned again to Lasari. "At 2:00 A.M., you'll get an order for a cigarette break. You use that break to take a nature call. The latrines will be five hundred yards south of your positions, approximately at grids A–14.

"Stay in the latrine for exactly five minutes. When you come out, a soldier will ask you for a light. Hand him these matches.'' Vayetch took a book of matches with the horned devil symbol of Teufel's Atelier on the cover and tossed it on the table. "The soldier takes the matches and leaves behind a duffel bag with your initials and ID number on it.''

"How will I know him?'' Lasari asked. "What uniform will he be wearing?''

"You don't have to know him,'' Vayetch said. "He has seen pictures. *He* knows *you*.''

Herr Rauch put his hand into his overcoat pocket, brought out a small plastic bottle and handed it to Vayetch, who said, "With the duffel in your possession, you will promptly swallow three of these pills. They are harmless but powerful emetics; they will not blur your senses but you will be completely nauseated and run a high fever for twenty-four hours.''

He held the bottle out to Lasari.

For the first time, Herr Rauch seemed interested, even amused. "Don't worry,'' he said to Lasari. "They are smart little pills. They know who their friends are.''

"Take your duffel bag and your sickness and get back to platoon headquarters immediately. Check in with a medic and get permission to bed down. In the morning insist that you be examined by a doctor. These pills will simulate all the symptoms of morbid dysentery and acute food poisoning. You and your precious knapsack will be back in Regensburg on sick leave two days from now. From then on, you're on your way back to the States. Sergeant Strasser knows how to do his job.''

Strasser spoke then, but his words had begun to thicken. "The next friendly face you see, Jackson, will be at O'Hare Airport in Chicago. Just one more GI on leave, carrying regulation duffel, right size, right weight, right initials, right ID number. You'll be met by friends.''

The sergeant passed the back of his hand over his dry lips.

"Customs *does* want to look at your gear, all they see is a couple of presents for the girl friend back home and a few changes of Army wardrobe."

"And the heroin, where am I carrying it? How do I know you're not tricking me?" Lasari said.

"That information is not relevant to your contribution to the project," Vayetch said. "You just don't need to know."

The doorbell rang, four short rings, and Strasser called out, "Hold it, Eddie." He turned a mirthless smile to the two visitors. "Change of guard reporting for the ginzo here."

Herr Rauch stood and Vayetch did the same, pulling on his overcoat and creasing the crown of a velour fedora between his fingers. He put his hand out to Duro Lasari and the two men shook briefly and formally.

"As I said, Herr Rauch and I are businessmen. We have been successful in our ventures because we keep the operations simple and leave nothing to chance. 'There is no greatness where there is no simplicity . . .' The great Russian, Count Leo Tolstoy, said that, and I honor his words. I like to think that Count Tolstoy would have found us interesting men, self-reliant and alive to the realities of our times."

Vayetch put on his hat, then took suede gloves from a pocket. He pulled them on slowly, smoothing the fine leather into the grooves between each finger, studying Lasari with a final, thoughtful appraisal. "I regret that we shall not meet again," he said. "But even though you do not see us, Mr. Jackson, please do not make the mistake of thinking we do not see *you*."

Eddie Neal held open the door with insolent courtesy and the two men passed him without speaking.

At a mumbled command from Strasser, Lasari helped the sergeant off the bar stool, steadying him as they walked toward the bedroom door. Lasari tapped the wood with the toe of his boot and Greta opened it.

She pointed to Strasser. "I'm not going to stay in here when he's drunk. He promised me he wouldn't spoil your last day."

"Do what you like, Greta," Lasari said. She slipped out of the bedroom and he pushed the door shut behind her. He guided the sergeant to the bed, letting him fall back across it, his weight creaking the springs.

"Let me take your shoes off," Lasari said in a loud voice. "You'll never get to sleep like that." Swiftly Lasari untied the shoelaces, slipped off the shoes, and swung the man's feet around onto the foot of the bed. Then he pulled open the drawer in a night table and rifled through the contents, a paperback novel, two candy bars, some loose Kleenex and a plastic flask.

He turned and ran his hands over the big sergeant's body, feeling every pocket and moving down the seams of his trousers. There was no gun.

"I don't need help from no ginzo," Strasser muttered. "Get away from me, you cockamamie. If I wanna undress, my girl will do it for me."

"Yes, sir," Lasari said and walked out of the bedroom, leaving the door ajar.

# Chapter Thirty-four

PRIVATE NEAL HAD positioned himself in the middle of the room, dominating the space with his lean, taut body. Greta stood facing him. Neither was speaking but Lasari could sense the tension between them.

"No need for you to be sassy with me, Greta," Neal said with a friendly smile. "I just asked for a stein of beer with an egg in it and some schnapps. Had an errand to run for your boy friend and I missed my lunch."

"It's the *way* you ask," she said, "like I was a slave."

"That's just your kraut imagination, kid. The soldier here and I got business. So go in the kitchen and fix me a little nip, okay?" He laughed. "Ernie don't always say pretty please with sugar on it, does he, fraulein? By the way, what did you do with First Shirt, Jackson?"

"He's taking a nap, Eddie."

"Fuck *Eddie*, ginzo. It's *Corporal Neal, sir.* You and the fraulein are getting pretty sloppy with your military discipline."

"Sergeant Strasser is taking a nap, Corporal Neal, sir."

"He real drunk?"

"More or less, maybe. I don't know."

"You don't know *shit*, do you?" The voice was still good-humored but there was a muddy look to Neal's eyes. "Everybody's scared around here and it's the wrong time for it. You, ginzo, *you* don't know *nothing.* Strasser's got his head in the bottle, the kraut cunt puts her nose in the air like I smell

252

bad . . ." He took a step toward Greta looking down at her with an almost affectionate smile.

"Let me tell you something, Greta. My old man was over here in World War Biggie, same country, same krautheads, hands out begging for food after they'd thrown their guns away. There was no fraternizing then, my old man told me. He was an MP. One night he's on duty and a German broad shoves her ass up against him and says, 'How'd you like to fraternize with that, Yank?'

"Know what he did? He rammed her in that fat German ass of hers with his bayonet, straight through the lard to her hip-bone. She didn't have anything very smart to say after that, Greta, just lay nice and quiet, waiting for an ambulance."

Lasari caught Greta's eye and with a slight nod signaled her to leave. "While you're fixing the corporal's drink, I'd like a beer, okay?"

When she left, Neal settled down in the big armchair, crossing his long legs at the ankles. Lamplight glinted on his shiny mid-calf boots.

"She handles nice and easy with you, Jackson. You fucking her?"

"No, corporal."

"How come, you afraid of Strasser? That rummy's getting so cockeyed, he wouldn't even know if you were fucking *him*." He looked thoughtful. "Maybe that's the way you swing, Jackson. You go for boys?"

"No, Corporal."

Eddie Neal grinned his down-home grin and rubbed a finger over his soft lips. "Maybe you're too scared to go either way now, ginzo. Little old Sicilian cock shriveled up and worried to death about what's coming. No need for that. We're not gonna let anybody hurt you. You're gonna arrive in Chicago safe and sound and I'll be part of the welcoming committee. Just put a pair of blinkers on, do what you're told—you got nothin' to sweat."

Lasari could hear the sound of Greta's gold mules tapping around the kitchen. "It's not Chicago I'm worrying about, corporal. What if I can't get the stuff through German customs?"

Neal shrugged. "Unless they're tipped off to something, they don't check you going out. We're guests in this country, here by invitation, billeted in more than three hundred towns.

The military just come and go like smoke."

"What you're saying is, customs *does* check on the American side . . ."

"Why should they? On the plane you get a routine customs declaration to fill out. What you declare is just *nothing*. They'll take your word for it. Nobody's gonna catch you dirty. You're red, white and blue, Jackson.

"If they *do* open your duffel, what are they gonna find? Nothing again. Strasser has those bags custom-made. They hold six to eight pounds of pure white in the lining. There's nothing suspicious, you sail through like a piece of cake. Customs gave us no trouble on the runs so far . . .

"You're worrying about the wrong things, Jackson. You got fucked-up priorities. In this operation, everything starts and ends with Malleck and I'm Malleck's man. That's what you should be worrying about. When you get the stuff and leave Lucky Thirteenth, don't bother to look over your shoulder for me. I'll be there."

Eddie Neal craned his neck to look down the hallway, then put two fingers in his mouth and gave a shrill whistle. "Where the hell is that broad with my drink?"

"Probably making sure the beer is cold, corporal. Greta knows the way I like it."

"But you don't know how she likes it, right?" Neal smiled his taunting grin. "You're gonna be our golden goose, but we didn't figure you for a faggot goose. No offense, for Christ's sake," he said as he noticed the burn of anger in Lasari's face. "Just joking, Jackson."

Eddie Neal stood and pushed open the bedroom door. Strasser was lying flat on his back, mouth open, snoring noisily. The man closed the door and shook his head in disgust.

"My old man used to say that a chain was only as strong as its weakest link. He told me that sitting behind wire in the visitors section of the federal pen in Anniston, Alabama, so maybe he didn't know shit from Shinola anyway, but it's something to remember." He looked at his watch and sighed. "Ernie's not pulling his weight. He's supposed to take care of these details but everything's on me all of a sudden."

The corporal opened his tunic and began to feel through the inside pockets. Lasari caught a glimpse of the handgun in a shoulder holster. He found what he was looking for and handed Lasari a packet of folded forms. "And here's a pen," he said, holding out a ballpoint. "Where I put the x's, you sign all four of them."

"What are these?" Lasari said, smoothing out the papers.

"What do you care?" Neal said. "It's part of the deal with Malleck. We want your signature and your ID number on each one."

The numbered forms were printed in German with blanks left open and an X-marked line at the bottom of each. Lasari shuffled the forms, letting his eyes run quickly over the unfamiliar words and concentrating on the individual row of numbers on the top of each page. Except for the numbers, the forms seemed identical.

"What's the matter, you read German?" Neal asked.

"No I don't, but I can put two and two together. Their word 'Register' is the same as ours, and I saw this word on a building; 'Postamt.' That means post office."

"Just a little something the sergeants have going on the side. They picked some nice loot for you to mail back to a friend in Chicago."

"Do I get to put in a card?" Lasari said.

Neal's hand made a move toward the top of his boot, then stopped. "Go on and sign, smartass," he said. "I'm getting nervous with Strasser passed out in there."

Lasari wrote "George Jackson, PFC" and his ID number four times and handed the forms and pen back to Neal.

Greta brought in their drinks, placing the tray on a table next to the armchair. Lasari stood to serve himself, picking up a bottle of dark lager and a goblet decorated with a border of toadstools and dwarfs.

Corporal Neal stared with disgust at the big stein in which Greta had made his drink. Large flakes of eggshell floated on the sudsy beer. At the bottom of the glass was a yolk marked with red streaks of blood. A small glass of schnapps stood beside it.

Neal stood, put his hands on his hips and stared at Greta. "Now what the fuck is that supposed to be?"

"It's what you ordered, Corporal Eddie. Schnapps and a beer '*mit ei*.' "

"Don't give me any of that '*mit ei*' bullshit!"

"You told me to put an egg in it. You *don't* want an egg, say so. You speak English, don't you?"

"I wanted an egg, you cunt," Eddie Neal said, "but no egg-shells and not a goddamn yolk marked with chicken shit."

He was still smiling as he spoke, moistening his lips, ducking his head as if this were a friendly misunderstanding, a humorous mix-up. But Lasari could see the color rising in his throat, the dangerous look in his eyes.

"Greta," Lasari said, "why not take the man's drink and dump it down the sink. Just build him one the way he likes it."

"Ginzo, if we've got a problem," Neal said, "I don't recollect asking you to help out. You hear me ask for advice?"

"No, corporal, I didn't."

Neal broadened his smile and said, "Greta, if that's your idea of a tasty drink, I'm not gonna deprive you of the fun of drinkin' it. You hear me, girl? Just pick up that stein and drain it back, eggshells and all." He poured the glass of schnapps into the beer. "Down the hatch," he said.

She shook her head uncertainly. "I don't want it. I don't like schnapps."

Eddie Neal caught the fall of hair tied at the top of her head and twisted it powerfully, forcing her to her knees. "If it ain't good enough for you, it sure as shit ain't good enough for me, fraulein."

"Leave me alone, stop it!" she cried. "Make your own drinks!"

"I warned you about that sassy mouth of yours, lady."

He plucked a switchblade from the cuff of his boot, flipping a catch that caused a four-inch blade to flick out like the tongue of a snake. He sliced through the golden braid of her slip strap, then twisted her head back, forcing her to arch her back with a gasp of pain. Half of her black slip fell away, revealing a soft, white breast.

"Maybe I should do something to help you remember your manners," he said, "like mommies tying a string around a kid's finger. Think you might pay more attention if I put my initials above your nipple?"

She began to scream, the cords straining in her throat. The bedroom door opened and Strasser took a lurching step into the room.

"What the fuck," he muttered. "What the hell is this?" He blinked at the scene as if he were peering through layers of fog.

Neal smiled and laid the tip of his knife against Greta's bare breast. He looked at the sergeant steadily. "My old man always told me, Top, that it don't matter who breaks a filly as long as she gets broke. If this is your woman, no argument, but somebody's got to teach this fraulein what a bridle and spurs are for. You teach her or me, Top, it don't make no difference . . ."

For a moment Strasser stared down at Greta, his eyes focusing on the blade touching her breast.

Lasari put his glass aside. He was watching a man die, he realized, not all at once and not completely, but in a small way a part of Ernest Strasser had ceased to exist. He wasn't going to challenge Eddie Neal and that decision would cause something inside him to shrink and wither away. He could live without it, maybe, Lasari thought. Sergeant Strasser might pull off the heroin scam, get his money, sit around a condo in Florida laughing and telling how he'd let one of his corporals in Germany put the fear of God into a nice piece of kraut stuff he'd had a fling with.

But at this moment, in a room crowded with cuckoo clocks and garish bric-a-brac, looking at a knife touching a soft, young breast and with three witnesses watching him, an essential part of the sergeant died.

Strasser laughed uncertainly. "Hell, you don't have to make jokes with me, Neal. This filly knows how to take care of herself . . ."

He turned on unsteady legs and walked into the bedroom, slamming the door. They heard his body collapse on the bed.

"I believe in offering a lady a choice, Greta," Neal said. "You want the initials above or below that cute little tit of yours?"

Lasari moved forward. "Put the knife away, Eddie. You touch her and you've got to kill me."

"Hold it, soldier. This ain't no concern of yours."

"I'm gonna talk real slow," Lasari said, "to try to get through to that Georgia peabrain of yours. You touch the lady and you've got to kill me. Maybe you can do that, maybe you can't."

"Hold it, boy!" Neal grinned and turned the blade toward Lasari. "I thought you said you wasn't fuckin' her. What the shit difference does any of this make to you?"

Lasari moved his hands out from his sides. "Try me, you cracker bastard. Then a couple of things are gonna happen real fast. You may try to cut my throat before I put a boot into that big buck mouth of yours. Or Greta runs outside and calls the cops. Or maybe Strasser has a nightmare, wakes up and takes your gun away, wastes me himself. But if the golden goose is dead, who picks up the stuff at the Lucky Thirteenth? Maybe I get buried in a deserter's grave, but you get a general court-martial and a few dozen years for murder.''

Lasari watched the confusion in Neal's face. "But I'll tell you what else there's no doubt about, Eddie. When you walk out of the federal pen, there's gonna be somebody waiting for you, and you better be ready to tell Malleck why you blew his multi-million-dollar deal sky high just because you couldn't keep your hands off Strasser's girl friend.''

For a moment the only sound in the room was Neal's harsh breathing and Greta's sobs. Then the corporal loosened his grasp on her hair, shrugged and took a step backward, touching a button on the shaft of his knife. The blade disappeared in a silvery flash.

"You got guts, ginzo,'' he said with an admiring smile. "A gutsy guy, a lot of sand to your bottom. You smart, too. First things first, you see that. Let's just call this unfinished business between you and me.''

He brushed the palms of his hands against his trousers, picked up his topcoat and walked to the door. "I'm gonna wait downstairs in the fresh air. When Strasser's driver shows I'll give you a whistle under the window.'' He paused at the door, his hand on the knob, his expression shy and awkward. "Yeah, Jackson, we still got some things to settle.''

Greta was crying softly. "It's over,'' he said. "You might as well forget it.''

He helped her from her knees and pulled together the ends of her slip strap and tied them in an expert square knot. She looked at it gratefully.

"It's almost like it's on purpose,'' she said. "Like a decoration.''

He brought a clean napkin and a glass of water from the bar. "Here. Fix yourself up, you'll feel better.''

"Eddie could have killed you, George.''

"The odds were against it. He's not that dumb.''

"Ernie wouldn't have stopped him, Ernie didn't care what he was going to do with me.''

"He's drunk, Greta, he probably won't even remember it."

"So then I should forget it, is that what you're saying? That man I live with, who's going to take me to the United States, that *dummkopf* who doesn't even care if someone carves initials on me? Ernie told me he has a cabin on a lake in Wisconsin. Do you know where that is?"

"Yes," Lasari said. "The Midwest, green country with fir trees and lots of snow in winter. Like Bavaria without mountains."

She looked around the cluttered room. "Ernie said there are lots of Germans there, that they like cuckoo clocks and strudel and they'd like me . . . He's a fucking liar, isn't he?"

"I think he means it," Lasari said.

Her eyes were suddenly wide and frightened; her voice dropped to a whisper. "I have something for you, George."

A whistle sounded from the street below. Lasari went to the window and looked down. He could see a jeep at the curb, Neal standing beside it.

Greta had gone into the bedroom. She tugged at Strasser's body till he rolled over on his back, coughing and moistening his lips with spittle. She took a key ring from his pocket and unsnapped it from the chain that held it to his belt.

Lasari stood in the bedroom doorway. "I've got to go, Greta."

"He won't help me," she said, as if talking to herself. She unlocked the double doors of a floor to ceiling closet, then selected a key to open a drawer. "He'll never take me to Wisconsin, he'll run out on me. Ernie'll give me a couple thousand DM and a teddy bear that plays 'Tannenbaum' or something and I'll never see him again."

Inside the drawer was a heavy metal box with a separate lock. She opened it.

"Nobody ever did anything for me in my whole life, not my family, not Ernie, no one until you almost let Eddie kill you," she whispered. She took something from the box, closed it and secured all three locks. Then she stepped back into the front room.

"Don't tell me a fucking thing you've got planned, George. Then they can't make me tell them anything. But I can see it in your eyes, I saw it when you looked at Eddie. You're not going to do what they say. You're going to take a chance and run for it . . ."

"You said to tell you nothing, Greta."

She held out an American passport. "It was supposed to be for me," she said. "He paid twenty-five thousand DM for it. It's a perfect fake, you just have to put your name and the right picture in it. There are machines at the PX that take those pictures." She sighed. "He'd have sold the passport back on the black market before he'd give it to me."

She put the passport in Lasari's hand and closed his fingers over it. "Who loves ya, baby?"

He shrugged. "Kojak, I guess."

She was beginning to cry. "I was never as dumb as you thought, George. Those TV people aren't real, they can't help you, I know that. But at least they can't hurt you."

The whistle sounded again and in the bedroom Strasser stirred and threw an arm over his face. "Listen, Greta," Lasari said. "If Strasser finds out, tell him I stole it. Better still, get out of here tonight, before he wakes. I never thought you were dumb, now for Christ's sake prove it."

She shook her head stubbornly. "Not yet. I've got to figure out how much he owes me."

Lasari went down the stairs to the street, where an icy wind was rising off the river. As Neal held open the door of the jeep, Lasari glanced up at the apartment windows. They were clear yellow squares against the darkness, bright but empty.

# Chapter Thirty-five

THE GENERAL SWAM a dozen laps in the Rhein-Baden pool, then took an icy shower in a stall fitted with crisscross jet sprays. In his third-floor room he opened the windows and looked out on the parks and graveled walks of the spa's expansive grounds. It was not yet eight o'clock, and sharply cold, but a few of the healthier guests were out in jogging clothes and an elderly man and woman in wheelchairs, plaid robes tucked around them, were being pushed along by uniformed spa attendants under the bare linden trees.

Weir did a half hour of setting-up exercises, then sat down with a towel around his waist for a breakfast of fruit, boiled eggs and toast that had arrived from the room service on the same knock as the items from the pressing room. Fritz Vestrick was not yet in his office when Weir registered, but the desk clerk assured the general that Herr Vestrick would be informed of the honored guest's presence the moment he arrived.

On the stroke of nine o'clock the phone rang and Vestrick's voice, showing traces of a southern accent, said, "Hiya, Scotty! Am I coming up or are you coming down?"

"Give me five minutes, Fritz. I'll be down."

"Can't wait to see you, pardner."

Tarbert Weir put on his freshly pressed Class-A uniform, gray twill trousers, cordovan ankle boots with buckled straps, khaki shirt and tie and an olive drab tunic with three rows of campaign ribbons and decorations and the stars of a general.

261

He checked the insignia on his garrison cap and slapped it across his knee to soften the folds. At the open window he took several deep breaths, then flexed his muscles so the fabric of the tunic stretched tight over his shoulders but moved with ease at the armpits. There was no need to look in the full-length mirror. Weir knew by the flex and stretch exactly how trim he looked.

Herr Vestrick's office, opening directly off the lobby, was furnished in bleached leather, shining wood and circular carpets with patterns woven in varying shades of blue. In the background, from a tape cassette, came the throaty, sugared tones of Al Jolson singing "My Old Kentucky Home."

The two men embraced and Vestrick motioned Weir to a chair while he seated himself behind the big desk. Vestrick nodded at the cassette player. "Just once through, Scotty, for old times' sake. I had it transposed from the old seventy-eight."

Vestrick was older than Weir by four or five years, a big man with high coloring. He wore the striped trousers and cutaway coat of a traditional boniface. He had been one of the first Luftwaffe pilots shot down over Britain after the United States' entry into World War II, and had spent the next four years in prisoner-of-war camps in the deep South. After his release, Vestrick had returned to Frankfurt and was working as a busboy in the dining room at the Frankfurter Hof when Weir and Maggie had stopped there on their wedding leave. Weir had been impressed with the German's fluent English, surprising accent and passionate love of the South. He had arranged for Vestrick to get work as a translator at the Am-Main Army Headquarters. The Jolson recording, now on tape, was one that Tarbert Weir had found in a second-hand record store near the Army College in Carlisle, Pennsylvania, and sent to Vestrick nearly twenty years ago.

On the last falling tones, Vestrick switched off the cassette and said, "I know about Mark, Scotty. I still subscribe to the Louisville *Journal*, they covered it under national news."

For a moment Weir did not trust himself to speak.

"I already called you in Springfield," Vestrick said, "but they told me you had gone to Virginia."

"You talked to John Grimes?"

"No, a young lady. I didn't ask her name."

"A friend of Mark's," the general said.

"Helga wants you at the house for lunch, Scotty. It's up to you, of course." Weir shook his head. "I'll do anything," Vestrick said. "I've got fine staff here. I'll take a few days off, we'll go to the mountains, I'll get drunk with you."

Weir shook his head again. "That just won't do it, Fritz. Not this time. There might be something, however. You still flying?"

"Yes, I keep an A36 Bonanza at the local airport."

"What are you cleared for?"

"Almost everything. What do you want, Scotty?"

General Weir put his garrison cap on his head and held out his hand. "Thank you, Fritz. I'll let you know later in the day."


A cab took him to the headquarters of Belgium's NATO mission in Germany, a three-story, salmon-colored building situated in the district of Wilhelmshohe, on the outskirts of the immense park which served as a frame for Ludensdorf's elegantly restored summer palace.

Captain Alain Tranchet-LeRoi was waiting for his visitor in an office on the second floor of the building, a corner room with narrow, leaded windows which faced the park and the shining curve of a river in the distance.

Alain was tall, though not as tall as Weir had expected him to be, and stocky rather than muscular, not quite the athletic appearance the general had expected to see. He must be twenty-nine now, nearing thirty, the general thought, younger than Mark.

They had last met when Alain was eighteen. It had been his birthday and the general had visited him at the university with his mother to celebrate that and a prized soccer victory. Emile LeRoi had been in Holland on business that weekend, Marta had explained to her son. Alain had played for his district and now the university and there was talk that day about a tryout with a professional soccer team in South America.

It had been a festive afternoon, as Weir remembered it, idyllic and mannered, like an Impressionist painting, the college buildings of Louvain purple in the sunlight, the quads emerald green, the soccer field lined with picnic tables.

General Weir offered his hand and then patted Captain Tranchet-LeRoi warmly on the shoulder. "So good to see you, Alain, after all these years. I would not have been surprised if our appointment had been at a stadium somewhere, rather than the military."

The captain smiled thinly, there was a touch of chill in his clipped careful English. "Establishment football was just a passing thing. I had a head for the game, no pun intended, but on the professional level I was outclassed. I think my father was more disappointed than I was."

He lit a cigarette from the embossed leather box on his desk and walked to the windows. "My mother told me how glad she was to see you," he said. " 'I feel almost young again, Alain' was the way she put it." He pinched the bridge of his nose, as if to relieve tension. "Christ! If we could give both generations prefrontal lobotomies it might be all to the good."

"We all have our pasts to live with," Weir said. "Marta's and mine happened to cross."

"Ah, yes, and our futures." The Belgian gestured with his cigarette, sending a whirl of smoke through the office. "May I show you, sir?"

Tarbert Weir joined him at the window and looked down to the area in the parking lot at which the captain was pointing. He singled out a Belgian staff car, a Mercedes Benz 300 Diesel with black panels, brown fenders and heavy-duty tires. It carried NATO license plates and NATO and Belgian flags bolted to the bumpers. Tranchet-LeRoi's smile was enigmatic, barely amused. "You couldn't get that from a soccer player," he said.

For the next ten minutes General Weir sat on one side of the desk while the captain spread out certain items between them. He was a chain smoker, and he sipped frequently at a coffee cup on his desk though the liquid was obviously cold. He must be more like his father than his mother, Weir thought; there was little of Marta's vitality and warmth in his manner. The general was aware that the younger man was not meeting his eyes and that his face could have been that of a man of forty rather than a decade younger. There was a look of weariness in the lidded expression. Alain's hair, while still full, was a fading ash blond, a shade away from gray.

When the items were lined up between them, the captain pushed each one across the desk toward Weir with a well-manicured finger. Besides the key to the Mercedes there was a leather case with NATO markings for the general's identity cards and a packet of documents with appropriate seals and stamps, defining the temporary assignment for General Tarbert Weir, U.S. Army, retired, now serving as an accredited observer at the NATO field maneuvers in the proscribed areas outside Ludensdorf.

"I would advise you to wear these at all times in the field," the captain said, pointing to a pair of stretch armbands, each marked: OFFICIAL OBSERVER. "Another one of the improvements since your time," he added. "These have reflecting threads, and can be seen in the dark."

He picked up a waterproof pouch, untied the binders and pulled out a small-scale grid map. A long gray ash from his cigarette fell on the map and he blew the residue away with impatience, sending a dust of ash onto the sleeve of Tarbert Weir's uniform. For a moment the two men's eyes met and it was Tranchet-LeRoi who turned away first. "My apologies, general," he said coolly. He made a cross with a pencil on the map. "I have checked rosters and here is where your man should be at 2:00 A.M.

"And you want this, of course," he said, dropping a pair of keys on a metal ring to the desktop. "The key to—what was the quaint phrase my mother said you used?"

" '*Maison Gris*' is what your group calls them, I believe," Weir said. "The United Kingdom uses 'Bluebirds' and the Germans say '*Falltur*' or 'Trapdoor.' The American code word has always been 'Case Ace.' "

"My mother tells me you were one of the bright military minds who helped organize this 'safe house' system, for top political personnel and high Army brass, an emergency escape route."

"Marta's wrong there," Scotty Weir said. "Those escape houses, old ski chalets, country schoolhouses, isolated farms —that route was selected, laid out and supplied in the late 1940s, the time of the first Berlin airlift, in preparation for a 'worst possible scenario,' an invasion of the continent by the Russians. It was a concern even then, captain.

"I didn't organize or pick these hideaways originally, but I did assist in reorganizing and relocating the system in the middle sixties."

Weir picked up the key ring and examined the small metal tag with the numeral two imprinted on it.

"There are three Case Aces within a fifty mile radius of these maneuvers," Weir said. "I requested number two because it's up the mountain, secluded, and the closest to Ludensdorf."

General Weir gathered the identification documents into the leather folder and put it, with the map pouch and armbands, into his inner tunic pocket. Then he hooked the keys to the Mercedes and the key to Case Ace, number two, onto his personal key ring.

The silence in the office stretched out. The general knew their business was not finished but he was determined the captain would speak first.

Tranchet-LeRoi lit a fifth cigarette with fingers that trembled in anger. "Goddamn your Yankee stubbornness," he said at last. "You're not going to ask about the gun, are you?"

"I figured you'd bring it up."

"All right. A gun is something else, Weir. So far the car, the observer's credentials, those things are harmless, almost official. But I can't issue a permit for a regulation service revolver unless you tell me exactly what your plans are."

"I can't do that, Alain," he said.

"Then I have only one option," the captain said and opened the top desk drawer. "I offer you something personal, something of a family heirloom on my father's side." He put a self-loading pistol, the barrel etched with silver inlay, and a small box of ammunition on the desk. "It is in perfect firing condition. I have checked it out myself." He paused. "It could do the trick for you."

Weir looked at the gun without touching it. "And it could also get me arrested for carrying an unofficial firearm, couldn't it? You could pick up that phone before I got out the front gate."

There were touches of color in the captain's cheeks and he ground out his cigarette in the ashtray with a savage twist. With the other hand he swept the pistol and ammunition back into the top drawer.

"Just one more question before you leave, my friend," he said. "*Where* do you get your guts? Why in hell did you expect *me* to put my ass on the line for you?"

The insolence, the hatred in the question forced Weir to pause, to try to read the Belgian's face, to put order into his own thoughts. Then he spoke firmly, but with restraint.

"Something happened a long time ago, captain. I thought

you knew that. For that action I was awarded the Medal of Honor by my own government. And I was awarded two decorations by *your* government. One gives me the freedom and courtesy of that city through the Order of Brussels, the other extends the gratitude of His Belgian Majesty, King Leopold, to Tarbert Weir in perpetuity. And I figured if your king was willing to lay his gratitude on the line, you—as an individual Belgian—also owed me something. It's an American concept, Alain. In Las Vegas it's what's called 'an open I.O.U.' I'm calling in my markers."

The two men stared at one another for a long moment, then Captain Tranchet-LeRoi nodded abruptly. "So be it. And since I've paid my debt, may I ask a special favor of you, general?"

Tarbert Weir nodded.

"Make this the last time you see any of the Tranchet-LeRois," he said. "My father was *not* out of town on business yesterday. He was in a pub in the village, waiting to see your car drive out of town. I may not speak for my mother, but I am *certain* for my father and myself. We have had enough. Can you imagine what it has been like to compete for a *lifetime* against the great and glorious Scotty Weir? What more do you want of us? A war that's been over for more than three decades and whose fire still blows through our lives, how long must we be grateful?"

His voice was shrill with emotion, and he stood abruptly, placing his hands flat on the desk, the knuckles pressed white with tension.

"We are *Belgique* and proud of it. We want now only to be ourselves. Is that not something you could force yourself to understand? Have you any concept, General Weir, how tired we are of Americans, how tired we are of *heroes?*"

Weir stood and walked toward the office door. His own anger was so sudden, that he put his hand on the doorknob to steady himself. He wanted to turn back and tip the desk onto the floor, spilling papers and files, and flinging the desk drawer with the antique pistol out over the carpet. He wanted to take the young officer by his tunic and shake him until there was no longer any look of judgment or rebuke in his pale eyes. He wanted to kill this smug, vengeful European who knew neither the young man Scotty Weir had once been, nor the young Mark Weir who was dead while this *Belgique* still lived.

Instead he forced himself to speak almost kindly. "Think sometime, captain, where you *Belgiques* would be, where all of Europe would be if it weren't for Americans *and* heroes.

"Most mortals, soldier and civilian, go through life on secret orders till a moment of crisis, when something bigger than human measure is asked of them. It's then they open those orders. That's how heroes find out who they are."

General Weir put on his garrison cap and opened the door. " 'A hero is a man who endures for one moment longer . . .' I'm not the first man who said that, Alain, but I'm obviously the first one who said it to you."

Weir nodded thoughtfully. "Yes," he said, "you have my word on your last request. I will not see you or your family again, but on one condition only." The kindness left his voice. "If you double-cross me, captain, if you fuck up my plans in any way at all, I'll come back here in person and break your *Belgique* neck with my own bare hands."

He walked down two flights of marble stairs, cut across the main courtyard and began the walk back to Ludensdorf. The staff car would stay in its official parking slot until later.

The general glanced at his wristwatch. The entire interview had taken less than half an hour.

# Chapter Thirty-six

IN LUDENSDORF CAFES were open and street traffic was brisk, but the sign in the airlines' ticket office still read closed in three languages, so Tarbert Weir made his first stop at the pharmacy.

Two young men in white coats were dusting shelves and polishing glass cabinets; there were no other customers. The air was cold and smelled cleanly of alcohol, emollients and horehound drops. Weir spoke to a clerk at a rear counter. The young man hesitated a moment, then said, "If it's for your dog, *mein Herr*, I could suggest a good veternarian."

"Thank you," Weir said. "It's for myself. I use a few drops of it in seltzer water as a carminative. Your German cooking is excellent but rich for my American stomach."

The man came back in a few moments with a small bottle of colorless liquid and put it into a green paper bag. Then he put the registry book for purchasers of controlled substances onto the counter and turned it to face the general. Weir signed it "John Grimes, Rhein-Baden Spa Hotel."

Weir pointed to the green package. "*Wei steht der dollar?*"

"*Drei, mein Herr*," the clerk said.

The general was aware the young German was looking at him covertly, examining his uniform and rows of medal ribbons. Weir took a ten-dollar bill from his wallet and said, "*Bitte geben Sir mir Deutsche Marks hierfur*."

As the clerk counted out the change in German currency, the general said, "*Name und Vorname?*"

"Gunther Maginer," the clerk said.

Weir smiled and gave the man a soft salute. "*Sehr angenehm und Guten Morgen, Herr Maginer.*"

The clerk snapped to attention and touched his hand smartly to his right eyebrow. "*Guten Morgen, Herr General.*"

Scotty Weir spent the remainder of the morning sightseeing. He looked into the Grimm Brothers museum, browsed through bookstores and then joined a tour group to inspect the paintings in the palace art gallery. The guide gave the information in both German and English and Weir trailed along with the crowd, studying the paintings leisurely.

Now and then he stayed behind for a longer look at a painting that held his interest. There was an oil portrait by Rembrandt of his wife, a stolid matron, and he stood longer at the Durers, feeling an empathy for the German's realism. The artist knew that men got hurt using their hands, and how those hands looked afterward, the fingers thickened, veins like swollen rivers, knuckles bruised and big as walnuts. Weir glanced at his own hands, hanging loosely at his sides, aligned with the seams of his uniform trousers. They were big hands, fingers strong and clean, the nails clipped short, with no rings on the fingers, no scars. Unscathed hands. It would have been wrong, a betrayal of the past, of his memories, the general realized, to have struck Captain Alain Tranchet-LeRoi with those hands.

The general took a corner table for a late lunch at the Hutten-Bar. He ordered cold meats, salad and a pot of tea, then leaned back in his chair to wait, letting his eyes wander over the dining room, past the fake bamboo wall that separated the table from the bar, until he became accustomed to the darkness. A man seated at the near end of the bar ordered a Johnny Walker Black Label with ice and soda. The voice was flat, slightly nasal, a touch of New Jersey. That meant the man was not German after all.

Weir's anger and then the long walk back to town had given him an appetite and he enjoyed his lunch. The Rembrandts and the Durers and the Grimm Brothers might be relics of another era, but they had served their purpose. He had got what he wanted from them, and from the bookstores, the museums, the old streets of Ludensdorf, and what he'd got was the fact that he was under surveillance.

The man at the bar had been on the periphery of his vision all that morning and he remembered him from the Liege airport and before that in Philo Park.

The man was about forty, bulky, muscled, with blond hair cut short, and oddly old-fashioned in his Ivy dress of twenty years ago, flannel slacks, Blucher brogues, a raglan topcoat and the buttoned down, fine cotton shirt and striped tie that identified Brooks Brothers like a thumbprint.

When Weir paid the waiter, he heard the clink of change being tossed on the inside bar. He left the restaurant and strolled to the airlines ticket office without turning around.

The clerk at Lufthansa was happy to take a credit card for flight 257 leaving that evening at nine o'clock from Munich to New York and Chicago. Weir spent some time checking out exactly what time the plane reached Chicago, whether this was a full dinner flight and could the fraulein check what inflight movie was scheduled?

When she obtained all the answers for him, she said, "We'll want you at the airport by eight, sir. Munich is about one hundred sixty kilometers from here. Would you like me to arrange ground transport?"

Weir looked at his watch thoughtfully. "No, I'll do that myself, thank you. Make out my ticket and send it to the hotel at five o'clock . . . the Rhein-Baden Spa, Room 333, General Tarbert Weir."

Fritz Vestrick was lunching on a tray at his desk but put it aside when he saw the general in the doorway. "I'll be checking out tonight, Fritz," he said. "I'd appreciate it if I could spend some time with you. How about a swim?"

Weir went to his room to change into trunks and a robe. From a pocket of his tunic he took the bottle of liquid from the pharmacy, plus the car keys and other materials Captain Tranchet had given him earlier, put them all together in the waterproof map pouch, tucking the packet into the pocket of his robe.

Vestrick had also changed and stood with his office clothes carefully draped on a hanger. From the hotel lobby the two men walked to a vast indoor pool, steam rising from the heated surface, and swam laps together, side by side, talking quietly between their rhythmic strokes. Then they saunaed, ordered salt rubdowns and showered.

Vestrick changed into his elegant working clothes and joined the general in the glassed-in fern gardens beyond the poolhouse. Weir gave Vestrick the map pouch, the two men embraced and the general took an elevator back to his room.

He shaved once more, put on the jogging suit he'd worn in Philo Park, collected his clothing and toilet articles and began to pack. He hung his wet swimming trunks on the bathroom door handle and put everything else in his suitcase, folding his uniform neatly and arranging his robe and slippers on top.

He checked his watch again, then lay back on the bedspread, staring at the ceiling and trying to will relaxation into his body; he remained as tense as a coiled spring, and his thoughts were racing, words forming almost involuntarily in his mind. "It's right for me to be here, Mark. Survivors feel this way after a battle, it's a known quality of combat. You look at your comrades, you count the casualties and you wish that you could be part of them in some way . . ."

A few minutes before five the general dialed room service and asked for ice, soda, a bottle of Johnny Walker Black Label and two glasses. "I'm expecting an airline ticket to be left with the concierge at five," he said. "Ask your man to bring it up with the drinks, if you will."

He stood at the windows, back to the door, waiting for the knock. When he opened it, the man from the Hutten-Bar was standing there, liquor tray in hand, the airline ticket on the tray.

"Do you mind if I come in?" he said.

"I sure as hell do," Weir answered. "If you're selling anything, whether it's black market currency or young girls or their brothers, I'm not buying."

"Come now, general," the man said. "I know you spotted me at least once this morning and I have a notion you've been on to me for some time, so I bribed room service to let me bring up your order. May I put it down somewhere?" He nodded down at the tray. "Johnny Walker Black. You're a thoughtful host."

"On the bureau then," Weir said. "And you must let me reimburse you for that bribe. Or is that an expense account item?"

The man put up a hand in mock protest.

"Please, general. My pleasure." He picked up the airlines envelope and handed it to Weir. "It's all in order, I've checked it. Munich departure nine o'clock, arrival at Kennedy, transfer to American for Chicago, then a twelve-seater down to Springfield in time for supper tomorrow night. The concierge put in the voucher for the ride to the airport. It's all there."

The man looked around the hotel room, checking the windows, glancing toward the bathroom. "I've called the home office. My people want you aboard Flight 257 and my orders are to stick with you till you're emplaned."

He put out his hand. "I'm Lenox Riley. I'd like our few hours together to be as pleasant as possible."

"There's no need to introduce myself," Weir said dryly. "You seem to know everything about me. But I'll tell you what, Riley, I'll buy the drinks if you'll tell me how you got onto me. Scotch all right? I could send down for wine . . ."

"Scotch will do nicely," Riley said. He removed his topcoat and dropped it over the arm of a chair. "Easy on the soda and a single ice cube."

"Hell, every time I'm pressed into service as a bartender I either make it too light or too heavy. Mind serving yourself?"

The general walked to the windows, humming, pretending to savor the sight of the lights twinkling beyond the darkened windows. In the reflection of a pane he watched Riley half fill a glass with Scotch, then take a long swallow from it, adding another ounce of liquor before topping it with soda and an ice cube.

"I'll make my own, thanks," the general said and walked to the bureau.

"This is a rare, on the job treat for me," Riley said. "If I drank like this all the time I'd have a liver the size of a coconut."

"Christ, enjoy yourself. It's the only way to relax after a hard day." Weir lifted his glass. "Cheers."

"Cheers," Riley said but set down his glass. He walked to the closets, opened them and ran a hand along the empty metal hangers. He pulled open each bureau drawer and searched them. He went into the bathroom, kicking the door wide open, then checked the medicine cabinet. He noticed the wet swim trunks hanging from the doorknob.

"Forget something?" he asked.

"No. I'm not taking them. I don't want wet luggage at thirty thousand feet."

The man opened the suitcase on the bed and felt through the layers of clothing. Then he picked up his drink, placed the straight-backed desk chair between Weir and the hall doorway and straddled it. "You're a neat packer," he said. Weir nodded.

"Before we start enjoying ourselves too much," Riley said, "I'd like to inform you that I'm armed at the moment with a .38 special, Smith and Wesson, for which I carry a German license, and like you, Weir, I'm karate trained."

Weir nodded again without interest.

"You look CIA, Riley," the general said flatly, "but I can think of no reason they'd have an interest in me."

"At the moment I'm an independent, though I still have a classified number in Langley and an operator who'll take a signal. It's one of your own confreres who asked me to keep an eye on you, general. There's no need to be secretive about it now."

Weir felt a jolt of anger and satisfaction. "How did Colonel Benton know I'd left the Greenbrier?"

"For about twelve hours, he didn't," Riley said. "Fortunately Captain Jetter is a light sleeper. When he finally realized you'd given him the slip, he remembered dreaming about a helicopter, then decided it had been a real one. A list was made of all airports with overseas schedules within a reasonable 'copter distance from Virginia. Lufthansa was checked for their passenger lists from those depots. They got Dallas, your flight, your destination and Benton put a call through to me in Frankfurt."

"But Germany, why did Colonel Benton believe I'd be going to Germany?"

"I asked the same question," Riley said. "Colonel Benton informed me that was not a need-to-know priority, I could complete my assignment without that information."

"And my trip to the Tranchet farm? I assume that was you in the pickup truck."

"Yes. I checked your background at the American military library in Heidelberg and got the material on the Medal of Honor and your friendship with the family. I was convinced you'd head there. It's a sixth sense that intelligence agents

develop . . . I can't think of a better word for it." He sipped
his drink. "Captain Tranchet-LeRoi is quite a fan of yours, by
the way."

"Did you see him before or after I did?"

"Just a short time afterward," Lenox Riley said. "He was
emotional, pretty shaken by your visit, said you'd always been
like a second father to him. My most sincere condolences on
the death of your son, by the way."

"Thank you. The Tranchets and Alain were part of this sentimental journey, I suppose. After my son's death I had a
great need to touch some familiar pickets in an old fence. It's
been a healing few days. I'm ready to go home now."

"The clerk in the pharmacy said you'd been experiencing
some stomach disorders."

"Emotions," Scotty Weir said. "Purely emotions gone
amok." He held up his glass. "But I find this helps."

"Good," Riley said. "Mind if I freshen mine and switch on
a few lights? It's gloomy as hell in here."

"Drink up," Weir said. "I don't want to put an opened
bottle in my suitcase. We've got time. The front desk said
they'd ring up when the limo comes round."

The two men sat in the back seat during the drive to
Ludensdorf's municipal airport. The chauffeur, wearing a
uniform and a visored cap with "Rhein-Baden Spa" on the
band, drove at a steady speed along the autobahn, the highway lit at intervals with antifog lamps that cast a yellow glow
on the roadside snowdrifts.

Neither man spoke for several kilometers. Riley held his
liquor well, Weir thought; in the hotel his speech had remained clear, his hands steady. But as the man turned to him
now in the back seat, Weir noticed a small tic had begun to
pull at the side of his mouth.

"I'm flattered that you thought I was CIA," he said. "That
was my berth for several years. It's like going to a good prep
school, the training always shows." Riley looked out the rear
window at the dark countryside and absently scrawled his
initials on the damp glass. "They assigned me a lateral, exotic
approach," he went on. "Arbitrage banking. I actually
worked in a bank in Calcutta for six years after Princeton.
Had a large gentleman's flat and half a dozen servants.
Couldn't even reach for a drink for myself. A twelve-year-old

boy in red pantaloons stood by my chair to do that.''

"Why would anyone leave that kind of plush assignment?"
Weir asked.

Riley was thoughtful. "I'm not homosexual," he said,
"just unmarried. But if you ask dozens of people dozens of
questions about anyone's behavior, you're likely to find some
touch of gossip, hot-tubbing in a drunken mood, a miscon-
strued invitation to spend the night." He shrugged. "In spite
of their investigation, I tested out like a bar of Ivory soap,
general."

"The top Army brass is still using you, Riley," Weir said.
"That's all the vindication a man needs."

At the airport the driver pulled past the main terminal and
took a narrow road behind the maintenance sheds to a corner
of the tarmac where a four-seater Bonanza was taxiing into
position. The two passengers stepped from the limo, while the
driver stowed Weir's single piece of luggage in the plane, then
left the field through a black and white striped exit gate.

Lenox Riley looked appraisingly at the plane, then said,
"You strap into the rear passenger seat, general. I'll sit next to
the pilot." He swung himself into the second cockpit seat, put
a hand inside his jacket and removed the .38 special from a
shoulder holster. He rested the gun on his knee.

"I'm presuming your German is more fluent than mine,
general. Tell our pilot I understand something about planes
and I can read flight plans and instrument panels."

"I speak English," the pilot said.

"Very well," Riley said. "We want to deliver Mr. Weir to
Munich by eight o'clock so he can be aboard Lufthansa 257
for a nine o'clock flight. And we want no mistakes."

The pilot nodded, turned the plane one hundred and eighty
degrees and began to taxi around the perimeter of the field. A
row of private planes stood parked at one side of the area,
dark and locked for the night. Two small feeder lines were
boarding passengers at the brightly lit terminal and in the public parking lot a pair of local taxis idled, while a few parked
cars shone under arc lights.

Riley sat beside the pilot, silent but alert, eyes traveling over
the expanse of air field. Suddenly the plane's headbeams
picked out the black and white striped exit gate.

"Goddamnit!" Riley said abruptly. "We're right back
where we started from!"

"I'm waiting for the control tower . . ." the pilot began.

"Listen, you swine . . ." Riley's voice broke into a yelp of pain as Tarbert Weir leaned forward suddenly and struck him a fast blow on the neck with the blade of his hand. Riley was dazed but struggling when the pilot knocked him unconscious with a second blow that caught a vital artery. The man slid sideways, breathing raggedly.

Weir reached forward and lifted the Smith & Wesson from Riley's limp hand. Fritz Vestrick turned in the pilot's seat to look at him. "Jesus, Scotty, you tapped him like some kid testing a ripe watermelon."

"I'd have got him the second time," Weir said. "He fooled me, he's as drunk and relaxed as a turkey." The general shook his head sadly. "I'll take my gear now, Fritz. Can you believe that poor dumb bastard thinks he's got a *sixth sense* going for him?"

Vestrick handed the waterproof pouch to Weir and a set of car keys. "My Mercedes is parked right in front of the terminal. There's a rabbit's foot tied to the mirror, you can't miss it."

"How much fuel do you have?"

"Enough to cruise at four thousand feet for a while, then enough to get him there and get me back. I'll have him on the ground in Munich at half-past nine sharp."

Weir opened the plane door and swung his suitcase to the tarmac. Then he reached out and gripped Vestrick's broad shoulder. "*Auf wiedersehen,* pardner," he said. "I'll call you from Springfield when it's all over."

# Chapter Thirty-seven

THE WEATHER HAD turned bitter, an early spring snowstorm sharp with wind and sleeting snow. Sometimes the flakes seemed to be falling from the dark skies; at other moments the flurries were lifted in gusts from the rock-hard ground and swirled against the assembled troops, tanks and guns with stinging force by mountain winds.

The patrolled area allocated for Combined NATO Forces maneuvers, several square miles of field and wood in southern Germany near the Czechoslovakian border, was crowded with hundreds of soldiers and tanks, guns, heavy equipment, plus temporary executive and housing quarters, but the organization and discipline, the limited communications between the polyglot troops and the demands of the rough terrain and weather seemed to isolate the region in a cone of near silence.

The Lucky Thirteenth, with its M60 tanks with 105mm snouts, stretched out on either side of Lasari's assigned position, hidden in clumps of trees or behind escarpments of rock camouflaged by cut fir branches and mottled canvas netting, shadowed under the night sky.

As Private George Jackson, Lasari's orders had assigned him to act as tactical observer and assistant scanner to a French tank technician with a sergeant's rank. That man sat now in a metal sling seat, legs swinging free, as he monitored the night beam and scopes of a Chaparral, part of the Army's air defense weapons system.

Above the military scene, the air was occasionally whipped and churned by Cobra choppers patrolling the activities of the various sectors.

Lasari asked to borrow a pair of field glasses from the Frenchman and trained them on the horizon, picking out the details of action on the Czech border. Electrically wired fences stood ten feet tall for as far as he could see, illuminated at intervals by yellow arc lights that silhouetted the NATO troops patrolling West German soil, and lit up the machine gun towers on the Czech perimeter of the snowy woodlands, both sides guarding a strip of no-man's land.

Lasari returned the glasses, flexed his stiff fingers and stamped his boots on the icy soil. He had stood in the same position for more than three hours and his hands and feet were almost without feeling. In the days since leaving Heidelberg he had tried to reevaluate his dilemma, to make judgments without panic. Now the potential of this unfamiliar locale, with its parameters and boundaries and searchlights, had stamped itself in his mind like a free-form map. The border crossover into Czechoslovakia was impossible, a deathtrap. To the north, troop deployments occupied the territory for at least five miles. If he could split south in the darkness and reach the Bavarian Alps, he might make it to the Austrian border. From there it could be Italy, Yugoslavia, a boat to Greece . . . Even though a deserter, he was at this moment an ordinary GI, absent without leave. At two o'clock he would become something else.

An American officer strode by and called out, "Everything normal at this grid?"

"*Certainement*," the Frenchman said. "The enemy is looking at us and we are looking at him." Lasari glanced at his watch. It was 0155 hours.

A few moments later a fresh-faced GI, a reddish cowlick sticking out from under his helmet, slogged over to Lasari and said, "I'm your relief watch. Take a break, soldier."

Lasari and several dozen soldiers on relief broke position and headed toward the makeshift canteens and latrines sheltered some distance away. Lasari knew he was expected to proceed five hundred yards to Grid 14, to the first latrine on his left, go inside and wait five minutes. Jesus, I don't even want the burden of choice, Lasari thought. Both decision and

indecision seemed equally impossible and he remembered
what seasoned GIs in 'Nam had said to newcomers with
troubles . . . just forget it, soldier, write it in your diary, dig a
hole in the ground and bury it, *but forget it* . . .

A short time later he stood before a urinal in the frigid
latrine, shielded on both sides by corrugated slabs of grayish
plastic. There were a dozen men in the shed, but no one spoke.
There was no joking, no feeling of camaraderie, just a chilled,
cross-section of men in different uniforms with different
signias, savoring a few moments of respite from the sting of
cold winds.

Lasari glanced about him, letting his gaze touch each
uniformed stranger. ". . . *even though you do not see us,
please do not make the mistake of thinking we do not see
you,*" Pytor Vayetch had said.

Lasari turned his watch so he could see the dial in the half
light. The sweat on his fingers made the watch feel cold and
slick. Almost three and a half minutes left before he could step
outside the latrine . . .

He felt like a man about to be executed, a victim without
emotional reserves. In an attempt to regain control, he tried to
think of memorable events in his life, events that would give
some importance and stature to his life. But his mind was a
blank. A cloudburst in Durham when he was a child, he
remembered that. His mother had come into his room and
hugged him. He was five. An old man in the minors, a kindly
coach named Dingo who'd been chosen to tell him he was cut
from the team—he remembered that man. But he couldn't
recall sunrises and sunsets, specific meals or music he'd enjoyed. He forced himself to think of Carlos and the checker
games at Mrs. Swade's rooming house and the way Bonnie
Caidin's lips had looked, moist and tinted, when she sipped
the wine.

It seemed an unbearable moment, the life he'd led before
this razor edge of time and what would happen to him when he
went through the door. Then a poignant memory hit him, the
moment Bonnie had told him about her dead brothers and the
sadness that had linked them together then, a compassion and
caring that was as endless as the universe itself, the moment of
love. He tried to fix that moment in his thoughts, but his time
was up.

The plan now seemed to have a life of its own, independent

of Duro Lasari. Just outside the latrine a soldier stood in the shadows, a duffel bag at his feet, an unlighted cigarette between his lips.

"Here, Jackson," the man said.

Lasari moved toward him, fumbling in his pocket for the book of matches from Teufel's Atelier. The man put out his hand but Lasari stepped closer, struck a match and held it to the man's cigarette.

The two men stood in the glow of the match, toe to toe, staring at each other, their frozen breath a floating halo to the scene. The stranger was young, no more than twenty, slightly built, sallow complexion and dark eyes, glistening now with alarm. The nails of the hand that held the cigarette to his lips were broken and seamed with dirt, almost the hands of a farmboy, and the tip of the little finger was missing.

The match burned short and Lasari dropped it to the snow. But in the brief light he had seen the markings on the soldier's field helmet, the cerise oblong with the white three-quarters moon and single star of the Turkish flag. Lasari closed the book of matches and put it in his pocket.

With a sharp intake of breath the Turkish soldier dropped his cigarette and fled the rest area, leaving the duffel bag on the ground at Lasari's feet.

Lasari quickly looked around. Snow flurries clouded the terrain but the immediate foot traffic seemed normal, the action routine. He picked up the duffel bag and walked to a clearing in the bushes behind the latrines, his boots moving with a whisper through the clean snow. With a second match he checked the outside of the duffel. It was marked in white stencil with the initials Pvt. G.J., followed by his Army ID number.

He unzipped the bag and felt through the folded GI garments inside, shirts, socks, shorts, a couple of wrapped gifts, a carton of cigarettes, shaving things. Then he tried to examine the lining, pinching the fabric, moving his fingers in a rubbing gesture. At first the material seemed coarse, almost felt-like, and then Lasari detected the sliding sensation of a substance between the layers of canvas, a movement like the shifting of fine sugar or powdered silk.

Lasari rezipped the bag, holding it on the ground between his ankles, his thoughts in a turmoil. From an inside pocket he took the small bottle of pills which Vayetch had given him in Heidelberg. He tossed the bottle on the palm of his hand. ". . . *take three*," the man had said.

Lasari thought he heard a footstep to his left, but misjudged. The movement was behind him. Two things happened almost at once. A man's arm circled him from the back, crushing his chest with such force that when the viselike grip was released, Lasari gulped and fought to take in breath. And at that moment a damp, bittersweet wad of gauze was pressed over his mouth and nose.

As he blacked out he heard a man say, "Your orders have just been changed, soldier."

# Chapter Thirty-eight

THE QUEASINESS WASN'T only in his stomach, Lasari decided, it was also at the base of his skull. There was a warm, almost fluid response in his spine, and he felt a sudden move might cause his head to disintegrate.

He tried to focus his eyes on the strange room. The ceiling was high beamed with a narrow balcony running around the second floor and a series of small doors that seemed to lead to bedrooms. A gray stone fireplace dominated the downstairs area, with two stuffed wild boars' heads over the mantel, as well as a pair of old-fashioned wooden skis, carefully waxed and preserved, with red pompoms on the ankle straps. An unlit fire was laid in the grate and the room smelled of dampness and old leather.

The man had opened the windows of the Mercedes, but the night air did little to clear Lasari's narcotic fog. He remembered sprawling in the back seat, half sick from the chloroform, fading in and out of consciousness. During the climb into the mountains high winds had been lulling, almost hypnotic, but the sharp turns in the road had sickened him and caused bile to rise in his throat. Once he had raised his head to see where they were going and glimpsed only giant pine trees, studded with upright cones, and then his mind slipped back into darkness.

Now he licked his lips in an attempt to speak and was repelled by the taste of the drug. His breathing was shallow and irregular, and when he tried to rub his numb cheeks his hands were chill and clammy.

"It's cold as hell in here," he said weakly from the armchair.

"You're all right. We won't be here long enough to burn a fire. Drink this tea."

Lasari focused on the man's voice and his vision cleared so he could make out General Tarbert Weir, the man from Philo Park, sitting at a table opposite him. A steaming mug sat on the table, along with the contents of Lasari's pockets, including the vial of pills, the matchbook and American passport. The general was in full uniform and he had placed Lasari's duffle bag in front of him, holding it firmly in place with a highly polished boot.

"You tried to kill me, didn't you, you bastard," Lasari said.

"That wasn't my intention," Scotty Weir said. "I gave you forty-five seconds on my pocket chronometer, then a few extra inhalations just to be sure. That was about an hour ago. Another sixty minutes or so of normal breathing, and you'll have exhaled ninety percent of the anesthesia."

"I can't see right," Lasari said.

The general struck a match and held it close to Lasari's face. "Your pupils are still dilated, but you're coming around."

"Where are we?"

"Schwartzwald, an old ski lodge, a kind of mom-and-pop operation that went out of business when the big resorts were developed in the Zugspitz area. It's an Army safe house, code name Case Ace Two. I have the key."

"How far are we from where you picked me up?"

"In a direct line, down the old ski slopes, about six or eight miles, but taking the mountain roads, I'd say about thirty-five. We're alone here, soldier, if that's what you're asking."

"I thought I heard someone. I thought I heard a car."

"A highway patrol passes on the main road once or twice a night, but you couldn't hear it from here," Weir said. He rose, slung the duffel bag on a couch and walked to a shuttered window, opening it a crack. He looked out over the snowy courtyard toward the parked Mercedes, pulled up against a windbreak hedge. There was one set of tire tracks coming in, then two sets of footprints approaching the front door. "It's stopped snowing," he said, "but there's a lot of wind out there."

"I still think you tried to kill me," Lasari said, his stiff lips barely forming words. He lifted an arm and winced. "I think you cracked my rib cage."

General Weir left the window. He took Lenox Riley's .38 special from his inner tunic and put it on the table. "If I wanted to kill you, soldier, I wouldn't have to do it the hard way."

He passed the mug of tea to Lasari and closed the man's chilled fingers around it. Lasari tried to sip but the cup chattered against his teeth. Weir took it from him, set it back on the table.

"We are not under surveillance here, there are no hidden microphones," Weir said evenly. "I want answers. Let me repeat what I told you in Philo Park. My son, Lieutenant Mark Weir, was shot and killed in Chicago about two weeks ago. He was shot because he knew *something*, but probably didn't know *enough*. A young woman calls my home and leaves an urgent message on my phone tape. She wants to talk to Mark about 'George Jackson, that soldier.'"

"I told you back in the park," Lasari said. "I'm a buck-ass private in the U.S. Army on assignment in Germany. I've got papers and orders . . ."

"Spare me that spiel," Weir said. "Within hours of that phone call my son is ambushed and executed, Miss Caidin is beaten bloody on the way to the hospital and within another forty-eight hours Private George 'No Middle Initial' Jackson, a new ID in Army records, gets rush orders to join the Lucky Thirteenth in Colorado and leave almost immediately for Germany."

Lasari reached for the mug of tea and took several hasty swallows. ". . . *Miss Caidin is beaten bloody.*" A rush of anger had surged through his body, leaving his mouth burning, his tongue parched and dry.

"You're involved in something you shouldn't be involved in," the general said. "You know that, I know that. You can save us both a lot of further pain and trouble by telling the truth."

"I don't know who killed your son, I don't know what's going on in Chicago."

"Maybe this will clear your thinking," Weir said. "My son

was working on a case involving four American soldiers. His jurisdiction was Chicago, but he suspected the key was in Europe. All four of those men were, as you put it, buck-ass privates in the U.S. Army doing their duty on assignment in Germany. They all had papers, they all had orders. And they all had one more thing in common. They were murdered in Chicago right after getting back from Germany . . ."

"I can't help you," Lasari said, but suddenly other words were sparking like electric shocks through the haze of confusion and sedation. Strasser, in his vindictive drunkenness, had said too much, had almost spelled it out. *". . . the next friendly face you, Jackson, will see will be at O'Hare Airport in Chicago. Just one more GI on leave. You'll be met by friends."* And Eddie Neal with his farewell message *". . . unfinished business between you and me . . . Yeah, Jackson, we still got some things to settle."*

The general picked up the passport and flipped it open to Lasari's new picture. "A new passport, soldier? Where did you think you were going? What name were you going to put in this one, George Jackson or Durham Lasari?" He waited for an answer, then said, "What name were you going to desert under this time? That's the long and short of it, isn't it? Even with trumped-up papers, you were going to betray your uniform again. You *did* plan to desert a second time, didn't you, Lasari?"

"You live in a tidier world than I do, general. You're talking about the Articles of War, I'm talking about survival. I'm facing the federal pen, or worse. I hadn't decided how to save myself."

The wind seemed to be circling the house, rattling shutters, sending a whistling draft down the chimney and stirring the fir branches that touched the roof. For a moment both men stopped to listen. Then Lasari broke the silence. "We had a motto in 'Nam, general, something you wouldn't understand. It applies only to the men who take orders, never to the men who give them. 'It don't mean *nothing*,' that was our motto, our fingerhold on sanity. Sure, I'm a deserter, but I wanted to make good on that desertion. I wanted clean paper. I was working with Miss Caidin in Chicago and got double-crossed by the Army itself."

"Exactly what does that mean, soldier?"

"There's nothing more I want to say. You think I'm scum, a yellow belly, a man who'd betray his uniform. Okay. What about *your* desertion, general? Bonnie Caidin told me you retired because you couldn't explain yourself or your wars to your son. What made *you* crack, general? Where the hell was *your* sense of responsibility to the Army? You took the good paper, the privileges, the pension and walked away. I just walked away with nothing in my hands but crutches. You're talking to me about loyalty and patriotism, I think you're trying to talk to a dead man. I'm not your son, general."

The general picked up the gun and walked to the windows. He cracked open the shutters and studied the darkness outside. Then he went to the front door, opened it and stood in silence. There were winds and the sounds of a stormy mountain night but nothing more. He closed the door and came back to stand opposite Lasari.

Scotty Weir pulled the receiver of the automatic back and released it to slam a round into the chamber, then pointed the gun at Lasari. "Whatever it is you're afraid of," he said, "I want you to be more afraid of me, soldier. Hear me good. You're a two-time deserter, and I wear four silver stars. If I decide to pull this trigger, we won't disturb anything more than a couple of snow owls."

"I've got nothing to tell you," Lasari said.

The general turned suddenly, pulled the duffel bag off the couch and tossed it at Lasari's feet. "You can tell me about that duffel, why it's so important to you."

"It isn't," Lasari said. "There's nothing in it but some GI gear and a couple of presents I wanted to bring back to the States."

"Not good enough," Scotty Weir said and pulled back one cuff of his shirt and tunic. Lasari saw the broad, strong hand, a glint of a silver ID bracelet, then the swollen flesh of the wrist, clawed with long scratches and scarred by tooth marks. "When I put the gauze over your face, you fought like a bull terrier to keep that bag . . ."

"I didn't know what I was doing," Lasari said.

"I think you do," the general said. He took out a pocket knife, flicked open the blade and reached down to slash the canvas side of the bag. "Let's see what you're carrying, soldier."

"No! Don't do that! It's my only way out!" Lasari stood, still groggy, and took a wild, looping swing at Weir. Weir backhanded him almost casually along the side of the head with the revolver, sending him slumping back into the chair.

He looked at his watch. "We've got time, Lasari, if you start talking pronto. And we're not going anywhere until you do."

"Against my will I'm part of a drug loop," Lasari said at last. "I believe if I could complete the loop, there's a chance to indict the people involved, do myself and the world a favor. But it's a tough gamble. I'm convinced I'll be killed and/or sent to prison along the way. Back there at maneuvers, I was trying to make up my mind how to figure my odds."

"Let me help you," Tarbert Weir said.

Lasari started with the first night at the Veterans' Bureau and told the general what had happened since then, from Sergeant Malleck to the armory, through Sergeant Strasser and Pytor Vayetch, the false illness, and the military papers already cut for transport back to Chicago.

The general's face was impassive, but the eyes were dark with growing fury as he paced back and forth in front of the fireplace.

"Heroin," he said, and the word was isolated like a bitter echo in the cold room. "Greed, lies, *murder*. Betrayal and corruption hiding behind the American flag. *It must be stopped.* My son wasn't born for this, he goddamn well shouldn't have had to die for it." His voice was rough with emotion. "We ask you men to join us, to raise their hands in oath . . . There are certain trusts that *cannot* be betrayed, soldier. *This is a matter of honor.*"

He moved to stand directly in front of Lasari. "And you believe that if you *could* get back to Malleck, if you completed the circle, you could tell the military everyone who is involved?"

Lasari shrugged. "I believe so. At least every name, number and order that I personally saw or heard from Chicago to Ludensdorf and back, the whole loop."

"You've kept a written record?"

"No. Nothing on paper, but I've got a freak memory. I know your identification number, for instance, 397-07-1991."

Lasari rattled off the nine figures easily. "I saw your ID bracelet in Philo Park."

"You have a photographic memory, you remember everything?"

"Only what I want to," Lasari said. "I don't go through life memorizing billboards."

For a moment the general was lost in thought. "It's like a medical technique. Doctors put a chemical dye in the bloodstream and then trace it through the body's circulating system to find cancers and malfunctions. You're like that little red blood stain, tracking and marking every step of the way."

He touched the duffel bag with the toe of his boot, then lifted it and tried the heft in his hand. "We can do it, soldier!" he said then. "*You* can do it. Do yourself, do your country a favor. Go back to Chicago on schedule, complete the loop . . ."

"You're offering me about the same deal as Malleck," Lasari said hotly, "except that you've sweetened it with some patriotic talk."

"Wrong," the general said. "I'll be in Chicago before you, I'll alert the right people. And I'll testify for you afterward. The Army will believe Scotty Weir, goddamn it. They'll hear what we've got to say."

He looked at his watch, then removed the Observer bands from a pocket and slipped them over his sleeves. "Get yourself together, Lasari, and I'll bring the car around. You're going back to the base. If there's been an AWOL report on you, I'll countermand it. This is one more time I put these stars to work."

In the far courtyard Lasari heard the Mercedes engine turn over, then the sound of tires crunching on the snow. He put the passport, pills and matchbook in his pocket, checked the zipper on the duffel and looked around the room. There was nothing but a half mug of cold tea on the table to show anyone had been there.

The general was behind the wheel of the car, coming up the circle drive leading to the Schwartzwald, headlights on low, the glow pinpointing Lasari against the lodge. There was a sudden squeal of brakes and the general's shout, "Look out there, soldier!"

As he threw himself to the snow Lasari heard bullets cracking around him as if he were the focal point of a three-way firefight. A bullet sliced through the empty air where he had been standing only seconds before. There were two more shots and something large and dark and full of pain fell to the ground a few feet from him. The Mercedes was still running in its own pool of light, surrounded by silence.

Lasari ran toward the fallen body near the front door. A moon had broken through the storm clouds with enough light to show the body of a big man in an open topcoat, lying face downward in the snow. Lasari used both hands to turn the body over and saw it was Herr Rauch, his collarbones smashed and his upper chest dark with waxy blood, a Mauser automatic still gripped in his hand.

Lasari felt through the man's pockets. There were no papers, no wallet, nothing but a set of car keys, several fine linen handkerchiefs and a roll of breath mints.

Lasari ran to the Mercedes. General Weir had fallen to his knees and was leaning against the car, a hand to his chest. "It's never as bad as it looks, soldier," he said.

"I'll get you to a hospital," Lasari said.

"No. The German highway patrol will be by within the hour." The general tried to rise but the effort was too great. "I'm giving the orders here. Take this car and get back to camp. Don't break that loop, Lasari."

"I can't leave you here."

"You've got to. Get those bastards, soldier."

"How can I go it alone? Who can I trust? Who'll trust *me*?"

"Call the States, use a public airport phone. Get John Grimes, my place in Springfield. He'll need General Stigmuller and Sergeant Gordon, tell him I said so. And here, soldier."

With ragged breathing and in obvious pain the general slipped his hand inside his tunic and took out a wallet, sorting through it with numbing fingers. Between bits of tissue paper he located the Medal of Honor, the Liberty head, stars and the single word Valor clearly visible in the moonlight. "Take it," he said. "That will show them Scotty Weir sent you."

Lasari hesitated only a moment. "I won't need the car, general," he said. "Let me help you out of this wind." He switched off the Mercedes engine, then lifted Weir into the car on the driver's side.

Back in the lodge Lasari took the skis off the wall racks, pulled a blanket from the couch and went back to the car.

"It's never as bad as it looks," the general said, barely audible, as Lasari bundled the blanket around him. Then he turned the headlights to bright, cradled the general's head on a folded arm and arranged the body to lean against the steering wheel. A shrill wail sounded in the night as the general's inert weight pressed against the horn.

Lasari strapped on the skis, picked up the duffel and glided over the snow to the top of the old ski run. There was just enough light to pick out the path down the mountain, lined on either side with pines and tufted with scrub growth. About six or eight miles down the trail, the general said, with twists and turns and unknown terrain ahead.

Lasari hoisted the duffel over his head, ignoring the painful spasms in his bruised chest, and tried a couple of tentative knee bends. It was not the challenge of the slope that worried him; it was the network of nerves that were tingling through the old wounds in his thigh and calf, a betraying sign of weakness or crippling fear.

Lasari pushed off and started down the slope, the cold wind bringing tears to his eyes and wetting his cheeks. It seemed to him a long, long time, dodging scrub and gliding past tall conifers, before the wailing sound of the Mercedes' horn faded behind him into the night.

He halted with a sharp christiana a few hundred yards above the maneuver area, where he could see lights and make out signs of movement.

Concealing the skis in deep brush, he took out the American passport and tore each page into a dozen pieces, letting the fragments mix with the wind. From his pocket he removed the bottle of pills (". . . *take three*," Vayetch had said) and shook out six small capsules, washing them down with a mouthful of snow.

For the first time he noticed heavy blood stains on his tunic and spent several minutes rubbing at the spots with handfuls of snow, leaving crimson stains on the ground around him.

Lasari had begun the final walk downhill, duffel in hand,

when the first wave of nausea struck him. He began to walk faster, breathing deeply and trying to focus on the lights below. The quantity of blood on his uniform had surprised and disconcerted him.

"*It's never as bad as it looks*" . . . the general had said that twice. And Lasari was determined to believe him.

# Chapter Thirty-nine

THE AIRPORT AT Frankfurt had been a maelstrom of confusion, hundreds of passengers hurrying in every direction toward the more than fifty international airline terminals that left from the aerodrome. The city itself, rebuilt from World War II rubble in neomodern style, was a sprawl of blocky concrete in the late afternoon light. As Lasari looked down from the plane window, the movement of cars and autobahns below sent spasms of nausea through his body, and when the plane passed over the broad band of the River Main reflections from the water sent slices of pain through his eyeballs. He would like to have shaded his eyes, tried to sleep, but he was hoping for at least a glimpse of the Am-Main Military Hospital. General Weir had been flown there from Ludensdorf in a military transport, John Grimes had told him.

Their conversation had been brief, a collect call made to the Tarbert Weir home outside Springfield from a phone booth in the airport. Even in the privacy of the booth Lasari had talked urgently, a hand cupped around his mouth and his back to the shuffle of traffic passing the glass door.

He had asked first about the general. "He's holding his own," Grimes had said.

"Did you talk to him?"

"No, he's not up to that yet. A doctor called."

"What do you think, Mr. Grimes?"

"He's got the constitution of a horse, always had."

Lasari hesitated a moment. The connection was good, Grimes' voice was clear, but Lasari had the impression that someone might be listening in on the line, at the Springfield end. It was not a noise that alerted him but rather a feeling of presence, the silence of breath being withheld.

"Is it safe to talk, Mr. Grimes?"

"Shoot, fellow. Say what you've got to say," the man said. "I've been expecting some sort of instructions from the general. He gave me a rough idea what he was up to."

Lasari gave Grimes the number of the Lufthansa flight, his arrival time in Chicago and a description of the single item he would be carrying. And then he gave him General Weir's instructions about Sergeant Gordon and General Stigmuller.

"I have their numbers," Grimes said, his voice suddenly hard. "I'll tell them what the general wants them to know." He broke the connection.

Before entering the waiting area for his flight, Lasari stood to one side and watched as passengers were guided through the metal detectors used to search out concealed weapons. On a moving belt attendants arranged hand luggage to pass through a separate detector, to be picked up on the other side of the barrier.

Two minutes before flight time he handed his duffel to an attendant and walked through the detector arches. A variety of luggage moved past him before he saw his duffel emerging on the belt. He stepped over to pick it up, as casual as any other traveler, then blended into the line of passengers holding boarding passes.

Sergeant Karl Malleck had rung for fresh coffee. Since five o'clock he had been out of bed and restless. With the business on schedule, it was too early for whiskey, yet he desperately needed a pickup. The waiting, the goddam silence, the creaking floors, the smells of the horse stalls that became miasmic in the damp—it was all getting on his nerves. He needed someone to talk to.

When Private Andrew Scales came in with the tray Malleck thought of sending him back for another cup. Instead he said sharply, "You been checking up on your mailbox regularly, Scales?"

"Yes, sir," the black man said. "I goes over every two days or so."

"You know I don't want those pickup notices lying around any longer than absolutely necessary."

Scales responded with a nervous chuckle. "No, sir, Top, I'm on the ball. I'm as worried as you are to pick up Uncle Andy's presents."

Malleck looked at Scales, experiencing a sharp distaste, not because the man was black, not because he stood there shuffling like some back-country Jim Crow, but because he was so dumb; because in a society where he'd been ass-kicked since day one, in a world where his only pleasure came from a needle, he was still dumb enough to take on worries for somebody else.

"You know what I'm really waiting for, Scales. The golden goose is coming in for a landing." He looked at his watch. "That fucker Salmi is late again. His wife says he's having stomach troubles, but I told him to get in here today."

"He'll be round, sarge, he's a good man."

"Well, you go out front and wait for him, Scales. Get him in here. And tell me the minute Neal and Castana pull into the courtyard."

"I can watch good from my window, sarge. It's raining outside."

"So what, so what, Scales? You never been wet before? Take a broom, sweep off the steps or something. If there's one thing I hate more than a dumb nigger, it's a lazy nigger."

Lasari fell in line behind several civilians at the farthest customs counter, where the queue was shorter. He gave the uniformed official his customs slip checked Nothing to Declare, then swung the duffel up on the counter.

". . . *just one more GI on leave, carrying regulation duffel, right size, right weight, right initials, right ID number,*" Sergeant Strasser had said. The customs official was young, Lasari noticed, probably not much older than he was, with a name tag, Kelsey, pinned to his twill pocket, ". . . *customs does want to look at your gear, all they see is a couple of presents for the girl friend back home and a few changes of Army underwear.*"

Kelsey unzipped the bag, looked inside, ran a hand through the garments and closed it again. He made a chalk mark on the canvas and pushed the bag toward Lasari. "Welcome home, soldier," he said.

*      *      *

Before the two big MPs fell into step with him, Lasari was
aware of someone else who seemed to have him under observation, a traveler in well-tailored clothes and carrying a briefcase, a middle-aged black man with skin the color of light soot
and lips that were almost purple. But when Joe Castana and
Eddie Neal came out of the crowd to walk on either side of
Lasari, the black man disappeared. Both men were in uniform
with shiny boots and MP armbands on their sleeves.

"You're looking downright sickly, Jackson," Eddie Neal
said. "You look like a bone the dogs worked over."

By the sheer bulk and press of their bodies the two men
guided Lasari away from the main airport lobby and toward a
side door leading to a maintenance parking lot.

"Don't try to run, Jackson," Neal said. "We're both
armed."

"Run? He's too scared to run," Castana said. "He don't
even ask questions. He even *try* to speak, he'd be spittin'
cotton."

Lasari's eyes swept the maintenance area, not knowing what
to expect but determined to be ready for it if he saw it. A
chain-link fence, twelve feet high and topped with coils of
barbed wire, circled the lot. A dozen or more employees' cars
were parked in a row, as well as one long limo with shaded,
opaque windows, several baggage carts, and a pair of food
and beverage trucks jacked up for repair. Four employees in
airlines overalls were tinkering with the mechanism of a mov-
able staircase.

Parked in a far corner of the yard, near an exit gate, was an
Army vehicle with a jeep understructure, high wheels and a
windowless van body on top. Lasari knew that was where they
were heading.

He felt a sudden urge to pray, to make a bargain with God,
promise some contribution or sacrifice so difficult or stunning
it would attract divine attention even down to this remote
maintenance lot. As a boy in North Carolina he had often
bargained with some imagined heavenly being for good grades
in school, or a day at the circus by promising to rake the yard
or paint a shed without being asked. Down in the minor
leagues, in the swamp country of Florida he had once offered

to do a hundred pushups before breakfast, every day, all
season, in return for a good batting average. In Vietnam he
had used pain as barter, offering to take any and all suffering
without recrimination or complaint if only he was allowed to
live.

But now, walking across the macadam, with the two MPs so
close that he could feel the warmth of their bodies, Lasari
thought with desperation that he had nothing left to bargain
with, nothing at all to offer a watchful or caring God. He was
a two-time deserter carrying an illegal cache of heroin, walking under armed guard across an airport lot, a man with no
job, no money and no future.

But suddenly he became aware of the parts of a picture for
which he had been searching. A stocky man in a tweed jacket
and leather gloves was standing outside an open gate, not far
from the Army jeep. The man was not coming closer, but he
was not walking away. John Grimes . . . And the four maintenance men had completed repairs on the staircase and were
pushing it in front of them, bending their backs to the task,
covering Lasari from the rear.

A flash of hope lit his thoughts, he knew what he could
bargain with, and made a silent promise more important to
himself than to God. "Let me out of this," he prayed, "save
me one more time, and I will go to her and ask her and love
her for the rest of my life."

Suddenly a door of the parked limo opened and the black
man with the briefcase stepped out, holding a gun this time,
shouting, "Hold it, gentlemen! I'll take that baggage now."

As the black man stepped forward, John Grimes dashed in
the gate, arms high over his head. Joe Castana made a dive to
wrest the bag from Lasari's grip, and the black man fired a
shot that caught Castana in the wrist and jolted him out of the
way. Lasari swung the bag in a looping arc toward Grimes.

The men in maintenance uniforms sprang forward with
drawn guns, and one shouted, "Chicago police officers!
Freeze!"

One officer tackled the black gunman from behind,
knocked the revolver from his hand, spinning him around to
sprawl face downward on the hood of the limousine.

Eddie Neal shoved Lasari aside and with a bellow of rage
threw himself forward to seize the duffel bag, but Grimes was

ready. He swung his boot in a powerful upward kick, catching Neal in the chest and sending him back on the macadam, stunned and fighting for breath.

Joe Castana was rocking on his knees, cursing through clenched teeth, trying to hold his shattered wrist together with his good hand.

"Take your man and split, Grimes!" one of the police officers shouted, and Grimes swung the duffel into the cab of the Army vehicle and signaled to Lasari.

"You'd better know where we're going, soldier," he said. "I never drove in this town in my life."

Private Scales had finished cleaning off the steps in front of the Armory. The rain was now hardly more than a mist, and he began to sweep the wet cobblestones of the courtyard itself, never lifting his eyes from his work as he edged himself toward the open front gate and street. He paused there, wiped his wet face with a khaki handkerchief and looked up and down the street. There was only the normal early morning traffic, no strange cars parked in either direction, but his attention was caught by three men standing in the doorway of a warehouse near the corner and three others, in civilian clothes, sauntering in the rain half a block away.

The sight of the strangers brought no surprise to Scales, only a feeling of deep melancholy and a decision that had been hiding in his subconscious for some months. He knew he wasn't going to tell Malleck anything this time.

One of the men at the warehouse was familiar to him. He had seen him twice before, at Cabrini Green, in uniform then, relentless, going from building to building, checking, rechecking, asking questions. There had been a lot of uniforms at the Green since Malleck ordered that lieutenant wasted, but this one Scales remembered most clearly. He was black and his face seemed more bitter and dangerous than all the others.

As Scales walked back over the courtyard he saw Malleck standing at the window, watching him. He waved and called out, "You just rest yourself, sarge. I'm watchin' for you."

At that moment Malleck spotted the Army vehicle as it slowed at the front gate and turned into the courtyard with a screech of rubber. And right on plan there were two men in the front seat.

A surge of relief swept through the sergeant's body, so rousing and satisfying that he felt as if he had had a sexual catharsis. His legs, then his torso trembled with an emotion so violent that he had to sit down. It was going to happen, the matching condos, the sea breezes, the choice of broads, the numbered bank accounts. Sergeant Malleck, Mr. Karl Malleck, was definitely going to be a rich and envied man. He folded his hands to control the shaking, fixed his eyes on the main entrance to his office, and waited.

He waited several minutes and though the delay was not long enough to cause alarm, Malleck was taken by surprise when the door to Scales' cubicle opened and Durham Lasari stepped into the room. He was in uniform, his face pale and expressionless, but his eyes were dark with derision.

He gave Malleck a snappy salute and said, "Private George Jackson reporting, sir. Private George Jackson making delivery."

Lasari took three steps toward the desk, duffel bag in hand, and then Malleck gasped with disbelief as he saw three men with drawn guns and Private Andrew Scales step into the room directly behind Lasari.

"Sergeant Malleck, I am Sergeant Gordon of the Chicago Police Department," a big black man said. "You are under arrest."

"Goddamn it, Scales," Malleck shouted, his voice almost breaking. "What the hell *is* this . . ."

With a panicked reflex he opened a desk drawer and found a gun. As he raised it, there was a sharp pop in the air, the sound of a single shot from an automatic pistol with a silencer, and Malleck's body jerked once, then spun around and he fell face downward on the rug, his gun falling from his hand.

He looked almost graceful as he lay there, head resting on one arm as though trying to sleep, but there was blood on the rug beside him and a perfect curve of mandible bone that had fragmented when Scales' bullet had shattered his jaw.

"You fucking idiot!" Sergeant Gordon said with fury as he snatched Scales' gun from his hand. "You had my orders, all of you. This was to be a lawful, a *peaceful* bust. We *needed* that man, we wanted him *alive*."

"You don't understand, boss," Scales said. "It had to be this way. Sergeant Malleck and I, we been together a long,

long time. We're something special. He'd of wanted me to do it for him, I know that."

Lasari set the duffel bag on a chair, as though it had become repugnant to him. Sergeant Gordon nodded and one of the plainclothes officers stepped over to claim it.

"I'm not sure what happens from here on," Lasari said. "Tell me, am I under arrest, Sergeant Gordon?"

"More or less protective custody, Mr. Lasari, like that shit we just confiscated."

# Chapter Forty

THREE DAYS LATER, after a four o'clock appointment, Laura Devers drove Bonnie Caidin home from the doctor's office.

"It's too early to tell really," Caidin said as they left downtown Springfield, "but the doctor agrees I'm probably pregnant. At first I told myself I'd been knocked off my menstrual schedule by that godawful beating, but, no, there are other signs. My breasts have been sensitive, and I felt ghastly three mornings in a row. I thought that might have been worrying about Duro and the general." She sat huddled in a tweed coat, a yellow scarf at her throat, and her face was pale and still. The older woman reached over and patted her knee.

"The doctor doesn't do abortions, he made that clear," Bonnie Caidin said. "He told me that under some circumstances he and a consulting physician might come to an administrative decision to prevent the birth. He acted as if, he just *assumed*, Laura, that I wanted to get rid of it."

"He'd never seen you before," Laura Devers said. "He must have wondered why you didn't go to your own doctor."

"I didn't want to wait," Caidin said. "I felt I wanted to know before I saw Duro again."

"Did you tell him you had a doctor's appointment?"

Caidin shook her head. "No, I haven't even talked to him. I asked Sergeant Gordon to tell him to do whatever he had to do, square himself away with the Army and the police before he got in touch with me. But I did hear his voice. I listened in when he was calling from Frankfurt." She laughed softly.

"He didn't ask for me. I'm not even sure he plans to call . . ."

"Would you like to have the baby?"

"I don't know," Bonnie Caidin said. "I'm not sure I want to love anything for a while. Right now I can't be sure what's truth and what's fantasy. Sometimes I think I just imagined the past . . . my brothers, Mark and even Duro."

It was dusk and lights from the Weir farmhouse laid flat squares of yellow on the gravel driveway when they reached the front door. Laura declined the invitation to come in for a drink.

"To tell you the truth, Bonnie, I want to go home and write a letter to Scotty. I feel better about him when I stay in touch."

"But you told me you called the hospital twice."

"Three times, actually, but I just get to talk to the floor orderly. He tells me Scotty's doing just fine, seeing no one except his doctors. You'd think at my age I could make up my mind," she said, "but I've been arguing with myself whether or not I should fly over to Frankfurt. Or at least fly over to bring him home when he's fit."

"Why don't you? I think he'd love that."

"And then again he might not," Laura said. "We're old, old friends, and good friends, and I know how I feel about him, but he's stubborn, you know. I wouldn't want to rile him. I've got a hunch Scotty Weir'd rather find his own way home."

"There's a number for you to call in Chicago, Miss Bonnie. It's Sergeant Gordon. He tried to reach you three times. Can I bring you a pot of tea? You haven't eaten a bite today."

"Tea would be just fine," she said. "Tea with lots of sugar and dry toast."

Grimes hesitated and the skin above his collar flushed red as he spoke. "You'll forgive me, Miss Bonnie, but is it Mark's boy you're carrying?"

"No, Grimes," she said, "it isn't. That just wasn't meant to be, Mark and I."

"The general would've been pleased," the man said. "We'd have made a fine pair of grandfathers, don't you think? Jesus, we'd have carried on . . ."

Bonnie Caidin sat at the general's desk and picked up the phone pad with Grimes' writing on it.

Gordon answered at once in a voice so booming, so vibrant that she said, "Doobie, what is it? Have you been drinking?"

"Drinking, hell, Bonnie. I'm just on one big success high. When you get to the bottom of a case as deep and rotten as this one, it's like sniffing pure oxygen. Get your pencil ready, lady."

"Doobie," she said, "I'm off duty. I haven't even called the office since Grimes drove me down here."

"Don't give me that, Bonnie. You're too pro to turn down a byline on something like this. The whole city is upside down, I've had a hard time protecting it for you, but remember, Mark said this would be your story."

"All right," Caidin said. "I've got a pencil and paper here. Shoot, Doobie."

"There's been a lot of coverage, but what I'm giving you is the nuts and bolts, the inside stuff on how we put the case together, the information the other papers don't have yet. And a lot of credit goes to your boy friend."

"Don't call him that, please," she said and scrawled "Durham Lasari" across the top of the page. "Start with the Chicago end."

"Okay. We'd been working round the clock, we didn't know exactly what we were looking for, but we were looking. There were shadows, we were getting an outline. It was part coincidence, part self-indictment, but last Friday we finally threw a net over Detective Frank Salmi, one of the city's own finest, the bastard, and he broke down and gave us some very pertinent details."

Grimes came in and set a tray of tea things on the desk. Bonnie Caidin blew him a kiss and said into the phone, "How'd you do it?"

"The damnedest thing, Bonnie. We had that voice tape and the man's voice we couldn't identify on it, right? Well, by chance I was on the elevators in the police building, on my way up to the office, sharing the ride with some civilian cats, and on the third floor Salmi gets on. Remember, Bonnie, how in those elevators, right over the regular floor number, there's a little brass plaque with the numbers in braille? It's the same in all the county buildings."

"I remember," she said.

"Well, Salmi sees me, nods hello and then he goes apeshit, puts on some kind of clown act, feeling those braille number plates, making cracks about Lady Justice being blind. He got a couple of laughs from the civilians and then he turned to me and said, 'I'd like to ask you for lunch today, Sergeant, but my wife sewed razor blades in my pockets. She don't want me bribing no cops.' Another big laugh, he's a real elevator comedian, his nerves just cracked on him.

"Salmi's a short guy, you know, balding, tan complexion, and I saw that he was sweating like a greaseball. All of a sudden I knew why. That was his voice on the tapes and the fucker was so nervous being in the same car with me that he couldn't keep still, he *had* to expose himself.

"So at the next floor I asked all the civilians to step out. Frank and I took a ride up a couple more floors and I pressed the emergency button to stop the cab between floors. I pulled the door open just a little to show him we were all alone between four brick walls. We had our chat. I never laid a hand on him, Bonnie, but in five minutes he was blubbering to get up to Commissioner McDade's office and give his story to a steno."

"Okay, Doobie," she said, "you talk fast but I've got that."

"Salmi told us what we'd suspected all along but could never prove. It was a heroin scam on both sides of the Atlantic, using military couriers, a growing business. They were expecting their fifth delivery."

"Just a minute," she said, and then asked a few questions to clarify details on the earlier deliveries. "All right, I'm clear so far. Where was Sergeant Malleck during all this?"

"Right where he should be, running his operation from the armory. We decided our best strategy was to simulate business as usual. Let Lasari try to get through to the armory with the payload and catch Malleck with the goods in his hands."

"And Detective Salmi?"

"We kept him on ice, so to speak. Once he started talking he didn't want to stop. He knew he was an accessory to Murder One for setting up Mark with that phone call, though he's pleading against collusion. He insists he didn't know an execution was planned.

"It was two of Malleck's men, Eddie Neal and Joe Castana, who pulled the trigger. We got them both right at the airport, along with that amateur gunsel Mr. M. sent over to pick up the shit for himself."

"Mr. M.? I thought he was straight syndicate."

"I guess he wanted something on the side. According to Salmi, Mr. M. bankrolled the operation for Malleck from the beginning. It was going to be comparatively small stuff, but profitable enough for both sides. But Malleck got greedy and careless.

"The first couriers brought in duffels with only three to four pounds of white in the lining. Malleck figured out a new angle for a profit to split between himself and a Sergeant Strasser in Germany. Before leaving Germany, each courier would mail home one or more regulation GI packages, little things, a teddy bear, a fancy pillow, a music box—each with its cache of heroin inside. There's no limit as to how many packages a GI can send as long as they're no heavier than seventy pounds maximum and are marked gift with a declared value under fifty dollars. He can take his choice, the German post office or APO, which is a little cheaper. Malleck wasn't worried about costs, and he was bypassing Mr. M. completely on this extra loot."

"How did you get onto the mail angle?"

"Lasari corroborated the information, but it came from Frank Salmi first. Finding Salmi was like getting a direct hit at the *piñata* with a baseball bat. Goodies spilled out all over the place. And, of course, Uncle Andy wanted a chance to cleanse his soul."

"Uncle Andy?"

"Private Andrew Scales, a soldier and a junkie, the man who shot Malleck. He was billeted at the armory but he hung around Cabrini Green. I'd been checking through Cabrini books and found that Scales had rented four different apartments in different buildings over a five-month period. Each time he got a new mailbox and a new key. He knew I was onto him, but I let him dangle. After the shooting he told us Malleck had alerted him to watch out for *four* presents from Germany for Uncle Andy this time."

"Packages they forced Lasari to send?"

"Yes, but the packages never left Germany, Bonnie. Lasari had the right information tucked in his memory bank. He'd memorized the file numbers of the four mail receipts he'd signed and the German officials caught the stuff right at the Frankfurt post office."

"How did they try to do it this time?"

"Same M.O., Bonnie. Separate packages, all to be mailed on different dates, all addressed to Andrew Scales. This stuff could have fooled anyone—four big expensive cuckoo clocks, painted in Alpine colors, crazy little birds inside, but each pair of swinging weights—they look like pine cones, the Germans told us—each cone is hollowed out and filled with about a pound and a half of heroin.

"The military in Frankfurt put the cuffs on Strasser, Malleck's opposite number, the German border police picked up the ringleader, Pytor Vayetch, as he tried to cross the Czech border near Cheb.

"Andrew Scales . . . that poor junkie brother's got more than heroin possession and Malleck's murder to worry about. It was Scales who gave Malleck the layout of the Cabrini apartment, the place they got Mark . . ."

Gordon sighed and some of the animation went out of his voice. "Well, Bonnie, it's an ongoing investigation, of course, but I think that covers the Chicago end up to date."

"And Lasari," she said, keeping her tone impersonal. "Has he been with you all this time?"

"Not exactly. We talked to him on tape the better part of a day, he's got a mind like a computer for details, you know. Then at Senator Copeland's suggestion, he and Superintendent McDade flew into Washington. They've been holding meetings with General Buck Stigmuller and a Colonel Benton of Intelligence, along with the senator. I'm strictly Chicago law-and-order and not privy to those meetings, but McDade says they're haggling over the best public relations approach for this matter, whether or not a full disclosure in this country and abroad is the best approach. Intelligence seems to favor a limited exposure, almost a coverup, but Copeland and Stigmuller like the bad apple theory and a major announcement that they've cleaned out the whole damned barrel.

"General Stigmuller has his special point of view on a lot of things," the sergeant said. "He contends he was working closely with Tarbert Weir and that Durham Lasari was in their plans from the beginning. Lasari's been cooperating in every way, he's holding back nothing. I thought you'd want to know, Bonnie."

"I'll explain what you just told me to the desk," she said, "and see how they want to handle it. Maybe they'll want to put someone from the Washington bureau on that angle, direct quotes from the three big names.''

"Okay, Ace. I'll be in the office for a half hour or so, and you've got my home number if there's anything you need to recheck," Gordon said. "McDade and Lasari flew into Chicago about an hour ago. We'll want him up here for more questioning and as a witness at the trials, of course, but McDade gave him a couple of days off. Lasari said to tell you he's driving down there tonight."

Bonnie paused, took a sip of tea to compose herself, then said, "One more important thing, Doobie. General Weir—are you going to send him a report on all this?"

"I already talked to him, Bonnie."

"You *talked* to him?"

"Well, it was rather a one-sided conversation but a nurse held a phone over the bed and I gave him an official report. I knew there were two things he was adamant about. He wanted those GI killings stopped and he wanted to find out who'd murdered his son. I said, 'Mission accomplished, sir' and that was that."

"You're sure he heard you?"

"The nurse said he made one hand into a fist, held it up like a victory sign. He *can* talk, she said, but he's still got those damned tubes in his throat."

"Just one last thing, Doobie. I'm not sure I have these numbers right. You said the first four couriers brought in three to four pounds of white, then Malleck got greedy. That means that Lasari's duffel had more?"

"Yes, they stuffed in seven pounds this time, all balanced out so the weight was even."

"And the cuckoo clocks with a pound and a half in each of two pendulums, that's another twelve pounds?"

"Right."

"So all together on this loop Malleck was trying to bring in nineteen pounds of heroin. In street money, when they're dealing, how much would all that be worth, Doobie?"

"Drug Enforcement figures quantity in kilos, and there's two point two pounds to a kilo so, in this case, we're talking about eight and a half kilos, a little more."

"And?"

"At retail level, with the stuff cut for street sale, this high-grade stuff sells, all told, for about two million dollars a kilo."

"I don't have a calculator, Doobie. What did you come up with?"

"We'll have accurate figures when the German agents send us exact weights and measures," Doobie said, "but this haul would have been worth from sixteen to eighteen million dollars, and if the market is dry, even a little more."

"And this was the fifth try," Bonnie said. "I'm speechless, Doobie. Thanks, and whether or not I get a bonus on this, I'm going to call you and take you out to lunch."

She hung up and dialed Larry Malloy on the city desk at the *Tribune* and talked with him for an hour.

Bonnie folded the notes and put them in a sweater pocket, straightened the top of the desk, switched the lamp to low. When she'd lit the logs and tinder in the fireplace, she decided to ask Grimes to chill some red wine from the cellar.

For the doctor's visit in Springfield her choice had been brown slacks and a cashmere cardigan set, but she wanted to shower and change into a dress. What had she been wearing when she saw Lasari last, she wondered. With a start she remembered her torn and bloody clothes had been destroyed at Henrotin Hospital. She had reached the foot of the staircase when the phone rang.

"I'm sure it's for me, Grimes," she called out. "Malloy must have found something I skipped. And, please, can you chill a couple of reds for us? Lasari's coming."

She picked up the study phone and was surprised to see Grimes watching her from the doorway. After listening briefly, she held out the phone. "It's for you. Person to person, the overseas operator."

As a voice sounded on the overseas end of the line, Grimes squared his shoulders, standing almost at attention. "Yes, sir," he said. "John Grimes here."

Bonnie saw the warning flick of shock in the man's expression, the sudden sag of his shoulders.

"Yes, I hear you, sir. I was just listening. But we'd been given to understand . . ." His face was ashen and she could see the shine of tears in his eyes. After some moments he said, "I see, I see. Thank you, major, and God bless you, sir. This can't be easy for you."

He replaced the phone and turned to Caidin. "The hospital

in Frankfurt's been trying to reach us for an hour or more, but the line was tied up.''

"I was talking to Sergeant Gordon in Chicago, and then my paper.''

"A doctor just told me, a medical major, that the general died an hour ago. Scotty Weir didn't make it after all, Miss Caidin. Can you believe that?'' Grimes watched the young woman closely, studying her eyes, her mouth, as if to find an answer somewhere in her expression. She nodded helplessly.

"He was so alive to me,'' she said. "I was just using his paper and pencils. There are some playbills in the desk drawer, a deck of cards . . .''

Grimes seemed not to hear. "It wasn't the gunshot wounds at all, according to the major. That skulking bastard never killed him. It was an embolism, the doctor said, a blood clot that got loose and went for the heart.''

"It's too much for me to take in,'' Bonnie said. "I know I should weep, but it's too soon, I feel I honor him by *not* crying.''

There was a flash of headlights across the windows, a crunch of gravel as a car pulled into the drive and Grimes went to the front door.

Duro Lasari came into the study, a rush of cold air around him, tired, his face troubled and dark. He put his arms around Bonnie and his lean, hard body felt hot, almost fevered through his clothes.

"I heard it on the car radio. I should have stayed with him, but goddamn it, he *ordered* me to leave him.''

"Please, Duro. You're hurting my shoulders. I'm still bruised there.''

He slackened his grip and said, " 'It's never as bad as it looks, soldier,' those were the last words. But he'd called out to warn me, he took that shot for me. He just didn't give a damn.''

"You're wrong about that,'' Grimes said. "Scotty Weir knew what he was doing. He *always* gave a damn.''

Lasari dropped his arms to his sides and began to pace the small study. "This is the last thing I expected. I had begun to understand him. I believed I would *see* him again.'' He paused. "Maybe it was a decision he made out there at Schwartzwald. Maybe it was a moral one, but it was an action he'd conditioned himself to take.''

"We were friends for more than thirty years," Grimes said. "I knew the man and respected him, but I'm just a snapass corporal. I don't know if he's the last of his kind or the start of a new breed."

He looked around the study, the walls of books, the empty trophy cabinets, the folders of maps and papers stacked on shelves. "It shouldn't end like this," he said. "It has to mean more than that. We should *talk* about him, remember him. Someone should put it all on paper."

"I've been thinking of little else for days," Bonnie said.

Grimes walked to the foot locker with the flag folded on top, touching it reverently. "There's more than a man's life in that trunk, there's history here, his speeches, his medals, his decorations. They should be sorted out, looked at, treated with respect. I'm too hurt by all this, it's like a terminal wound to me. I wouldn't know where to start."

"Maybe I would," Duro Lasari said, and took a packet from his pocket and placed it on the desk, folding back the leaves of tissue paper.

Bonnie Caidin bent close, then touched the object with the tip of her finger. "That's a Medal of Honor, isn't it? I never saw one before."

Lasari put his hand on her shoulder lightly, but he seemed to be addressing someone beyond the shadows of the room. "You're right, Bonnie, a Medal of Honor. The Army gave that to General Weir years ago, when he was just a kid, a private. The reason you never saw one before, well, there are just too damned few medals around these days. That's the way I see it."

John Grimes nodded and Bonnie Caidin said softly, "You're right, Duro. And that's the way I see it . . . far too few."